Chasity
A NOVEL

Tamika Cole

Chasity Copyright © 2016 by Tamika Cole

Editor: Jennifer Sim

Photography: Dscanphotography Savage

Cover Girl Cristyn Uno

Cover Design: Hotbookcovers.com

Interior Design and Typesetting: InteriorBookDesigns.com

ISBN 978-0-9857562-3-9

Dedicated to
Sheldon Gavin Ogle
and
Earnest Bynes

Acknowledgments

Giving glory and honor to the one and only God. Thanking Him for His son Jesus Christ, my Lord and Savior.

I would like to take this time to thank my mother and father for always being there. Gwen and Derrick, you did a wonderful job with me, and I'm tooting my own horn. Special thanks to my test readers LuveraTrumpler-Kelly, Cheron Freeland, Rashana Burr, Picola Ray, Debbie Johnson, and Alicia Robinson. Thanks for your support and feedback. Yolanda Best, Cheron, Gwen Jackson, Bernadette Wallace, and Alma Kinnard, thanks for investing into my dream. Words can't express my gratitude. Thanks Ms. Cristyn for gracing my cover with your loveliness. You're a sweet girl and you will make an awesome mother. To my sister Brenda Bynes, I love you and my prayers are with you. RIP Earnest Bynes. God has you now and He will comfort your mom in due time. Also, Natasha Smith, you mentored me in our very technical job, and I'm truly grateful for your expertise and support. I give thanks for my partner that God designed specifically for me, my hubby, Paul. I'm fortunate to be able to spend my life with you and the kids. You keep my head above water with the blessings of Jah! Lastly, I give thanks to all my kids, step, and biological. And, a special shout to my granddaughter Jewells. Her cute face brings so much joy into my life and she's so smart.

Chapter 1

Chasity

"Chasity, listen closely sweetheart. I need you to hide in our special hiding place. No matter what, don't come out until I come get you," my mother instructed.

"Come with me, Mommy!" I pleaded, jumping up with excitement.

"I'm coming in a minute. Go now… and remember what I said. Don't come out unless I come get you—do you understand? And don't make a sound!"

"Okay," I replied, as I raced off to my mother's closet. I went through the secret door that led up to the attic. It was mommy's secret play place for me and we played up there often. Especially when daddy made her mad, or the police visited.

I was playing with my dollhouse when I heard loud fire-crackers inside the house. Voices drifted up the stairs and invaded my secret place. I heard mother crying and begging for her life. I wanted to help so badly, but I remembered she said not to move until she came for me. Several more firecrackers went off before I heard my father's voice. "Cathy, no! Oh God, nah! Not my baby! Nigga you killed my wife and your childhood friend. Do whatever the fuck you want, traitor, cause I don't have nuttin' to live for now."

"You will die, Tray, no doubt. But not before I kill your daughter in front of you. How old is she, around ten? Yeah, that's old enough for my men. You should've just given me the connects' info, my man. Where's your daughter, Tray? I will only ask once."

"My daughter ain't here, pussy, and you will never touch her. See, my instincts told me your punk ass was coming, King, so I took the necessary steps to keep my daughter safe. You will never see my money, or my connects, because I took care of that too. When Jon-Jon receives that video I sent with you fucking his wife, you will join me and my wife, pussy!" One more firecracker went off, and everything became silent. Mommy and Daddy's voices ceased and quiet loomed through the air.

I was only ten years old, but old enough to understand the severity of what happened downstairs. Quietly, I clutched my doll and curled up in the corner of the room. A while later, smoke clouded the air and I coughed, searching for an exit. There was no window for me to escape, so I crept back downstairs. The smoke blinded me, causing me to fall over my father's dead body. I glanced into his eyes one last time and longed to say goodbye, but I needed to escape because smoke was filling my lungs.

I could see the glare from the moon shining through the window. I bolted to the window and opened it. After climbing onto the roof, I saw my entire house in flames. I cried and yelled for help, but we lived in a secluded family mansion in the suburbs of Alpharetta, Georgia. The closest house was a quarter of a mile up the road. The flames roared and a part of the roof where I stood collapsed. An oak tree that stood as high as my house was my only chance. My friends and I climbed the tree often when we played in the yard, but never to the top. I leapt into the tree, but my stunt sent me spiraling twelve feet to the ground, each branch grazing my skin.

When the ambulance got me to the hospital and the doctors examined me, they discovered I had a broken leg and cuts that required over fifty stitches. During my stay at the hospital, police and social workers badgered me, wanting to know what happened to my parents. I felt victimized by all of the questions, but my mother's angelic face comforted me.

On the third day of my stay, an unknown man came to the hospital and introduced himself as Uncle Kenny. He said he was taking me back to Philly to live with him and his family. He appeared to be a nice man, but I was unfamiliar with him. My parents grew up in Philly and they always talked badly about that place. However, Uncle Kenny assured me we would get through this together.

"Chasity, the doctor said you'll be discharged soon. I know you must be scared and so am I, but I promise I will give you a good life. I'll be back tomorrow. Here's the number to the motel where I'm staying. If the cops, or anyone else try to harass or ask you any more questions, tell them you need to call me. You understand, Chass?"

"Yes, I understand," I replied.

When we arrived at his home a few days later, I noticed it was not the big house I had become accustomed to in Georgia, but it was a nice single-family home in Jenkintown, a suburb of Philadelphia.

A gorgeous woman waited at the door. "This must be Chasity!" she greeted with a friendly smile. "My name is Denise, but most of my friends call me Dumpling. You can call me Aunt Dumpling. Come on in, you must be tired from the long trip," she said as she grabbed my hand and escorted me inside. When we got inside, I spotted a young girl sitting in the recliner. "Destiny, come over and say hello to your cousin Chasity. She'll be living with us from now on."

"Her can't stay in my room!" The little five-year-old barked.

"I don't want to stay in your room! I want to go home, Uncle Kenny!" I cried, feeling displaced.

"Sweetheart, this will be hard for everyone. When your mother went into labor, I stood right there beside her. Did you know that?" I shook my head no. "Your father was in route, but your mom couldn't hold on any longer. I held you first, even before your mother. The doctors mistook me for your father, which caused a whole commotion with your father and me, but when he saw you for the first time, he forgot about the whole argument," Uncle Kenny laughed to himself.

"You were there?" I asked, wiping my tears.

"Yes, and I love you. I can't bring back your parents Chass, but as long as I'm alive, I will take care of you. Now, your Aunt Dumpling will show you to your room, and I'll be in to check on you before you go to sleep."

Pink and yellow was the theme of my bedroom decor. It reminded me of a princess room, and I smiled for the first time all week.

"Tomorrow we'll go clothes shopping and have a great time. Are you hungry, Chasity?" Aunt Dumpling asked.

"No thank you, but I'll take something to drink." I replied.

"I have fruit juice and orange juice, which would you prefer?"

"I'll take the fruit juice. Thanks," I replied.

"Okay, I'll be right back. Tomorrow you can tell me the kinds of foods and snacks you want," she said, as she exited the room.

I jumped into bed and cried from the pain of losing the only love I recognized, until I heard a knock at the door. With the pillow, I wiped my face and yelled, "Come in." Uncle Kenny was standing there with my glass of juice.

"Hey Pumpkin, you okay?" he asked as he wiped away my tears. "I know it's hard now, but I promise time will heal your wounds. We'll have so much fun, you'll see. Tomorrow we can go to Dave & Buster's and get the fun started. What do you say? Is it a date, Pumpkin?"

"It's a date, Uncle Kenny. And thanks for the juice," I replied with excitement

"Sure. Whenever you're ready, we can talk about your parents.

They wanted the funeral to be held in Philly, and it's in three days. I know it will be painful but I will be with you the entire time," he reasoned as he left the room.

Uncle Kenny and Aunt Dumpling kept their word. They bought me a new wardrobe and took me to every amusement park from Pennsylvania to New Jersey. I even enjoyed having a younger sister. Destiny worshiped the ground I walked on and she listened to every word I said. I had a new family that showed me unconditional love and that love carried me through college.

Chapter 2

Chasity

Eleven Years later

T oday, I was graduating college with a business degree. Still, carpentry was my first love, and I had Uncle Kenny to thank for that. An expert artisan, he could build anything, and he specialized in woodworking. He built our kitchen cabinets from oak he had delivered specially from Malaysia, and he taught me everything about construction and woodworking. My masterpieces were the coffee and end tables I made for my bedroom right before I left for college. Thinking back over the years, I thanked God for my Uncle Kenny often.

I was graduating from Lincoln University, a black college, and it had been six months since I saw him or Aunt Dumpling. Destiny came up early to stay with me for my last week on campus. She had grown into a lovely young woman and she still adored me.

"Destiny, are you ready girl? The mirror will break if you keep staring at it," I teased.

"Everyone can't be as gorgeous as you. You wake up pretty and you still look like you're sixteen."

"I'm twenty-one, young girl, so you better respect your elders. And Destiny, you are beautiful too. Stop comparing us," I said, gently turning her towards the mirror. "I see a pretty girl with cute dimples and hazel eyes."

"Yeah, but you," she countered. "Your skin tone is the perfect shade of hot chocolate with a touch of cream."

"Hot chocolate though?" I repeated.

"Yeah, let me finish, please," she said, bobbing her head. She was spoiled and sassy. "Your body is something that the Lord made, and your lips," she continued, but I stopped her, knowing we could be there all day.

"That's enough, Dee. We have to go. I wonder where Uncle Kenny and Aunt Dumping are. They should've been here an hour ago. Let's go to the auditorium, maybe they're already seated."

I didn't see them when we got downstairs, but it was time for me to join my fellow graduates on stage so I told Destiny to take her seat. The ceremony took forever, but when I received a $20,000-dollar Honor Award in business from the Blake Corporation, it was worth the wait. I searched for my family after the graduation to no avail.

"Where are they?" I asked when I found Destiny.

"I don't know, Chass, but I'm starting to worry."

"Alright, let me call them," I said, searching for my phone in my purse.

"I've been calling them throughout the ceremony and they're not answering," she retorted.

"Calm down, Dee. They probably got stuck in traffic and will be here any minute."

Dean Matthews walked towards us with a concerned look on his face. "Chasity, can I speak to you in my office? It's very important."

"Sure, but I have my sister with me and I don't want to leave her alone," I explained. Even though she was my cousin, we called each other sisters.

"Yes, it's best you both come," he said, as he led us to his office. Dean Matthews asked us to have a seat. "Chasity, we just got word from the police department. I'm sorry, but your aunt and uncle were in a fatal car accident not far from the school."

"Fatal? What do you mean fatal? They're going to make it, right?" I asked.

"Yeah, they have to be okay! What hospital are they in?" Destiny asked.

"I'm sorry I have to be the one to inform you, but they didn't make it. From the report the police gave, they died on impact."

"Nooooooooo!" Destiny's shout pained me even more, and I felt every part of my body breaking.

I pulled her into my arms to try to comfort her, but her world was crushed. Destiny was not my Uncle's biological daughter, but he was her dad in every other way. Aunt Dumpling loved both of us, and I felt the pain of losing another mother. Our hearts and minds were slaughtered and we had no one but ourselves.

Chapter 3

Chasity

I had mixed feelings as we sat in the attorney's office going over Uncle Kenny and Aunt Dumplings assets. Uncle Kenny left specific instructions on how he wanted to rest. The insurance policy was divided between myself, Destiny, and Aunt Dumpling had she survived. The attorney explained that Uncle Kenny purchased the policy for one-hundred thousand dollars; however, since it was an accidental death, the policy had doubled. Destiny and I would receive equal shares after the funeral expenses. The estimated funeral costs ran between twenty and forty thousand, leaving Destiny and I the balance. He and Aunt Dumpling wanted to be buried side-by-side in the same cemetery where my parents lie.

Destiny had me worried. She shut me out and performed disappearing acts, going missing for hours. This chick stopped eating and going to school. With just three weeks left in the school year, I received calls from all of her teachers. Once I explained what happened, a few were sympathetic, while others said she still had to do extra assignments if she planned to pass to the twelfth grade. My pain was severe, but I tried to be strong for Destiny. Obtaining full custody of her was the singular positive from the meeting with the attorney. I glanced over and saw the relief on her face, even though she had been acting distant towards me. Aunt Dumpling's sister Yvette said she had no room for us. Destiny's grandmother died last year, and no other family members volunteered. We had no one. The attorney handed me a letter from Uncle Kenny before we left. I wanted to read it at once, but waited until I got home.

I asked Destiny if she wanted to have lunch, but she declined. I didn't know how to comfort or assure her we would be fine. I was twenty-one and unaware of how to take care of myself, let alone a sixteen-year-old, but separating us was not an option. After the meeting, I drove Uncle Kenny's Honda truck home and raced to my room to read his letter.

Dear Pumpkin,

If you're reading this, then you know I'm gone. Chasity, when you came to stay with us, I wanted to show you a love that could equal your parents'. My heart was heavily burdened when I found out about Tray and Cathy. I promised myself that I would care for and protect you. I kept my promise and I believe I did a good job raising you into a magnificent young woman. Before your parent's murder, your dad hid some money away for you. It was eighty-two thousand dollars, which paid for your college education. Chasity, we both know I'm not your biological father, but you are my daughter in every other way. I love you more than life itself and I would die for you, my love. I spoiled you and Destiny, and I pray that God will lead the two of you into the right path. Take care of Aunt Dumpling and Destiny until I see you again. And Chass, take good care of yourself. I was there to protect you from them little knuckleheads, but I can't protect you any longer. I expect you to be responsible and don't give away what God blessed you with until you're married. That may be unrealistic, but I have faith in you, Daughter. I want you to find the man you asked me about named Jon-Jon. There's information in my safe that can help you. The combination is your birthday. Remember who loves you. Uncle Kenny

I collapsed on my pillow and sobbed. The reality of losing four parents was too much to bear. I longed for my uncle and aunt to be back in my life, and the agony inside turned destructive. I blacked out and vandalized my room

"Chasity, what are you doing? Stop!" Destiny yelled as she wrapped her arms around me. We both sobbed for hours, eventually falling asleep on my bed

The next morning, I took Destiny to school. After I dropped her off, I went to the funeral home. I chose a platinum coffin for Uncle Kenny and pink for Aunt Dumpling, her favorite color. The funeral director tried to sell me on less expensive models, but my uncle and aunt deserved to go out in style. The total bill for the funeral came to thirty-nine thousand dollars. Once I took care of the details, I raced home to meet Aunt Dumpling's best friend, Olivia. She was bringing over food for Destiny and I, and she wanted to help get the funeral invitations out.

When I pulled into the garage, I saw Olivia waving at me from across the street. I escorted her into the house and we got started. Three hundred invitations later, we were finally done. She asked if I wanted her to warm up a plate of food, but I told her I had to pick up Destiny from school. She extended her generosity by offering to cook for us for a while. I agreed because I was not a chef by any means. Aunt Dumpling was an excellent cook, and I wished I had taken the time to gain a few cooking skills. Olivia and I walked out together and I went to pick up Destiny.

As soon as Destiny got inside the truck, she started crying. "What's wrong, Dee?" I asked concerned.

"My teachers said if I don't finish the missed and extra credit assignments, I won't pass to the twelfth grade. There's no way I'll finish in time!"

"Yes you will, Destiny. I will help you, even if I have to do them myself. You will pass to the next grade because you didn't. When we get home, I'll look to see what needs to be done."

"Thanks, Chass. I don't know what I would do without you. I'm so happy you came to live with us because I can't imagine life without you."

"Aww, that's so sweet, Dee. Ditto, life without my sister would be unimaginable."

I warmed up the food when we got home and reviewed Destiny's assignments. Those teachers were insensitive assholes to expect her to finish all the required work. However, they did not know she possessed a secret weapon — me. It wasn't impossible, but it would take a few days to finish everything.

The funeral was one of the saddest days of my life since losing my real parents. Uncle Kenny and Aunt Dumpling had a good turnout. There was not an available seat inside the church and people came far and wide to pay their respects. The funeral dragged on due to everyone wanting to speak on their behalf. Things suddenly got real crazy when an unknown woman took the mic. She broke down, saying she just lost the love of her life. She continued to embarrass herself by lying on my Uncle, saying she was pregnant with his son and that he promised to marry her. Murderous thoughts ran through my mind as I contemplated whipping this bitch's ass and dragging her out the church. She had me hype. Right before I went ballistic, a handsome man dragged her ass away. Wherever this chick came from, she was unwelcome. How dare she spit those lies on my Uncle! Once things settled down and the crazed woman was forced to leave, they announced the final viewing of the bodies.

"Chasity, I don't want to see the bodies. Can you walk me outside to get some air?" Destiny asked.

"Sure, I can't take it either. Let's go," I said as I escorted her from the church.

Destiny broke down on the church steps. Friends of my uncle and aunt tried to console us, but I said we were fine, knowing how disrespectful Destiny could be. Her mouth was lethal and if provoked she would spit venom. Still, the handsome man that escorted the crazed woman out grabbed my hand and gave his condolences.

"You must be. Chasity. You look just like your mother, Cathy. We all grew up together - me, her, Kenny, and your father, Tray," he explained, while staring at me as if my mother had been resurrected. When he realized he was gawking, he said, "I'm sorry, it's just…your resemblance to your mother is remarkable. It's as if she spat you right out." He continued to stare.

"Thanks," I replied. He was handsome for an older man.

"Here, take my card. Don't hesitate to reach out if you need anything." Without looking at the card, I tossed it in the Michael Kors bag that my Uncle bought for me last Christmas. "I mean it, no matter what it is I want you to contact me right away."

He told Destiny the same thing as he walked away. I continued to comfort her until the funeral was over. When we got back home, it was full to capacity. I had never seen so many people gather in one house. From the front porch to the backyard, mourners swarmed our home.

They played oldies, danced, sang, and drank plenty of liquor. Yet, what caught my attention was when someone turned on a video that stilled me and touched my heart. It was a video of my mother and father, Uncle Kenny, and the man from the funeral. They were having a cookout and everyone appeared to be enjoying him or herself. My mother looked so gorgeous and I finally saw the resemblance.

Around ten that evening, most of the guests were gone, but some stayed to help clean. I tried to find Destiny with no success, until I looked in her bedroom and found her sound asleep. I left her alone because neither of us had gotten much sleep since the day of the crash.

We only had each other to lean on and I prayed for strength to care for her, knowing she could be a handful. I thought about the future, wondering how we would survive without our rock. I adored Uncle Kenny and admired his persistence and endurance. He was there for me when I needed him the most and never stopped until now. The pain and loneliness inside was fresh, and I craved for release and resolve.

Chapter 4

Chasity

A Year Later

Destiny was graduating high school and proud was an understatement. When she entered the twelfth grade, she got serious with her work and excelled. Our parents would have been proud of her even though she wanted to attend college away from home, in New York. She received one rejection letter after another, but New York University accepted her. She was still debating, so I intended to do everything in my power to keep her close to Philadelphia.

After the graduation ceremony, I stood off to the side and watched as she took pictures with all her friends. She was happy, which gave me pride in knowing I did good a job with her this past year on my own.

"Chasity, come over here and take a picture with me," she demanded.

"Okay, boss, I'm coming!" I replied, hurrying before she snapped.

Once she took enough pictures, she told everyone goodbye and we left. I had two surprises in store for her, even though I was unable to get the car she hinted about. After we split up the money and I paid the bills, it was impractical for my bank account. Destiny still had her share because I refused to allow her to spend any of it. I set that money aside for her first two years of college. We would have to figure out the rest. I just needed her to inform me of what college she chose.

I took her to the Cheese Cake Factory in King of Prussia, which was her favorite restaurant. When they seated us, I handed her the huge box I lugged inside the restaurant. She danced in her chair once she saw the pocketbooks inside. I got her two *Louis Vuitton* handbags, though she only asked for one. I felt guilty about the car, but we would have to share Uncle Kenny's truck for now.

"Thanks Chass, even though I thought I'd be pushing my whip. But I understand our financial sorrows, so don't start with the broke song," she said, knowing me so well.

"Well since you know that, I'll save it for another day. Today is your day."

"Since it's my day, I would love to go to my girlfriend's graduation party with no curfew. Please?" she begged.

"You're not grown yet, but you deserve to have fun. I remember when I graduated high school and Uncle Kenny shot me down when I asked. You know what, that was the only time I can recall being pissed at him," I replied as memories resurfaced.

"Yeah, I remember. You stopped speaking to him for two weeks. He was miserable and couldn't stand not talking to you. He would have me spy on you and report back. I wasn't mad though because we got a Disney World trip," she laughed.

"I'm not him, so you can go to your little party. But there will be a curfew, sweetie. Two o'clock and not a minute later," I warned. "So what's the plan, boss?"

"Let's go home. I need to find something to wear that matches one of my new pocketbooks. Plus, I need to take a nap."

"You're too young to be napping during the day," I replied, knowing how lazy she was.

When we got home, I thought about the interview I had at the Blake Corporation. The Dean at my college encouraged me to apply for the internship they were offering. He explained my chances were good because they were the sponsors of my scholarship money. The thirty-day internship came with the possibility of a permanent position. I needed this opportunity because money was getting low.

I made a few thousand dollars completing Uncle Kenny's orders, but making cabinets was hard work when you're flying solo. I worked slower than my Uncle did and the customers showed no mercy. Once they found out he died, their business died with him. My first love was woodworking, but I wanted to dabble in restoring homes down to their original bones and flipping houses. Uncle Kenny showed me the importance and value of wood, and it pissed him off when he went into homes and saw painted wood. He'd say, "This is some bullshit. These dumb muhfucker's don't have a clue. You can't even get this wood no more and they cover it with paint. Dumb muhfucker's."

I missed his horrible mouth, and I had just realized where Destiny got hers. My Uncle cussed up a storm, but underneath the exterior he was a teddy bear. The three of us monopolized his world, leaving him no choice but to please us. Although his mouth and demeanor could be foul, he feared God and he read me the Bible often. I prayed and asked God to make a way for us because our futures were uncertain.

The next morning, I happily prepared for my interview, knowing I did not have to wake up Destiny. That was like hitting a brick wall. I happily put my face on, but I had hated wearing make-up until I found a well-known mineral foundation that I loved. It gave me a light coverage that looked and felt natural. I put on my new cream suit, along with a cream and brown striped silk shirt. I glanced back at myself in the mirror and approved of my interview outfit.

When I reached the eight story high-rise building in South Philly near Penn's Landing, there were two parking lots, one for the employees and the other for the visitors. Near the back of the building was a wide lot filled with construction machinery. I saw several excavators, forklifts, compactors, dozers, and every other machine capable of doing any construction job. Seeing them in person was impressive. My Uncle insisted I major in business, but my first love was working with my hands and getting dirty just like him.

When I walked into the lobby, I spotted a guard and the front desk receptionist. I walked over and informed her of my appointment with Mr. Junior Blake.

"What's your name?" the woman asked, dressed in her street wear.

"Chasity Smith," I smiled.

"You can have a seat and I will let Junior know you're here."

"Thank you!" I responded.

A few minutes later, she called me back to her desk. "I'm sorry but there's a problem with your appointment time. Junior said your appointment is at two o'clock. If you'd like, you can have a seat in the waiting area, or you can come back," she explained.

I looked at my phone. It was twelve thirty. It took thirty minutes to get here and I was not about to waste my gas. "I'll wait," I replied, as I took a seat.

"We have a cafeteria in the basement. You can get something to eat while you wait," she offered.

"Thanks, I think I will get some lunch."

"Take the elevator to the basement, then it's on your right. You can't miss it."

When I got on the elevator, a handsome man dressed in jeans and a t-shirt greeted me. He quickly sized me up and pressed the B button. I was happy that I wore my suit and my ego continued to grow. When the elevator stopped and the doors opened, he held the doors, allowing me to get off first. I thanked him and saw the cafeteria to my right.

I ordered a grilled Chicken Caesar salad and a bottle of water. I picked up the free Metro paper and sat at an empty table. A half-hour later, a woman disrupted my thoughts and lunch. "Excuse me, do you mind if I sit with you? I don't want to sit with those ignorant bitches," the unknown woman asked.

"Sure, I'm almost finished anyway," I responded.

"Don't let me scare you away, I'm just trying to enjoy my lunch break in peace," she explained as she unwrapped her turkey sandwich. "Did you transfer from one of the other offices? You don't look familiar."

"No, I'm here interviewing for the intern position."

"Oh, well, let me be the first to warn you, Junior is an asshole—I mean a real bastard. We call him Iron Man because he does not give second chances, the heartless monkey. And don't be fooled by his handsome face or sexy body. He's an evil narcissist!"

Damn! "I believe I saw him on the elevator, but he seemed okay. Is that him right there?" I turned her attention to the man from the elevator.

"No, that's his bother Domencio. He's cool, but he's not in charge of hiring or firing people. Junior takes pleasure in those duties."

"You got me scared now," I joked.

"You should be," she replied and stood up from the table. "My lunch is just about over, and he only gives us a half-hour—son of bitch. Good luck though!"

Her information haunted me, but I was up for any challenge. I headed back upstairs to the waiting area. Ten minutes later, the receptionist got a call, and she informed me that Junior was ready. "Catch the elevator to the eighth floor and the secretary up there will further assist you," she instructed.

Once I reached the eighth floor, a Caucasian woman greeted me. "Chasity Smith, Junior is ready for you. His office is through those glass doors and on the right," she explained.

When I knocked on his door, a young voice told me to enter. "Hello, Mr. Blake. It's a pleasure to meet you," I said as I crossed the room. I extended my hand, but he refused. *Damn he is fine as shit, if not one of the finest men I have ever seen.* I stood there a moment too long staring into his grayish eyes before he asked me to have a seat. His skin color and hair were flawless, and he was definitely mixed with something. What, I didn't know. There was no doubt that he was a black man, but his thick wavy hair deceived me. He reminded me of a black David Beckham with a slim but fit build.

"I see here you graduated a year ago with a bachelor's degree in business."

"Yes, along with carpentry skills," I replied, keeping it short and allowing him to lead.

"Carpentry," he repeated, while rubbing his chin. *Oooh don't do that, you're about to make me cum all over myself.* "Why has it taken you so long to start an internship? Shouldn't you have a job by now?" he asked, staring straight into my eyes.

"I had death in my family and I had to adjust to several life changes. But I'm getting by and it will not interfere with my job performance," I replied.

"Good. The position can change daily. There are no specific duties, other than doing what I instruct you to do. Do you understand?"

"Yes, I do what you say."

"You can start tomorrow. And Chasity? Don't come to work dressed that way again. We have a dress code, but it doesn't include suits of any kind. Keep it casual. Jeans, t-shirt—you get where I'm coming from," he said, disregarding anything else I might have to say. "Nine o'clock sharp and not a minute later, Chasity."

"Yes, Sir."

"Don't call me Sir or Mr. Blake. Junior will be fine. Goodbye, Chasity."

"Goodbye, Junior and thanks for giving me a chance. I promise I'll work hard." He only half nodded in response, but I left satisfied.

When I walked into the house, I hollered out for Destiny but got no answer, so I went to my bedroom and changed my clothes. While I looked for my slippers under the bed, I heard moaning sounds. I stopped dead in my tracks when I heard it again. I crept to Destiny's room and peeked through the peephole. It was horrific. A boy was fucking Destiny hard, and she was enjoying it. I stood up and banged on her door. This little hot box had lost her mind.

"Destiny, what the hell are you doing in there?" I yelled through the door.

"Give me a minute, I'm coming! Get off me, Khalif! My sister is here." I heard her say.

I waited downstairs so I could confront them with this blatant disrespect. Destiny graduated, but she was not an adult yet. Twenty minutes later, she pranced down the stairs with Khalif in toe. He tried to walk right past me and out the door, but I was not having that.

"Excuse you, where the hell are you going? You think you can fuck my sister and walk right past me?"

"It's not like that at all. Destiny told me to just leave."

"How old are you, Khalif? That is your name, right?"

"Yes, and I'm eighteen. I wanted to get your permission to date Destiny."

"You just fucked her in my house. Don't you think it's a little too late to ask for permission?"

"I see your point, but Destiny and I are serious about each other and I want to marry her."

"Marry her! Get the fuck out my house," I barked as I pushed him out the front door.

"Why did you do that, Chass? I'm in love with him and when I turn eighteen we're getting married."

"Did you bump your fucking head? You're too young to get married. You can't even pick a college!"

"That's where you're wrong. I'm going to New York with Khalif and we're getting an apartment together."

"Oh my God! Uncle Kenny and Aunt Dumpling must be rolling over in their graves. I'm too young for all this stress."

"Haven't you ever been in love? Of all the people in this world I thought you'd understand! I don't care what you say anyway. I have no parents and you're not my ruler. Khalif loves me and he's my support system."

"Destiny, I'm right here. I support you—always. It's running into the arms of a boy that will hurt you," I rationed, thinking back to my ex-boyfriend, Terrance.

"Chass, I love you. You're my sister, but it's not the same. Khalif makes me feel alive, as if I can do the impossible. He's different from most boys out there. Khalif is smart and he comes from a good family. He shows me things that are amazing and he is so mature."

"Yeah it's clear he's showing you things, but I don't care how amazing they are. You shouldn't be having sex, Destiny. Have a little self-respect. If Khalif loves you as much as you claim, then he should be able to wait."

"He would have waited, but it was my decision. I wanted to do it. And I have been making love to Khalif for over a year, so he ain't going nowhere." She rolled her eyes with confidence.

"I hope for your sake you're protecting yourself because Lord knows we can't afford a baby. I came home to share my good news. Instead, I'm greeted with this teenage bullshit. I'm done, since you got it all figured out. Do you, Destiny."

"Chass, what did you want to share?"

"It's not important. Good night," I spat, storming up the stairs.

When I got inside my room, memories of Terrance flooded my mind and brought back hidden emotions. I met him in my sophomore year at college. He was majoring in architecture and engineering while being groomed to take over the family business. He came from a wealthy family and his father was a pastor at a well-known church in Philadelphia.

Terrance was handsome, smart, and we did everything together. Our problems didn't start until I wanted to make love. We had been dating for six months, but the most we engaged in was cuddling and kissing. I was sick of the intimacy without the penetration. Terrance, being a God-fearing man from his upbringing, took his beliefs seriously. Sex before marriage being the main commitment.

I acted like the man in the relationship, pressuring him for sex. Although I understood his faith, I wanted to share my virginity with him. I became bored with his shit because other cute boys were checking for me. I broke up with him, but a week later he was at my dorm room begging me to come with him. He asked me to pack an overnight bag, and I packed with the quickness.

We pulled into a motel parking lot and when we got inside the room, he wasted no time asking me to undress. As I stood naked in front of him, he explained that we were not indulging in sex, but he had something else in mind. I was nervous until he threw me on the bed and spread my legs. He dove into my vagina with his tongue and took my body to the abyss. I had never experienced an orgasm so pleasurable. I thought the ones I gave myself were spectacular, but I realized the tongue ruled the planet. Terrance continued to feast on my vagina to avoid breaking his abstinence and I obliged, hoping with all my heart he would ask me to marry him. But that engagement never came. Instead, two weeks before graduation, he broke up with me and told me he had to focus on the family business. He said he had sinned with me and he needed to repent, putting the past behind him. He wasn't saying that shit when he was deep sea diving, and I had stopped pressuring him about sex. On the flip side, he hadn't crossed my mind much, and I realized I didn't love him as much as I thought I did.

After going down memory lane, I cut the television on, pulled out my *Seven* jeans, and prepared for work tomorrow. Junior said he wanted casual, and I had no problems with that. I looked under my bed, grabbed my white High Ends, and thought about my day. Junior seemed tough, but I planned to obey and please him. I needed to secure a job, and if the internship goes smoothly, I should have permanent job in a month.

Chapter 5

Junior

I was on my way to our monthly meeting with my father, the infamous Johnathan Blake, better known as Jon-Jon. My father started his business ten years ago and named me CEO when I got out of jail after serving two years. The charge should have been life, but my father worked miracles and got me a large decrease in my sentence. When you have money, connections, and a ruthless family backing you, prison is much easier to survive. Still, no matter how you sliced that bullshit, I would never be returning.

Jon-Jon used to be one of the heads of the largest and most lethal drug empires in Philadelphia. Loyalty and honor had vanished, and snitches and bitches had risen from the womb. Pops' intuition of the drug game was solid. He left the game and started a new family business, which I had turned into a construction empire. The drug game had changed and I was living proof of its outcome. My father pulled out at the right time and we left that bullshit for the dumb and dumber. The Philly police wanted my family for years, but were unsuccessful in their attempts to bring us down. Still, that changed in 2004 when I was arrested for drug trafficking, murder, conspiracy and many other miscellaneous charges. A few of the young soldiers sold their souls, and I went down for the entire organization, facing life in prison. By the grace of God, my father worked his magic and got me a three year bid. Pops demanded that I school myself on everything regarding the construction business. I spent ninety percent of my time reading and educating myself. In 2006, they freed me a year early for good behavior.

My father sent me books and literature on our business. I poured all my frustrations and energy into learning every aspect of my new position. When he made me CEO, I thought heads would roll. My cousin Wayne and little brother Domencio were already prominent leaders in the company and I figured they would be my greatest opposition. Yet they welcomed me, and we became the three musketeers with me as the leader. I believed ruling with iron fist was effective and it kept people out of my office with the bullshit. Instead, they complained to Wayne and Domencio, which was how I liked it.

I drove up the long driveway to my father's eight thousand square foot home and spotted Wayne parking at the same time.

"What's up, Wayne?" I greeted.

"This hot ass weather. What's up with you? Did your father tell you why we're meeting at his house?"

"Nah, he just explained it was big."

"That shit sounds like dollar bills, and my ears are ringing. Let's not keep Uncle Jon waiting."

We walked into his study and all the elite administrative staff had arrived. My father sat behind his desk, looking agitated when he spotted me.

"Hey, Pops. What's up?"

"Junior, I will talk to you later, but I can't delay anymore. Take a seat," he demanded. "Folks, we landed the contract of the century. It's a contract for two billion dollars." Everyone in the room sat up straight, and if my father did not have their attention before, he had it then. "The contract is for an extremely challenging building in Dubai. This is the most lucrative deal this company has seen since its birth in 2004. I have full confidence in all of you. I need more than your best on this project, and I set up a meeting in two days with an engineering consultant group. Junior, I need you to be at that meeting."

"We have our own engineers, Pops. We don't need to consult with another firm" I said, confident in our team.

"Junior, this isn't your ordinary soil and we have never taken on a project of this magnitude. These engineers are experienced with building in Dubai and they will simply be there to consult. With that said, meeting adjourned." He looked at me and said, "Junior, I need you to stick around for a few."

I respected and looked up to my father. He embodied the image of a real man. The one significant difference between him and me was that he loved women hard. My father was not a player; he was a lover. My mother died knowing how much my father loved her. I remember when she would walk into a room, my father's whole demeanor would change and a smile of wonder and adoration would show on his face. We were opposites in that aspect of our lives; I never saw myself settling down with a woman. I've had every type of woman from the gold digger to the dream seeker. They all came with headaches and my tolerance level for anything other than sex was minus zero.

"How you been, Pop?" I asked, preparing myself for a lecture.

"I'm great son, but I need to discuss your attitude at work."

"My attitude at work? Where is all this coming from, Pops?" I spat, annoyed.

"Junior, don't look at me with that smug expression. Everyone is complaining and no one feels comfortable around you. This new contract is very important, and I need my staff happy and efficient. I can't afford for people to be fucking up because you want act like King Henry," he scolded as he poured himself a glass of expensive Scotch.

"I didn't bring the company as far as I did by playing nice. I'm not their friend—I'm their boss, point blank."

"Yes, you have done exceptional work being CEO, but no one is free from constructive criticism. Enough already. You will treat people with respect and dignity. Learn to be a team player. I know you can do it, Junior."

"Is that all?" I asked, thinking I was the team, and they were the assistants. Change did not come easy for me unless I was the one making the changes.

"Yes, Junior," he sighed, knowing he failed to convince me.

I pondered what my father had said, but I was not that bad. No one complained to me, so I didn't see the problem. Rarely have I had confrontations with the staff, and their issues were meaningless. Wayne and Domencio were the go-to guys for those migraines. Nevertheless, Pops made a small bit of sense. This new contract would change the game and the staff needed to be at their best. I would try, but I was not promising anything.

Chapter 6

Chasity

It has been three weeks since the start of my internship and the staff was excited about the contract with Dubai. Honestly, the internship was bullshit on a stick. I fetched coffee and did more clerical duties than anything of substance. However, at lunchtime, I researched Dubai's history and the building infrastructures on my iPad. This would be a challenge for all involved, requiring substantial attention to detail. I was interested in the building products and I had discovered ways for the company to save money. My plan was to share it at the staff meeting this afternoon.

Junior was unapproachable but my Uncle always said, "A quiet mouth don't get fed, Chasity." If he was not interested in saving his company money, not only would I consider him a bad executive, but a major dickhead. The staff sought after Wayne or Domencio with any ideas they wanted to pitch, waiting for approval from the fake God, sitting on his throne. The difference between them and me was my services were free with no guarantee of a permanent position, so I couldn't give a fuck. By now, someone should have approached me about a full-time position. I hoped the research I put into my pitch would result in the perfect opportunity I needed.

Everyone piled into the conference room one by one. I was nervous and excited to offer some input, even if it was unwanted. Junior sat at the head of the table with Wayne and Domencio on each of his sides. The conference table did not have enough seats, so I sat in a chair near the back wall. Captivated by my own thoughts, I missed the entire meeting and before I knew it, Junior adjourned the meeting.

I stood up and said, "Wait, I have something to share. I discovered a way for the company to save a good portion in building materials." Junior had a disgruntled expression on his face. I glanced around the room, and a few members of the staff just shook their heads. Others smirked aloud as if I had just said the unforbidden.

"Who are you again?" he asked, agitated.

"My name is Chasity. I'm the intern, remember?" *You know who I am, bitch*, I wanted to say.

"Intern—listen, intern. The next time you want to have an outburst, I encourage you to keep it to yourself. You should be more attentive to my coffee because it's been weak—if you know what I'm saying."

Son of bitch! "No, I don't know what you're saying. My name is Chasity not Intern, and I believe that I had a suggestion as opposed to an outburst. I was trying to help the company and myself because I didn't spend four years in college to get anyone's coffee or run errands."

"Chasity, you have been weighed and measured, now get the fuck out my office. Actually, get your belongings and never return to this building."

"Weighed and measured? What's that supposed to mean?"

"It means you hold no value here, and you depreciated when you walked into this meeting."

"Yeah, well—well you can kiss my black ass, you smug dickhead!" The room emptied fast. "You act as if I'm being paid to fetch your whack ass coffee. You're an insensitive jerk who can't even entertain my money saving idea. Dumb ass."

"Domencio, call security." Domencio looked at Junior as if he had dropped from the sky.

"Security, you're calling security on me? You punk ass nigga! Call security! By the time they get up here, you'll be stabbed to death with that envelope opener," I barked. "I know your type all too well. You're that pretty boy bitch type, who sit behind the desk and bark orders because he got a little dick. Yuck, what is that smell?" I asked, covering my nose. "Oh, I know what it is. It's your pussy ass." The psychotic demon inside overpowered my sane mind.

"What did you call me?" he asked, as security arrived.

"What part didn't you get, Pussssssssy?" I screamed.

"Chuck, close and lock the door behind you." *Oh shit*! I panicked.

"No, Chuck, that's okay, I'm leaving," I said, but Chuck ignored me and locked the door.

"Say that again, Chasity. I didn't quite hear you," he said, as he walked towards me with a sinister look on his face. "What was the word you used to describe me?" He was in my face damn near breathing down my throat. *Damn, he smells so good*. His cologne swept me off my feet and I couldn't catch my breath. He placed both of his hands against the wall, blocking my escape and whispered, "Pussy, yes that was it. Please—repeat yourself so we both understand."

"Listen, I was out of order. I'll just leave and you won't ever see me again," I replied, as I try to pry myself away from him. However, he was not budging.

He pinned me on the wall and said, "No, not before you say it again." His penis was poking my stomach through his jeans, and his demeanor turned me on in a sick and fearful way. His aggressive and unruly behavior sent a bolt of energy through me, so I continued to test the waters.

"I said, Pussy. You're a pus—". He wrapped his hands around my throat allowing just enough space for me to breathe.

"You know, you should watch that slick tongue of yours with someone of my stature. See, I'm sensitive to that word and coming from a bird like you, it's unacceptable. A few years ago, they might've found your body lying in the alley with your tongue cut out, so thank God for better days. You get a pass today, but next time you may not be so lucky," he said, as he turned me loose.

I grabbed my pocketbook and unlocked the door. "I'm look-ing forward to the next time. And just so we understand each other, if you ever invade my space again, they may find you with your tongue wrapped around your dick." I gave him the meanest face I could muster and got the hell out of dodge.

I felt depleted when I got home and reflected on the ordeal. My behavior was despicable and the way I handled the altercation with Junior was irrational. He pissed me off by saying I wasn't worth shit, so he had himself to blame for my rowdy unleashing. My uncle always told me how beautiful and smart I was. He would say, "Chass, you got the whole package and you can thank your momma for that." Junior tried to steal my confidence, unaware of the strong woman Uncle Kenny had raised, and I was not about to be humiliated by the likes of him.

I walked into the kitchen and cleaned the wingdings I thawed out before I left for work. Destiny's behind was not home, but I knew she was with Khalif. While I prepared dinner, I replayed the day's event. It still amazed me that someone who was so handsome was one of the most insensitive men I had ever met. Still, I was just fooling myself, because he could have had me bent over the conference room table, had he continued to entice me with his dangerous persona.

I studied his moves whenever the chance arose, which normally happened when I slaved to get his coffee. He was not the type that wanted to hear his own voice nor was he obtrusive. What he was, was an unapproachable, pompous, hazardous man that if given a chance, I would give my virginity to. When his breath rubbed against my face, I wanted him so bad. His even, dark brown sugar complexion and slim frame was a turn on. Add a pair of bowlegs, thick eyelashes and gray eyes, and he was enough to send any woman insane. But once they got a taste of him, I'm sure their impression changed. I'm positive he has an Affective Disorder that is undiagnosed and untreated.

When I finished taking the last pieces of fried chicken out of the pan, I heard Destiny come in and turn on the television. "Chasity!" she yelled. "What's for dinner?"

"Come see, and I'm not fixing your plate!" I hollered, as I put a spoonful of rice, corn and string beans onto my plate. Olivia taught us the basics and I was happy she did, knowing we could not afford take-out or delivery anymore. Destiny and I took turns, and the cooking was working out fine.

"Why aren't you eating downstairs?" she asked, once she saw me taking my plate upstairs.

"I have some stuff to do on the computer before tomorrow," I lied, because I was still mad over the whole Khalif ordeal and avoiding her. Especially now that I was back at square one, stuck in the house with no money or prospective job.

I meditated for hours, but I came up with nothing. Working for Junior was no longer a choice, and I thought about Uncle Kenny because I missed him so much. If he was here, I know I would receive the encouragement and support I desperately needed. Uncle Kenny was my rock, and he held me down from the time I was ten. He was more a father than my biological father was. He molded me and taught me to depend on God, him, and myself.

I thought about flipping houses while I was still in college. I composed a business plan, but I needed the startup money. My uncle was against getting loans of any kind. He encouraged me to stay away from it, but my back was against the wall.

I tried to think of a quick get-rich scam, but came up blank. Then in an instant, I thought about the letter Uncle Kenny left me. He told me to check the safe and to contact Jon-Jon. I could not believe a whole year had passed and I was just remembering! I bolted to their room, but stopped when I got outside the door. I had not been in their room since they died and it was awkward and uncomfortable. I mustered up the courage. Once inside, I went straight for the safe. In the letter, Uncle Kenny said the combination was my birthday. I put in the date and the safe opened.

Inside were three envelopes and jewelry. I grabbed everything and took it back to my room. The first envelope said 'Emergency Cash', and it contained fifteen thousand dollars. *Hallelujah, thank you, God and Uncle Kenny.* The second envelope contained photos, and one in particular got my attention. It was a picture of Uncle Kenny, my father, the man from the funeral, and another man posed holding money and guns. I turned the picture over and it read, *Jon-Jon Million Dollar Party*! I wondered if the man from the funeral was Jon-Jon or if it was the other man standing beside him. I opened the final envelope and there was another letter from Uncle Kenny.

Dear Chass,
   Do you remember when we talked about your parents? Well, Jon-Jon was a close friend to your father and me. If you desire answers about your parent's death, he is the man you want to reach out to. Also, Chasity he owes me and your father. If you ever need anything you should contact him immediately. I love you my sweet daughter and I pray for your happiness!
   Love Always, Uncle Kenny.

I sat there dumbfounded for a moment until I remembered that the man from the funeral had given me a card. I raced to my closet and pulled out my pocketbook in hopes I still had the card. I dumped everything on the bed and found the card crinkled up. I opened it and it had the name Johnathan Blake written on it. *Johnathan must stand for Jon-Jon. Blake? Blake! No, it can't be*, I thought. I looked at the number and decided it was too late to call, but I would contact him first thing in the morning.

I made a batch of pancakes and turkey sausage that next morning. Destiny was asleep, and the house was quiet. I put aside her plate and called Johnathan. When he answered, he sounded pleasant and businesslike.

"Jonathan Blake here, how I can I help you," he asked.

"Hello, Mr. Blake. You might not remember me, but you gave me your card at my aunt and uncle's funeral. I'm Chasity, Tray and Cathy's daughter."

"I know who you are, Chasity. How are you?"

"I'm fine, but I was calling to ask you something."

"Shoot, I'm all ears," he replied.

"Is your nickname Jon-Jon?"

"Yes, that's what some call me. Why did you ask me that, Chasity?"

"Because Uncle Kenny told me I should reach out to you if I ever need anything, or need questions answered about my parents."

"Do you require both requests?" he asked.

"Yes, but I'm more in need. I was hoping you would be generous enough to invest in my new company. I have my business plan and proposal ready for review, and I can email it to you right now. But as far as my parents goes, I only have one question."

"What's that, Chass?"

"Did you have my parents murdered?"

The phone went silent for a few seconds before he said, "Hell no! What gave you that impression?"

"It was something I heard before my parents' murder."

"Listen, Chasity. I want to hear more about this business plan, and I think it's a good idea we meet immediately. I can have my chef prepare anything you desire and we can talk more. Is tonight too soon?" he asked.

"Tonight?" I repeated.

"Yes, I hope your schedule is free. I would love for you to meet my family. Why don't you bring Destiny along?"

"Sure, I just need your address."

He gave me the information and asked if I could be there by six. I agreed and hoped Destiny would come. Her mind, body and soul belonged to Khalif and her whereabouts were unknown often. Just then, Destiny walked into the living room and plopped down on the sofa.

"I put your food in the microwave. I'm sure it's cold by now."

"Thanks, but I'm not that hungry. Plus, Khalif should be here soon to take me to breakfast."

"I guess you're going to do exactly what you want and follow behind that boy."

"Yup," she smugly replied.

I rolled my eyes and said, "I need you to come with me to meet one of Uncle Kenny's friends tonight. He might invest in me, but he asked that we both attend."

"What time and where is this meeting?"

"In Newtown Square by six o'clock."

"Okay," she replied as she headed back upstairs.

We got lost, and it took an hour to get to Jon-Jon's home after making a wrong turn. I pressed the bell on the gate and it opened after I introduced myself. Destiny was in awe, and she stayed as silent as a lamb, which was unlike her. I too admired the beautifully crafted home and its custom made brickwork. It had that Old World charm and was built with the finest quality construction. It reminded me of the home I lived in with my parents.

"Dude must be a baller to live in a house like this," Destiny said.

"You probably don't remember him, but you met him at the funeral. He came over, introduced himself, and gave me his card." She shrugged her shoulders.

Johnathan greeted us at the door, and he was even more handsome than I recalled. "Chasity and Destiny, welcome to my humble abode," he said as if he lived in a shack.

Once we got inside, I could not help but bask in my exquisite surroundings. The incredible millwork, moldings, stonework, and cathedral ceilings placed me in wonderland. It was a carpenter's dream to see all the attention to detail, and it was obvious this house had no budget.

"Thanks for inviting us to dinner, Johnathan. Your house is spectacular. I love the Belizean mahogany and grey marble. The streaks match the wood to perfection."

"I see you know your materials," he said surprised.

"Yes, I do. Did you pick out the trimmings? They're exceptional."

"You're making me blush, Chasity. I take that as a compliment. Come, I want to introduce you both to the family. I thought we could start out with a drink. Follow me. Destiny, I'll have Janice bring you something of your choice. Chasity, are you old enough to drink?"

"Yes, I'm twenty-two, but I wouldn't even know what to order."

"I see—a virgin," he said, and I was wondering if he could see through me, until I realized he was referring to the alcohol. "I have the perfect starter drink. Trust me, you will enjoy my margaritas, and I'll make one special just for you."

"Thanks, that sounds good," I replied, feeling at home. His house was warm and smothering in a positive way.

When we walked into his study, it was empty. Jon-Jon walked over to his mini bar and whipped up my margarita. Moments later, the housekeeper came in and asked if we needed anything. He instructed her to have the family join us in the study. Jon-Jon handed me my drink, and it tasted delicious. He made me a strawberry margarita with sugar around the rim.

"Good?" he asked.

"Yes, very good, and sweet." A pretty woman walked in with a little girl in hand as I took another sip.

"Chasity, this is my lady, Carlton and her two-year-old daughter, Anastasia."

"Nice to meet you," I greeted, shaking Carlton's hand.

"The pleasure is mine," Carlton responded.

"Where are those boys of mine?" Jon-Jon asked, sounding impatient.

"They're coming, Jon. Just calm down, honey," she replied.

I took another sip of my drink because it was so good, but what walked through the door next caused me to spit the drink out and cough uncontrollably.

"Are you okay, Chass? Carlton get her a glass of water. Okay young lady, no more margaritas for you," Jon-Jon comforted, showing affection like a concerned father. Once I caught my breath, he said, "I want to introduce you to my sons, Junior and Domencio. Guys, this here is Chasity and her sister, Destiny." The room got quiet and Jon-Jon caught whiff of the awkwardness. "Maybe we should head into the dining room, I'm sure dinner is ready." He left, and everyone followed.

It was uncomfortable and exciting sitting at the table with Junior. He wore his jeans well and commanded the room with pure sexy. However, I was not about to consort with the enemy. He had better keep his mouth shut, and I prayed I kept my cool. In addition, I had to refrain, because I needed Jon-Jon to make that investment with me, and I did not want to risk him finding out about my behavior. If he discovered my emotional breakdown the other day, it may have an adverse effect and cause him to back away.

"Chasity, you sure you're okay?" Destiny whispered when we sat down at the table.

"Yeah, Dee. I'll tell you all about it when we leave."

Jon-Jon said the prayer when dinner arrived, and I glanced over at Junior to see if the Devil prayed. Shockingly, he had his head down. I felt sure he was pretending. As disgraceful as he acted, I suspected there was no relationship between him and God.

After prayer, Jon-Jon said, "Chasity has a business proposal prepared, and she wants me to invest in her company. Junior, I was thinking you could look over her plan for me."

"Nah, I'm good, Pops. We have our hands full and we don't need the investment. And I'm not interested in doing business with this woman."

"Junior, give it a chance, son. Remember what we discussed the other day."

"Yeah, but that was different. You were referring to our employees, not her."

"I was one of your employees two days ago. You see, your precious son fired me and called security on me like the little bi—." He stood up and gave me that familiar menacing look from the day before. One to which I looked forward. I stood up as well to stand my ground. Admittedly, I wanted to be reprimanded by him and I was willing to test his limits.

"What in Heaven's name is going on here?" Uncle Jon demanded.

"You were free labor and never an employee, Chasity," Junior spat, but I loved how he said my name.

"We need not rehash the other day, Mr. Blake. I know what I am, and you know how I feel about your sorry ass," I replied while rolling my eyes. "If you all don't want to invest into my business, I will find another source. If you would excuse me, I need to use the powder room before I commit murder."

"Do you want me to come with you, Chass?" Destiny asked, looking confused as ever.

"No, I'll be right back, just stay here until I return."

"I'll show you where it is," Carlton stated, just as dumbfounded as Uncle Jon.

When I got inside the restroom, I washed my face to calm my nerves. Junior was getting the best of me tonight and seeing him made me want him even more. Being torn between kicking his ass and allowing him to take my virginity was getting on my nerves, not to mention the margarita was affecting me. I didn't have to use the bathroom, I just needed to get away from Junior. I glanced at myself one last time and opened the door. I almost fell back when I saw Junior leaning against the wall outside the bathroom. He pushed me back into the bathroom and locked the door.

"Chasity, when you left my office, what did you say? Oh yes, now I remember. After you insulted my manhood, you said you looked forward to the next time, and something about invading your space—right? And let's not forget the threat on my dick."

"I think it's obvious you need some meds. Who cares what I said. I see you, and I looked forward to it. So what now?" I was not backing away.

Before I could say another word, he pulled me into his arms, grabbed the back of my head and forced me to kiss him. I tried to resist at first, but the smell of his cologne and the taste of his lips restrained me from denying him. He twirled his tongue inside my mouth while lifting me up and placing me on the double vanity granite sink.

"You think I'm a pussy, huh?" he asked, as he kissed my neck and unbuttoned my shirt. "I want to show how much of a pussy I am, Chasity. You want to see?" he asked, while pricking my nipples and staring precariously into my eyes. I was in shock. "Cat got your tongue, huh. Where is that big bad Chasity now? You think you can come up in here wearing those tight jeans and back talking a nigga. Say the word, I'm daring you."

"What, you mean pus—pussy," I moaned from the pleasure of his touch.

"There we go," he said, roughly pulling off my jeans. "I'm going teach you a lesson, Chasity. You ready?" His fingers were toiling my clitoris, serving delightful sensations.

"I think we should stop," I said, in between moans.

"Nah, you don't want to stop now, do you? We wouldn't want anyone to get the impression you're a pussy. That's your favorite name—right?" he replied while nibbling on my ear lobe.

"You made me mad and you embarrassed..." He cut me off.

"Shhhhh, this isn't the time nor the place to back down. See, I know your type too. I sized you up from the day you walked into my office," he continued, as his finger was doing work on my clitoris. "Girls like you come a dime a dozen, Chasity. Look how easy it is for me to have you right where I want you. You're about to let me fuck you right here and now. Who's the pussy now, Chasity?" He stepped away from me, leaving me trembling on top of the sink. *WTF!* I thought. "Oh wait, did you think I wanted you?" he laughed. "I'm particular, Chasity, and I don't waste time with easy goers."

"I'm far from that. But if I'm honest with myself, I can admit that you are very handsome man, and any woman put in this position would find you hard to resist, too. So don't think you're disrespecting or degrading me. You are sexy, but you're an asshole and you act like--."

"Choose your words wisely, Chasity," he interrupted.

"A wimp! Junior, there is something about you that lights my fire, but I can also see myself pushing you off the Walt Whitman. I'm glad we had this little talk, because I'm over it, and you," I said, while putting back on my clothes. "I was a fool to want to share my virginity with you. Thank God my angels appeared and stopped this atrocity."

"Virgin?" he repeated, but I was out the door. He pulled me back into the bathroom and said, "Look inside the bottom drawer and you'll see a comb. Fix your hair because it didn't look like that when you left." He walked out the bathroom and closed the door.

I looked in the mirror and my hair was wild. I did a quick makeover and walked back to the dining room. "Destiny, get ready, we're about to go. Jon-Jon, I'm sorry we didn't get to talk, but we have to leave."

"We haven't had desert, and I was still hoping we could talk, Chasity," he reasoned.

"I know, but some other time. Preferably alone."

"I'll walk you ladies to the door," Domencio chimed in.

"Take your hands off her, Domencio," Iron Man barked, when Domencio gave me a proper escort by putting his arm underneath my and Destiny's arms.

"Junior, what's up bro? Get it together man," he responded, while everyone looked at him as if he were crazy.

"I'll walk the ladies out," Jon-Jon butted in. "Chasity, we still need to talk, and I want to get to know you better. Your leaving, does it have anything to do with Junior?" he asked.

"Yes. It's complicated and right now I'm beside myself. It's not your fault that your seed produced a bad one. Here is my business plan, and if you're interested, my number is included. I would love to build on our relationship, Jon-Jon. However, I would rather do it with just the two of us."

"Fair enough, Chasity. Maybe we can get together sometime this week for dinner. I know a nice intimate place where we can talk. Oh and Chasity, don't misconstrue the word intimate. You can count on me the same way you did with your Uncle Kenny and your father."

"I didn't take it no way, Uncle Jon-Jon." We both laughed aloud.

"Destiny that goes for you too, sweetheart. You should be off to college soon and I want you to contact me when you decide on a college."

"I already decided. I'm going to NYU and I'm moving in with—," I nudged her arm because she was about to ruin things with her news of moving in with Khalif. Jon-Jon was trying to be a father figure, and we both needed a daddy. Trying to be every figure to Destiny for the past year had stressed me out.

"Uh, what she meant to say is, New York is one of many she's considering."

"Very good then, let me know what you ladies decide," he said, holding the door open. I glanced at the immaculate home one last time and wished I could stay forever.

Chapter 7

Junior

"What was that all about, Junior?" Pops asked when he came back. "What did you say to Chasity when you followed her to the bathroom?" He looked at me knowingly.

"Pops, I don't know what you're talking about."

"Junior, I warned you about your attitude. You're not in the streets running corners no more, Son. You need to get that chip off your shoulder before it destroys you. Tell me, why did you fire her?"

"She had an idea on how to save the company some money, but Junior disrespected her in front of everyone," Domencio snitched.

"Yo, Dee, I believe he was talking to me, Rat."

"Call me what you want, but I'm tired of cleaning up your messes. The staff hate you brah, and I know you don't care about that, but it's starting to affect me."

"Affect you? Get the fuck outta' here. I'm the one that took this company from flipping houses to building skyscrapers, so all you need to do is handle business as usual."

"What idea did Chasity have about saving my company money?" Pops asked, reminding us who was really in charge.

"We didn't get a chance to hear it before he fired her and called security," Domencio responded.

"You called security on her, Junior? What did she do to deserve that?"

"She threatened me and called me a pussy several times. I don't play those games, especially at the workplace. And ah—I see you've taken a liking to her, Pops... but honestly, she's lucky to be alive. That uncontrolled mouth she has is going to be her downfall, disrespecting me!

"If the shoe fits, oh well," he shrugged as both he and Domencio burst into laughter.

"I'm glad y'all find this shit funny. Pops, I can't stop you from building a relationship with her, just make sure you keep her away from me. I'm not about to play games with this young girl, and I definitely don't want to go back to jail."

"You're not going back to jail, Junior, and you will not lay one hand on Chasity," he cautioned.

"What's the deal with this? I know you have history with your past partners, but that was a long time ago and they're all dead now."

"Dead, but not forgotten. Except for that snake, King. May that bastard rot in hell."

"Whatever, Pops. I don't feel like visiting memory lane. Keep Chasity far away from me," I warned. "Carlton, thanks for dinner."

I parked in the parking garage of my condominium on Columbus Blvd. It included all the amenities I desired, and it was close to work. Only my closest family members had my address and when the time came for pleasure and entertaining a woman, I splurged on a nice hotel. My home was my sanctuary, and I refused to lead these women on or give them false hope. Investing into a long-term or committed relationship was never on my radar. My teenage crush Kali was the only one who came close before I went away to prison. She proved to be an unfaithful, backstabbing bitch who could drop off the face of the earth. Nevertheless, my emotions were slightly unkempt and Chasity was to blame.

The first time she walked into my office I thought 'here comes another pretty face thinking she can win me over with her beauty and body', but during the interview, something about her made me want to love her. Those foreign emotions had me bothered and confused but I set that aside, still planning to make her a permanent employee because she appeared to be hungry. Each encounter with her brightened my day, though that kind of change in my world was unwelcome. I had a solid life and I enjoyed being me.

Chasity had something I couldn't quite figure out. Her body was right and tight. She had a dimple in her chin and even her tacky nose ring was sexy. When she smiled the room danced, and as her expressions changed that dimple went along for the ride, igniting my entire body. Her lips were perfect and when I kissed them tonight, she further fueled my desire. After she dropped the bombshell about her virginity, she had me hook, line and sinker. I loved her fearlessness towards me, which only made me want her more. I didn't tell my father, but I took her plan home because I was curious of where her head was at. I poured myself a glass of Henny and reviewed her plan.

I wrapped up twenty minutes later and was amusingly impressed. Her ideas were cute, and it reminded me of when I took over the company. We started out flipping houses, but that was child's play for our empire now. It only took two years to bring in unforeseen profits and necessary expansion. The company escalated courtesy of me. Her business plan and the research she did was thorough, but her budget was a joke. The city had intentions of tearing down a single family home in Germantown and Chasity wanted to save it. Honestly, she would do better demolishing the house and rebuilding, but her interest lied in restoring the home to its original state.

I had to give it to her; she was ambitious if nothing else. The house foundation was in jeopardy and there was no telling what the inside entailed. At that moment, I decided to invest. I would make Domencio handle the details. I had a lot on my mind with the trip to Dubai approaching and my 30th birthday party right around the corner. I needed to be at peace with myself. I changed my clothes and went downstairs to the gym, one of the many amenities I enjoyed at my condo. Once I finished working out, I retired for the night. However, Chasity's sweet lips came to mind and I tossed and turned, trying to get her out of my head.

Chapter 8

Chasity

When I woke up the next morning, I heard Destiny and Khalif downstairs watching a movie. I gave in and allowed Destiny to have company, but her bedroom was off limits. I washed my face and brushed my teeth before I headed to the kitchen.

"What's up," I greeted.

"Good morning, Ms. Chasity. Did you sleep well? Because you look great." Khalif asked.

"Stop with the fake compliments, Khalif, and I told you not to call me Ms. I'm just a few years older than you, boy."

"He's just playing with you, Chasity, damn! My man is smart and he has a great sense of humor. Just relax," Destiny defended.

"Whatever," I replied, leaving the room. My cell phone was vibrating on the counter. I picked it up and looked at the screen, which showed an unknown number. "Hello?" I answered.

"Can I speak to Chasity?" the male voice asked.

"Who's calling?"

"This is Domencio Blake."

"Oh hey, Domencio. Why are you calling? Did Jon-Jon ask you to call?" I asked before he could reply.

"Actually, I was calling to inform you that the Blake Corporation will invest in your company. I was hoping you could meet me for lunch. Let's say around twelve thirty."

"Sure, but I can come down there. You don't have to take me to lunch."

"It's better this way, Chasity. Junior doesn't want to cross paths with you. I hope you don't mind."

Punk ass, I thought. "It don't matter where we meet," I replied.

He gave me the information for the meeting and when I hung up, I danced around the kitchen. I assumed the deal was off the table due to Junior's persistent protest, but I guess Jon-Jon had the last word.

A week later, I checked my account, and the balance revealed one-hundred fifty thousand dollars. I was overjoyed because I only asked for one-hundred. The city sold me the house for a dollar on the condition I bring it up to code, but the timeframe they gave was short. I had six months to complete everything, and I needed to get started right away.

My first step was a meeting with my foreman, Jeff, because I was not experienced in remodeling an entire house. Jeff worked with my uncle and I needed his technical help. Plus, I trusted him and he was giving me a great deal. His expertise would cover what I lacked. Jeff was standing in front of the house when I pulled up.

"Hey, Jeff. Were you waiting long?" I asked as I greeted him.

"Not too long, about five-minutes."

"Okay. You see what I'm working with? It's tore up from the floor up."

"I agree, but it's not impossible. I've seen worse. The structure needs to be sound. We will have to raise the house and lay a new foundation before we can even tackle the inside."

"How much will that cost?"

"That will run you around ten grand."

"Ten grand? For some cement! We can jack up the house and do it ourselves for that price."

"You're kidding me, right?" Jeff laughed.

"I agree that she is very naïve to believe the two of you can lift a house alone," the familiar voice sneered. I turned around and saw Junior's handsome face.

"This is none of your business. Why are you even here?" I spat.

"That's where you're wrong, Chasity. This is my business, especially when my money is involved."

"Your money?"

"Yes, my money. The Blake Corporation is me all day, and I'm here to check on my investment."

Play nice, Chasity. Don't blow this, I rationed. "Yes, you're absolutely right. You should know what you've invested in, and here it is. It doesn't look like much now, but I promise you when I'm done with it, I will get double if not triple the investment."

He smirked and said, "You're reaching, but I'm glad you're optimistic. Listen, you may be in slightly over your head, so I will help you out and lend some additional resources."

"I'm not in over my head, Junior, but I'm willing to accept the help," I replied, trying to keep it professional. It was a thin line between lust and hate with us, and I was tired of fighting with him.

"Regardless, I'm sending my team to help you with the foundation. They'll be here in the morning, and you'll be able to enter the premises afterwards."

"Thank you, but I thought you didn't want to see me again," I said, wondering what his motive was.

"I still don't. Like I said before, I'm just checking on my investment."

"That's what I wanted to clarify. There is no you and me, other than me paying you back when I make a boat load of money out of this house."

"For your sake, I hope so. Anyway, I was wondering if we could have lunch to discuss your plan further. I have some questions, especially about your budget. You seem to be somewhat delusional and I came to set you straight," he said as he scanned my attire, looking densely amused by my get up. I had on a pair of Timberlands, jean shorts, and a wife beater because it was hot as hell outside. "I see you came ready to work."

"I guess you can see I'm not dressed for lunch, so maybe another time."

"Nah, I'm a busy a man. Another time won't work for me. I know a place where you'll fit in just fine."

"Okay, as long as you bring me back." He nodded in agreement. I told Jeff I'd meet him tomorrow, and we drove off in his CL 600. The car was so beautiful that I was afraid to move. At work, he always drove his Range Rover, but he pulled out the big guns today and succeeded in shutting my mouth.

We pulled up to a small seafood restaurant in Bala Cynwyd and he parked. I took off my tool belt, placed it on the floor of the passenger seat, and followed him into the restaurant.

"Chasity, we can sit over here in the corner," he directed. A few minutes later, a waitress came over all googly-eyed for him.

"Junior, it's good to see you as always," she grinned a little too long. "It's been awhile. Where you been hiding?" she asked, obviously familiar with him.

"I've been around, Latoya, and I will have my usual. Chasity, do you know what you want yet?" he asked, redirecting the conversation.

"I'll have the crab cake special."

"It comes with corn, broccoli and your choice of mashed or baked potatoes," Latoya explained.

"I'll take a baked potato with butter."

"Okay, I'll be back with your food soon. Can I get you some drinks?" she asked.

"We'll take two bottled waters," Junior said.

"Actually, I'll have a diet Coke." Junior mean grilled me and I looked down at the menu, pretending to be preoccupied.

"Diet sodas are no good for you. Have you ever taken the time to research what's inside? You like researching everything else," he said, less of a question and more of his own fact.

"Humans are born to die, Junior. I refuse to waste precious time obsessing over what is inevitable." I rolled my eyes. "You said you wanted to discuss our investment, so I suggest you stick to that." I screw faced him.

"Fair enough. Can you share with me how much you plan to make?"

"I'm thinking at least three-hundred thousand."

"After you wake from that dream, realistically, how much?" he laughed.

"I'm being as real as they come. I did the comps in the neighborhood and the last house that sold in the area sold for three-hundred fifty thousand. Based on that, I'm already underpriced. That price was based on market value, but once I'm done restoring it back to its original glory, there's no telling what I can get."

"Two-hundred fifty is the most you'll get. I also did the comps, and the house you're talking about was renovated from top to bottom, including the exterior."

"I plan to do the same thing, so you can crawl back under the rock you came from. There is no way I'm putting a five bedroom, two and half bath home on the market for less than three- hundred thousand."

"Chasity, get ready for that house to sit on the market for a while. I'm telling you, you're over compensating, but as my father used to say, a hard head leads to a soft behind. Carry on, but when it's time for me to collect, I don't want to hear the sob story."

"Ye of little faith. I'm glad I had a strong and wise man raise me because you really know how to bring a sister down. Uncle Kenny always told me I could do whatever I wanted, and here you are trying to throw a monkey wrench into the program. I will prove you wrong and make you eat your words," I replied as the waitress placed our food on the table.

"Will there be anything else?" she asked, smiling at Junior.

"Nah, we're good Latoya. You can bring the check too," Junior instructed. We ate in silence and as soon as we finished he drove me back to my car.

"Thanks for lunch, Junior. It was a blast and I can't wait until we meet again," I smirked, while I got out of his car.

"Likewise, Chasity. Likewise," he replied and sped away.

Chapter 9

Junior

We were having our last meeting before the trip to Dubai to complete the final details. As promised, Pops was making his presence known and I expected him to arrive any minute. When he walked into the office, the staff treated him as if he was a God.

"Junior, you can start the meeting," he instructed, and an hour later, we had most of the details accounted for. Me, Wayne and Domencio remained in the conference room while everyone else left.

"Pops, are you satisfied with everything?"

"So far we're good, Son, but I have something I want to run by you in private. Domencio and Wayne, can you give us a moment?" They exited the room and Pops asked, "How's Chasity making out?"

"Pops, how the fuck would I know? I don't keep tabs on her. The only thing we have between us is business."

"If that's the case, Junior, why are you so defensive whenever I mention her name? You two didn't get off to a good start, but you need to respect my next decision. I'm adopting her into the family."

"Adopting her into the family? Pops, that sounds absurd! She's a grown ass woman, with a smart ass mouth. She doesn't need anyone to adopt her."

"Yes, she does. She needs me—she needs us. Chasity has lost so much and I owe it to Tray and Kenny, but more importantly, I owe it to her mother, Cathy. Cat wasn't just Tray's wife, we all felt as if we had a stake in her. We grew up together from kindergarten, and Cat was a part of the gang. You know, we treated her like one of the boys. Until she grew up and started getting attention from other boys," he smiled, recalling the memory. "That's when we took notice, so we betted on who would win her over."

"It's obvious Tray won, Pops."

"Not that simple, Junior. She found out about the bet from King when he realized his chances were slim to none. She stopped speaking to all of us until we had to whip Beatles' ass, this chump from Southwest Philly, for putting his hands on her. After that, I met your mother, so the bet was off the table for me. However, Kenny and Tray were still in the running. Cat and Kenny dated first, but Kenny's love for women made it impossible for them to be together. Cat was running around beating the shit out of every skank who fucked Kenny. She eventually dumped him and ran into the arms of Tray."

"So she ended up marrying Tray. I still don't get the strong connection and your need to take care of this girl."

"Junior, you can act like a real idiot. You will never get it, because you have no sense of team. Let me simplify. Cathy was my sister and Tray my brother. I will make sure their child is well kept as long as I'm alive and even after I pass. And don't take me for a fool, believing I'm incompetent. You're in love with her."

"Get the fuck outta' here! That's bullshit, Pops, and you shouldn't be assuming shit."

"Deny it all you want, but you will play nice. It's good you are in denial, because we wouldn't want her to get heartbroken over the likes of you. She's a nice young lady and her future will be promising. Stay away from her sexually, so there's no problem between you and me. Got it?"

"Don't worry yourself, she's safe for now."

"Now that we've agreed, are the details set for your party next weekend?"

I nodded.

"Just so you know, I'm inviting Chasity and Destiny as my special guests. I'll talk too you soon, Son. Good day," he said, and I knew the conversation was over.

My father saw right through me. Before he walked into my office and forbade me from seeing her sexually, I had planned to do just that. Despite his warning, his mention of Chasity prompted me to make an in-home visit to check on my investment.

When I pulled up to the Victorian style single-family home, I was pleased with her progress. The exterior of the house was complete. She repaired and painted the shingles on the home and replaced the entire roof. The weeds that stood as tall as the house were gone. She even added flower boxes under the front windows for old-world charm.

I walked up the newly cemented steps and stopped in my tracks. Chasity was bent over screwing a nail into the sheetrock. Her legs were plump and her ass was the perfect size for me. I wasn't into oversized asses, but it was round enough for me cup in my hands when the time came. Her workers were on the same page, standing around in a daze like zombies.

"Chasity, I guess you're the only one working around here?" She stood up and rolled her eyes at me.

"What do you want now, Junior? Don't you see I'm hard at work to meet the City's deadline, along with yours?"

"I never gave you a deadline, but I'm impressed."

"Really. Let me give you a tour then." She smiled, which turned me on as I let her body lead me into the kitchen.

"I had to demolish the walls because the plaster was falling apart and unsalvageable. There was water damage and mold, which was a cost I didn't expect, along with the asbestos found in the basement."

"It sounds as if you had some setbacks, but you're moving forward."

"Yes I am, but I still have a ton of work to do. The woodwork, including the floors, has to be stripped and sanded, but I'm comfortable with where we are."

"What about the cabinets? Are you replacing them?"

"No!" she yelled. "Why would I do that?"

"Calm down. I think you should replace them with new cabinets."

"I make cabinets, that's what I specialize in. I have it all mapped out. The tour is over. You should come back when it's done before giving your unnecessary criticism. You might just be more impressed than you are today."

"True dat. You have a valid point and I didn't expect you'd be this far. Good job," I responded, impressed with her more than the house.

"That must have hurt your pride to admit."

"Why do you say that?"

"Because it was not entirely convincing, but I guess it's a start."

"A start to what, Chasity?"

"A start to a better working relationship. Sometimes—no, majority of the time, you make me uncomfortable, feeling as if I have to be on the defensive with you. I'm tired of arguing or whatever it is we do when we are together. I want to apologize for calling you out your name all those times, and I don't blame you for hating me," she said sincerely.

"I don't hate you, but your mouth is hateful. To show I'm willing to let bygones be bygones, I'm inviting you to my birthday party next Saturday."

"For real? I'd love to come. But um, what should I wear? I would hate to disobey your dress code," she laughed.

"I'm sure you can figure out something," I said with a wink.

"That's what up, Junior, but if you don't mind, I need to get back to work," she said, starting the cordless drill.

"Yeah, I'll let you handle that," I replied, starting for the door. Before leaving out, I couldn't help myself and said, "Chasity, you should rethink those shorts. I think you're distracting your workers, and your one squat away from an ass cheek popping out. Cover up a little more. And don't tell my father I invited you to the party, he wanted to be the one to extend the invite." I exited before she freed that brash tongue of hers.

Chapter 10

Chasity

It was the day before Junior's party and I was meeting up with Jon-Jon at a restaurant called the Rose Tattoo. He explained that we could talk, as he had something very important to ask. I wondered what it could be, but I was more interested in Junior's Birthday Bash. They had been promoting his party on the radio and it was by invitation only. The last time I partied, I was in college and I looked forward to this event.

I parked on 19th Street and spotted Jon-Jon waiting for me in front of the restaurant. He greeted me with a hug and said, "Hey, young lady. How are you?"

"I'm doing okay thanks to you and Junior. He surprised me by the investment, and so far there have been no major issues."

"I'm happy to hear that. Let's go inside, I have a private table waiting, where we can talk without being disturbed."

We walked up to the second floor, which revealed a botanical garden with trees that stood as high as the ceilings. The waiter escorted us to our table in the back and asked if we wanted drinks.

"Do you have strawberry margaritas?" I asked, and Jon-Jon smiled.

"I see you liked my drink, but I must warn you, I doubt it will be as good as mine."

"You're probably right, but I'll take my chances."

"You are your mother's child. She had a direct approach to everything, and I miss her and your father."

"I miss them too, but the crazy thing is, I don't remember them as much as I use to. I remember the night they passed away vividly, and how my mother made the best pancakes, but everything else is foggy."

"Chasity, I don't want you to relive that awful night, but do you mind telling me what you remember?" My body shuddered involuntarily, and Jon-Jon said, "If it's too uncomfortable, we don't have to go there."

"No, it's not. It's just that I'm not sure you're ready for my questions."

"I have nothing to hide and I promise I will be as honest as I can. Now, tell me your story."

"That night, I could feel the tension between my parents. Daddy was running around in a panic while my mother tried to calm him down. It was Saturday, and my friend Malika was supposed to sleepover, but mommy told me I couldn't have her over. I was mad and asked if I could stay at Malika's house instead, but she snapped and screamed at me, which was my first encounter with that side of mommy. I saw it before when she dealt with daddy, but I was never subject to it. Anyway, she must have realized she hurt me, so she promised to play with me. She told me to hide in the secret attic which she called our secret play space."

"I'm sorry to interrupt, but why was your father so frantic?"

"I have no idea."

"What happened after that?" he asked, hanging on to my every word.

Tears fell from my eyes as I continued. "My mother was begging for her life and then I heard gunshots, thinking they were firecrackers. After that, I didn't hear my mother anymore, but I heard my father scream when he realized my mother was dead." He handed me his handkerchief.

"What did your father say? Take your time, Pumpkin." I glanced at him awkwardly and he said, "Did I say something wrong?"

"No, it's just that Uncle Kenny always called me Pumpkin and I miss him so much. I loved him and Aunt Dumpling more than my own parents, and I haven't fully healed from their passing."

"I recognize the love in your eyes for them. But can I tell you something?"

"Sure," I laughed, trying to cover the pain.

"When we received the heartbreaking news about your parents, Kenny and I fought over who would raise you. I wanted you, badly, but Kenny was one-step ahead of me. He got to Atlanta before me and got the paperwork squared away. When he brought you back, we had a heart-to-heart, and he convinced me you would be better off with him. I had the boys and since he was raising a daughter, Destiny, he convinced me it was the perfect fit. Obviously, he was right, because you turned out to be a beautiful and intelligent woman, who reminds me so much of a stunning sister named Cathy. Chasity, tell me what Tray said."

"Oh, yeah—he cried and told King that he had nothing to live for and he could kill him. King responded by saying he planned to do just that, but he wanted me first."

"Wanted you? For what?" he asked puzzled.

"To have his men rape me, I guess."

"Jesus! That motherfucker wanted to harm you. Son of bitch. He turned sour, but I did not know he'd gone ballistic. Sorry, Chass. Continue."

"My dad yelled that he would never find me or his money, and when you received the tape of him screwing your wife, he was as good as dead, or something to that effect. I heard one last shot, and it became silent and smoky."

"Pumpkin…I hope you don't mind me calling you that. We gave that nickname to your mother. Listen, I'm sorry you had to go through that horrific experience, but King will never hurt you again."

"Why, is he in jail?" I asked.

"He's not in jail, he's in hell. I wanted to ask you and Destiny to be a part of my family. You're a grown woman, so I can't legally adopt you, but I want to do it unofficially. And it would give me great pleasure if you'd call me Uncle Jon."

"I love that! Yes, I will. Trying to be a parent and get my career jump started has left me feeling defeated and unaided."

"Well, you can rest assured that you are not alone. You have me now. Destiny's leaving for college soon, what are her needs?"

"Since we're family now, here's the thing. Destiny has fallen in love with a young man named Khalif. She's planning to go to school in New York and get an apartment with this boy."

"How hold is she again?"

"Seventeen, and you can't tell her nothing. She acts just like the female version of Uncle Kenny. I gave up because it causes friction between us, and I have so much other stuff on my shoulders."

"We'll see what we can do to resolve the Destiny problem, but I plan on lightening the other weight. What do you need, Chasity? I see you driving your uncle's truck. Wouldn't you prefer a more feminine car?"

"Feminine," I laughed, not considering myself feminine. "I'm good, Unc. I love driving his truck. It's as if he's riding with me. Plus, the truck is fully loaded and Uncle Kenny maintained it well. Thanks, but I'm okay. However, Destiny asked for a car when she graduated, and I didn't want to take it out of her college fund."

"College fund. She has one?" He looked surprised.

"It's the money from the insurance policy. We put her portion in the bank. I wanted her to enjoy that same opportunity my father and uncle gave me."

"You're a very responsible and unselfish woman, Chasity. Two traits near and dear to my heart. Junior is having a birthday party tomorrow, and I want you and Destiny to join me. You may not fancy Junior, but I need you both to resolve your differences. We're family now!"

"Family, that sounds so sweet."

"Since you won't allow me to spoil you with a car, what do you say we go on a mini shopping spree? I want you to be fabulous when I induct you into the family tomorrow night."

"I don't think Junior's party is the place or time, and I'm positive he will have a problem with that. Junior and I are taking baby steps and the announcement may put us back to first trimester pregnancy."

"Don't be silly, Chasity. Leave Junior to me," he demanded.

We enjoyed a delicious lunch and he was right, his margarita was much better. Before we left, I blurted out the last questions on my mind. "Uncle Jon, did you kill King? And your wife, was she Junior and Domencio's mother,"

"Watch your mouth, Chasity. I see the apple don't fall far from the tree! You act just like your mother. Nevertheless, I did not have them killed, and she was my second wife. My first wife, their mother Lela, died from breast cancer. The rumor was they overdosed in a motel somewhere in Jersey. Don't worry your sweet head over that anymore. It's in the past now and we'll make new memories. Come, let's go get you a pretty dress."

Forty-five minutes later, the driver pulled up to the King of Prussia Mall entrance. Uncle Jon told me there was no budget and to just enjoy myself. Excitement was an understatement for my feelings and I prayed I found the perfect dress to get Junior's attention.

When we walked inside Niemen Marcus it was like the Land of Oz. Everything was so new and out of the ordinary for me. I was waiting for the wizard to tap me on my back and say welcome. But Uncle Jon was the wizard, and he was making dreams come true.

He couldn't decide on a dress after I tried on over ten so he said, "We'll take them all. You look beautiful in each one. You take them home and decide what you want to wear to the party."

"That's not necessary. I mean, I can choose one now," I replied, because the dresses I tried on were no less than fifteen hundred dollars each.

"Chasity, you are family, and we have more of these overpriced parties to attend. Take it as a future investment. The next big gala, you'll be prepared."

"Thanks, Uncle Jon. I'm ready now."

"I'm not a fashion expert, but you'll need a pair of shoes and accessories to go along with whatever dress you decide on for tonight. Take my card, Chasity, and the woman will help you. I have to take this call," he explained as he answered the phone.

"Okay, I'll be right back," I said, as Carolyn the sales representative showed me the way. She stayed by my side the entire time, working hard for the huge commission coming her way.

I snuck in a dress for Destiny and she would worship me with the shoes I was about to get us. I picked a pair of Christian Louboutin's Lawrence Lace Ups for me and the Gold Pagalle Spikes for her. Carolyn helped me pick jewelry that would match any of the dresses I chose. The clutch bags in the store were so expensive, but even though I felt a little guilty about the price, I settled on a beaded fold-over clutch bag in black, by Moyna. It would go with most of the dresses I selected.

Jon-Jon found me as Carolyn carefully bagged my dresses and shoes. The total with the accessories came to twenty-two thousand dollars. I turned and looked at Jon-Jon as if he had lost his mind, but he was all smiles.

"I'm glad you find it funny. I would never shop in this store voluntarily," I smirked.

"In that case, we'll come at least once a month."

"Deal," I laughed.

"You got a deal, Pumpkin. Are you hungry? We can get a bite to eat before we go."

"No thanks, I'm still full from earlier and I'm too happy to eat. Uncle Jon, thanks for the magnificent day. I feel like Julia Roberts in *Pretty Woman*, except you are my uncle." He embraced me and kissed me on my forehead.

The driver was waiting in front of the mall when we reached the front. He took my bags and placed them in the armored Evade that resembled a black mini tank. It was sleek, but frightening. I wondered why he needed protection.

When he dropped me off, my car was sitting in the driveway. I glanced over at Jon-Jon and he explained that he had one of his workers tow it to my house. It was a nice gesture from a distinguished man and it amazed me that Junior shared the same DNA. Destiny was waiting at the door as I grabbed my bags full of expensive shit. When she saw the name on the bags, her eyes beamed.

"Chasity, we forgot to get something for Destiny!" Uncle Jon exclaimed.

"No we didn't, I took care of it. She has something proper to wear to the party."

"Your mind is always working, I love it. I can't wait to see what dress you select. I may have to hire additional security to keep the sharks away! I'll see you tomorrow night. A car will be here to pick you up at eight sharp." He kissed me on my cheek and waved goodbye to Destiny.

Destiny didn't give me a chance to catch my breath before she said, "What's in the bags and why didn't you take me?"

"Chill, I got you something nice to wear to Junior's party."

"Where is this party and what did you buy me?"

"At the Kimmel Center. A car is coming to take us. Follow me to my room so you can pick the dress you want."

I lay all the dresses on the bed, except the black and white Herve Leger rhinestone knit dress. My accessories and clutch matched that one the most. I also placed the silk Gucci Carly jumpsuit to the side. When I tried that on I had to have it. It was elegant and more my style than the frilly dresses. Heads would turn when I wear that beast. Destiny had her choice of Valentino, Alexander Wang, Alexander McQueen and a nice little dress by Akris Punto. She chose the other Herve Leger dress, the one I predicted she would pick. It was a cream bandage dress with gold studs around the bodice.

"This is the one. Let me try it on real quick," she said as she stripped down. She put the dress on and modeled in my full-length mirror, admiring her curves. "When Khalif see me in this dress he will want to marry me on the spot."

"I don't want to hear that bullshit. Here," I said, handing her the shoebox. She saw the name and pulled the top off with the quickness.

"Oh my God! You got me a pair of Christian Louboutin's. They're a perfect match. Thanks, Sis!"

"If you play your cards right, I might get you that car sooner rather than later. Uncle Jon is going to lighten the load and include us in his family. We could use some other people in the mix, don't you agree? Plus, you have Khalif now and I can't compete with him."

"You're my sister, Chass. There is no competition. I'm just growing up at a rapid pace. Don't get mad at me, but I read your journal. I can't believe you're still a virgin and in love with Junior," she giggled as a high school student would.

"Why would you invade my private thoughts? Do you see me snooping around you and Khalif when he's here?" I barked.

"I'm sorry, but you never talk about boys or yourself. Please forgive me, Chass. It was childish, but that's what little sisters do."

"Take your stuff and get out. You get on my last nerve, Dee. Stay out of my shit."

"I said I was sorry. But check this out...if you need any advice I can give it to you. The first time hurts like hell, but you get accustomed to it pretty quick."

"Bye, Destiny! Don't make me whip your ass," I spat. *The nerve of her.*

When she left, I hung the dresses in the closet and went to fix myself a sandwich. I should have taken Jon-Jon up on his offer to get something to eat because I was starving. I called Jeff to make sure he finished the floors and the house was still in one piece. He explained that the inspector was coming first thing Monday morning to check the plumbing. I went to bed early, but gained a sudden case of insomnia. I tossed and turned all night, thinking about the party and Junior.

Someone was ringing the bell like a mad person, scaring me out of my sleep. It woke Destiny too because she stumbled out of her room at the same time as me, looking cray-cray.

"Who the hell is that this early in the morning!" she barked.

"It better not be Khalif cause your ass will be sorry."

"It's not Khalif. He would have called before he came. He knows better." She was ready to defend her man.

"Shut up, Destiny," I replied, agitated. "Who is it?" I yelled.

"It's Calvin, Jon-Jon's driver." I opened the door, and the same driver that dropped me off yesterday stood in the doorway. "Jon sent me to take you ladies for a day of pampering at the spa. Also, he requested that you bring a change of clothes, because he would like the two of you to be his guests overnight at his home."

"Okay, we'll be ready in fifteen minutes," Destiny said, excitedly dashing off to her room.

"We'll be out in a few," I confirmed.

"Take your time," he replied, walking back to the car.

Forty-five minutes later, Destiny and I headed to the spa, happy as two kids at Six Flags Great Adventure. I assumed massages were a part of the package but anticipated the unknown. When we arrived at the exclusive spa, Calvin informed us that Uncle Jon took care of the tab and that he would wait for us in the lobby.

The spa was heavenly, and the service was superb. The staff catered to us as if we were royalty, placing smiles on both of our faces. I was relaxed from the hour-long full body massage, and the facial exfoliated my skin, leaving it feeling smooth and rejuvenated. Destiny talked me into the Brazilian Bikini wax, which was the Debbie Downer of the day. We both regretted it, but it was vindication on my part because Destiny cried real tears. That served her little ass right for trying to act grown.

"Are you okay?" I asked, inwardly laughing as we went to get manicures and pedicures.

"I know you think it's funny, but it's not."

"What did you expect? Waxing causes pain, dummy! Next time do your research before jumping in head first."

"I'm not the only dummy, because you followed right behind me," she replied, rolling her eyes as hard as she could. She had me there.

"We need to wrap this up because I still need to get my hair done."

"We have a hair salon on campus if you need that service. There is no limit, all your expenses are prepaid," Beverly the manicurist interjected.

"No offense, but are they familiar with styling African American hair? It's probably better I wait," I said, skeptical about the stylists.

"We do all hair types. Our stylists are top in their field and I can call ahead for you lovely ladies."

"Okay, that sounds good. You can schedule it." I replied.

After we got our nails and feet done, we headed over to the salon. I was still uncertain but prayed they would come through, because I had something special and different in mind. The hair salon had two sides and Destiny was getting her hair done on the side opposite me. Honestly, it was for the best, because I had no tolerance to hear her mouth about me cutting my hair. It hung about twelve inches below my shoulders and it was getting on my nerves. When I worked it was a constant distraction, even in a ponytail. I wanted a curly Mohawk style, but that would be too drastic.

"Now, Miss Thing... tell me how you want your hair," my stylist James asked.

"I was thinking you can cut it shoulder length."

"Are you sure you want me to cut your hair?" he asked, while combing through it with a wide-tooth brush.

"Yes, I'm sure. Unless you can't do it the way I want."

"Oh, honey chile, I can do anything. I was just making sure. Do you know how many people come in here wanting their hair cut and leave regretting it?"

"We're good. I know what I'm doing and I know what I want. Shoulder length and not inch higher," I commanded.

An hour later, James put the finishing touches on my hair and turned me around to face the mirror. It was a whole new me and I loved it. The curls were shiny and soft, giving me the look I desired. I was dying for Junior to see.

"James, you did an awesome job. I love how my curls look. You know I can never get it like this. What did you put in my hair?" I asked, needing that product in my life forever.

"Just a homemade concoction I invented. People can't get enough. I sell it for fifty dollars a jar, but it lasts a long time. If you apply a small amount of my magic potion after you shampoo and condition, you can achieve the same look."

"Sold, I'll take two bottles," I responded, just as Destiny walked up.

"Oh my God. You cut off all your hair! Are you going crazy, Chass?"

"No, girl but I wanted a change. You don't like it?"

Once she did a full inspection, she said, "It looks nice, but you're beautiful anyway, so anything would look good on you. I, on the other hand, would never cut my hair that short."

"Okay, we get the picture. Are you ready? Because I'm starving! I have a taste for seafood."

"Red Lobster it is then. Let's go find the driver."

When we got inside the car, I asked Calvin to take us to the restaurant and he agreed, explaining that our wish was his command. Destiny and I smiled at each other as we used to do when Uncle Kenny took us to the Toys R Us.

We realized after dinner that it was almost eight and the party started at ten. I asked Calvin to take us home because I forgot to pack my Gucci jumpsuit, and our house was closer to the party.

By the time we dressed and got out the door, it was almost ten o'clock. Calvin drove the Escalade with precision and speed. When we arrived, he opened the door for us and told us how beautiful we looked. I believed it and received it. Destiny was stunning with her hair pulled to one side and curls flowing down her shoulder. Her hair was long, and I believed her when she said she would never cut it.

My stomach was doing somersaults thinking of seeing Junior again. He had an unbreakable hold on me, but I wanted to change all that and just have him hold me. Destiny noticed my apprehension and said, "Don't worry, Chass, you look beautiful, and if Junior don't want you someone else will."

"Thanks, Dee. I guess you are more mature than I give you credit for."

"It's about time you recognized this, but at the end of the day, you're the boss big Sis!"

"Thanks, now let's go show off these gorgeous dresses."

When we entered the crowded ballroom I searched for Jon-Jon but it was like looking for a needle in a haystack. Destiny and I walked to the bar. I ordered a strawberry margarita for me and a Coke for her. Just as the bartender handed me my drink, a dark handsome man approached me and asked me to dance.

"Um, actually, I just got here, and I need to find my uncle, but maybe later."

"Now, later—I'll take you any way I can get you. Beautiful, what is your name?"

"Chasity, and yours?"

"Linwood, but everyone calls me, Track, but you can call me anything you want."

"Okay, Track, I'll talk to you later."

"Why do you need to talk to him later?" I heard a voice ask from behind. I turned around and Uncle Jon stood looking handsome as ever, but slightly displeased.

"Hey Uncle Jon, I was looking everywhere for you."

"I see I showed up in the nick of time—Track it's good to see you again. It's been a while."

"Yes, it has. Listen I didn't mean no disrespect—is she yours," he asked, looking at me.

"All me! Come Chasity and Destiny. I want to introduce you to a few people," Uncle Jon explained, dismissing Track. "You ladies look stunning," he said, when we made it over to the terrace.

He introduced us to several of his business partners and friends. It was a happy occasion and Uncle Jon had a bright smile on as he introduced us as his nieces. Everyone told us how beautiful we were and he was cheesing from ear to ear as the compliments poured in. With all the attention, we were getting I forgot about the man of the hour.

"Where's the birthday boy. I haven't him see him all night," I asked Uncle Jon.

"I'm sure he's around here somewhere with his date, but don't worry about him."

Date, WTF. I can't believe he bought someone with him. I thought we understood one another. Although we were connecting on a dysfunctional level, I believed we were connecting. My mood fell flat at the sound of him bringing a date.

"Uncle Jon, I'll be right back. Do you want something from the bar?" I asked, needing a moment to myself.

"No, I've reached my limit, but don't take too long, Chasity. I'll be ready to make that announcement soon."

"I won't. Come on, Destiny, walk with me," I said as I grabbed her hand.

"What's wrong with you, Chass, and why did you grab my hand so hard?"

"Junior, he came with someone and I need a drink before I see him."

"What did you expect him to do? I'm the only one that knows you're in love with him."

"I'm not in love with him. I just thought something was there, but I guess I was wrong. Anyway, forget about that. Track will be my saving grace tonight."

"He is fine and if I were old enough, I'd date him."

"Yeah, I just need to get his attention." Right than, Uncle Jon told us to follow him.

He escorted us over to the DJ stand and grabbed the mic. "Can I have everyone's attention please? Junior and Domencio will you join me," he asked, and I spotted Junior for the first time. He was wearing the shit out of that suit and I wanted him now. His stunning date acted as if she wanted to come along, but Junior quickly whispered in her ear and her ass stood still. *Yeah, bitch, this is family business so stay in your own lane,* I thought.

Junior surveyed me and the twinkle in his eyes said he was pleased. I wondered what he thought about the new haircut and hoped it didn't scare him away. Actually, he could not take his eyes off me and I was feeling myself.

"First. I would like to say happy birthday to my first born, Junior. I thank God for you and Domencio every day, and I stand before you all as a proud father. Will everyone raise your glasses — Son, Happy Thirtieth." Everyone raised their glasses and followed up with an applause. Uncle Jon silenced the crowd with a hand signal and continued. "Secondly, The Blake family has two new lovely additions and I would like to take this chance to welcome them to the family. These are my nieces Destiny and Chasity." Cheers rang out, but when I looked over at Domencio and Junior, neither one seemed happy. Domencio whispered in Junior's ear and the looks on their faces said it all.

I knew this would happen but I never expected to see the disdain on Junior's face. I wanted to crawl under a rock and hide.

"Pops, can we speak to you alone," Domencio asked.

"Not now, Son. Everyone, I'm not finished." He spoke through the mic again.

"Destiny is on her way to college and I wanted to send her off the proper and decent way. Also, Chasity is a college graduate and a shrewd business woman. I'm very proud of these ladies and the evening wouldn't be complete without the appropriate welcome gifts. With that said, Carlton, sweetie come," he summoned his woman. She handed him two pink crafty wrapped boxes, and said, "If you would all turn your attention to the screens." You could see smoke coming out of Junior and Domencio's head, but kept my focus on the gifts coming from Uncle Jon. A picture of a BMW 320 I appeared and Carlton handed Destiny the gift box. When she opened it, revealing the car key, I thought we would need an ambulance the way she reacted. She went ballistic jumping up and down and screaming to the top of her lungs. I was so happy for her. "Where not done," he said, and everyone turned his or her attention back to the screen. The next picture revealed a black Infiniti Q 50. Now it was my turn to act a fool. I joined Destiny in her celebration dance and we were over the top.

Once I regained my senses, I said, "I thought I told you I didn't want a car. You're something else, Uncle Jon."

"I know that's what you told me, but I also know what woman enjoy. Are you happy — I mean was it too much," he smirked.

"You know it was too much and by the look on Domencio and Junior's face, I believe you have a problem."

"Chasity, don't get this thing twisted. I'm the boss and I run this family. I want to spoil my nieces and put smiles on their beautiful faces. Don't worry about those boys of mine. If they have a problem, they know what's up. Now go and enjoy yourself. And ah, Chasity, stay away from Track, he's not the right fit for you."

I looked at him strangely because he was blocking me from my redeemer for the night. Track was my back-up plan. I just shook my head and got away from him fast, thinking he was taking this uncle thing seriously. I didn't want to disappoint him, but I am a grown ass woman who takes care of a rebellious teenager. I deserved the Super Woman Award for that shit.

I spotted Junior dancing with his date and surprised to see he knew how to dance, which only made me want him more. My anger temperature was rising while he appeared to be enjoying himself. It was time for a bold and unexpected move. I pranced over to Junior and tapped him on the shoulder. When he turned around, I knew he was shocked.

"I'm sorry, do you mind if I cut in. I haven't spoken to my cousin all night," I asked his date.

"Sure, I don't mind. My name is, Cashmere. That was a wonderful display by Mr. Blake. You must be on cloud nine."

"Yes I am, Junior, shall we dance," I said, cutting her conversation short.

"Yeah, Cashmere, give me a minute," Junior replied.

Yeah bye, girl. Go stand over there and look pretty, while I deal with Junior, I thought. When she walked away, I said, "First, let me say happy birthday and I'm wishing you many more. I don't know if it was just me who thought we connected, but I was hoping the feeling was mutual."

"Dear cousin, I don't know what would give you that impression." He had a devilish smile on his face. "Chasity, I only made an effort for my father's sake, so I wouldn't push it if I were you."

"Okay, if you want to play this game—I'm in, but let me give you a forewarning, I'm a virgin and I'm horny. I will not wait around and I will give my virgin pussy to someone less deserving than you." I looked him straight in the eye. "Anyway, we should at least dance so it don't look no way."

"Who said I care about you or your alleged virgin pussy. As far as dancing goes, it would look inappropriate for me to be dancing with my cousin on a slow song. You can thank your, Uncle Jon for that," he responded. Leaving me on the dance floor. I watched him walk over to Cashmere, and Track was standing on the opposite side of him. *Game time,* I thought.

Chapter 11

Junior

Today was my thirtieth birthday, and I expected tonight would be eventful and satisfying. It had been a while since I hung out with my boys and clubbed until the sun came up. A known fact was that the City of Brotherly Love had changed for the worse and was now a killing field for the youth. The game was much different when I began and at the end of my reign desperate circumstances caused for unruly behavior. Loyalty vanished, while greed and gluttony possessed the young soldiers, creating snitches and bitches.

Shit was so bad that I couldn't enjoy myself without security. I hated that shit. It just enhanced the spotlight on me, and the extra attention got me locked down for two years. The streets and I have a long history together, but when it was time to revisit them, I had to protect myself. I was a prime target for thieves and kidnappers. Believe me, I have seen it happen too many times.

I planned to enjoy myself tonight and my gear was no exception. My black Valentino suit had just arrived from the tailor and Connie, the beautiful sales woman, assisted me with all the accessories. Suits were not my thing, but if I had to wear one, I was wearing the best. I had a change of clothes for the after party, knowing the first half of the party was more for my pops and our business associates.

Secretly, my desire to see and touch Chasity was burning my insides and that unfamiliar passion was becoming the norm. She was unlike any woman I encountered since my teenage years, where young girls came out the womb cussing niggas out. The women I dated bow down to a nigga, hoping to win my affections. Chasity, however, did the exact opposite, forcing me to be more attentive towards her. Money can't buy you love, but it can buy you peace of mind. The women I dealt with accepted anything I said, knowing their time was limited. This girl, however, had fire and an impudent boldness that lured me in. My intuition nagged at me, which was why I was bringing a date. I needed the normal to break up the confusion and temptation named Chasity.

Hours later, Cashmere and I arrived an hour late to my party, and it was just as I had expected. A bunch of executive's brown nosing and making deals. Tonight the wives were in control, accompanying their mogul husbands. This was a first lady event, no side hoes allowed. They were honoring me, but this party was beyond even my luxurious taste, and I had Pops to thank for that. This was my new circle. I loved that it made me a shit load of money *and* kept me out of prison.

"You finally made it, I see," Pops commented as he approached me from behind.

"Pops, I'm only an hour late, but I'm here. This is Cashmere, my escort for tonight."

"Escort! I'm no one's' escort. I'm his date and it's a pleasure to meet you, Mr. Blake."

"The pleasure is mine, beautiful, but do you mind if I steal him away for a moment?" Pops asked.

"Of course I don't mind. I'll be here waiting until you get back," she responded, ready to do anything I required.

"Are you pleased with everything?" Pops asked when we got to the bar.

"Yeah, everything is good, Pops! The place is nice and I'm feeling the ambiance."

"I'm glad to hear that, because I spent a fortune on this place," he replied.

"Do you want me to pay you back?" I snapped. Because that's the second time you mentioned the money, and no disrespect, Pops, but I don't take kindly to that shit."

"Calm down, Son. That irrational temper of yours will come back to bite you in the ass if you keep it up. Listen, tonight is your night and I don't want to damper the mood. Enjoy yourself and drink, Junior. I don't think you should keep that gorgeous woman waiting any longer. I see Steven over there talking to Byron, which could be a recipe for disaster. I'll see you later. Oh, have you seen Chasity and Destiny? I can't seem to find them."

"Nah Pops, but I wasn't looking either."

"Junior, if you see them please let me know—that's all," he said and walked away.

An hour later, my father asked Domencio and me to join him for his big announcement. I knew he was up to no good when I saw Chasity and Destiny standing beside him.

"You know anything about this?" Domencio asked as we made our way to the front.

"I have an idea."

Pops introduced the ladies as his nieces and wanted to welcome them to the Blake Family.

"Pops done bumped his fuckin' head! We need to talk to him and straighten this shit out," Domencio whispered in my ear.

"Hold on, let him finish his theatrics. We will deal with him later," I replied, pissed but not wanting to spoil my party.

The betrayal was rubbed in even further for Domencio when Pops revealed the cars he purchased for the girls. I didn't have the same problem as Domencio. I was mad that Pops beat me to the punch. My father was taking this whole niece matter to the extreme. Destiny reacted as any young girl would in her position, but Miss Back Talk surprised me with her equally excited response. She wore the shit out of her dress and by the looks of that expensive get up, I knew Pops had sponsored her. She had beautiful legs, but what captured my attention the most was her new haircut. I loved the way it framed her perfectly shaped face. I wanted to run my fingers through her hair and take her body to a place where she would desire me alone. Acknowledging my strong feelings towards her was just the first obstacle; acting out on them would be like climbing the Alps.

I needed to clear my head, so I took Cashmere on the dance floor to take my mind off Chasity's fine ass. A few minutes later, my distraction was ruined when Bold-and-beautiful cut in. She put her feelings on display as she voiced her displeasure about Cashmere's attendance, further throwing me off with the invite to her virgin walls. She had my dick hard as steel and each time her mouth moved it was hypnotizing. *I can't let this girl into my heart,* I thought. My response was not acceptable in her eyes and it took strength for me to walk away.

I rejoined the slightly annoyed Cashmere, careless to her feelings. Luckily, Track was standing right next to me and I sparked up a conversation with him to avoid her inevitable questions

"Track, it's been while, Fam. How's everything going?"

"Stackin' paper brah. All day every day. You know how we do."

"Yeah, I know. So ah, you still majoring in Pharmaceuticals? The last I heard you was still kidnapping and murdering niggas."

"You got jokes, Junior. It's your birthday, so I'll let you enjoy yourself and keep your life right now."

"Track, don't get it fucked up, my man. I may have left the game, but I still know how to play."

"Junior, me of all people know how you used to get down and I don't want no problems tonight. Plus, I see the answer to my prayers coming my way," he said, as Chasity approached us and asked him to dance. *I'm about to fuck her little ass up and kill his bitch ass,* I thought, furious at her behavior.

"Track, I believe you promised me a dance, and we wouldn't want the night to slip away before you fulfill that promise," she stated seductively.

"Your wish is my command, beautiful. Come on baby, let me show you how it's done," Track responded as they walked away from me.

It was clear what she was trying to do, and the shit was working. I had to check her before shit got out of control and Track lost his life. I text Domencio telling him to come find me immediately. Cashmere's time had expired, and I needed Domencio to escort her out.

"Dee, listen man, have Calvin drop off Cashmere. I'll be at the bar. Let me know when she's gone."

"Yes, Sir—Massuh, Sir. I will get right on it," he mocked.

"Domencio, stop acting like a little bitch and do me this favor."

"Fuck you!" he spat, while walking away.

I had a clear view of Chasity's performance before I closed the curtain. I had to give her credit though; she was very convincing the way she threw that ass around for Track, knowing that pussy belonged to me. I ordered two shots of Hennessey, ready to get turned up. Domencio returned, shaking his head, and I didn't feel like hearing his mouth.

"Junior, next time you need to handle your own business. I'm tired of explaining shit to these hoes and tidying up your dirty laundry. Why the fuck did you invite her?" he asked. When he got no answer he continued, "What are you staring at?" He turned in the same direction and saw what I was looking at - Chasity, making a fool out of herself and enjoying it. "Oh, I see what's going on. Nigga you sprung on Chasity!" he laughed while covering his mouth. "Yo, you drawing, Son. That's our cousin, Junior."

"Stop with that bullshit. You know damn well she is not our cousin. And I don't know what you're talking about."

He smirked and said, "Whatever, here come Pops and he doesn't look too happy."

I gulped down the two shots and turned my attention back to Chasity. The Deejay slowed it down and played *Neighbors Know My Name* by *Trey Songz* and Chasity was letting this nigga touch all on her.

"I told Chasity to stay away from Track but it's like she's totally defying me," Pops said, when he saw the freak show. "I'll deal with Track directly."

"Nah Pops. Let me handle this please" I insisted, ready to put to a stop to this bullshit.

"Junior, I don't want no problems with you and Track. I would hate to end King's son life. You know what I mean."

"I got this, Pops. Why don't you check on Destiny? She looks lost."

"She does look a bit bored. I'll be right back."

I had stomached all I could and stormed over to end this bullshit.

Chapter 12

Chasity

After Junior shot me down, I decided it was payback time. I pranced over to Track and escorted him onto the dance floor. Minutes later, I had forgotten Junior dissed me, because Track was handsome and charming. He had the gift of gab, engaging my soul and grabbing my attention.

"As soon as I spotted you, I said to myself, I would break down the walls of Jericho for that woman and show her the stars. I'm hoping I can get your number and take you out on a real date," Track said as we moved on the dance floor.

"I'll consider it, but I just met you, and we only shared one dance," I replied coyly, thinking he might be a potential cherry buster.

"If I'm lucky to share a second dance it would be more than I deserve," he whispered.

"Aww, that's sweet," I replied, absorbing his swag. When *Trey Songz* came on, I moved into his chest and he wrapped his arms around me. *Umm, this feels good.* The comfort of his arms sent me into a small daze until someone pulled me by my waist. "Junior, what are you doing?" I asked when I turned around and saw him in front of me.

"Yeah, dog! What the fuck is your problem?" Track demanded.

"Nigga, I ain't got no problem, but you're about to have a disaster strike you if you don't back the fuck off."

"Junior, we were just dancing. What is wrong with you?" I asked, secretly thinking that it sure took him long enough.

"What the fuck, y'all kissing cousins or some shit? I'm still trying to figure out how I'm allowing you to breathe after snatching a woman away from me."

"You figure that shit out, Track. This one," he said, pointing at me, "is not a possibility. No disrespect my man, but you need to shop somewhere else. And, um, she's not my cousin. She belongs to the Blake Family, and that's that."

"Chasity, is that the case? Because if you say otherwise, then we have a problem."

"You're about to start a war and get this nigga killed. Walk away and wait for me in the lobby. I'll be there in five minutes. Make sure you're down there," he whispered in my ear.

"Track, it's probably for the..." Junior silenced me by pulling me to the side.

"What part of go downstairs and wait in the lobby did you overlook? Don't make this situation any worse. For the last time, I'll meet you downstairs," he commanded, gently pushing me towards the elevators. I watched him walk over to Track before I exited.

I felt bad for Track because he was only a pawn in my plan. I practically had to fuck him on the dance floor to get Iron Man's attention. Still, I was on my way to the lobby as instructed. I hurried to avoid running into Destiny or Uncle Jon. Calvin pulled up when I reached the lobby doors and looked surprised when he saw me. He got out of the car and told me to enter while talking on his cell.

"Junior should be here in a few minutes." He ushered me into the back seat of the jeep. A few minutes later, Junior strolled through the door.

"Come on, we're leaving in another car," he said, pulling me out of the back seat.

We jumped into his Mercedes and he drove away. We headed towards Penn's Landing and Junior remained silent the entire ride. Now that I had him exactly where I wanted him, I was at loss for words, trying to map out my next move.

Ten minutes later, we pulled up to a condominium complex on the waterfront. I drove past this building many times and never took notice that it was a residential property.

"Chasity, you need to know that I don't bring women to my home, so don't get too comfortable," he explained as he opened the door to his condominium. "However, your deadly behavior and bad attempts to get a rise out of me caused this one-time emergency. I need to talk to you, but that's all we're doing."

"That's fine because I want to talk to you too. If you don't want me, why would you interfere with me and Track?" I asked, while taking a moment to view my sterile surroundings. He remained silent.

Junior took the industrial, mad scientist look to the extreme. His place had no character or warmth. Everything was gray and minimalist. I'm positive the price tag disagreed with the Spartan appearance and represented him to the tee. A gray suede sofa sat in the living room, along with a black leather chair trimmed in chrome and a glass coffee table, all incorrectly placed. *Why he didn't just get two chairs to balance it out and a throw rug to take away the coldness?* I thought. His living room looked like the lobby of an executive building.

Since the kitchen was in view, I decided to help myself to a tour. Junior stood against the wall looking uncomfortable in his own apartment. He surrounded himself with gloom. If I thought the worst was over, the kitchen continued to disappoint me. Gray gloss laminate cabinets with stainless steel appliances haunted me. The floor had charcoal leather tiles, which added to the tackiness.

"You enjoying yourself?" he asked. He was close enough for me to feel his penis touching my spine.

"Ah, no," I replied, and when I turned around I was in his chest. I looked into his gray eyes and melted. "Where's your bedroom?" I asked, trying to stay calm and control my breathing.

"My bedroom is off limits, Chasity. I told you we're only talking."

"I understand, but I have to see how Iron Man sleeps."

"Rule number one, don't call me Iron Man and like I said, my bedroom is off limits to you."

"I need to use the bathroom. Is it down there?" I asked.

"It's the one on the left," he replied as I walked away.

"You said the one on the right?" I quickly opened the door and walked inside.

His bed was the first thing that caught my eye. Outside of the lifeless gray comforter, it looked extremely comfortable. I turned my attention to his walk-in closet and surprisingly, it was not as organized as I assumed it would be. It was a mini mall inside and he had a ton of clothes and sneakers. Before I could snoop around the master bathroom, Junior stopped the tour.

"You're hard-headed and disobedient. Didn't I tell you my bedroom was a no go?"

"It was an accident, Junior. You know…your bed is the only thing that looks comfortable in this apartment." I jumped on the bed and my dress rose just above my butt cheeks. I rolled around and hugged the pillows as if they were my man. "This bed is so comfortable and soft. What kind of mattress is this, memory foam?" I asked.

He didn't respond. Instead, he came over to the bed, picked me up, and said, "It's a bed not meant for sharing." He tried to put me down, but I held on tight. I wrapped my arms around his neck and forced him to kiss me, returning the favor from the other night.

When he finally submitted, I released my tight hold and gave him a long, heated kiss. We came up for air and I attacked his neck, sucking and kissing all over it. I heard the moans he worked so hard to conceal and I went in for the kill.

"Junior," I said, staring into his beautiful eyes, "please make love to me tonight and take me out my misery. I want you badly and I hope you want the same thing. Let's just stop the charade and enjoy each other. No strings attached," I pleaded, hot as a pepper.

"See, this is the problem." He released his hold and placed me on the floor. "You're too desperate and hungry for this right here," he explained, holding his penis. "Other than the fact that you're a virgin, you come on strong, Chasity, and I don't like that shit. Stop trying to take the lead from a leader."

This bitch, I thought. "You're right, and I don't know why I even bothered. You don't have to worry about that happening again. I was overly anxious for a man not suited for the job. I guess I'll keep interviewing until someone fills my walls. Can you take me to Uncle Jon's? He's expecting me."

"Nah, Chass. You're sleeping here tonight. I'll take you in the morning. I have an after party to attend. We can talk when I get back."

See, this is the bipolar shit I'm talking about with this dude. "Are you insane? You really expect me to stay here after you just said what you said? Clearly, you're not interested and we can just be friends. You say I'm hungry and I agree. I was desperate to be with you, but trust and believe, you're not the only fish, baby. Lucky for me, I'm an excellent swimmer and Uncle Kenny taught me how to fish. He showed me the ones you throw back in because there immature and need time to grow." *Meltdown time again.* "I'm sorry that I came off too strong for you, Mr. CEO. I guess first impressions are lasting in this case. Just take me to Uncle Jon's!" I snapped.

His expression changed, and he backed me up against the wall. "Let me clarify. I need you to stay put until I get back. We need to talk and I never said I didn't want you. Calvin will be here shortly with the bag you left. Please take a shower before I return. I can still smell that motherfucker's cologne on you." I stood there looking baffled.

"Why can't I go with you?" I asked, wondering why I was uninvited.

"Don't you think that dress caused enough trouble for to-night? Stay put and I'll be back before you know it. Cool?" he asked, but it was not a question.

"I guess," I replied, still wanting to stand my ground.

"Guessing is for game contestants, Chasity. I'll be back in less than two hours. In the meantime, don't burn down my home," he said, before he changed and left.

Junior was special in a non-gifted way if he supposed that would work on me. As soon as Calvin comes, I'm telling him to take me to Uncle Jon's warm and inviting mansion, where love awaited. If he thought I was staying in his ice cave after he refused to give me some dick, he was even more mentally impaired than I imagined. While I waited for Calvin to come, I snooped around in his closet again.

His jeans took up one side of the closet, stacked to the ceiling as if they were books. I inspected the prices on the ones that still had tags on them. *Diesel $228.00, True Religion $298.00, Dolce and Gabbana $658.00.* Damn I've been living in the land of cheap, I thought, because there was not a pair of Levi's anywhere. On the opposite side of the closet, he had an array of sweatshirts, leather jackets and a few suits. At the far back of the closet, he kept his autographed sneakers on a glass shelf with the rest surrounding the room in a border.

A skinny glass shelf held his many colognes, and I noticed a picture of a woman. I opened the door and studied it. She was stunning, with dark skin and Indian-like hair. It was like staring at a female version of Junior. I turned the picture over and it read, "My beautiful mother, Lela." The year was 1986. I placed it back inside the shelf and went into the dull and uninspiring master bathroom. Just as I got bored, I heard my phone ringing. I reached into my clutch bag and saw an unknown number.

"Hello?" I answered.

"Chasity, this is Calvin. I'm downstairs with your bag. If you buzz me in, I'll bring it up to you."

"That won't be necessary, Calvin. I'm coming down now, and I need you to drop me off at Uncle Jon's house."

"But ah, Junior said I should just bring you your bag."

"I know, but remember what Uncle Jon-Jon said earlier. He wanted me stay at his house tonight and I don't want to disappoint him."

"You're right, Ms. Chasity. I'll be waiting for you outside."

"I'll be down in a few minutes," I said as I grabbed my purse and dashed to the door. Junior would return and find his home empty and alone, as it should be.

Thirty-five minutes later, we pulled up to Uncle Jon's estate and I instantly felt better. He was waiting at the door when we drove through the gate.

"Chasity, where did you and Junior disappear too? I saw you on the floor dancing with Track and the next the minute you vanished. And didn't I explain he is no good for you? Let me rephrase, stay the hell away from him. It's for your own good."

"I got it, Uncle Jon. Junior already drilled that into my head."

"Junior, huh?" He clinched his jaws. "Chasity, he's another one I want you to stay clear of. He's my son and I would do anything for him, but he will never make you happy, which is what I desire for you."

"Thanks for considering me that way. It will take a little more time to get used to a father figure in my life, but I'm happy to have you, Uncle Jon." I reached in and gave him a hug.

"I'm on top of the moon to have you, Pumpkin. Come inside where it's cool. Can I get you a cold glass of fresh lemonade?"

"That and a bed. I'm exhausted. I'm not used to hanging out this late, but I had a good time."

"I'm happy to hear that. Calvin, that will be all. I'll see you in the morning," he said as we went inside the house.

He showed me to my room and said, "Chasity, if you want to stay permanently, this will be your room. You can change it or do whatever you want."

"That's kind of you to offer, but I would need some time to think about that," I replied, unsure if I could live there with him being so overly protective.

"You do that. Tomorrow we'll have a big breakfast and go shopping. Destiny is elated and can't wait. If you want to check in on her, she's right down the hall," he said, as if Destiny was a toddler. "Oh, I almost forgot! They will deliver the cars tomorrow, too. Good night, Pumpkin."

"Good night, Uncle Jon," I replied and closed the door.

The room looked like a picture from an upscale magazine. When I touched the fabric on the bed, my hands melted into the sheets and the champagne colored baby soft suede headboard. The elegant metallic gold comforter accented it perfectly and there were six pillows calling my name. The wooden bedside tables were painted in light metallic gold with long stem crystal lamps on top. It was a room designed for me. The attached bathroom was spa heaven. Uncle Jon's taste was beyond anything I had imagined. One would have thought that this was the master because it had a separate shower, double vanity sinks, and a deep soaker jet tub. The custom cream glass tiles sparkled and I could definitely see myself living here. After a quick shower, I bonded with the bed, knowing I would sleep well.

Chapter 13

Junior

What the fuck is Chasity trying to pull? I thought to myself as I walked over toward them. I grabbed her away from him and my glare dared his punk ass to say shit. I was ready for Chasity's smart-ass mouth too. Track was talking, but I wasn't that concerned with what he had to say. I gave her specific instructions, and she was still trying to be problematic.

When she left, I turned to Track and said, "Listen, nigga, I know you thought you found you a nice little piece of ass tonight, but I told you she belongs to the Blake Family, which means she belongs to me. You need to respect it, and back the fuck off."

"Junior, your ah funny dude. I tell you what. I'll let you have her tonight, but if I happen to see her outside of your presence, well—all bets are off."

"With that said, let the games begin." He shook his head in response as I left. Track would have to die now.

I saw Chasity sitting inside the jeep and I told her to get inside my car. When we got back to my apartment, she disregarded everything I had to say. She threw her pussy at me, but somehow I resisted the temptation. I wanted Chasity, but I wanted her my way, which would require me in the lead. She was up in your face and bold. Her heroism excited me, but she would learn her place in time. I was stepping into the abyss, hoping I could find my way back. I insisted she stay her ass put until I returned, but of course that went on deaf ears. Calvin said she insisted on leaving and he didn't want any problems with Pops. I respected my father, but I didn't fear him, so I headed to Newton Square.

It was almost dawn, and the house was dark and quiet. I used my keys and went in search of Chasity. I knew she was in one of the guest quarters so I hurried up the steps and found her sleeping like a baby. She looked so comfortable that I almost didn't want to wake her.

"Chasity! Wake up, Chasity." She opened her eyes. "Why did you leave me? I told you I'd be right back."

"Junior, it's too late or too early in the morning for this," she groaned. "We can talk tomorrow. Come back for breakfast," she said, pulling the comforter over her head.

I yanked the comforter back and dropped it to the floor. Her sexy legs greeted me with a smile and I wanted to take her virginity right then. "Get up, you're coming with me. Since you don't know how to behave properly, I'll have to teach you. Get dressed," I commanded, and surprisingly she obliged. She huffed the entire time as she slid on her slippers and grabbed her bag. I noticed she wouldn't look at me.

"I'm ready," she said, still not looking at me.

"Here, I'll carry your bag. I didn't mean to scare you," I said, standing in front of her, forcing her to look at me. "You hear me?"

"Yes," she answered, slightly agitated. "We better get going before Uncle Jon wakes up, because he warned me to stay away from you."

"Oh, I get it now? You're afraid of him, but not me?"

"I'm not afraid of either of you. If that was the case, Junior, why am I leaving with you?"

"True, let's go."

When we got back to my apartment, I wanted to talk, but Chasity ran straight to the bedroom and fell asleep in my bed. That was okay with me and I was happy knowing she would be there when I wake later. I slid in the bed and gently pushed her over some because she was taking over the entire bed. I was tripping off the entire situation and it took me a minute to get to sleep. Having a woman in my bed was foreign, but it felt right.

When I woke up, I felt an unfamiliar warmth. Chasity's body buried into my spine and I welcomed her softness. I didn't want to wake her because she was sleeping so hard, and admittedly, I wanted to feel her next to me for a while longer. I was in my zone, thinking of ways I could please her, until my phone vibrated. I glanced at the number and it was Pops. By the time I answered, it stopped ringing. I eased from under Chasity's shield and went into the bathroom to call him back.

"Pops, what up?"

"Junior, please tell me you didn't come to my house and take away one of my guests. I know fucking well you're not that unwitting that you thought you could get away with it."

He's pissed, I thought. "Pops, I didn't make her do anything she didn't want to do. She wanted to come."

"Boy—you—you, Junior, are going to make me fuck you up! Bring Chasity to me now. And Junior? You don't want me to have to come for her," he barked, then disconnected the call.

I walked back into the bedroom and Chasity was still sleep. I gently nudged her until she woke up. "Hey, sleepy head. The king has summoned you to the castle. Your Uncle Jon is pissed at you for disobeying him. I guess now he'll know how I feel. Are you hungry?"

"Not right now. But why is he mad at me and not you? You're the one that kidnapped me and brought me here," she replied, still half asleep.

"Kidnapped? That's the story you're going with?"

"Sure is! Move," she commanded, shoving me to the side. "I'll be ready in ten minutes, so hurry, Junior. I should've just listened to him and stayed put." She continued to talk, but more to herself. She grabbed her bag and went into the bathroom.

I took a quick shower in the guestroom because I wanted to get Chasity to Pops as soon as possible. I wrapped the towel around my waist and walked into my closet. I grabbed a pair of jeans, a t-shirt and boxers. I heard Chasity come out, and when she saw me standing there in my towel she stared at me for a few moments too long. She looked sexy in a perfectly tailored burgundy jumpsuit, heightening my desire.

I threw on my clothes quickly and we headed to the door. She picked up her bag, and I asked, "Why are you taking your bag?"

"What do you mean? I'm not about to leave all my stuff here."

"You're right. We will have to go shopping to get you some clothes. You're staying with me until my trip to Dubai."

"Says who? Are you asking me, or are you telling me?"

"Both. Now come on. We can't keep Pops waiting. And when we get there, just follow my lead."

"We'll see," she replied as she rolled her eyes, having to have the last word.

Chapter 14

Chasity

I was dreaming about Junior, and when he woke me up from my sleep, it was certainly a dream come true. He was irresistible and undeniable. Although I could be snide and resilient, I wanted Junior exclusively and in return, I was willing to compromise myself. I desired the all-inclusive package and refused to settle for anything less. His forceful nature lit a fire between my thighs, blinding my sensibility. Junior was strong, handsome, and mysterious. His features far surpassed mine, and I felt privileged that he kidnapped me in the wee hours of the night.

Back at his place, we fell into a deep sleep. When the sun shined through the window, I peeped over at Junior and he was slightly snoring. I spooned him and went back to sleep, but he interrupted me shortly after. He explained Uncle Jon wanted me home and he was angry. I was unnerved, but Junior would never know, because I was blaming him for everything if backed against the wall by Uncle Jon

Before we left, Junior explained that I was staying with him, which was music to my ears and confirmed he was feeling me. His prior comment about me being easy and hungry was unsettling, and I made a note to self to be less aggressive.

Uncle Jon's house was cheerful and when Junior parked, he leaned over and briefly pecked my lips. "Remember, follow my lead," he instructed. We walked into the eat-in kitchen and Destiny was stuffing her face with what looked like a delicious buffet. Uncle Jon was reading the paper until he spotted us standing their hand in hand.

"Chasity, were you drunk last night? Because I remember telling you specifically to stay away from Junior. And Junior, you are treading on thin ice, son. I'm disappointed in the both of you."

"We're just trying to get to know one another as you suggested, Uncle Jon," I replied like a child caught with her hand in the cookie jar.

"Young Lady, when you're trying to get to know someone, it's not supposed to happen in the wee hours of the morning! I put you to sleep, only to find you gone hours later. I didn't know what happened to you until I spoke to Calvin and he put my mind at ease."

"I didn't mean to disappoint you, and I know you want the best for me. But I like Junior and I want to get to know him better."

"She loves Junior, and she wants to give her virginity to him," Destiny snitched.

"Shut the hell up! You don't know what you're talking about, Destiny." *This little winch.*

"You're a virgin, Chasity? And you want to give a precious gift like that to Junior! Oh, my shallow niece. This thing is worse than I thought."

"Pops, you outta order disrespecting me like that. Chasity will be fine and we're both grown. You can't control everything and you can't control me. I don't want this to come between us, but, Chasity is right, we plan to spend a lot more time with each other," Junior strongly stated, finally giving his input. He told me to follow his lead and until now, I thought I was the leader.

"Chasity, do you understand that staying a virgin for as long as you did is a blessing? Why would you throw that away for someone other than your husband?"

"I'm not a virgin, Uncle Jon," I replied, trying to end this topic of conversation.

"Yes she is, Uncle Jon! Unless Junior took her virginity last night, because she was virgin when we came to the party!" Destiny spat, betraying me.

Payback, hoe! "Destiny, why don't you tell Uncle Jon how you're not a virgin? And how I caught Khalif fucking your brains out in your bedroom! Talk about that! Tell him how you offered advice on the subject because you're such an expert," I snapped.

"I can't believe you, Chasity!" she cried, stunned.

"And I can't believe you either! If you want to throw a rock, bitch, expect a brick to be thrown back!" I spat.

"Okay, ladies, enough already!" Uncle Jon barked. "It's obvious that your loss has caused all this dysfunction. You were barely adults when you had to take on adult issues. Chasity, Junior is right. You are grown. But when this bossy nigga breaks your heart, come on home and I will be there to mend it. I'm done with this. Help yourself to something to eat," he said as he exited the room.

I went in on Destiny as soon as he left. "Why the fuck did you tell him my business? First off, you were wrong for even going through my shit, but to expose me in front of him is unforgivable! I thought we were sisters, but I see you got your own agenda. Do you boo because you will need me before I need you."

"Chasity, I'm sorry you feel that way. And just so you know, you don't have to take care of me anymore, because I'm moving in with Uncle Jon and he is my new caregiver. Just like he said, when *this person,*" she emphasized, "breaks your heart, we will be here with open arms to take you back. But until then, we are distant sisters and you can kick bricks, bitch, and masturbate until you turn blue in the face. Maybe now you'll get some real dick and throw away all those buzzing toys I hear every night." She stormed out the room, leaving me speechless.

Junior was staring at me in disbelief. "What," I yelled.

"That's how sisters do, I guess. Toys and diaries—I wonder how many more skeletons are locked away. You wrote about me in your diary?" he asked intrigued.

"No, I wasn't thinking about you like that," I lied.

He grabbed my hand and pulled me into his chest. "Are you sure you weren't thinking about me? Why do I find that hard to believe?" he asked, sucking my earlobe while holding my head steady. It was aggressive and enticing. I had to get away, knowing he was just teasing.

I used force to pull away from him and said, "None of that—remember where only in the talking stage and I'm more than willing to hear your voice, but your touch is off limits until you're ready to take me out my misery."

"You're handing over the keys and allowing me to drive?" He looked surprised.

"Yes, you're the boss for a week. Lead me and free me, handsome," I replied and hugged his neck.

That was the first time a real smile evolved, and I was in love, lust—fuck, I was a goner "I'm about to throw down on this food, will you be joining me?" I asked.

"Yeah, I'm starved and if you keep up that behavior, you'll get what you want real soon," he said, looking sexy as ever.

"I'll make your plate, would that make you feel good," I asked, grabbing one of the stacked plates on the island.

"I want some of everything. Can you warm up the waffles? They look cold and I'll take a glass of orange juice."

"Yes, Sir—right away," I smirked. I warmed up his plate and handed it to him along with the orange juice. I loved it because he never took his eyes off me. His extended gaze verified his interest in me and I knew I had him. I just had to figure out how to keep him. "Here you go, Sir, is there anything else I can assist with," I asked.

"Cut the bullshit and just allow me to have you my way this week. If you listen, I promise to make it a week you won't forget, now kiss me," he insisted.

"If I kiss you, will you promise to make love to me?"

He grabbed my waist, pulled me close, and said, "I promise to make sweet love to you. Sit down and eat your food because we'll be leaving soon."

"Are you taking me back to the ice—?" I caught myself and said, "To your condo."

"See, there you go. I thought we understood one another," he replied. Destiny walked in and said Uncle Jon wanted me out front.

When I spotted my car, I lost my mind again. Seeing the car in person was far more exciting than watching it on a screen. It was beautiful, and I wanted to drive it right away. I thanked Uncle Jon again and gave him a big hug, but he was still mad at me.

"I know you want to drive your car so just follow me," Junior said.

"You read my mind. Let's go," I responded, as I watched Destiny drive away and roll her eyes. It was unclear what she was going through, but I was embracing the new selfish me and didn't care. Do you boo, I thought?

I followed Junior back to his condo, we switched cars and hopped into his Range Rover. When I asked why we were changing cars, he explained we were going shopping and needed the extra space.

We reached the Cherry Hill Mall in Jersey and a smile spread across my face. I was in my element because Uncle Kenny brought us here many times. When we entered, I spotted Forever 21 and asked if we could go inside the store. Junior followed behind and watched as I went through the racks. He touched the dress fabric and looked down at the tag.

"Chasity, I view you as a smart woman, so I'm confused why you would bring me into a low budget store like this?"

"I don't want you spending mass amounts of money on me. I thought I was doing you a favor because they have cute clothes and great bargains. They even have a men's department. You don't want to look?" I asked, embarrassed and pissed that he was calling me cheap.

"Not only are you beautiful, you have a great sense of humor, but I don't have the time nor the patience," he replied, as he took my hand and led me out of the store. Letting him lead was bullshit and I didn't know how long I could play this game. We ended up in Nordstrom's but my mood had dissipated, so I watched him shop.

"Chasity, stop playing and go find enough clothes for the week. Please don't tell me you want to go back to that hideous store. If you insist, we can." He laughed at his own joke. "Nah, but straight up, you need to find something now."

"Okay, Junior, but I will return to that store another time, so I don't offend you."

"Did you give my father this much trouble when he took you out?" I gave him a surprised look. "You thought I didn't know, Chasity. You walk up in my party in a $1,500 hundred-dollar dress and the first store you walk into is an updated flea market. Of course I knew he funded your outfit."

"I'll go find something to wear, before I transform back into me again and we be arguing." I walked away and went to the women's department. Once alone, I had to admit the difference in the fabric was astronomical, but I never cared about the material before today. If it was cute, I wanted it, but just like in Neiman's, I was in a whole other world.

An hour later, I had enough clothes to last for the week. All Junior had to do was take me home to get my own clothes, but he had other plans. I was happy with my finds and successful with picking the least expensive items, but Junior still paid more than I wanted.

We walked through the mall and I spotted a well-known lingerie store. After selecting panties and bras, I snuck in a pink teddy to use as bait if Junior tries to back out. He was in front of the store talking on the phone and I wondered if it was another woman, but quickly dismissed the thought. I paid for my stuff and met up with Junior.

"You ready? I think I have everything I need except personal items."

"We can stop at the Walmart when we get home."

"You shop at Walmart?"

"Yeah, I need personal items too" he laughed. Are you hungry?"

"Starved. Can we go to Red Lobster?" I blurted, and he sighed. "Listen, I don't want to go to a fancy restaurant and eat shit—I mean food. I never heard of before. At Red Lobster, you get a salad, bread and entrée for a reasonable price. I always leave full and satisfied."

"Calm down, I thought you were following my lead. I eat anywhere the food is good. I love seafood too and I know just the spot. There's a nice little spot on Broad Street called Route 66. Their food is tight."

"Okay, I'm in."

Junior's choice of restaurant was on point and the food was delicious. The crab balls were to die for and the wine had me intoxicated. Back at his place there was an awkward silence between us. "Do you mind if I take a shower? Which bathroom do you want me to use?" I asked.

"You want permission now?" He was being smug. "You can use any one you prefer. I have a few calls to make but if you need me, I'll be here in the living room."

"I need you! I'm just kidding," I lied. He smirked and sat down on the couch.

I took a shower and washed my hair. I let it air dry and used a small amount of the magic pudding I received from the spa. I put on a pair of cotton pajamas, grabbed the remote and surfed the channels until I found one of my favorite Alaskan shows. I loved everything about Alaska. It amazed me how they lived off the land, hunting for food and trying to stay warm for the entire winter. An Alaskan cruise was an item on my to-do list and I couldn't wait. I dozed off, but Junior woke me up a few minutes later.

"Hey, wake up, Chass," Junior's hand was on my shoulder and he gently nudged me. I played sleep a little longer just so I could feel his touch. "When I get out the shower we'll finish our talk

And I know you hear me," he said as he went into the bathroom.

He came out the shower with his towel wrapped around his waist and I noticed the huge print poking between his thighs. *Do I really want to lose my virginity to that?* I thought, but briefly terminated the doubt. *Hell yeah, he's the one.*

"What, you see something you want?" he asked mischievously.

"I'm checking you out, Junior. You are very sexy and you shouldn't do me like that."

"Do you like what? I don't know what you're talking about."

"Coming in here with your big dick poking through that towel. You should've taken a pair of drawers in with you instead of teasing me."

"My bad, I'll be more mindful the next time," he said, as he let the towel drop, giving me the big picture. He went inside his closet, leaving me hot and bothered. When he got into the bed, I moved over and allowed him to get comfortable. He placed the pillows behind his back and said, "Come closer, Chass. I promise I won't bite," he said, but he had my permission to break that promise.

I scooted over and he wrapped his arms around me, something I longed for all day. "What do you want to talk about first?" I asked, loving his embrace.

"You, me, us. Okay, question number one. Why did you stay a virgin for so long? Now don't get me wrong, I'm happy about that, just curious is all. Was it because your uncle would've killed a nigga?"

"Yes and no. I knew Uncle Kenny wasn't going for that, but I met someone in college. I thought I was in love, but later found I was in lust." I had his full attention. "My boyfriend in college was a devout Christian, and he didn't believe in sex until marriage. I did everything I could to make it work, thinking he'd ask for my hand in marriage. What a fool I was."

"His stupidity is my gain. Have you ever experienced an orgasm?"

"Yes, I'm a virgin but I know how an orgasm feels."

"Your toys?"

"That and other things."

"Other things? Don't leave me in suspense, Chass." That was the fourth time he called me Chass tonight. Maybe we'll work our way to baby or sweetie before the end of the week. "Spill it," he demanded.

"After a while, I got tired of snuggling and kissing. I wanted to feel the real thing, and he was not willing to break his oath to God. I felt like Satan in the relationship and it made me feel unloved, so I broke up with him. Anyway, he came back with a great idea to keep his celibacy and me, which was eating my pussy."

"Did you return the favor?"

"No, he refused, not wanting any penetration, so it was all one-sided."

"What happened between y'all?"

"He broke up with me right before graduation, saying he had sinned and needed to repent."

"Just like that, huh? How do I know you won't pull the same thing on me if I don't give you none?"

"Because, you promised and he never did."

"Is that all you want, Chasity? Because I can give you your wish and then we're done…"

"No, why do you say that? Honestly, Destiny was right. I do have strong feelings towards you, and I hope it don't scare you away. Although, I'm used to nothing being permanent in my life." Tears fell from my eyes.

"Are you crying, Chasity? I didn't mean to make you feel sad. I'm just trying to get to know you."

"It's fine, Junior. I guess you never get over a loss like mine, but I'm doing the best I can."

"You're doing damn good, girl. I'm looking forward to getting to know you," he said, as he ran his fingers through my hair. "Chasity, I love your haircut. Was that for me?" he asked.

"Yes," I lied, knowing I did it more for work.

"I think that's enough for tonight. We can come back to this tomorrow evening when I get off work," he explained.

"Junior, I have some business to take care of tomorrow too, so are you going to give me a key?"

"What business? I want you here at my disposal. All I asked for was a week," he replied, looking slightly panicked.

"I'm giving it to you, but the inspector is coming out tomorrow. If I miss him, who knows when he'll come back! It took three weeks to get this appointment, Junior."

"What time is the inspector coming?"

"You know how they are, Junior."

"I know, but we'll figure that out in the morning. I'm ready to get a little shut eye. Do you mind cutting off the TV?" I obeyed, and he didn't turn his back. Instead, he pulled me into his chest and we fell asleep knotted together.

The next morning, Junior woke before me and I heard him talking on the phone in the living room. I went into the bathroom to wash my face and brush my teeth. When I heard my special ring tone for Jeff, I ran back to grab my phone. He was just calling to remind me about the inspector. I told him I would be there in forty-five minutes, knowing Route 76 would be off the chain and swarmed with rush hour traffic.

Junior came into the room, still talking on the phone, but once he saw me ironing my clothes he told the person to hold. "Where do you think you're going? I want you here today. I want to try something new."

"Did you forget that fast, Junior? I told you about the inspector coming. You should know better than anyone that I can't miss them."

"Yes, I remember and I know how important getting the approval from the inspector is. However, I also know you don't have to be there. Your foreman can handle that," he replied after he told the person on the phone he would call them back.

Calm down, bitch before he makes you turn into an alley cat, I rationed inwardly. I took a deep breath and said, "I understand, but that's my baby, and I want to be there to hear what he has to say. Don't forget you have your money invested. You should come," I rationed, trying to lighten the weight of me rearing into his ass.

"I'm needed at the office, though the invite is tempting. Let me try a different approach. Chasity, please stay put until I come home from work. We're experimenting and you don't want to fuck up the progress."

"I'm good, but obviously you bumped your fuck--," I stopped myself and regrouped. "I think you're being irrational and stubborn. I'm trying hard to be chill, but it's like you're trying to bring out my dark side."

"Nah, Chass, you don't need me for that, but you're right. Do your thing and I'll see you when I see you." He turned and left.

Whatever, I thought. I dressed and rushed out because I was excited to drive my car. I needed time to figure out all the features but for now, my only mission was to get to my house.

When I pulled up, Jeff was sitting on the steps smoking a cigarette. I noticed he put flowers in the flower boxes, which added the perfect extra touch. Jeff took pride in the house, knowing he was the one that did all the hard work.

"What's up, Jeff?" I asked. "You look tired."

"I am tired, Chass. You know you're not my only client, but I'm proud of you and I would do anything for your Uncle Kenny. Come inside, I want to show you the bathroom. I'm proud to tell you everything is complete."

The house was beautiful. A big chunk of the budget went towards the bathroom and the kitchen appliances. If the inspector says everything is a go, I can put this house on the market next week.

When I walked into the bathroom, I was pleased. Jeff had exceeded my expectations. It was huge, which was one reason it cost so much. The white basket weave marble tile set a sister back, but it was worth it. It matched the kitchen counter tops and I loved it. I invested in a soaker tub and surrounded it with glossy white subway tile. I chose a chocolate brown theme and Jeff installed the double marble top vanity. To give it more life, instead of matching the mirrors with the vanity, I selected two mosaic-trimmed glass mirrors with lighting sconces on top. Jeff added a stand up shower with the same subway tiles and marble on the shower floor.

It was bright and inviting. "Jeff, I can't tell you how much I love the work you did. When I imagined it, it was beautiful, but to see you bring my vision to life is far better than I could've dreamed." A tear fell from my eyes because I was so grateful for his help. He was giving me a great deal, but I intended on hooking him up with a bonus as soon as I sold the house. I needed Jeff in my life and I wanted him along for the ride. He was another father figure who I trusted and respected.

"Don't cry, baby girl. It was my pleasure and I look forward to working with you on other projects."

"You better, because I wouldn't have it any other way," I replied and hugged him.

"I see we're giving out love today." Junior interrupted. "Can I get some love?" he asked.

I let go of Jeff and said, "Junior, I'm surprised to see you here. I thought work was more important."

"Baby girl, I'll take one last look around before the inspector comes. I'll see you guys downstairs," Jeff said.

"Okay, I'll be down soon, and thanks again for all the beautiful work we did together." He shook his head and left the bathroom.

"It's obvious you're a lovable person, so tell me, what is required from me to get some of that love.? Do I have to bang a few nails or what?"

"That would be sexy but you really don't have to do much. You know how I feel and I don't appreciate you teasing me all the time."

"You think I'm teasing you?" he asked as he ran his fingers through my hair. "Don't worry, baby girl. I got you."

"Are you jealous of a man that's old enough to be my father? Only my elders can call me baby girl. If you want to make my day, you can call me baby or sweetie."

"Since you dragged me down here, show me around, but I can already see you did your thing. The place is tight," he responded, ignoring the last part of my comment.

"Whatever, Junior. As you can see, the bathroom is spectacular. Let me show you the bedrooms," I said as I led the way. I gave him a tour of the upstairs and he was pleased, but I wanted to show him my masterpiece, the kitchen.

I stood there with a bright smile, full of pride at the hard work I put into the cabinets. I refinished them and added a center island which had a white marble top with shiny streaks of silver sporadically catching your eye. I added sleek brush nickel hardware that popped against the dark stain. I put in a white farmhouse sink to match the character of the house. The hardwood floors were the original floors and after we stained, sanded and applied polyurethane, they were beautiful.

"I like! You should have no problems selling this house. I'm still skeptical about the asking price, but I guess we'll see what happens. If I could suggest one thing that would sell this house faster? I think you should stage it."

"That's not happening, plus there's no more money in the budget. Matter of fact, the budget is depleted and I'm praying the inspector passes this house."

"You can stage this whole house for three thousand dollars."

"Junior, I don't have the money and I want the person to imagine what they will do with the house, not see one that's already staged. I want them to see that although I kept the integrity of the house, I also gave them quality materials that will last a lifetime." Jeff interrupted us, informing me the inspector had arrived.

"Hey, Scott, long time no see. How's everything?" Junior asked.

"Junior, it has been a long time. I'm doing well. How is your father? I was meaning to call him. I have some good news and I'm glad I ran into you, because that refreshed my memory. I'll call him this evening," Scott replied.

"Hello," I said, getting their attention. "I'm Chasity, and I believe you're here to see me."

"Yes, Chasity. I didn't meet you the last time I was here, but the pleasure is all mine. If you two will excuse me, I'll get to it. Junior, when I'm done, can I speak to you alone?" Chuck asked.

"Sure, Chuck." Junior responded.

When Chuck walked away, I asked, "How do you know him?"

"Chasity, I've been in this business a while, and Chuck has done many inspections with the Blake Corporation. We go way back."

"Well, I hope everything is all good because Lord knows, I don't have another dime to drop into this house."

"If it's a problem, I'll take care of it, and I'm willing to pay for the staging as well."

"Thanks, but I know I don't want that. I fell in love with the house when I saw all the space, and I want the buyer to envision their dreams for the place."

"You're the boss, Chass and in this one instance, I will follow your lead."

"Thank you. Was that so hard, handsome?" He smiled. "I like your smile. You should do that more often. You look happy when you smile."

"Who don't look happy when they smile, Chass?"

"Many people, Junior, but I'm not about to argue over your smile. It just made me feel good."

"I'll try to smile more, just for you. Let me go talk to Chuck and then we can leave."

"Are we going somewhere special?" I asked, hoping he had a surprise for me.

"I believe so, and it's a place where I never go. It should be interesting," he responded as he walked away. I couldn't wait and I loved that he was becoming friendlier by the day.

Ten minutes later, Chuck gave me the good news. I was ready to celebrate, and happy Junior showed up and surprised me. His mood was faint when he left for work, but he was back in the game. I locked the house, told Jeff I would be in touch, and we left.

We pulled up to a supermarket on Columbus Boulevard, confusing the hell out of me. But once he parked, the suspense was over and out the window. He grabbed a cart and we made our way through the aisles getting enough food to last a month. *We must be going somewhere else after*, I thought.

When we stood in line he said, "Chass, did you get every-thing you wanted? I'm not used to having food in the house, but since you're staying with me temporarily, I think it's a good idea," he said as if he were asking himself.

Hell no, dick for brains. I want to eat out. Instead of expressing my disapproval, I smiled and said, "Great idea."

We had two carts of groceries as if we were paying with a food stamp card. The bill came to over four hundred dollars and I wondered who was carrying all this stuff inside. I helped him load everything into his Range Rover and we drove down the street to his home, less than five minutes away. When we reached the condo, Junior had to make two trips, and I aided with as many bags as I could carry on my first trip. I told him I would put the food away.

The task went quickly due to Junior's refrigerator being emp-ty. The only things inside the cabinets were glasses and dishes that appeared unused. After I put the food away, I heard him arguing with someone on the phone and his tone and rhythm changed. *Damn, now he'll probably be a dick towards me*, I dreaded.

He walked into the kitchen as I was finishing up and said, "Chass, what's for lunch? I thought we could cook together and talk more."

"Okay, but I'm not that great a cook and I don't want you talking about my food."

"You're not alone. I can't cook either, but between the two of us I'm sure we can come up with something."

"You're right but it's still early. Do you want breakfast or lunch?"

"Lunch, baby," he said as he pulled me into his arms. "You know you're beautiful and sexy as shit." He applied soft pecks on my neck, increasing my desire for him. He massaged my ass cheeks as he lifted me. I assisted by wrapping my legs around his waist. *This is it. It's going down*, I thought. His arms were solid and his hold was strong as he kissed me straight into stupid. I was drunk in love, minus the alcohol. "Chass, I want to get to know everything about your body before I enter it," he whispered, as he unbuttoned my cotton shirt and devoured my breast with the swirl of his tongue.

"Aww, Junior, stop teasing me. I can't take it," I moaned.

"It's called control," he replied while pecking my lips. "You need to find it within yourself, and when the time is right, I'll invite you to lose control," he explained, placing me back on the floor. "Come on, let's cook. Why are you standing there like that?" he asked when I stood trembling in the middle of the kitchen.

"I'll be right back. I have to pee," I said, running to the guest bathroom. I had to clean myself from the unexpected orgasm and calm my nerves. I was tired of those types of orgasms. My handy bullet and vivid imagination could stimulate me all day, but I wanted the real thing desperately. *I want some dick, damn it!* I rejoined Junior in the kitchen. "So what are we eating?" I asked.

"Surprise me. You can lead on this one."

"Typical, how about chicken tacos since you don't eat red meat that often. It's quick and we'll be eating in no time. But for dinner, I wanted to make the salmon we bought while it's still fresh."

"Do your thing ma. Tell me what to do." He appeared eager.

"Where are your pots and pans?" He opened the stove and a brand new set of pots stared back. I looked at him strangely.

"What? That's where my mother kept all the pots."

"Did I say anything, Junior? Just grab those seasonings we bought today and the box of soft taco shells," I instructed as I washed my hands and opened the package of chicken breasts. After cleaning them and trimming away all the fat, I cut them into small chunks with Junior's unused chef knives. I had to be careful not to cut myself because they were professional, sharp as shit knives.

I placed the chicken in a bowl and seasoned it with pepper, seasoning, and garlic salt. The taco sauce would do the rest. He snuck up behind me and hugged my waist again. "What do I do now?" he asked, nibbling on my ear.

"Hand me a tomato, the lettuce, and sour cream out the fridge. I saw a cutting board in the top cabinet. You can cut the tomatoes up in small cubes." He grabbed the cutting board and the biggest knife he had. "Use this serrated knife. It will cut the tomato better. You're about to make tomato juice."

"Is this right?" he asked as he cut the tomato with precision and expertise. I don't know if it was because his knives were so sharp or if he was playing me.

"Perfecto!" I said as I browned the chicken. We sat down at the all glass dinette table and enjoyed a healthy, homemade meal together. I was ready to talk, and it was my turn to inquire about him. "Junior, don't get mad at me, but why do you treat your employees so horribly? You know, they call you Iron Man...and a few other things I won't mention."

"I'm shocked, Chasity. I thought you were the only one who named called," he replied as he took a bite of his taco. "My feelings are butchered," he continued with a mouthful of food.

"Don't be smug, Junior. I know you don't care, but you should. Your employees are afraid of you and they perform under command instead of authority."

"That means the same thing in my world, Chass. Oh, wait, I'm sorry. I meant baby."

"Don't say it unless you mean it. In fact, don't say it at all, because it doesn't even sound right coming from your mouth."

"It sounds like you're getting a little upset, and here I thought we were getting along so well," he smirked.

"I can get upset if I want to. Plus, you're not playing fair. You wanted to talk, but I see that was one-sided. You want to know everything about me, except how my pussy smell," I grabbed my plate and stood up from the table. "If you can't be open and honest about yourself, then you might as well take me home. I'm tired of you holding my pussy hostage. I can't do this with you and I need time to get you out my system," I said, walking into the kitchen to discard my plate. When he continued eating, I went into the bedroom to pack my stuff. He had me fucked up. I was a virgin, but I was not gullible. I went into the bathroom and grabbed my toothbrush. Just as I was about to grab my keys, Junior walked into the bedroom.

"Where the fuck is you going?" he asked, as if the last few minutes wasn't a dysfunctional fantasy.

"Home," I said, loud and proud.

"Chasity, you are home for the rest of the week. I thought we agreed and now you're reneging on the deal."

"Junior, you don't want to talk, you don't want me... I don't know what kind of sick game we're playing, but I give up, you win. I'm going home."

"Okay, you want to talk, let's talk, sweetie." He looked at me with those sexy, crazy eyes I loved. "The day you walked into my office, you had a small piece of my attention. However, the day you took your stand at my meeting, I wanted to fuck you on the wall where you stood, and do all kinds of things to your body. But what scared me to death was wanting more than the usual of just ravishing a woman's body. It was an unfamiliar feeling that scared me, but I'm trying to face those feelings directly. This is unheard of for me, baby."

"So you're afraid of falling in love, being in a relationship, or both?"

"Both. Not to mention you're a virgin, which is even more frightening."

"Why is that scary? I should be the one afraid."

"Chasity, I never had sex with a virgin. I fucked my babysitter when I was ten, and throughout my teenage years, I only dealt with older girls. I'm cautious of entering virgin walls."

"But I'm ready, and every woman has to go through this. I'm excited to endure what is inevitable."

"It's noticeable. Trust me, Chass. Give me my week, and I promise to give you want you want."

"Okay, one week and then I'm moving on, Junior."

"Don't threaten me, Chasity. You know what affect that has on me. Not only does it make my dick rock hard, it makes me want to bend you over and spank that ass for the disrespect," he whispered, as he patted my behind hard enough for me to glance back. "Behave yourself and be a good girl for Junior." He kissed my neck.

"I can do that," I responded, trapped under his spell again. His eyes were my weakness, his body my lustful torment, and his crazy ass personality my mental challenge. Still, I was head over heels.

"I don't know about all that. Just do the best you can. Come on, I want to watch TV. I never have time for that," he said, as he tackled me to the bed.

For the next couple of days, Junior and I talked, cooked, watched TV, and enjoyed each other's company. By the time Wednesday arrived, he had to go back to the office and I was disappointed.

"Chass, I know you're tired of being in the house. I arranged for Calvin to take you anywhere you desire, except to see another man."

"Junior, what's the deal with that? Wherever I go, I'm coming back to you—as long as you want."

"That's sweet. Calvin will be here shortly. You should take advantage of it because what I have planned for the next few days, will require you all to myself."

"That sounds mysterious and sexual. I can't wait."

"Take your mind out of the gutter. I'm serious. Get ready to give me the same dance you gave Pops. I liked that dance."

"Oh, you'll enjoy my dance, trust me, handsome!" He kissed my lips and left, leaving me hanging once again.

Chapter 15

Junior

C hasity got me bugging the fuck out. First, I bring her back to my sanctuary, then she got a nigga up in the market buying groceries and shit. Now, she had inspired me to address my staff, something I never did before. Not to mention what I had planned for her ass, I thought, as I walked into my office.

I instructed Domencio to gather everyone in the conference room to discuss a few issues and put smiles on their faces. As they entered, I noticed their visible stress for the first time, and realized they hated being in my presence.

"Thank you all for stopping your work for this emergency meeting. As you know, myself, Domencio, and a few other executives will be leaving for Dubai on Monday. Wayne will be in charge and will keep me afloat on everything." Relief settled on their faces. "This is my last day, but I'll be back when I return from Dubai." Domencio shot me a look of surprise and the room smiled. "Also, I want to extend my gratitude for your dedication and commitment. Because of your hard work, a bonus is deserved and long overdue. Wayne will issue out the checks today. I hope you have a great week." *That felt good*, I thought.

"Thank you, Junior." Rosilyn showed her appreciation first and everyone else followed suit.

"You're welcome. Ladies, if you would be so kind to stay behind, meeting is adjourned." When everyone else left, I addressed the women. "I don't want to offend anyone, but I was hoping to get your personal opinions. My friend and I had an intense conversation, which turned into a lengthy debate and I was hoping you ladies could help clarify the issue."

"Shoot, we're all ears," Antoinette, the head of resources, said.

"Okay, remember I warned you. At any time, you become uncomfortable, we can stop the conversation," I explained, hoping I wasn't digging a hole for myself. "I begged to differ with my friend when referring to a woman losing her virginity." There was a slight distorted look upon their faces. *Fuck it. I'm in too deep to turn back now.* "My good friend believes a woman's first time is unpleasing. I was wondering if you fine woman could give your input." The room got quiet, and I regretted my decision. *Damn, Chasity had a boss fucked up,* I thought. I'm out here doing the unthinkable for this woman.

"Your friend is right. My first time was horrible, and I try my best to suppress that memory," Bernadette broke the silence.

My receptionist, Kristina, added "Yeah, it was bad and if I could turn back time, I would've done things differently and chose a different partner."

Amen sang throughout the conference room. I was starting to get discouraged until Cheron said, "I disagree. My first time was special and I've been happily married to him for seven years. I guess it depends on the man. My man was gentle, and he took his time to make me feel comfortable. Before we even got to the sex, I was ready to explode from the intimacy. For me, it was one of the best nights I've had with my husband."

I was smiling internally because Cheron had brightened my mood. My dick was not for the weak and weary, so virgin pussy was foreign. I enjoyed experienced woman, and I never sought after a virgin or a relationship. *Look how shit is evolving now.*

"Okay ladies, that was very informative and I apologize again. I plan to change the way I interact with the staff. I don't want to you to be afraid of Iron Man anymore." They were unaware I knew about the name by the shy expressions on their faces. "Don't get me wrong, I won't have an open-door policy, but I want you to be comfortable in my presence. I'll inform my friend and see you all when I return. Thank you again."

When I got back to my office, I called Calvin to get the company jet ready. Chasity's first time would be special and where better than the most magical place in the world? I called her cell phone and it rang until her voicemail picked up, which instantly agitated me. I called my house phone and she picked up, sounding out of breath.

"Why didn't you answer your phone?" I asked at once.

"I was in the shower and when I got out I saw that you had called, but then your phone started ringing, so I figured it was you. Why did I just have to explain all that," she said aloud, but I believe it was more for her own ears.

"You need to explain because I asked you to. That's normally how this thing works. Be ready when I get home and pack an overnight bag. We'll figure out the rest when we get there."

"Get where?" she asked.

"Just get ready and stop misbehaving."

"Junior, you just back pedaled on your own words. I asked a question and now I want an explanation. Don't be a one-sided bully."

"Chasity, I'm not telling you because it's a surprise, so don't ruin it," I replied sternly.

"One minute you're sweet, but in an instant you act sour?"

"See, this is the bullshit that gets under my skin and kept me single. Don't spoil this opportunity, baby."

"Bye, Junior," she slammed the phone down, which excited and angered me simultaneously.

The drive to my house was a short distance, and I arrived home in no time. I walked into my room and Chasity was spread across my bed watching *Alaska, The Last Frontier*. She was different from the norm. The average woman wanted me for my looks, but more disheartening, my money. She was different and more interested in making her own money. I admired and hated it at the same time, wanting to be her provider. Over the past few days, I discovered she loved Alaska and planned to take a cruise there. I looked into the trip but it would entail more time than I had, so I was going for the alternative. She said she loved when her Uncle Kenny took the family for vacation.

"Hey, you. Why aren't you dressed? You trying to defy or test me? Which is it, because I'm sure I told you to be ready."

"No, I'm trying to surprise you by not being ready. Surprise," she said, opening her arms as if it was my birthday.

"Stop playing, ma and get ready. Don't forget to pack a bag because we won't be able to shop until tomorrow. And I'm not asking again, Chasity." She got up and opened a suitcase I hadn't seen before and started throwing stuff on the bed.

"Where did that come from?" I asked.

"Calvin. He took me home since I had a day of freedom."

"That was a smart move because you belong to me for the next four days," I explained, invading her space. I stood behind her, placed my hands on her healthy hips, and whispered, "Why are you acting like you're not happy to see me? Since our phone call, you been acting unhappy and defiant. What's up? Talk to me, baby."

"I don't appreciate being treated like a child. Today you reminded me of that day at your office. I don't have a problem trying to make you happy, but you have to trust me. Having Calvin drive me around is not gonna work. I want to drive my new car and be normal. You should take your own advice and treat me the way you want to be treated."

"That's what I'm trying to do, trust me. You have no idea how out of character this is for me. Listen, we're both doing the best we can. Let's just agree to disagree for now, because we need to get going. I want to reach our destination early."

"Okay, Junior," she responded and started moving at pace that was satisfactory.

When we arrived at the airport, the puzzled look on her face pleased me. When Calvin drove up to the company jet, her look went from baffled to stimulated. That look delighted me and I couldn't wait to connect with her sexually. Four of my most trusted bodyguards came along for the ride. It was apparent she was uncomfortable because she kept asking me why I needed them in the first place. Truth be told, I've made plenty of enemies over the years, and my current status did not mean people forgot. Death threats were the norm for me and I was sure to take every precaution to secure my safety. And I damn sure didn't want anything to happen to Chasity. I got word that Track had been saying some unforgivable shit on the street. I was trying to be cool and let my pops handle it, but I hated for shit to be lingering.

When the plane landed, I could see the relief on Chasity's face because it was an unusually bumpy ride. "Come on, baby, your chariot awaits," I said as I picked her up and took her off the plane.

Chapter 16

Chasity

Once Junior left, Calvin took me home and I picked up some essentials. My goal was to talk to a realtor about listing the house, but I didn't feel comfortable with Calvin driving me around. He reported everything back to Junior, and it was obvious Junior thought I was his possession.

When we spoke on the phone, he was acting shady so I returned the favor. When he walked in and I saw his unmistakably handsome face, bowlegs and perfect body, there was no way I could stay mad at him. Now, we were on our way to the surprise and I was getting anxious.

When reached the airport, I knew we were flying somewhere, but never in my wildest dreams thought it would be on his private jet. I was nervous, giddy, and had a newfound respect for Junior. He provided the all-star treatment, but the four football-player-appearing bodyguards were misplaced.

"Junior, what's up with the entourage? I thought it would be just us two," I asked once inside the plane.

"They're here for our protection. You never know these days." He shrugged his shoulders as if it was nothing. "Folks are hungry and ready to eat, Chasity."

"But why are you a target? I mean, I could see if you were a drug pin or major criminal, but you're not. I don't get it," I replied, puzzled.

"These days' they target businessman the same as drug pins and criminals. I'm a target as well as my whole family, including you now."

"I'm your family?" I asked, smiling at the compliment.

"Absolutely, you're my cousin so that makes you family."

"You know what!" I punched him in the arm. "You treat me like a cousin so I'll rock with that. Oh shit, why is this plane so bumpy? Is the plane experiencing engine problems, Junior?" I asked frantically.

"Calm down Chasity, it's just a little turbulence. We're good, sweetie," he comforted as he came over and sat next to me. "Don't worry, I'm right here and this jet is the best of its kind. When you're with me, no harm will come to you. Give me a kiss," he demanded and the sinister look was back that fast. I hated to admit it, but that was fifty percent of why I was in love with his ass. As soon as I get some quality time to myself, I have to research Bipolar Disorder and its effects on relationships, so I can be more prepared.

When we landed, he whisked me out of my seat and carried me off the plane. I was so happy being in his arms and he always smelled so good. I laid my head on his shoulder and enjoyed the moment. I noticed we were at the Orlando International Airport and I had to pinch myself to make sure it was real.

Two SUVs were outside waiting and Junior and I hopped in one while the others got in the one behind us.

"Junior, thanks for the private plane ride. It was off the chain, except for the turbulence. What's next on the list?" I asked.

"Nah, I'm not telling you. Just sit back and enjoy the ride. Have I failed you yet, even with your uncontrollable behavior? I'm trying to impress you, which is like pulling teeth, and this shit is hard on me. I need you to stop trying to invade my mental space and let me experiment with you in peace."

"So, I'm an experiment, Junior? You really know how to steal a sister's joy," I smugly replied.

"Don't start, come here," he commanded, pulling me into his magnificence. "I don't want us to get off to a bad start, Chass, because I'm looking forward to the events as well. Play nice and be a good girl. Junior promises to fulfill his promise to you, and make you happy doing it," he said, speaking of himself in the third person.

"You're right. It doesn't matter what you have planned. As long as I'm with you, I'm happy." I rest my head on his chest and he wrapped his arms around me. Seconds later, I was asleep.

"Chasity, wake up, babe. We're here," I heard Junior say. I looked out the window and saw a luxurious two-story estate that was inexpressible. It looked more like Fort Knox than a house. "This is your home for the next four days. We'll be heading back Sunday."

"Words cannot describe what I'm feeling. You planned this all by yourself?"

"Yes, Chasity. I vacation sometimes, but it's been a while. Come on, let me show you around."

"Is this your house?"

"Nah, this house belongs to a good friend and business associate."

"What is he, a gazillionaire? This is way out of my league!"

"You're with me, and as long as you continue to be in my presence, nothing is unreachable for you."

"That's sweet, Junior. Now let's go see this house," I responded gleefully, feeling on top of the world.

As we approached the entrance of the Spanish style estate, typical for Florida homes, two massive columns that framed the entryway greeted us with grandeur. It was spectacular, and I was enjoying it with the finest man walking the face of the earth. The inside of the home had an open flow and a full view of a lake was visible through the massive glass windows. I headed towards the glass doors that led out to the backyard. The view was picture perfect, and the estate sat on a chain of lakes. The crystal blue infinity pool was impressive, but I didn't pack a bathing suit. Although I had no problem swimming in the nude with Junior.

"It's beautiful, right?" Junior asked as he stood beside me and held my hand.

"That's an understatement, Junior. This place is indescribable. Thank you for bringing me here. I will never forget this as long as I live."

"You could've fooled me. I was expecting the dance Pops received! I guess you have to be special to receive such a gift."

"I have a private dance in mind for you, and only you."

"I'm chomping at the bit, baby. Come, let's get settled in. I have another surprise for you."

"Nothing can top this except having sex," I replied.

"Here you go. Let me be as frank as I can, we won't be having sex. I'll be making love to you, even though I don't love you. You won't repeat how your first time was horrible. You will remember me."

"You're talking like you plan to hit and run, and I was hoping you'd stick around for a while, like forever," I replied and he laughed. "What the hell is so funny?"

"You, baby. I'm not laughing at you, but you need to pause your steps and let Junior lead the way."

"Whatever, man. I'll follow until I get bored." I faked a yawn.

"What?" he retorted, pulling me into his arm. "You ain't going nowhere, you hear me?" he said, kissing me behind my ear.

"Stop, I can't take the teasing and mocking. Don't touch me until you're ready to make love." I pushed him away.

"Are you mad from my show of affection, or is it because I said I don't love you?"

"Both, but I know what I'm getting myself into with you. Nothing is definite, I got it. I think it's best we move on before things get heated."

"Finally, we see eye-to-eye," he replied, and I followed him into the master bedroom.

My anger progression had diminished when I saw our room. Similar windows to the ones downstairs lined one side of the room, providing a remarkable view of the lake. Everything was top notch. *Dreams do come true, even temporary ones*, I thought. The master bath was fit for a king and queen. I thought Uncle Jon's house was untouchable, but this was by far as good as it gets.

"Junior," I started, but couldn't get the other words out.

"I know, baby. This leaves you speechless and I appreciate your humble reaction. I love seeing that look of amazement on your face. It turns me on. I hope to see more of that tonight. Now go freshen up, we're going out," he commanded, patting me on my ass.

It took a minute to figure out the shower's computer. I was soaked by the time I turned off the jets and the rainfall shower-head. I was trying to be quick, knowing Junior lacked patience. After my shower, I changed into a pair of tie-die short shorts and a matching shirt. I smeared my lips with lip-gloss and went into the bedroom. Junior had changed into a pair of cargo shorts he wore so well over his sexy, hairy legs. Staring at him was like living a fantasy. He was masculine and irresistible. However, my dream faded when he saw what I was wearing. His expression transformed, and I knew he had a problem.

"Yo, where you think you're going dressed like that. Fuck is you, crazy? See you got me cussing and shit. Go change before I lose control," he retorted. That was his real mad face and not the dangerous, seductive face I awaited. However, I continued to push his buttons.

"What's wrong with what I'm wearing? It feels like a sauna outside."

"I don't care if it feels like fire and brimstone. Did you wear those stripper shorts at school, or is this a new rebellion? I bet you got them from that hideous store you took me into."

"No, you're wrong. I got them from Nordstrom's when you took me shopping. These shorts weren't cheap."

"Yeah well, remind me to burn them tonight when we get back."

"You think I look like a stripper, Junior. Well, I got news for you. All the shorts I brought fit the same way." He strolled towards me in a haste, looking as if he was about to knock my ass out. *Oh shit!*

"Did you bump your fucking head, Chasity? Where's your bag?" he asked, searching around the room.

"It's in the bathroom," I replied, still as the sky. I watched as he grabbed the bag and threw my clothes on the bed.

"Here, wrap this shirt around your waist until we can get to the mall," he instructed, handing me my beige plaid long sleeve shirt. He grabbed my hand and escorted me out the mansion. The SUVs were waiting outside, and we left with an awkwardness between us.

An hour later, I lost my mind when we pulled up to Universal Studio in Orlando. I danced for Junior and he smiled. The Universal Studio globe guided us through the entrance and I was trying to figure out where to start first. We headed over to The Rip Ride Rockit and I thought I saw a pinch of fear in Junior.

"You okay? You don't have to get on if you're nervous. I can go by myself or you can send one of your bodyguards with me," I explained, being complacent.

"Scared of what, Chasity? I came to ride, baby. I'll let you lead."

After waiting in a long ass line, we took our seats, and I was ready for the thrill ahead. When the ride took off, I closed my eyes, regretting I let it be the first ride.

"Open your eyes, Chasity," Junior yelled. "You're afraid? Woohoo!" he hollered, throwing his hands in the air. When the ride ended, so did the thrills, and I was over it. That shit was fun as a child, but I didn't enjoy seeing my life flash before my eyes. I opted to go to KrustyLand to get on The Simpson's Ride, which was more my speed, but Junior wasn't having it. After we left, he led me to The Incredible Hulk. By the time we got off the Doctor Doom's Fearfall, I wanted to die.

"That shit was crazy, man. I haven't felt this alive in a long time," Junior said.

"I know right. That took me back to my childhood," Bip, the bodyguard, agreed. The other three bodyguards, James, Truth, and Stew also concurred.

"What's up, ma? You good?" Junior asked devilishly.

"Yeah, I'm good, but I'm hungry."

"Me too, babe. Let's find somewhere to fill your belly," he replied.

At dinner, the bodyguards blended in and no one would've suspected that they were protecting us. Junior interacted with them normally, which shocked me. I thought he dealt with everyone with an iron fist, but I guess I was wrong. The conversation was refreshing as I witnessed Junior unwind. He was relaxed, without a care in the world.

"Tomorrow we're heading over to Epcot after I get you some appropriate gear to wear," he said, somewhat embarrassing me. That would've been the perfect time to put him in his place, but lucky for him I was behaving. "Let's go check out the fireworks and call it a night," Junior suggested, but everyone knew it was a command. The fireworks were romantic and Junior stood behind me with his arms magically wrapped around my waist. "It's rumored that this is where dreams are made. You ready for your dreams to come true?" he whispered, at the height of the show.

"Yes, but I'm willing to wait until you're comfortable," I replied, not wanting to build up my hopes. Junior had proven himself to be a seductive teaser, and I was not buying his bullshit.

"I'm comfortable and the wait will be over soon. I just hope you're ready, Freddy. No turning back now, Chass. Do you understand what I'm saying?"

"I think so," I responded, wondering if he thought I would back down. I was in, regardless of his monstrous manhood.

"I don't need you to think, I need certainty," he explained, spinning me around to face him. "We're clear?" he asked, and his expression was undeniably hypnotizing.

"I'm sure, Junior, but I don't want to get my hopes up too high. You're always throwing a monkey wrench into the game you know."

"Tonight, it'll be you I'm throwing it into. Yo, let's get out of here now. No more games, as you call them."

"I'm ready whenever you are." We departed Universal Studio and headed toward my promise from Junior. It was on and popping.

When we pulled up to the mansion, my nerves were getting the best of me. My body was ready but my mind was bitching up. When we stepped inside the foyer, white rose pedals spread out on the floor and led down several paths. Huge lit candles were scattered throughout the massive family room, adding romance. I chose the lake path and there was a beautifully decorated table set for two with a bottle of *Cristal* chilling on ice.

"Junior, everything is beautiful. There are no words," I said, falling deeper in love with this psycho.

"Words are sweet, but I need something more tangible. Come here." He pulled me into his arms and knotted his tongue with mine. I was his for the taking and any doubt I had previously floated down the dark lake into the unknown. The way he caressed my upper extremities as he grazed me sent an absorbing sensation through my soul that felt astounding. I opened my eyes so I could memorize the moment and surprisingly his eyes were staring at me. "Finally," he said, taking a breath. "I want you to see everything I'm going to do to you tonight." He reconnected with my lips and sporadically kissed my entire mouth softly, pulling my bottom lip with his teeth while gently biting down. "You taste so good, baby. I can't wait to taste your other lips." He snatched the shirt he forced me to wear from around my waist. Between kisses, he reprimanded me about my shorts in a seductive maniac manner that turned me on. "These panties you call shorts — ," he grabbed my ass, "are not to be worn for anyone else but me," he menacingly stated as he continued to ignite his power over me. "We understand each other?" he asked, while standing back and looking at me with the most innocent, but devilishly sexy grin. I loved his mental instability.

"Yes, I understand," I responded, winded. His touch was everything I longed for since the day he backed me up in the corner of his office. *He better not find a reason or give me one to back down,* I thought as he stared at me. "I said I understand, Junior. What else do you want me to say?" I asked.

"Nothing at all, Chasity. I much rather hear you sing, particularly my name. And to show you I am a nice guy, I will let you keep these shorts, but you have to promise me you will model them for me, and only me, because you do look sexy as shit in them."

"I promise," I responded. *Now take me to the bedroom, living room...just take me!* I thought.

"Let's toast," he replied as he popped open the bottle of Cristal and poured it into the champagne glasses. He handed me my glass and said, "To tonight—may all your dreams come true."

"To tonight and many, many, many more, because I'm not going anywhere, Junior," I corrected. He was trying to act as if it would only be one night, but I knew I had more than his interest. I planned to sit back, let him make a fool of himself, and enjoy the crazy ride.

"Freedom of speech, sweetie, so you get to say whatever you like, despite how I feel."

"This place is truly beautiful," I said, changing the subject. "I don't know how you expect me to go back to my little house in Jenkintown after bringing me here."

"You don't have to worry about that. You'll be staying at my condo. At least for now."

"Junior, don't start with that. We haven't discussed it and I thought earlier you said I was an experiment. Let's just stick to that for now."

"We are." He lifted me up and carried me into the house. "The experiment is not over and while we're dissecting each other, I need you where I'm comfortable," he said, walking into the bedroom. Yellow rose pedals led from the entrance to the bed. More candles, champagne, and chocolate covered pineapples sat on another beautifully decorated table.

"When did you find time to do all of this?" I asked, awestruck.

"What's my name, babe? I told you, I'm the dream maker. But what I need you to do is strip."

"Strip," I repeated, and he nodded his head with a smirk on his face. I took my clothes off with the quickness and stood before him. He smiled and stripped with me. When he stood up, I glanced down at his elephant trunk and started second-guessing myself again.

He noticed my reaction and said, "I want you to be honest with me, Chasity. Are you scared? It's okay you know, I understand." I stood there speechless, no comeback or quick tongue to rescue me from dinosaur dick and the unknown. "Helloooo, is anyone home?" he asked, knocking on my head.

"Scared is too strong a word. I would describe it as somewhat skittish."

"Skittish huh? Don't be nervous, baby. If shit gets out of control, just tell me to stop." He strolled over, took my hand, and led me into the master bathroom. I watched as he turned on the entire shower system. He reached his hand out, signaling for me to come.

I joined him and said, "I think I am a little scared."

"Don't be. Nothing will happen that you don't want to happen," he replied, swooping me up and kissing every part of my body. He turned me around with my back facing him and pecked my neck with his wet lips, sending tingles through my spine from the cervical to the lumbar. His fingertips tickled my nipples as his tongue ignited trigger spots I didn't know I had. "Does that feel good, Chasity?" he asked, while kissing the center of my lower back. He moved down to my ass cheeks and kissed them.

"Yes," I moaned, because there was something surreal about having your ass kissed. It was warm and soothing, along with erotic and shameless. The combination of his touch and the water trickling on my body left me breathless.

"Chasity, you're beautiful..." He could barely get it out, "sexy, and you're all mine." He spun me around and lifted me up. I placed my legs around his waist and in one swift move, he lifted me on top of his shoulders and backed me against the shower wall. His face landed in the right place. I rested my head on the wall, ready for any stimulation to touch my vagina.

Junior's outstanding skills as a clitoris miner were noticeable. In fact, it was magical, delightful and unbearable at the same time, but I tried to endure the pleasure he gave. The licking, twirling and gentle bites were a recipe for insanity. "Oh, Junior, ooooh, help me Lord." *We'll be coming around the mountain, we'll be coming around the mountain, we'll be coming around the mountain when we come.* I sang in my mind trying to tune out the agonizing pleasure. His tongue continued to ripple across my clitoris, making me want to squeeze his face in between my legs. "Junior, Junior," I moaned.

"Say my name," he demanded when he came up for a brief breath.

"Junior," I gasped, and he went in for the kill. I glanced down as he bobble headed me like a programed robot. *Please, God, don't let me fart on him*, I prayed, knowing there was nowhere else for the lust to release itself. Junior tasted every inch of my woman-hood and took me into a black hole, lost and forgotten. I thought Terrance's immature oral was the bomb, but evidently he was inexperienced and uninformed, because Junior was on a whole other level.

He positioned me back on the shower floor and slightly bent his head to excite my breast. With his useful mouth, he sucked the tip of my nipple, pulling just enough and repeating the process bilaterally. My vagina had just experienced several seizures. "You like the way that feel, baby?" he asked, sticking his index finger inside me, toiling, and opening my vagina walls. He teased my labia, touching it mildly before placing two fingers inside me.

"Yes, Junior, I can't take no more," I pleaded, hoping he would enter inside me soon.

"You can't take no more, baby? But we're just getting started," he explained as he sponged up my neck delicately. "Are you ready for the bed, Chass?" His look was flirtatious yet erotic. He didn't wait for me to answer before he turned off the shower and swept me off my feet. Junior placed my wet body on the bed and kissed me as if he loved me. At least I hoped. "Did you come, baby?"

"Yes."

"How many times?" he badgered while spreading my legs.

"Too many," I replied, but it was a cry for help. With the tip of his penis, he rubbed my wet kitten, which sent it into over-drive. Just as I was about to have another orgasm, he slid inside me slow, pulling in and out of the entrance of my vagina.

"Look at me, Chasity," he said, staring at me as if I were a dream. "You feel so good and I haven't even touched the surface," he said as he pushed further inside me.

"Aaaaaaah, shit," I squirmed. He pulled back but not completely out before he inched in again.

"You okay, beautiful? Tell me if you can't take it. Your pussy feels so sweet. Let me in, please baby. I need to feel your walls smother my dick," he begged, but instead of pulling back, he stood in one spot and we were at a dead lock. He slowly rocked and rolled his penis until he broke through.

"Ooooooooh, Johnathan," I bawled when he popped my cherry. Junior zoned into me.

"What did you call me?" he asked as he continued to drive his manhood inside me. His rhythm was steady and his pace picked up.

"Johnathan," I cried.

"Say it again." He stopped his movement when he arrived at the reaching point of my pussy. There was no space between us and we were hip-bone-to-hip-bone, pelvises latched. In a circular aggressive motion, he took away any sign of my virginity, smothering me with stiff stabs and hitting all my g-spots. He touched one in particular, bringing out another orgasm that was palpable

"Ooooooooh, Junior, I've never felt so good," I yelled, while squeezing my walls, trying to savor the moment.

"You came all over me, Chasity," he said, flipping me over and positioning me on top. "Is this my pussy?" he asked as he slammed into my vagina, causing my body to react to his motion. "Tell me." He slammed into me again.

"This is yours, baby. Anytime of the day!" I sung, ramming him the same way he did me.

"Oh, shit, you're so wet." He turned me over and entered me from behind. "Chasity, you don't know what I want to do to you. Stay right there, don't move," he instructed.

"Have your way with me, Junior." When I gave him the go ahead, he fucked me every way imaginable, except for my ass, because that was staying a virgin. Once he ejaculated, I enjoyed the last few jolts as he fell on top of me.

"You're magnificent, babe, and I can't wait to experience more of you. Kiss me." I obeyed, and we engaged in a long wet kiss before heading to the shower again.

"Turn off the rain shower," I said, wanting to just bathe and go to bed because he wore me out. He lathered up the tan bathing sponge and painted it on my body.

"Open your legs," he said as he washed my vagina. There was something sensational and refreshing about having your man wash your privates. He washed my entire body, grabbed the handheld shower, and sprayed me down. But, instead of opening my legs, I lifted my left leg past my head and stood like the letter L. Ballet school helped me in that aspect. He sprayed the soap from between my legs and I moaned from the ticklish sensation. I closed my eyes and soaked up the moment, but when the water stopped, I felt something that was now familiar enter inside me. I opened my eyes and Junior was sliding in and out of me. He lifted my other leg and I straddled his waist, allowing him to have his way. When he came that second time, I knew I had him.

"Junior, you're too much. I love you and I don't mind that it's not mutual. I just wanted you to know." He kissed me instead of responding and we retired for the night. I was in a sleep coma when Junior woke me up the next morning.

"Wake up sleepy head. We have a full day ahead of us. I know you're hungry. What do you want to eat?" he asked, bending over me and kissing my forehead. *What's up with that*, I thought. "You need to freshen up your mouth, babe, so I can give you a proper kiss," he said knowingly.

"Anyway, are we going out to eat? I'm so tired, Junior"

"Nah, a chef is here ready to prepare whatever you want."

"In that case, I want pancakes, eggs, turkey sausage and bacon. Oh, and a side of grits with cheese," I replied, placing the pillow back over my face.

"Anything else, Your Highness?"

"That will be all for now."

"I'll get on that and by the time I get back, you should be dressed and revitalized. Put on the jeans you wore down here until we can get you some appropriate gear."

"Okay, Junior, I'm getting up."

When he left, I did as he instructed and met him downstairs. The sweet smell of breakfast lingered in the air, and I was starving from the sexual workout last night. Junior was sitting at the island watching the news while the chef was getting everything together.

"There you are, come here," he summoned and kissed me properly.

"Stop, Junior. We have company," I said, pointing to the chef.

"Don't tell me to stop again, Chass. He works for me. Now give me some more of those sweet lips before you upset me." I leaned in and submitted. After last night, I would crawl for him. "Good girl, but um, real talk. Did I hurt you last night? Be honest."

"A little, but after a while I loved it. It was all that imagined and you're right, I will never forget it."

"You weren't so bad yourself, you were nice and I enjoyed being inside you. I want more of you, which is unbelievable, but you got my attention, baby."

"Should I assume that I'm your woman since you stole the cookie?"

"You're something, but I haven't quite figured out what."

I pulled away from him and jokingly said, "You get on my nerves."

He pulled me back into his arms and whispered, "You're something special and I'm blessed to be with you right now. Let's eat so we can hit the road, sweetie."

After breakfast, we found the mall and shopped until I was ready to drop. When we arrived at Neiman Marcus Junior said, "Chasity, this is one of those times you need to follow my lead. I'm going to dress you, so no back talk, but I want to compliment you on a great job so far," he said, leading me into the Disney World of clothes.

Junior picked out an array of shorts, dresses, jeans, and shirts for me to try on, which ended up taking most of the day. I was getting agitated because he didn't even like the stuff he chose. I pleaded with him to let me try, but he was adamant and unwilling to compromise. Finally, after many tries and rejections, he was satisfied with his final selections. I walked away with enough shit to last two months and learned to keep my mouth shut about the astronomical prices.

"You want one of those bags?" Junior asked when he saw me staring at the Louis Vuitton handbags.

"Nah, I'm good."

"Stop lying, go pick out a few bags and don't make me ask twice. We need to get a move on."

I ended up getting three Lou's and two Chanel bags he chose. Between both of our stuff, the bill came to one sixty-five thousand and change, which was ridiculous. Although I was mute, I was uncomfortable with the price.

"Junior, you're making me fall deeper in love with you. Although you spent too much and went overboard, I appreciate the new clothes, the trip and just everything."

"I know you do, Chass. I peeped that about you, which makes it easy for me to spend some change on you. Your worth it to me. Plus, I can't have you running around showing the world my goodies, now can I?"

"I guess not. Do you think I can change my clothes before we leave?"

"Sure, right this way," the saleswoman replied.

"Junior, do you have a preference?" I asked, being smart.

"Everything I picked out is appropriate so knock yourself out."

Since we were going to Epcot, I changed into one of the overall jean shorts and a half-white tee. I put on the black and white Chanel sneakers and met Junior in front of the store.

"I'm ready whenever you are." I said.

The bodyguards carried the many bags back to the SUVs and we left.

For the next three days, we visited Disney World and Junior indulged in activities out of character for him. We had a blast taking pictures with different Disney characters and engaging in the attractions. Sunday came so fast and I was sad that the vacation was ending. Junior and I made love daily, and I hated that he was leaving for Dubai.

I was resting in his arms when he said, "Chasity, please reconsider coming with me. Two weeks is too long for me to be away from you. You can list the house when we get back."

"Junior, I don't want to go to Dubai. When I was doing my research, I was impressed with how the country had developed, but I don't want to bothered with the culture. I don't have time to be covered from head to toe, feeling uncomfortable."

"It's not like that at all, we'll be together most of the time. Other than a few business meetings, you will have my undivided attention."

"I want to be with you too, but I've done everything you've asked on this trip. Be reasonable, Junior."

"Point taken, but I'm not happy. I want you with me."

"I know, but I'll be waiting for you when you get back."

"At my condo, right?"

"Yes, as long as you give me my car back and allow me to drive alone."

"But I'd feel better if Calvin escorts you around while I'm gone."

"If that's the case, he can escort me from my house. You can't have it both ways, Junior."

"Not yet. Okay, you can have your car back, but you need to be available to me at all times. Keep your phone charged so we can Facetime."

"Aww that's so sweet, Junior, Facetime."

When we reached his condo, we made love again, and it continued to improve. What Junior didn't know is that I was planning on surprising him by joining him in a week. I figured by then I would have had the open houses and just be waiting on an offer.

That next morning, Junior informed me that The Home Restoration Project was featuring the house in their weekly article, which should generate more traffic. In addition, he informed several real estate agents about the first showing tomorrow. If I didn't know any better, I'd think he was trying to get me to sell this house fast.

"Be good and stay out of trouble," he said as he was about to walk out the door.

"What kind of trouble could I get into, Junior? You act like I'm a wild child or something."

"That mouth of yours is always a problem. Don't forget when I call, you answer." He sternly glanced at me.

"Can I have a kiss goodbye? You just gone leave me hanging like that?"

"Yes, it's already hard for me to leave you, so don't get upset. Maybe this time apart will be beneficial. I definitely need space to figure us out."

"Forget about it. Make sure you call me as soon your plane lands. I won't be able to sleep if you don't."

"I got you," he replied and exited.

I jumped back into the bed when he left and fell asleep shortly after.

Chapter 17

Junior

The trip to Florida was good for me, and Chasity was my new inspiration. She gave me the luxury and honor of relishing her virgin walls, and her sweet pussy was an unexpected delight. Her tight walls and sexy body fucked my mind up, and just thinking about it made my dick hard. Although she submitted and gave into my wishes, I knew she was a ticking bomb ready to explode, given the right opportunity.

Chasity robbed my heart like a thief in the night. She wanted to know if we were official, but I was afraid of hurting her because my heart wasn't up for grabs. But, I noticed a certain calm within myself whenever she was in my presence. Once the jet landed in Dubai, Muslim mogul officials responsible for the contract greeted us.

"Greetings, my friends. Did you have a good flight?" Abdul Hakeem, the head of resource and development, asked.

"Yes, we did. Your state is beautiful and we appreciate the wonderful accommodations you provided us. On behalf of my father, Johnathan Blake, we would like to extend this gift of gratitude," I responded, handing him a bottle of *Tom Ford's* most expensive brand of *Oud*. Abdul opened it immediately and extended his thanks.

When we reached *Atlantis, The Palm* I thought about how wrong Chasity was about this place. *If I could just get her down here to experience it, I'm positive she would have a change of heart* I thought. I settled in my room and few moments later, I heard a knock at the door. A member of the hotel staff handed me an envelope and I thanked him. I poured myself a drink and opened it. Enclosed was the itinerary for the next two weeks. Just looking at the list was getting on my fucking nerves. I knew of only one person who could remedy my stress, and her ass stayed behind to sell her little house. *Since when you needed a woman for anything?* I thought, traumatized with the realization that I needed Chasity.

I grabbed my cell phone and dialed the number. "What up, Calvin? What did Chasity do today?" I asked, wanting to know her every move.

"Nuttin much, Junior. She didn't leave the house until this afternoon after they dropped off her car."

"Where did she go?" I barked, because he needed to get to the point.

"She went to Home Goods and back to the market."

"Home Goods, what the fuck is that?"

"I don't know, man. They sell shit for your home. Like pillows and candles, you know, girlie shit. She came out with tons of bags."

"Did she go back to my place?"

"Yeah, she's been at your condo ever since."

"Thanks, Dog. I'll check in with you tomorrow." I hung up and called Chasity.

"Hey, Junior, did you have a good flight?" she asked when she picked up.

"I did, but more importantly, how was your day, and what did you do?"

"I went to the market. Thanks for leaving me your credit card. I can pay you back after I sell the house."

"Chasity, that won't be necessary. I explained this to you already, but let me refresh that brain of yours. As long as you're under my care, the sky's the limit. I put some money in the top drawer you took over. You may need some cash on hand. But check this out though...I need you to join me. Trust me babe, you will love this place, and I'm not taking no for an answer."

"Junior..." I didn't allow her time to whine.

"I don't want to hear you call my name that way unless it's an emergency or I'm fucking you. I'm giving you a few days to

wrap up the open house before I send the jet for you. We understand each other?"

"I guess, Junior. Whatever you say," she sighed.

"What's your problem, you don't miss me? I'm starting think
you're happy I'm away."

"I do miss you so much and I can't wait to see you, Johnathan. You just send too many conflicting signals and I want to
have a career. Woodwork is my first love, but until I can get a
warehouse to set that up, I'm giving flipping houses a chance."

"I'm not trying to stomp on your dreams, baby. I understand
about ambition and passion, Chasity. I know what I'm asking is
selfish, but I need you all to myself. I want to help make your
dreams come true. If you're worried about money, let me put
your mind at ease. Don't."

"I'm not worried about money. I stopped worrying about that
when Uncle Jon adopted us into the family. For me, its gratifica-
tion and knowing you did something that is useful and wonderful. Kitchen cabinets are in demand, along with wood furniture. I
want to take advantage of that market. You say you need me, but
what happens when I'm not needed anymore. Am I supposed to
put all my stuff on hold for your uninsured heart?"

"You tryna' come at nigga with that ole' sensitive bullshit.
You see, that's why I don't let bitches into my world." I said,
harshly.

"Did you just call me a bitch, Fucker? You don't have to worry about me, Junior. I see you got some emotional shit going on
that I'm not medically capable of handling, nor willing."

"You right, get your shit and go the fuck back home. That's
where you want to be anyway, and I'm definitely not about to
beg your ass to spend time with me. You had a nigga trippin' out
for a minute. Enjoy your career." I slammed the phone down,
angry with myself.

I regretted it instantly, but she was pushing my buttons. Any
other woman would jump at the chance of being in my presence.
This struggle and resistance she displayed angered me and I
needed to get my mind off Chasity. I called Domencio and told
him to meet me at the club I saw on the hotel magazine.

Chapter 18

Chasity

The morning after we returned, I was on top of the world. I went to the market and brought a few accessories to spruce up Junior's place. That next morning I was rejuvenated and happy. I played off the gray dull scheme and added life with coral and cream-striped throw pillows that I purchased from Home Goods. The abstract throw rug I chose popped against the floor and the place was coming alive. I placed a sleek mirror above the couch, which was perfect. Just those few items made me feel more comfortable and at home. I stood back, admired my quick fix decorating skills and went into the kitchen. I put the salmon that was marinating in olive oil and rosemary into the oven along with a baked potato. I prepared a quick garden salad and placed it in the fridge. After my shower, I caught the end of *Deadliest Catch*. *Damn, I missed it*, I thought, wanting to know how much each deckhand had profited.

After dinner, I thought about Junior and why he hadn't called. I prayed his flight went well and hoped that during this time apart, he'd discover that he can't live without me. However, that dream was shattered after he called and we got into it. It felt as if he stuck a knife in my heart when he called me a bitch and kicked me out of his condo.

We were right back at square one. He was definitely a challenge and I wasn't sure he was worth the grand prize. I took most of my belongings and left. I was happy to be going home until I remembered Destiny was at Uncle Jon's house. Honestly,

Junior's condo was growing on me, and it was unfortunate we couldn't grow together as a couple.

The open house was today, and I had to get my mind right. When I arrived at the flip, I turned on the central air, boldly showing off that new feature. These homes weren't built for central air, but the unit added value. The broken radiators were unsalvageable, and it was cheaper to install the unit as opposed to thirteen new radiators. As the day progressed, I became discouraged because no one had come. However, after lunch, several realtors and potential buyers arrived, easing the tension.

They all agreed I had done an exceptional job renovating the place. However, they disagreed with the price, explaining it was overpriced by twenty grand. That was fair since I listed it for three hundred fifty and all I wanted initially was three hundred. Either way I was profiting.

I was ready to shut it down for the day when trouble walked in. I could see it before it happened, but I stayed professional. "Track, what are you doing here?" I asked with a confused expression.

"I'm here to see the house, but if you want me to be here for you, that's my first choice," he grinned, looking sexy and dressed expensively. Outside of Junior, he was the second sexiest man in the world. "You know I have strict instructions to stay away from you, but I never heard it from your mouth," he said.

"Uh, you know that night was crazy. But um, I think we should keep our distance. I don't want to upset my uncle. Sorry," I replied, feeling uncomfortable. Track was cool and I didn't want to hurt him.

"Is it your uncle or your fake cousin, Junior? If it's your uncle, I can respect that. But if it's the other one, well, I have a problem with that," he explained, shaking his head.

"Actually, it's me. I'm focused on my career, selling this house in particular, and my time is very limited."

"If I buy the house, that will free up some of your time," he disputed.

"You haven't even seen the whole house and you're ready to buy?" I replied, surprised and happy.

"You're right. Lead the way, sweets. Take me on the grand tour." He signaled for me to go ahead with a hand gesture.

"Follow me," I replied, and I couldn't help but wonder if I had met Track first, would Junior even be an issue? He was funny, charming, and clear about his feelings towards me. In my opinion, he had no hidden agenda or ill motive. He appeared to want to love me and give me all that I desire. "What do you think?" I asked after the tour.

"I know I love it. This house will be perfect for my mother, sister, nieces and nephews. This house can accommodate them and its exceptionally renovated. Did you do all the work yourself?" he asked, truly amazed.

"Yes," I responded proud. "Sike, I'm lying, but I restored all the wood, lay some sheetrock, and did minor repairs that I could handle."

"I bet you can handle a lot more than you give yourself credit for. Listen, I want this house, and I will give you full asking price, all cash. There's just one catch though."

"And what would that be?" I asked, ready to snap.

"We have to discuss it over dinner tonight. Bring me the papers and I will bring you the money."

"I don't think that's such a good idea, Track. We can handle this in the morning," I replied, annoyed.

"Chasity, this is a business dinner. No strings and no pressure. I want the house, but I want to discuss it over dinner," he responded sincerely.

"Business dinner and that's it."

"Just business. What time should I pick you up?"

"I have the paperwork in my car, but I'll meet you because I have a stop to make." I was not about to jump into his Audi TTS Roadster to go anywhere.

"Fair enough. Do you have a preference?"

"Bonefish Grill, I'm in the mood for fish." I smiled just thinking about it.

"Bonefish it is. Can you meet me in an hour at the one in Deptford, NJ if that's not too far?"

"That's cool. See you there."

An hour and a half later, I pulled up to the restaurant and once I got inside, I spotted Track seated at a table. He summoned me to join him and I strutted over with the paperwork in hand.

Chapter 19

Junior

I left the building site pumped for the first time since my unfortunate conversation with Chasity. The freedom for creativity was a builders dream in Dubai. The more extreme, the sweeter the deal. We received the approval on what our engineers and architects presented, which was fucking delirious, and the work was due to start in one month.

It was unnecessary for me to stay for the entire two weeks because Domencio and the other executives could handle the rest. But I wasn't in a rush to get back after telling Chasity to leave my place. I intended on enjoying what this new and beautiful state offered. In addition, I had a two-day trip set to spend in Abu Dhabi, which I expected to do with Chasity until I ruined it.

When I got back to the hotel, I ordered in and reflected on the way I dealt with her. I fucked up by wanting everything my way and being unwilling to settle down, but I didn't know how to be anything else. I had jumped leaps and bounds for her, but she couldn't see that shit. Her concerns were centered around selling that house and buying more so she could spend less time with me. *When did I become soft about a woman sharing her time with me?* I thought, right before my cell rung.

"Calvin, what's good?"

"You ain't gonna like this shit, Junior. But ah, Chasity is out on a date with Track."

"Fuck is you talking about, Calvin!"

"They having dinner right now at Bonefish Grill in Jersey."

"This muhfucker done lost her mind. How the fuck that shit happen!" I barked.

"I don't know, but he popped up at the open house. She showed him the house and made a stop at the bank. Shortly after, I followed her here and saw the two of them eating dinner."

"Yo, I'll take care of it. Just watch her ass, Calvin." I hung up, ready to kill somebody. She wanted her and Track to end up in a mortuary. I dialed her number right away, but she didn't answer. I was ready to fuel up the jet and leave that night. I was enraged. I called her back, and this time her sneaky ass picked up.

Chapter 20

Chasity

I knew damn well this meeting with Track was a recipe for disaster, but I still agreed to meet him. Junior had dumped me and I needed to sell my house more than ever now. If Track's offer for the full list price was solid then it was on and popping, and I could prove Junior wrong.

"Sorry I'm late, but 76 was a bitch," I explained as I sat down at the table.

"I would've waited until the restaurant closed for the chance to be in your presence, beautiful."

"Business, remember? So stop flirting, even though I appreciate it. You have a way with words and you're very charming."

"Is that a compliment I hear?"

"No, more like a friendly gesture. It's a compliment, but don't read too much into it."

"Oh, it's like that. Okay, sweetheart. It's a good thing I came armored."

"You don't need to shield your heart, Track. I'm not looking to damage it."

"What are you looking for?" he asked, never dropping eye contact.

"Your check and these papers signed," I replied trying to be smart, but I think he believed I was flirting back. *Was I?*

"I got you on that already. I'm talking about after you steal away a small portion of my riches, what then?"

"I'm not a thief, but I plan on living my life and finding the next house to flip. Work consumes me."

"I feel you on that, you're only trying to get yours. But you know that saying. All work and no play makes Jane a dull girl."

"I'm cool with that because I have plenty of time to play. I'm young and the work I do requires upper body strength, so I need to get it in where it fits in. I think we should order and you should look over this paperwork," I said, getting back to business.

"In due time, Chasity. Can we at least enjoy a nice meal before we discuss this contract? Would you like a drink? I can call the waiter."

"I'll take a glass of water with lemon." Once the waiter took our orders, we conversed in small talk until the food had arrived.

After we devoured the food, he asked, "Do you want desert, Chasity? I mean, you're already so sweet, you don't need that. Can I ask you a personal question?"

"Shoot," I replied, taking my cell phone out because I felt it vibrating.

"What's up with you and Junior? Be honest with me, is he your man?" he asked, but my attention redirected to the number coming through my phone. *Oh shit*, I panicked inwardly. I sent it to voice mail and was ready to wrap up the dinner. Either he wanted the house or not. My phone rang again and something told my ass to answer. Junior was unpredictable and borderline psychotic. I wouldn't be surprised if he walked in the restaurant at that moment.

"I'm sorry, Track, but I have to take this call. I've been waiting all day. I'll be right back." I dashed away and answered the phone before he hung up a second time. "Hello," I said, trying to slow down my heavy breathing.

"Where the fuck is you, Chasity?" he barked. "Do you know I will whip your little ass? No, you don't have a clue."

"Why do you care, Junior? You put me out and think you can bipolar me to death."

"Let's try this again, Chasity. I advise you think before you speak and it better be the right shit. Tell me where you are and who you're with, now!" he yelled. *Schizophrenia arrived,* I thought.

"You need to calm down before I tell you this, and it's not what you think. Track—."

"You were warned to stay the fuck away from him. Is this some revenge shit? Trust me, Chasity, you don't want to play that game" he interrupted.

"If you would let me finish, he stopped by the open house and made me an offer for the full listing price. We came to the restaurant so he could sign the papers and hand me the check. It was a business meeting."

"Is that little brain of yours so ingenuous that you can't distinguish between fact and bullshit? Since when did dining after hours become a requirement to sign papers? Let me tell you what's about to happen since your unconscious. Let him know the little dinner date is over, you ain't selling him shit, and you have to go. I'll be calling you back in ten minutes, and you better be in your car." He hung up. *Damn.* My instincts are always right, and now I had to hurry and make it to my car in ten minutes. I would deal with Junior when he called me back.

I rushed back to the table and frantically said, "I have to leave now. I'm sorry, but there has been an emergency. I'm really sorry," I explained, rushing away.

"But Chasity, I haven't signed the papers," I heard him say. I continued in a haste and when I got outside, I ran to my car. I started it and drove out the parking lot just in case Track tried to run after me. The phone rang as I was sitting at the light.

"Junior, what's wrong with you?" I asked when I answered.

"Seven minutes, Chasity. That had to be a world record. However, your messy behavior could be deadly. I held you in high regards. Since this evening, that has dwindled down, but you have a chance to redeem yourself before I catch the red eye and break your fucking neck."

"We've resorted to threats, Junior? You kick me out of your condo and to add insult to injury, you call me a bitch."

"Drive straight to my condo and Calvin will transport you to the plane. I had to call in a few favors to get a private flight for you, so make sure you're on it," he commanded, ignoring me.

"The way you're talking is crazy, and I don't know if I feel like getting my neck broken or my ass whipped. You're scaring me."

"You should be petrified if you're not on the plane. Listen, it's been a long day and you have a thirteen-hour flight ahead. I suggest you bring something to occupy your time until you fall asleep. I'll be waiting for you at the airport. And I don't desire your fear, but I require your respect. As long as I see your beautiful face in the morning, fear not, Chasity."

"I'm sorry I upset you, and you're right, I should've known better. I was hurt and desperate to sell the house. I admit I made some poor choices today, but you left me somewhat broken," I said, trying to soften him up because I loved him.

"Yes, your choices were disastrous. I just hope we learn from our mistakes so life can be peaceful. Don't ever try to play me like that again, especially with Track. I'm not sharing you with anyone and I'll take care of his ass because that nigga was warned too. Let me apologize for yesterday. I didn't mean to call you a bitch, or refer to you as one. In my eyes, Chasity, you're this new light of inspiration, and I can't turn the shit off no matter how much I try. It revealed itself when I discovered you were having dinner with that piece of shit."

"I didn't have dinner with him to get back at you. I wanted to sell the house quickly and secure my finances. And how did you know where I was? You had me followed, Junior? I should've known."

"You're no bitch, you're precious to me, and I have to keep an eye on my valuables," he indirectly explained.

"So does that mean we're official now, or are we still experimenting?"

"You're my significant other."

"That's some bull, Junior. What is that supposed to mean?"

"It means you hold a great amount of significance in my life."

"That sounds like a business answer. I don't like that."

"We are whatever you want us to be," he exhaled loudly.

"I want you to be my man, or better yet, my fiancé." I know I was reaching on the last part.

"I make dreams come true, but I can't perform miracles. You're hilarious, Chasity. But I'll tell you what. I can handle being your man and believe me that's like moving mountains. But I'm cool with you as my lady. Is that sufficient?"

"Yes, it is. I can live with that for now."

"Good, now be a good girlfriend and pick up the pace. Call me when you get on the plane," he said and disconnected the call. He was breaking down walls, showing me the real Junior. *Slightly cray-cray if you ask me, but okay.* I allowed my heart to lead me, got my ass on the plane, and met my man in Dubai like I had common sense.

The plane ride was everlasting and I could not sleep. When I got off the plane, I spotted Junior. I couldn't make out his mood because his facial expression was deceiving, but I planned to play nice.

I walked over to him and said, "Hey."

He smirked and surprisingly didn't say anything. Instead, he grabbed my hand and escorted me to the limo that was waiting. Once inside, I remained silent, unsure if he was mad, or worse, still wanting to break my neck. *Why does that turn me on? Maybe I'm the one with the mental problem,* I thought.

"How was your flight, did they take good care of you?"

"Yes, but it was long and I couldn't seem to fall asleep" I yawned.

"Disobedience and disrespect fuck with your sleep."

Okay, he's still mad. Say nothing. Let him vent. I just smiled and put my head down, allowing him to think I was shamed. "Look at me," he demanded. "Why? That's all I want to know, and don't give me that nonsense about selling the house. You're well aware that there is bad blood between us from my birthday party."

"I don't know what you want me to tell you, I told you the truth. Would you rather me make up a lie?"

"Let's try the lie because I don't believe you. You didn't feel a hint of excitement to see the man you let put his hands all over you?"

"I thought we settled this on the phone, Junior. Why are you trying to ruin our reunion? I want to enjoy being your woman peacefully, as you suggested."

"Then you shouldn't have started a war, Chasity. Track wants you because he knows he can't have you as long as I'm around. He's been running his mouth, which is a problem. I'm telling you for the last time to stay away from him. Track is a drug lord with many people on his payroll. Some were my old combatants."

"They used to work for your company?" I asked, oblivious to what he was trying to say.

"No, they use to work on the street corners for me, along with Track. Before I became the man I am today, I was not a nice man. I did things that I regret and fucked up people's lives, but I also enjoyed life, power, and control. Fortunately, I was incarcerated for two years, which transformed me."

"What's so fortunate about that?"

"I was on two paths—prison or the grave. Prison captured me, but it didn't possess me. It woke me up and showed me life is short and precious." He paused a moment, and I didn't know how to respond. I wasn't no ride or die chick. Uncle Kenny loved me so much and I never sought the street life. I didn't even become interested in sex until l left for college. "Why are you so quiet? Tell me what you're thinking."

"I'm actually surprised, but it does make sense. You talk about my behavior, but you need to distinguish between the old and new life. I think you bring your past into your future and nobody wants to deal with that." He started rubbing what used to be a closely shaven beard that had grown over night. The beard excited me because he looked sexy in all forms.

"You think you're smart, don't you? But what I am sure about, and this you can store in your memory bank: If I hear, see, or think you been around this nigga, I will introduce you to the old Junior." With one swift move, he pulled me into his lap. "You see me and you don't give me no love. You didn't miss me?" He nibbled on my neck. "You need to learn how to greet your man," he moaned, kissing my lips. "You taste and feel so good, baby. I can't wait to get you back to the hotel."

"You better wait. I did my research on this country and you're not supposed to display affection in public."

"We're never leaving the room then. So get ready to hibernate."

"Whatever, Junior." I kissed him back.

The Atlantis hotel was crazy. All the sculptures and expensive trimmings seized my eye, and the hotel suite was rich people shit. Too bad I had no time to enjoy it before Junior undressed me and reminded me why I should never look at another man. He made the trip to Dubai wonderful. We rode camels, skied indoors, shopped, and made love. He had full control over me and I embraced it with open arms.

The last three days of the trip, we stayed at an eight-star hotel in Abu Dhabi. We shopped and out of respect for the culture, Junior picked out an array of beautiful silk headdresses, which I used to cover my head. A portion of my hair was visible, but I noticed the response from the residents was different once I covered up. Now don't get me wrong, it's me and Jesus all day, but I respect all religions and covering my head was just for a minute. Junior loved it, because not only was my head covered, but he bought me some nun clothing as well. I had several floor length sundresses that I planned to donate to charity back home.

"You might want to start dressing like this when we get back," he said when I modeled my new mummy look.

"You're taking things to the extreme, but I don't mind it down here."

The pressure of appearance was not present in the United Arab Emirates, only with the tourists. Most couldn't care less about the culture and just showed up because of its high end attractions. Junior was right in that I did enjoy the trip, but I wasn't totally off with my initial impression.

The plane ride home was crowded with Domencio and the other executives. I tuned them out because Junior and I were inseparable. He was outwardly showing his feelings for me and everyone took notice.

"So, Chasity, you and Junior. Y'all a couple now?" Domencio asked.

With the quickness I said, "Yes we are, Domencio."

He glanced over at Junior and when he didn't say anything, Domencio said, "Congrats. I hope it work out for you." He looked at me specifically.

"Nothing beats a failure but a try." When I said that Junior squeezed me into his arms even tighter, putting on a show. When I realized he was toiling with Domencio and getting a kick out of the confused look on his face, I joined in. I kissed his lips and rested my head on his shoulder, but he turned my head with his hand and French kissed me in front of everyone.

"Yo, y'all need to take that shit back to the hotel," Domencio barked. Junior ignored him and started nibbling on my ear.

"Junior, don't do that. You know what that does to me. You don't want me butt naked in front of your brother and staff, do you?" I whispered.

"And you don't want to end up getting spanked all night," he whispered back.

See this is what I'm talking about with his sense of humor or lack thereof. His thought process was intriguing to me but I'm sure a psychologist would disagree. "Whatever," I replied, softly punching him on the leg.

"Do you want to hear the good news or the great news first? Tell me." He spoke softly.

"Since you put it like that, I'll take the good news first."

"The house sold, so you can move on." His expression was stern and serious.

"Awesome, Junior! Who bought it?" I asked, wanting all the details.

"A Dominican family, and you were on point about the kitchen. From what I hear, the kitchen is what sealed the deal. Forgive me for doubting you."

"Forgiven! I'm so proud of myself. I remember that family, and the mom really did look interested. Now I can look for another house to flip and make more money. What's the great news?" I asked, ready to explode.

"The house sold for four hundred and twenty grand. It seems as if there was a bidding war, and the Papi's won."

"Thank you, God, I'm rich," I thought aloud and everyone on the plane laughed aloud. The joke was on them because I was laughing straight to the bank. Several ideas swarmed my brain, and I was ready to hit the track running. "Once I pay you back, I can get to work on my next house," I said.

"Chasity, don't insult me with the repayment of your loan. Especially when I've spent more than that just entertaining you. We'll talk about it another time." He dismissed me.

"I'm not trying to do that. I just wanted you to know that I pay my debts and I appreciate you taking a chance on me. You know things were different between us back then."

"We'll talk about it later," he kissed me, letting me know to cease and desist.

"Chasity, since you guys seem to be very close, do you mind sharing that money saving tip you had before it was shot down?" Domencio asked, messing with Junior.

"It was nothing and I rather forget that day," I responded.

"Speak, let's hear this great idea that caused so much trouble," Junior insisted.

"Okay. I was focusing on the interior of the building, woodworking specifically. Everything is high-end over there and the finishing's could be astronomical, depending on what the developer wants. My idea was to make all the cabinetry here, which would eliminate third parties, thus cutting costs in half. There's enough usable space in the basement for a workshop. In addition to the Dubai contract, it would be a future investment for the Blake Corporation right here in the homeland." Everyone was silent, and I wished I kept my shit to myself.

"So you believe it would save us money after we hire the workers and buy all the equipment for this wood shop?" Junior asked.

"I know it sounds unbelievable, but yes. You won't save as much on this contract as you would future projects, but you would still save Anyway, it was probably a silly idea and just me off in Woodworking Wonderland. That's my real passion. From the smell of freshly cut wood, all the way down to the grain is what I crave," I responded, realizing I said that a little too sensuous.

"Don't go having orgasms on us, Chass. You can save that for Junior," Domencio stated.

"Back up off her, Dee. She's good."

"I'm done. You all can have a laugh at my expense. I'm a big girl, I can handle it. Junior, I want to try to get some sleep." He leaned back in his chair and I placed my head on his shoulder.

"Yo, Dee, put in a comedy tape. I'm in the mood to laugh my ass off." I heard Junior say just before I dozed off.

Junior woke me up, and I was happy to be home. When we reached his condo it was six in the morning and I just wanted to sleep. But Junior was hot for me. After we made love, he was a good boy and went to sleep. I followed and when we finally woke, it was dark outside.

"Damn, Junior, we slept all day. I'm starved."

"That's because your pussy is so good, which is bittersweet."

"Why bittersweet?" I asked.

"Come on, forget about that. I'm starved too. Let's get dressed and have a late dinner."

"Okay, but where?"

"I know this nice little spot where we can eat and listen to the locals sing. Sometimes a singer will blow the crowd away. I go for the mussels though. They're off the chain." When we got outside, the two SUVs were back, along with the bodyguards.

"We need them to go to dinner, Junior? Are you serious?"

"Dead, and you have yourself to blame for the extra security."

"When did I become the cause?" I asked, dying to know.

"When you wore that dress to my party. It caused a war, but we're not getting into this conversation. I need security for now, which means you're in need too. Let's have a good evening, babe. You look very pretty tonight. Kiss me." He leaned in and I submitted. He was nostalgic and captivating, yet daunting.

The lounge-type atmosphere was cool and the singers weren't bad. No one blew me away or brought tears to my eyes, but it was tolerable. Junior's expression caught my attention when I saw a twinkle in his eye. He was happy and content.

"You're enjoying yourself, baby?" he reached over and touched my hand.

"Yes, Junior as long as I'm with you, I'm happy. You're something different and I hope this never ends."

"I love that you're never shy about your feelings. There's no underlying motive, just pure boldness. Your loyalty to me doesn't go unnoticed and I will do everything I can to do right by you."

"You say it as if you know you will eventually hurt me."

"That's unclear, but what I do know is I can't be without you. For how long, that is the million-dollar question, Chasity. You hope for forever and hope you're right," he replied, agitating me and messing up the mood. Nonetheless, the mood turned deadly when Track made his presence known with a beauty queen on his arm.

Chapter 21

Junior

All was well with my new status with Chasity and I enjoyed the trip to Dubai once she arrived. The whole Track fiasco opened my eyes. I recognized my feelings for her were strong and the thought of losing her to him or any man was unthinkable. Chasity could say what she wanted, but I saw her attraction for Track and I had to dead that shit. I was in a sticky situation, committing to be her man while knowing I had reservations. However, the doubts I had seemed miniscule compared to losing her. God sent me a gift I didn't ask for, nor did I desire—a virgin. It had been a long time since I prayed, but last night I had a talk with God before I fell asleep on the plane. Tonight, there was an abundance of happiness spilling out of me.

We had slept all day, and I was hungry. I woke her and took her to this spot that served good food and catered to the elite. Not everyone was welcomed due to the three hundred-dollar door fee, which paid for the talent. A place I normally frequented alone, but I was willing to share this experience with Chasity. I was comfortable having her by my side and when she took notice, telling me she loved when I smiled, I made a personal vow to do it more often. It was like a scene out of a romantic movie, which I would never entertain, but the scene went dark when Track walked in with my old girl, Kali. A match made in hell.

What were the odds of these two showing up? I thought. I stopped guessing what people's motives were long ago, but mostly, I trusted no one. The waiter escorted them in our direction and within minutes my bodyguards surrounded us, trained to operate as ghosts.

Kali pranced by as if she didn't see me, but I knew she spotted me before I even saw her. She stopped, doubled back and exclaimed, "Junior, oh my God! I haven't seen you in years. You look great as usual. Life looks like it's been good to you."

I glanced over at Chasity and she was mean-mugging Kali. "Life is good. I'm his woman, Chasity. And you are?" she asked before I could answer.

"His woman?" she laughed. "You look more like a groupie, but if you must know—he was my man first, sweetie."

"Clearly, coming in last in this situation makes me the winner, bitch. You don't know me or what I've been through to be calling me a groupie. It would be in your best interest to keep it moving and mosey your monkey ass over there with Track," Chasity stood up and pointed in Track's direction.

"Calm down, baby. You hyped," I stood up to make sure she wouldn't leap across the table on Kali. I would talk to her about her behavior in public later, but for now she was turning me on, standing up for what belonged to her.

"Junior, since when did your standards become so tasteless? I thought you had more ambition than this," she said, referring to me. "You need to put a muzzle on this dog." *Bad move, Kali.* Chasity lifted the table up and beat her silly. My bodyguards weren't quick enough to stop Wonder Woman. Track tried interfering, but they were on his ass. I looked to my left and saw Track's soldiers coming and knew it was about to go down. I had to get control of my crazed woman.

"What the fuck, Junior? It's like that, nigga, you got ya peeps all up on me. I was just trying to stop the fight."

"Nigga, I don't know what's on your mind, but I know what I been hearing. Word is, you want me dead, so let's settle this shit right now."

"If I wanted you dead, you'd be six feet under. You're no threat to my organization, Junior and the reason you still have your life is because I remember when your fam took me in and made me a lieutenant when I didn't have shit. But times have changed, old friend, and I'm the boss on these streets now."

"What, you want a standing ovation? Fuck you and these streets," I responded as I snatched Chasity off Kali, but Kali's head came along for the ride. "Let go of her hair, Chasity. That's enough, stop." I demanded.

Chasity punched her in the head one last time and barked, "Dogs fuck people up. If you ever come near my man or me again, I will beat you non-stop, first and old girlfriend." We were at a standoff and Chasity was blinded by her rage.

"Chasity, I need you to chill, shit is about to get real, babe. Remember what I said about your boyfriend, Track," I whispered. She glanced around and realized the severity of the situation. "This is when I lead and you follow, you feel me."

"Chasity, what happened to the sweet girl that wanted to work away her life? As I recall, you said you didn't have time for fun. I'm surprised and amused by your performance tonight. What, you can't talk now? This nigga got control like that. I'm more of a freedom of speech nigga myself."

Six more bodyguards appeared, along with the owner. "Track, we both know where we stand. We can have a good old fashion shootout, where innocent people get killed, along with you and your crew, or we can handle this another day," I reasoned, as Track caressed Kali. She was fucked up bad. Chasity had beat her silly. She couldn't even stand up on her own. Blood was leaking from her face and in the morning that shit would be worse.

"Yes, that's the best news I heard all night," the owner, Fat Barry, intervened. "You know I respect the two of you and I don't want to choose. Therefore, I'm asking you both to leave, and take your entourage with you. My guests come here to have a good time and feel safe doing it. This Scarface shit ain't gone work up in here."

"You right, Barry. I didn't mean no disrespect to your establishment. I just came to catch up with an old friend, but it appears some peeps are caught up in their feelings." Track glanced at me.

"Come on, Kali, let me take you to the hospital," he said, as he carried Kali away and his rodents followed.

"Junior, I'll get you and Mayweather over there two takeout containers, and then I'm gone need you to leave," Fat Barry explained.

"We're good. Come on, Chass. You calm down yet? I asked.

"No, I'm not calm. Get me out of here," she spat, mad as hell.

When we reached the SUV, I instructed Calvin to take me to my pops house. My instincts were telling me to stay away from the condo for a while. The way Track and Kali just showed up out of the blue had me on full alert. Chasity needed protection, and Pop's was the safest alternative.

"Yo, where did that behavior come from, Chasity? I knew your mouth lacked control, so I shouldn't have been surprised when your body let loose. Why you let her get to you like that? That's exactly what she wanted, babe. She played you."

"What the fuck is you talking about, Junior? I'm sure she didn't want her ass kicked like that, so she's the one who got played. Every time that bitch see a dog, she'll remember me." She rolled her eyes.

"Why are you getting an attitude with me? You were silent this whole ride as if I caused this. I can't be responsible for who approaches me. You may be with me and run into someone I dealt with. You can't go around beating up every chick I fucked."

"You're not helping your case, Junior, so just zip it. As long as these bitches don't disrespect me, I can be cordial," she replied as we pulled up to Pop's house. "Thank you for bringing me here Junior, because we need some space." She hopped out the car and ran to Pops, angering me.

"Yo, Chasity," I yelled, "come here." She ignored me.

When I walked into the study, Pops was comforting her and she was more than eager to tell him all the gory details. I made myself a drink and just watched the actress perform.

Chapter 22

Jon-Jon

"Tell me everything that happened, Pumpkin. You're safe now, and I'm going to make sure you stay that way," I said.

"We were at some hideous place where the local talent sucked. Anyway, Track and Junior's old ass girlfriend showed up and called me a dog. And, she told Junior to put a muzzle on me," she cried as she explained.

"Fuck is you crying for, Chasity? Not a tear fell when you were pounding into Kali's head. Stop the bullshit," Junior cut in.

"Junior, let her tell me her story, please," I warned.

"Yeah, Junior let me speak, because you had little to say when everything went down. Why didn't you check her? It looks like you're more concerned with her. My knuckles are bruised and my back aches, but you haven't once asked me if I'm okay. Fuck you, Junior. Go check on your little girlfriend."

"Chasity, I don't like your tongue. Please stop cussing. You're too beautiful for that, Pumpkin," I reasoned.

"Okay, Uncle Jon, I apologize. I'm just so hurt and confused."

"I know you are, but I promise you will feel better in the morning. I will have my private doctor come first thing to ensure no broken bones or fractures. It's been an unfortunate night for you and you should get some rest. Tomorrow we can shop or do whatever you want. I mean it, if you want to fly to Paris, we can do that too. Would that make you feel better?" I asked as I watched Junior's nostrils flare.

"Yes, you're the best. I'm so happy you adopted us and I love you, Uncle Jon. Thanks so much."

"You trying to make a grown man cry, Chasity? I love you too and Uncle Jon is here to make it all better, just as I promised."

"This is bullshit. Chasity, don't piss me off and don't sit over there acting like the victim. You ain't no victim in this shit, you're the cause of it. Listen, we need to talk so let's go to bed and handle this," Junior barked.

"I want to be alone, Junior. Sleep by yourself," Chasity replied.

"Yes, Junior, you should probably go home. I got it from here," I said.

"Got what, Pops, her? She's my responsibility and we need to clear this up tonight. Chasity, don't do this after all our progress. I promise, if you walk away from me, I'm done."

"Walk away from this nigga and go to bed, sweetheart. I need to talk to him." She left, and I addressed Junior. "What is your problem, Junior? I told you to leave her alone. You hurt everything you touch. Can't you see the poor girl is traumatized?"

"Pops, Chasity is not the victim and she can hold her own. I regret bringing her here because she's playing you."

"What happened tonight, Son? She mentioned Track and I haven't seen Kali in years. That was the one girl I thought you'd marry."

"Fuck her, but Track's time is up. We were seconds away from a gunfight. Ever since I got word of his beef with me, I beefed up security. Track was outnumbered, so we agreed to save the fireworks for another day. Pops, this shit has got to end now."

"I told you to let me handle it. I don't want you mixed up in any way. From the sound of it, people have seen the beef between you two, and I need you to lay low, Son. This needs to be handled clean without too many questions."

"Pops do you, but if my back is against the wall all bets are off. Chasity was my woman before we showed up here, and you can thank yourself for fucking that up too. Good night, Pops. Tell Chasity I won't be bothering her again," he explained as he exited.

Chapter 23

Chasity

I was distraught from the whole incident. First, Junior's ex entering and getting her ass beat, but then the standoff was something straight from a gangster flick. I wasn't sure why I was mad at Junior, but I needed time to myself.

In the morning, I woke up to a knock at my door. "Come in," I said, yawning.

"Hey, Chass. I heard you was here, and I was hoping we could talk and clear the air," Destiny said.

"Sure, let me take a shower real quick and we can talk. Damn, I just remembered I don't have a change of clothes."

"I have clothes and new panties. I go shopping like every other day, and Uncle Jon gives me anything I want."

"I bet he does. Let's see what we're working with," I replied as we headed to her bedroom.

Destiny and I had similar rooms, but her massive walk-in closet was bursting with clothes and unpacked shopping bags. "Destiny, did Uncle Jon buy you all these clothes? My God, there's no room for anything else," I said, astounded. This chick had stepped up to a whole other level.

"I'm running out of space, but Uncle Jon said he'd enlarge the closet for me if need be. I believe I have enough clothes for now though."

"You think?" I responded as I shopped in her small boutique. I chose a pair of hot pink short-shorts that would never fly if Junior were here and spotted a cream silk sleeveless tank that matched my sandals. My feet were smaller than hers was so we never could share shoes.

"Chasity, I'm sorry for telling Uncle Jon you were a virgin and exposing your private thoughts. It's just, I had a feeling you and Junior would get serious and leave me out. I figured if I blew your cover, Uncle Jon would insist you stay."

"That's selfish, Destiny. When you chose Khalif over me, I had to grin and bear it. You were never in danger of losing me because I would never choose a man over you. I accept your apology and I missed your crazy butt. I have no one to talk to and I had to beat Junior's old girlfriend up last night."

"What happened?" she covered her mouth, shocked. I gave her a synopsis of last night events, leaving out the standoff because I didn't want her worrying about me. "So what's up with you and Junior? Uncle Jon says it's only a matter of time before Junior hurts you. We've been preparing for this day."

"Uncle Jon needs to chill, and what do you mean by preparing for this day?"

"He said when you came back, we would treat you so good, you'd want to stay by default."

"Yeah well, I'm not staying, Destiny, but I'm happy for you and you're welcome to come home anytime."

"This is my new home, Chass, but I'll come to visit in my new BMW." She danced around and I realized I missed my sister. There was a knock at the door. "Come in," Destiny yelled.

"Chasity, the doctor is here. As soon as you can, come down to my study. I need to make sure you're okay," Uncle Jon said.

"Okay, I'll be down in a minute. I just need to freshen up real quick."

"Okay, I'll see you in a few," Uncle Jon replied as he left.

"See, don't you want to be treated like royalty? Uncle Jon will give you anything you want. All he requires is respect and love," Destiny said.

"Where's Carlton?" I asked, wondering how she felt about Destiny's intrusion.

"She took Anastasia on a family camping trip. They should be back next weekend."

"How is she treating you?" I asked.

"She's cool, but I barely see her. She spends Uncle Jon's money by taking trips everywhere. They just got back from Disney World last week, and now this unexpected camping trip. You tell me," she replied sarcastically

"Aren't you doing the same thing? I mean, from the looks of your closet, you're not lacking in that department."

"The difference is, I love him and I can't say the same for her. When she's here, she caters to him and he appears content, but something is off. I stay out of it because it doesn't have nothing to do with me. Uncle Jon told me my place is secure in this household and yours too, if you decide."

"What's up with Khalif? Aare you still madly in love?" I asked, changing the subject.

"Yes, he's not going anywhere and Uncle Jon knows his parents. He's allowed to visit and I see him almost every day. I have a curfew and as long as I don't break it, Uncle Jon keeps me laced."

"I'm happy to hear that everything is working out for you. I haven't seen you this happy in years, other than when you look at Khalif. I know he's a good kid, and that's why I never forced you to stop seeing him."

"Thanks, Chass. I'm glad we made up because I missed talking to you."

"Me too, now let me get downstairs before Uncle Jon has a heart attack."

"I'll be down in a few," she replied as I left. I raced to my room and freshened up before heading downstairs. The doctor checked me out and gave me a clean bill of health. Other than my sore knuckles, I'd live.

Uncle Jon took us to Atlantic City, and we had a wonderful time on the beach. He was handsome for fifty-two, looking more like forty. Junior got his eyebrows from him, but his dark complexion came from his mom. Uncle Jon favored Rick Fox and his body was on point. It became obvious how he landed Carlton. Strangely, he received more attention from the white women, and

Destiny and I got a kick out of him flirting. He was a smooth operator, charming and distinguished.

"Ooooh, I'm telling Carlton on you, Uncle Jon!" I said when he rejoined us.

"Chasity, a lady never tells and besides, I'm just having a little fun. I'm a one-woman man, except for my beautiful nieces."

"We love you too, Uncle Jon," Destiny responded.

"Okay, ladies, Uncle Jon came to try his luck. I'll meet you back at the hotel. Here's my card. Have fun, darlings." When he left, Destiny and I headed to the outlets. After spending a good sum of money, which Destiny was a pro at, Uncle Jon's driver took us back to the hotel. We called room service, rented movies and stayed up all night like old times. When Uncle Jon called and told us to get ready for the drive home, we were too tired to move. I dragged myself out of the bed and realized I missed Junior. I thought about what he said and prayed he didn't mean it. I planned to call him when I got back to Uncle Jon's home, but for now, I was enjoying my free time.

Later that day, Uncle Jon said he wanted to speak with me in private. I met him in his study and he had all these VHS tapes sitting on the table, along with a strawberry margarita.

"Pumpkin, I want to show you these tapes of me and your parents. You think you can handle that?" Uncle Jon asked.

"Sure, I can handle it," I responded, and we watched tape after tape.

My mother was a piece of work and based on the videos, she appeared to run shit with these men. In one scene, she was cussing them all out, and I watched as each one hit her off with a stack of dough. I didn't remember this bossy and fierce woman, though her beauty was everlasting in my mind. He placed the final tape in the VCR, and I had a million questions.

"Uncle Jon, why is my mother kissing Uncle Kenny! And is that King cooking on the grill?"

"To address your first question, your mother, May God bless her soul, dated your Uncle Kenny first. Later, she married your father, had you, and moved to Georgia."

"I'm confused. I can't believe this! Why would she date daddy's best friend?"

He sighed and responded, "Chasity, your mother was special to all of us and we all wanted her. She chose Kenny, but when that failed, Tray made an honest woman out of her. Listen, it's time you know everything and then maybe it'll make more sense."

"I'm listening," I replied.

"Kenny was always a ladies' man, but he tried with your mother and when he lost her to Tray, only then did he realize he made a big mistake. She too had a way with her hands and beat many women up. Women from here to Mississippi, over Kenny," he laughed. "Kenny and Cat grew up in a foster home, on the same block where King and I lived. We formed a lifetime friendship that was unbreakable. Unfortunately, not everyone was loyal."

"King?" I asked.

"Yes, the Judas. Chasity, none of us had good intentions back then. Everything was about the money and we were all hungry. We took the city by storm and made a boatload of cash. But shit was getting hot with the police. We met and agreed to stop all illegal activity, if you know what I mean?" I nodded, showing I understood. "Everyone came up with their own exit plan to keep the money flowing, except King, because he was illiterate."

"Just tell me why he killed my parents, Uncle Jon," I blurted impatiently.

"Tray was the only one who dealt with our distributors. He was the key to our success. King's exit plan flopped, so he went back to the game, but he had no connections and became desperate. His bitter, unsuccessful ass believed your father caused his misfortune. Obviously, he found your parents and you know the rest." I couldn't help but cry after that punch to the gut. My whole life has been lie and my parents and Uncle Kenny were not who I thought they were.

"He killed my parents because my dad wouldn't give him the information he wanted. I'm glad he's in hell, Uncle Jon, and I hope he burns forever."

"Trust me he will, but don't focus on the dead. Other than the scars imprinted on your heart, he can never hurt you again. You needed to know the full story, Pumpkin. There is one last thing. Track, he's King's son, and that's why I was so adamant that you stay away from him."

"Damn, the story continues to get worse. Does he know who I am?" I asked, wondering if he was being genuine when approached me, or if he had another motive — like revenge.

"I don't think so, but you can never be too sure. I hate to reprimand, or say I told you so, but had you just listened, we would not be standing in this position, young lady. If I was vague or inexplicit before, let me clarify. For the last and final time, you are to stay away from him. This situation is serious and you need to know he's a problem for the Blake's. Understand?"

"Yes, I understand now. I'm still trying to digest Uncle Kenny and my mom. No wonder he took good care of me."

"Yeah, and there's more. I don't know how you're going to take this, but I too received a letter from Kenny, instructing me to tell you everything."

"What more could there be?" I asked, overwhelmed.

"When your mother and Kenny broke up, straightaway Tray locked her down, in so many words. Once we found out she was pregnant with you, he married her right away. Basically, Pumpkin, Kenny believed he was your biological father."

"My father. You must be kidding," I replied, delirious from all the unwanted information. I thought back to our first encounter at the hospital. "I remember when I first arrived at his home, he told me he was at the hospital when I was born, and held me first. He said something about the doctors confusing him to be my father, and my real father being upset. But he said once he looked at me he forgot about the argument."

"Hum, not quite. Kenny wanted DNA testing, but when they found out what you would have to go through as a baby, they compromised and agreed Tray would raise you as his own. Your mother was against the testing, believing with all her heart you were Tray's. I never believed Kenny either."

"Uncle Jon, that was a TMI moment, and now I'll be wondering for the rest of my life, which one was my real father."

"That's where you're wrong. Kenny always prepared for the future. I have his DNA and you can find out anytime. I had to use a sample for another test." He threw that in.

"For who?" I asked, ready to find Junior so I could escape this sad revelation.

"Chasity, you may not want to hear this, but we've come too far to stop now. You may remember the woman from the funeral I escorted out."

"Yeah, the liar."

"Actually, she may have been lying about Kenny loving her, but she had a baby four months ago and he's Kenny son."

"Are you sure, Uncle Jon?" Tears poured down my eyes.

"Yes, Pumpkin. One hundred percent. He may be your brother, Chass, and I wanted to give you the opportunity to meet him. Other than the Blake's, you have no family. Even if he's not your brother, he's your family. Please stop crying, sweetheart. This aging heart can't take that," he replied sincerely.

"I can't help it, Uncle Jon. Nothing is as it appears," I replied, wiping my tears away.

"I am what I appear to be and I love you as if you were my own. You stole my heart with your honesty and sincerity," he replied, rubbing my shoulder.

"I leave you for less than twenty-four hours with Pops and already he got you crying. I never made you cry, did I?" Junior asked as he entered the room. He was a welcome sight. I got up and ran into his arms, taking Uncle Jon by surprise. "You miss me, babe? Because I missed you."

"Yes, Junior. Are we back together now?" I asked desperately.

"You were never in any danger of losing me. I'm the ass, Chass. Why are you crying, baby?" he asked as he took a step back and stared into my face.

"Memories and revelations. I just received some crushing information and all I want is to be with you. I feel safe with you, despite all your mental disorders."

"Thanks, I think?" He looked at me sideways.

I glanced back at Uncle Jon and he was astonished. "Chasity, you sure you know what you're doing? Remember what Junior said last night," Uncle Jon recalled.

"Pops, chill with that. You need to get used to this, to us, because I'm a permanent fixture in her life, and I came to get my woman." *Yeah, Uncle Jon, chill. I want to be babied, but I want Junior to provide that luxury,* I thought. I hugged him tighter while he ran his fingers through my hair.

"Junior, you're right. I'm out of line. The two of you are grown. Chasity, your safety and happiness is more important than my opinion. I must say, you two look good together, but looks can be deceiving. I hope you mean what you say, Son. Chasity, I'm sorry for today. I didn't mean for it to turn out the way it did. Maybe I should've waited a while longer to tell you."

"It's okay, you were just following my uncle, or father's, wishes. I just don't know where I fit in or who I belong too. But with you, I feel at home and I love Junior. He knows how I feel because I tell him every chance I can. He hasn't returned the favor, but I know in my heart he feels the same, even if he refuses to acknowledge it."

"Pumpkin, I agree with you there. I knew Junior loved you even before you did. But loving someone on an impulse differs from completely loving someone. You deserve to have a man who will appreciate and respect you. Someone that will bend over backwards to make sure you're happy so your life together is full of bliss. There's more than just the mediocre, run of the muck physical attraction. Any fool can fall for that; it's a spiritual connection that's lasting. Whatever happens between you and Junior, good or bad, please don't shut me out. I don't deserve that."

"Never, and I promise to visit at least once a week."

"Once a week, I can live with that. I'll make sure your visits are special." I walked over and hugged him, not wanting to let go. I knew he would always be there for me, even if Junior was not.

"Pops, I'm that man you just spoke about as it relates to Chasity. Stop trying to put bullshit into her head about me. I'm not trying to hurt her. Chass, you ready babe? I want to beat rush hour traffic." Junior asked, disturbing my bonding moment with Uncle Jon.

"You want to leave with this pushy negro, Chass, so be it," Uncle Jon said.

"Love you, Unc! I'll call you soon."

"I look forward to it." Destiny walked in just in time. "Hey, Dee, I'm about to hit the road, but I'm happy we made up. I missed you." Instead of responding, she ran over and hugged me as if she would never see me again. "What's up, Dee? I'll be back. Now that we're friends again, you can come stay with me and we can hang out like old times."

"You better not be lying. When I call you, I'll expect for you to answer. We can go shopping, my treat. Right Uncle Jon?"

"That's right, precious."

"Dee, you're a mess, but I love you. Call me later on, okay?" She agreed.

"Junior, step up the security for Chasity. I'll stop by the office tomorrow because we have some things to discuss."

"She's safe with me, Pops. Trust me. Where I go, she goes."

"Whatever, Junior! Destiny, Paul will drive you where you need to go for a while," Uncle Jon instructed.

"Why, did I do something wrong?" she asked, disappointed.

"No, you've been a little angel. I'm just taking additional measures to protect you. It won't be permanent, just for a little while," he explained.

The interaction between them was as if he had known her all her life. Destiny had Uncle Jon wrapped around her pinky finger and there was no way she would leave all this for me.

"Destiny, Uncle Jon, I'll talk to you soon," I said as Junior rushed me out of the room.

"I got a surprise for you," Junior whispered.

"Are we flying away somewhere romantic?" I asked, ready to explore the world with him.

"We won't be flying today, but if you have something in mind, I'm all ears."

"No, I'm more interested in your surprise."

"Good girl," he replied as he held the door open.

Chapter 24

Kenny

22 years earlier

I was about to bust a nut when a blunt object smashed into my head. I was fading away, but I could see Cathy whipping Tina's ass.

"Wake up nigga, ain't nuttin wrong with you," Cathy barked. "I swear on everything I love, I'm done with your cheating ass. I'm tired of your bullshit, Kenny. You woke nigga?"

"Yeah," I responded, rubbing my head. "What the fuck you hit me with, Cat?" I painfully asked.

"Pussy, you lucky I didn't end you and that bitch life. I'm too good for you, Kenny. We grew up like brother and sister, and I shoulda never gotten involved with you. But it's over for sure. You got until tonight to get your shit out my apartment before I call the man on your sorry ass."

"You mean our apartment. The last time I checked, I was the only motherfucker paying rent. Where am I supposed to go? I'm not going anywhere."

"You're right, I'll leave. But you better leave me the fuck alone!" she spat, kicking me in my head one last time. She showed her ass but I loved her. Even so, I loved new pussy more.

Within a month she was dating Tray, and five months later, her growing belly was on display. If Tray wasn't my man shit wouldn't have gone down like that. They say you never miss a good thing until it's gone, and I missed Cat. It was hard digesting them together, but I only had myself to blame.

However, shit got crazy the day of Jon-Jon's million-dollar party. Cathy was talking with her girlfriends and I couldn't help but notice how beautiful she was pregnant. Her girlfriend asked how far along she was in her pregnancy and she said five months. Five months ago, we were in a relationship, so unless she was fucking Tray while we were together, that was my baby she had in her belly.

I was fuming, ready to confront Cathy and Tray, but Jon walked up just as I was about to pull her to the side. "What's good, Kenny? You look pissed. Listen, don't start no shit at my party. I know you're not over Cat, but tonight is not the night, brah."

"Tonight is the night, Jon. That baby in her stomach is mine, and she needs to explain that shit. Tray outta order too, keeping a secret like that. I should beat the black off that bastard."

"You buggin yo! You think Pumpkin is carrying your baby? You need to get over her and let this shit go."

"Fuck you, Jon. I don't give a fuck about Cat or Tray, but if that's my baby, they better recognize. Look at her ass over there laughing and giggling and shit. Well, I'm about to take that smile off her damn face," I replied, and stormed over to Cat. "I need to talk to you. Now!" I demanded, standing in front of her.

"Kenny, there's nothing for us to talk about, and I warned you to stay away from me."

"Like you want me to stay away from our child you're carrying! You think I'm fucking stupid."

"This is not your child in my stomach," she defended. "What would give you that impression, Kenny? You're losing it boo. You need to get it together."

"Nah, I think I'm dead on. If you think your disloyal ass will get away with it, you better think again, Cat. When our baby is born, I want a paternity test!"

"Fuck you talking bout, Kenny?" Tray asked when he walked in on the conversation.

"I'm talking about my child she's carrying. And Tray, you harboring secrets. I know she got your nose wide open, nigga, but this shit is foul, unforgivable shit," I responded.

"Kenny, I never pegged you for a sore loser, my man. You're looking desperate and you need to slow your role. This is my baby, and no one is getting a paternity test. I suggest you go seek help before I fuck you up."

"Yeah, Kenny, take your punk ass somewhere else. All you do is hurt the ones close to you and ruin a good time," Cat interjected. *What is a man to do?* I slaughtered Tray with jabs and uppercuts. He put up a good fight, which I knew he would, but my anger allowed me to get the best of him. "You see why you can't keep friends, Kenny? It's because you're insecure. You couldn't appreciate me when you had me, and now you stoop this low." She sucker punched the shit out of me, defending her man.

"Kenny, I warned you not to fuck up my party. Follow me, man. You need to calm down," Jon reasoned. I followed him to his study and admired the view of the massive new mansion he purchased in Newton Square.

"Jon, I'm telling you, that baby is mines. I did the math and there's no way Tray is the father. I overheard her say she was five months. In order for Tray to be the father, they had to be fucking for two months before we broke up. All I know is, when the baby comes, I'm claiming it."

"I'm at a loss for words, but the side of your face is swelling, my man."

"Cat and her deadly punch."

"We taught her how to fight years ago. She sure mastered that shit. Honestly, I'm certain she can whip all of our asses," he laughed.

"I'm glad you find this funny. In four months, I'll have the last laugh." I rolled out before I killed someone.

Four months later

"Kenny, I'm tired of coming to motels to spend time with you. It makes me feel cheap. I'm starting to think you got a wife tucked away somewhere," Melissa said, after we finished having sex.

"Melissa, don't fuck up the vibe, babe. I told you before, I live with my mother," I lied.

"And I told you I don't mind. I would love to meet your mother. We've been dating for like what? Four months now? It's time we take things to the next level."

"Melissa, let me be clear and please don't take offense. There is no next level, baby. This is as good as it gets. I thought we had a nice arrangement. What, you need money to go shopping?"

"No, I can buy my own shit! I want to be with you, so if this is as good as it gets, I'll pass," she replied while gathering her things.

"You want me to call you a cab?" I asked, trying to be polite.

"No, I drove like I do every time. Something you never noticed." She slammed the door behind her and I left shortly afterwards.

On the ride home, my cell phone rang. I glanced down and saw it was Jon-Jon. "What's good?" I asked when I answered.

"Yo, Cat is about to have that baby and Tray plane hasn't landed yet. He's coming in from Mexico and me and the family are in the Bahamas. She has no one, Kenny. You need to put aside your differences and support her."

"I'm there. What hospital is she in?"

"The University of Pennsylvania. Call me when you get there."

I raced down to Penn, excited to see my son or daughter. When I arrived in the maternity ward, I asked for Cathy Peters' room.

"Who are you?" the nurse asked.

"I'm the father," I responded proudly.

"Oh, come this way, quickly! She's minutes away from giving birth. She may have already had the baby."

When I stepped inside the room, Cathy was in so much pain. It hurt me to see her in that much agony. "Cat, Tray is on his way, but I'm here to support you."

"Push, Mrs. Peters! I can see the head," the doctor said. I ran around so I could see my baby for the first time, but doubled back when I saw her vagina spread like something out of a horror flick.

"Kenny!" she screamed. "Kenny, help me. Please!" she begged.

"I'm right here, babe. What do you need me to do? Push, Cat! The baby is almost out. Listen, that was some nasty shit down there, so please take everyone out of their misery," I said, trying to be funny.

"I never liked your sense of humor, Kenny. Where is Tray? Oh God, please make him come soon," she moaned between pushes.

"Sorry," I replied, gently holding her hand. Her grip got tight on the last push, and I was sure my finger was broken.

"It's a girl!" the nurse announced. They cleaned her up, and instead of giving her to Cathy, they handed me my daughter. She was beautiful, and I knew she was mine.

"He's not--." I shot her a look that could kill.

I placed her in Cat's arms and said, "You know we're getting that test done, right?"

"Don't start with that bullshit again, Kenny. She's Tray's baby and we're moving from this Godforsaken city. I just had a baby and all you ever bring is drama. Let's just say hypothetically that she is yours. You never gave a damn about me, and you would make a horrible father. My child will be raised by a man who loves me unconditionally and don't sleep around with every pretty face he sees!"

"So you're punishing me because I fucked around on you? Bottom line, the timeframe don't add up. Unless you were fucking him while we were still together, I'm getting a test."

"I was, okay! Are you satisfied now? You barely touched me, nigga."

"You stopped allowing me to touch you and I had to take it. And you're wrong, I cared about you. I loved you and I still do, but that's beside the point. You can't keep my baby away, Cat. You know we come from nothing. If that's my baby, I need her in my life."

"If she was yours, Kenny, I would never keep you away. Please, let me live in peace. I love Tray more than life itself, and I would hate to see you two fall out over a misunderstanding. If you love me like you say, let us go, Kenny."

"Baby, my plane couldn't land quick enough," Tray interrupted as he burst through the door. "What's this nigga doing here? You won't stop until one of us ends up dead. It's a wrap, Kenny. She's my lady, and that's my daughter Chasity she's holding." He bent down, kissed Cat, and picked up my daughter. They were in lovers' land and I was standing there stuck on stupid.

"Her name is Chasity?" I said aloud as I exited the room.

Six Years later

I was on my way to talk to Jon-Jon about King, because he was taking matters into in his own hands and we couldn't have that. He went on a killing spree last night, knowing we all agreed to hold off on the hits. No one knew for sure who was robbing our spots, so there was no need for unnecessary deaths. I stopped at the gas station to fill my tank and pick up a pack of cigarettes. As I was waiting for the tank to fill, I noticed a sexy woman crying. She was holding a one-year-old toddler in her arms.

"Hey, sis! How is it that someone as beautiful as you have tears falling down their face? Who did it? I will fuck them up, for real." She laughed. "There we go, beautiful. Explain how I can keep that smile on your face," I reasoned, while making googly eyes at her little daughter. Oddly, she reached her hands out for me and cried when her mother held her back. "Can I hold her? I mean, she is crying for me." She reluctantly allowed me to embrace the little girl, and she hugged my neck tightly, not letting go. "What's her name? She's sweet."

"Destiny," she replied.

"Destiny, that's ironic since I believe its destiny that caused this encounter. What's your name?"

"Denise, but everyone calls me Dumpling. Listen, I'm sorry that we had to meet this way, but I really need to call a friend to come get me. My car won't start, I got fired today, and to make matters worse, I have ten days to vacate my apartment. Trust me, my life is fucked." She took Destiny out of my arms. She was trying to make a call while Destiny was hollering for me and fighting her mother. It was hilarious.

"I tell you what, Dumpling. With your permission, I insist on taking you to your destination. I will have your car towed and repaired My treat of course. The only thing I ask in return is that you and Destiny have dinner with me. I have to take care of something, but once I'm done, I'm all yours."

"Why are you being so nice?" She eyed me suspiciously.

"What? I see a beautiful woman and her adorable child in distress, and you question that?" I asked.

"Yes, I'm not used to men showing me kindness unless they want something. So what do you want?"

"Where's Destiny's father?" I asked, shifting the conversation.

"Dead! Someone took his life before she was born, but he wasn't claiming her then, and his family never did after he died." She looked like she was ready to cry again and my heart went out to her. I was falling for this woman and her sweet persona.

"I'm sorry to hear that, I didn't mean to bring up any bad memories. What do you say? My chariot awaits," I said, opening the passenger side door.

"I don't even know your name, and you expect me to get in your car."

"I'm Kenny, and it's a pleasure to make your acquaintance. I suggest you get Destiny's car seat and we be on our way. I have an important meeting I can't miss, but I definitely want to take you two to dinner."

"I can get a babysitter if it's too much."

"Nah, I met you together, and we all rolling together. One big happy family." She smiled.

When we reached her apartment, I was ashamed for her. Poor thing, she was living the struggle, and it took me back to my childhood. I couldn't allow her to stay another night in this dump. She had me from hello and I pondered the possibility of a happy home. I inspected the one-bedroom apartment, located in one of the worse parts of the city, Southwest Philly, and knew I was not picking her up from this location again.

"Dumpling, check this out. I don't know you and you damn sure don't know me. For all you know, I could be a psycho nigga tryna' hurt you and your baby. However, I'm not that man. When I saw you at the gas station, something unexpected happened. You and your daughter stole my heart. I'm asking you to trust me and get your shit, because you won't be returning here."

"Kenny, thanks for the ride home, but we'll be fine. You don't have to take us to dinner. God will provide for us. My faith was slightly shattered, but He didn't bring me this far for me to give up now."

"I like that, you're a religious woman. Let me ask you something? Is it possible that God is working through me, and you could be potentially blocking a blessing? See, I don't know about losing hope in Him, but I do know prayer works. Maybe I'm your saving grace."

"You're something else, Kenny. If I'm honest with myself, I find you to be very attractive. I'm afraid of being hurt, and this situation is crazy."

"You're right, but one day we'll look back and have a great story to tell. Now please, pack up only what you need and we'll figure the rest out."

"You're serious. You want me to leave with you and go where?"

"Somewhere safe for Destiny to lay her head and where I can take better care of you. We're taking a chance and going out on a limb, but I'm always up for a new adventure." Right then, Destiny wanted me and I swooped her into my arms. She lay her head on my shoulder and fell asleep, Dumpling started packing with the quickness.

"This is crazy," she continued saying. "I can't believe I'm about to leave with a man I don't know. God this better be You like he said, because if it's anything else, only You can bring me through," she prayed.

"Make sure you get enough stuff for the night. We can start over tomorrow," I explained, ready to bounce. The place wasn't dirty, I mean you could tell she tried her best, but there was no way to dress up raggedy.

I took her back to my apartment in Chestnut Hill and watched her get settled. I went into the bathroom and called Jon-Jon. "What's up man? I know I'm running late, but something important came up. I'll be there in an hour."

"I was about to have dinner and retire for the night. You're never on time, Kenny."

"Retire for the night? You sound like a ninety-year-old man. I told you something came up. I'm on my way." I hung up, trying to be patient with him. Since Lela's death a year ago, he hadn't been the same. I walked into the living room and it was empty. I followed the noise to the bathroom and Dumpling was bathing Destiny.

"Are you comfortable for now?" I asked, watching as she toyed around with Destiny.

"Yes, but we need to get something clear. I'm not sleeping with you. I appreciate what you're doing for me and my daughter, but as soon as I can secure a job, I'll be out of your hair."

"Is that so? Check this out, I have to meet my business partner, but when I get back, we can go to dinner."

"It's getting late, and I have something for Destiny and I to eat. Maybe tomorrow, because I'm tired," she replied.

"Okay boss lady, I'll be back soon."

When I pulled up to Jon-Jon's home, I could see Junior and Domencio playing video games through the window. I rang the bell and was taken aback when a vision of loveliness greeted me. "You must be Kenny. Jon-Jon is expecting you. Right this way," she directed, and I let her ass guide me to my friend.

"Take your eyes off my lady's ass," he warned as soon as I walked into his office. "Kenny, this is Renee. This is one of my business partners, Kenny." He introduced us.

"The pleasure is all mines, beautiful. Yes, you are lovely."

"Thank you," she responded, and Jon-Jon quickly dismissed her.

"Now I understand why you wanna turn in early, nigga. That bitch is fine as shit!"

"Watch ya mouth, yo! You need to learn how to treat a woman and maybe you'll have one for more than five minutes."

"I'm working on that. More importantly though, King is out of control. He on some solo I-AM-GOD shit. He forgot he works with a team. Now we have heat coming from the five 0 and beef with niggas who we have no proof hit our spots."

"Here's the deal. His Judas ass can go on his own and start his own shit. Without us, specifically Tray, he has no resources. No major connect will deal with his no-name ass. I was reluctant to put him on from the start. You and Tray vouched for him. I never cared for him back on the block, but I embraced him on the strength of y'all. As far as I'm concerned, he can disappear, if you know what I mean."

"I hear you."

"You talk to Tray about this?"

"Fuck no, that nigga still holding grudges, when I'm the one that should be mad that he took my daughter to fucking Timbuktu."

"You still on that shit? You need to let that go, Kenny."

"I'll never let it go. When you know something, you just know. Why is it they never bring Chasity with them when they come home? I'll tell you the reason, Chasity probably looks just like me, and they don't want their little secret revealed." Jon-Jon was looking at me as if I had my head screwed on backwards. "Fuck you, I'm out. You call Tray and let him know we're severing ties with King." I headed back to my apartment, eager to see Dumpling and Destiny.

For the next few weeks, Dumpling and I bonded on a whole other level, and not having sex wasn't that bad. This was my first relationship where sex was secondary. I showered her and Destiny with shopping sprees and gifts. We turned my second bedroom into a toddler's room, and I was trying to assemble the convertible crib I had just purchased.

"Ken, you want me to bring your plate in here, or are you joining us for dinner?" Dumpling asked.

I put the automatic drill down and said, "Nah, I'm coming to eat with my family like we been doing." She tried to hide her smile but I saw it. She was one of the most beautiful women I'd dealt with since Cat.

"What's for dinner?" I asked as I sat down at the table. Destiny was sitting in her high chair saying dada.

"Roasted chicken with rosemary, wild rice, and broccoli," she replied, sitting my plate in front of me. I was about to dig in until I remembered we pray before we eat.

"I'm sorry Dee, I don't know why I forget that every night."

"Practice and repetitive actions will lead to habit-forming behavior."

"What? Just say the prayer, Mrs. Prolific."

"I think you should say the prayer tonight. Remember, practice."

"Okay, I got this. Let's see. Heavenly Father, I thank you for this food and the beautiful hands that prepared it. And Lord, thanks for sending me two blessings. In Jesus' name, we pray. Amen."

"Amen! Kenny, were you referring to us?"

"I don't see no other blessings around here, do you?"

"That's sweet. You're more a blessing than anything. You were right, you are my saving grace."

Later that evening, I was flipping through channels as I enjoyed a cold Corona. Dumpling had put Destiny to sleep, and the apartment was finally quiet. I heard her turn off the shower and moments later, she was standing naked in the living room.

"Kenny, I was hoping you could bless me one more time," she seductively stated, pointing to her nicely shaven vagina. Her breasts, in their entire splendor, saluted me like the Star Spangled Banner. They were the size of mangos, with nipples slightly darker than her cinnamon skin. She was weaning Destiny off the breast milk and it showed. I tried to see through her clothes many days, but she was sexier than I had imagined. There was no trace of giving birth on her and I knew her pussy would feel good. "I'm sorry, I thought you wanted me," she covered her breasts with her hands when I didn't get up right away. I was just enjoying the view.

I jumped up, ran over to her, and said, "Are you mad? I wanted you from that first day," I said, gently licking her nipples. "You're sexy. You know that, baby. I was dying to touch you," I groaned. I covered her body with intimate kisses, exploring every part of her.

"I wanted you from the moment I saw you as well," she whispered as she got down on her knees and swallowed my dick. I had to stop her before I came. The anticipation from the long ass wait had me ready to prematurely come. It was my turn to return the favor. I picked her up and placed her on the sofa. She spread her legs, and I gave her something she was obviously craving. I entered her sweet walls and knew I was a goner. A few months later, I was shopping for rings.

Four years later

I had just purchased a four-bedroom single family home in Jenkintown for my wife and daughter. Dumpling and Destiny provided the fairytale life I dreamed of when I was child living with my foster parents. They never gave a damn about me or Cat. I had everything a man could ask for, but the one missing piece was my daughter, Chasity. Over the years, I came to my own personal resolve and prayed Cat and Tray spoiled her the way I would have.

"Babe, you're going to be late. Remember, you have to meet Jon-Jon and the man about the bathroom cabinets. He wants eight custom vanities. I told him his timeframe was ridiculous, but you should talk to him."

"Thanks, sexy girl. Now get over here and give me some sugar," she pranced over and kissed me with those full lips, reminding me why I married her.

"Let me go before you start something. I love you. Don't spend too much money decorating this place. Sike, I'm just kidding. Enjoy yourself, but nothing pink, orange--."

"Kenny, stop already. Everything will be white, okay?" she replied, getting agitated.

"You're fucking with me right?"

"Yes, but we already went over the color scheme in detail. You gave me full control, but every minute you're voicing your opinion. I allow you to be the man in every other aspect of our lives. Let me be the woman and decorate our home my way. One of the extra bedrooms will be yours to do whatever you please, along with the garage."

"That's why I married you, Dumpling. You and Destiny are the loves of my life. If you have time, do you think you could make me a small batch of your famous banana pudding?" I asked, knowing that was another reason I married her. She was a good girl and her cooking skills were bananas.

"Kenny, you know that's for holidays. You should've told me earlier. I guess I can stop fun shopping for the house and go to the supermarket," she pouted.

"Never mind," I replied, hating to see her upset. "I should be back around seven. I'll take you out to dinner instead."

"Love you, honey." She smothered me with hugs.

When I jumped on the expressway, my phone vibrated. I glanced down briefly and saw it was Jon. "I'm on my way, nigga. Why you always nagging?"

"Cat and Tray were murdered last night." When he said that I lost control of the car, but luckily I was going at a reasonable speed. "What about Chasity?" I asked once I regained control of the wheel. "She's good," he replied. "Hurry the fuck up!"

My mind didn't fully intake the severity of what he said. The entire way there, I prayed there was a mistake. Over the years, our relationship was cordial and respectful when it came to business, and I never would have wished death on either of them. Shit, I loved Cat, and at one-time Tray was like my brother. This had to be someone close, because the main reason Tray moved to Georgia was to keep a low profile. He alone dealt with the distributors and we all agreed that he should lie low. Cat thought he was doing it for her, but I knew the truth.

For the past couple of years, we all prepared to leave the game. Everyone was on board except King. We cut all ties with him, and he was too stupid to come up with a plan to legitimize his finances. Six months ago, Jon-Jon's oldest son Junior got pinched. He refused to talk and went down for the entire organization. Jon-Jon had been on edge doing everything possible to help his son. That was the final blow. We severed ties and went our own way. Most of my savings paid for my new house and brand new cars for Dumpling and I. I started out making cabinets for Jon-Jon until I found my own clientele. Once folks saw my skills, they told a friend who told a friend, and the trickledown effect was alive and well.

My heart was breaking, but if this was true, I had to get my daughter. I pulled up to Jon-Jon's house and his new wife, Renee, greeted me. When I walked into his study, he had a bottle of scotch sitting on his desk with two glasses.

"What the fuck happened, Jon, and do you even know if this shit is true?"

"My entire family lives down there and heard rumors, but the runner we had in the stash house verified the incident. He said it was all over the news. Execution style, and they burned the house down after the massacre."

"Who the fuck would do some shit like that? Was everything cool with the distributors? I mean, there wasn't an outstanding balance we didn't know about, right?"

"Come on, now. You know better than that. Tray had a good relationship with them. Many times, they gave us shit free for moving the weight so fast. They're not responsible, but I'm almost sure I know who did it."

"Spill it. Fuck you got me waiting for?"

"Two weeks ago, Tray called and said King had been pressuring him for the connect information, which was never going to happen. They had words, and King threatened to come down there. At the time, I offered my services because if it were left up to me, he would've been history when he did that unauthorized hit. I should've never let the peasant live. Now, Judas has reared his ugly face again."

"If he did this shit, you gone have to beat me to the punch. It'll be first come first served. That nigga didn't even consider my daughter. How did she escape?"

"I pulled it up on the internet so you could see for yourself." I walked over to his computer and looked at the screen. I took note to get one of these for my house. The report said that a husband and wife were found burnt and shot in the head execution style. It continued by saying my daughter had escaped by climbing out of the widow and jumping from a tree.

"What the fuck! I need to scoop her up quickly. I'm catching the next flight out."

"Slow your role, Kenny. I think it's best she stays with me. Don't nobody believe that shit about you being her father, and I have plenty of room, as you can see."

"Jon, you or no one else can stop me from getting my daughter. I don't give a fuck what you think. I know, and I can finally prove it to your ass. Don't get in my way, Jon. You're like my brother, but you're crossing the line."

"We can get shared custody. That way we both can raise her."

"Hell no. I'm not sharing her with you or anyone else. I will raise her the same way I'm raising Destiny. She will know that I always loved her from the moment the doctor placed her in my hands. It's been ten years, and I haven't seen my daughter. Cat and Tray made sure of that, but for no longer, my friend. Destiny needs a sibling, and since Dumpling can't have any more children, this unfortunate fate will work out for the best."

"Since you put it like that, I'll fall back for now."

"Yeah, you do that. I'll deal with King's ass when I return, but my daughter is my main priority. I'll call you when I reach down there."

As I was leaving Jon said, "Yo, Kenny. I don't think it's a good idea for you to tell her you're her father. I know you believe that with all your heart, but she's been through a lot and don't know you from a can of paint."

"Noted. Before I forget, congratulations on your recent nuptials," I replied before leaving.

I drove home doing ninety miles per hour. When I pulled into the garage, I raced to find Dumpling and found her knocked out on the sofa.

"Babe, wake up. I have something important to tell you."

"I'm woke, what's up honey? Why you look so frazzled?"

"You remember my friends Cathy and Tray? You met them at Jon-Jon's wedding. To make a long story short, I used to date Cat right before she got with Tray."

"Damn, what was y'all doing, sharing her?"

"Nah, it wasn't like that. Anyway, when she got pregnant, I knew it was my baby. I was all ready to get a paternity test, but when I saw the bond between her and Tray at the hospital, I painfully walked away. They died last night, murdered, but my daughter escaped and I need to get her."

"Oh Lord! I'm so sorry for your loss, Kenny. Go, honey, and get your daughter. Do you want me to come with you?"

"Nah, babe. I need to handle this one alone. She don't know us, and I want to feel her out first. I just need you to love her the same way I love Destiny. I need her to know she is welcome, because I never stopped loving her."

"Kenny, anything that comes from you, or belong to you, I will love. I love you with all my heart and will love her the same."

"I don't deserve you, babe but God still blessed me. He's a mighty man."

"Yes He is. I love it when you get all religious. That shit turns me on. Ooops, forgive me Lord."

"Watch your mouth woman, and save those lips for kissing me," I responded and took her to the bedroom.

"I guess we don't have to worry about one of the extra bedrooms."

"Nah, but I need you to have her room done when I get back. Make it special babe. You know what little girls like." The next day I caught a flight to Atlanta.

Chapter 25

Junior

I t was extremely difficult sleeping without Chasity, and I was angry at Pops for fucking up the program. No other woman had affected me and placed a spell on my heart like her. My desire to consume her entirely had me doomed. She was trying to listen, but I needed her to try a little harder. This behavior of controlling a woman was normal of me, but I couldn't regulate my emotions, and my need to possess everything about her was ruining everything.

I gave her two days for Pops to pamper to her needs, but his time had expired, and it was time for her to tend to my needs. When I walked into his study and saw tears in her eyes it angered me, and I wanted to fuck Pops up. I bet he pulled out all those videos and bored her to tears. When she ran into my arms and held me tight, I felt justified, and I was ready to take my woman home.

When we got inside the armored rental car, I instructed the driver to take us to my workplace. The past couple of days, I had been working on a plan, and I believed it would make all parties happy. We drove the entire ride with her head snuggled into my chest, and she was trying hard not to cry. I hoped that my surprise would change her mood.

"You okay?" I asked, while caressing her arm and kissing on her forehead.

"I don't know. How can I be okay when I don't know where I come from or who I belong to?" she tearfully replied. It broke me to see her in so much pain.

"You got me and the rest of the Blake's. When people ask about your family, you tell them you belong to us. Chasity, life don't stop because bad things happen. You can always start over. God gives second chances, look at me. I could've spent the rest of my life in prison, but He had another plan for me, and it wasn't until recently that I could fully appreciate it."

"What happened recently that made you feel this way?"

"You. You bring me an insatiable amount of joy. If I never told you before, thanks for allowing me to be your first. It was an honor and privilege to experience an untouched woman. The effect it had on me was unexpected, so you have to forgive me if I'm a bit overprotective."

"I know, Junior." She held me tighter and closed her eyes. She understood me well, which allowed me to be me.

"Don't fall asleep on me yet, baby. I'm turning those tears into a smile."

When we got to my office building I cut the alarm off, because the building had officially closed for the day. Chasity tried to put on a good front, but she was still sad, and the surprise couldn't come fast enough. When we got on the elevator with a couple of my security team, I pulled her to my arms. She felt so good and her hair smelled so fresh. I loved this woman, but I was not quite ready to confess. Instead, I hoped she would accept this gift as a sign of my love for her.

"Why are we here, Junior? I'm tired, and I have a slight head-ache."

"You'll see," I replied as I escorted her off the elevator. Instead of turning towards the cafeteria, I directed her down the opposite hall. When I opened the door, I said, "Surprise." I waited for her response.

"Junior, you did all this for me? I'm speechless!" She cried again, confusing me. I thought this would cheer her up.

"Why are you crying, Chass? I did this to make you happy. I can't take the tears, babe."

"Junior, these are tears of joy. You thought enough of me to take my advice. I know you love me, and you can deny it all you want, but this helps me to wait patiently until you pronounce it." She jumped me and wrapped her legs around my waist while kissing me with her sweet lips. "I missed you so much. I promise to listen to you from now on," she whispered as she pecked my neck with her tongue. "I'll be a good girl," she moaned, in her own zone. It was as if she was turning herself on.

"Y'all can wait outside for us. We'll be fine." I instructed security to leave. "Are my ears deceiving me, or did you just say you will listen?" I asked while massaging her ass. I put her down and said, "Undress, quickly." I mean-mugged her. She obeyed, and I never tired of seeing her body. It drove me insane knowing I was the sole owner of such sweetness. "Go sit on the table saw and spread your legs for daddy." Her ass cheeks bounced from left to right, hardening my penis further. I dropped my pants, and when she turned around, I was right there. "Let me help you out," I said as I lifted her up and sat her on the table saw.

"I can't wait to feel you inside me. I missed your touch," she cried, with pleasure laced on her tongue.

"You missed this?" I asked, holding my dick. "Open up wide," I demanded.

"Yes master," she replied as she spread her legs like eagle wings.

I slid inside her festival of fun, anticipating the adventure awaiting. The potent pleasure smothered my manhood at each turn and from every angle weakened my knees. I anchored my hands between her thighs and with a fast steady pace I took ownership of her pussy and devoured it with my dick. "You're magnificent, baby!" I moaned. "Show me how far your legs can spread." She extended her legs, giving me a full view of her womanhood and turning me into a lunatic. I stuck and jabbed, hitting all her walls. She was a good girl and allowed me to knockout her vagina. Satisfaction exuded through her face, further turning me on. "It feels good, baby?" I asked.

"Yes, so good, Junior," she responded in a lust-filled mode.

"Tell me how good. I want to hear it."

"More than my dreams, baby. You're my life and there will be no other," she whispered, and then she did something with her vagina that sent my penis into and orgasmic frenzy. She pushed her muscles down as if she was resisting me or pushing back my dick. A new sensation had stricken my penis, and I craved to feel it again.

"Did you come, baby?" I asked, wanting her to come with me always.

"Yes, you never disappoint me. Each time is better."

"I'm happy to hear that. Now, look around before we head home. I want to know what you think."

"Junior, I think it's wonderful that you took my advice. I guarantee you'll see some savings."

"I don't think you understand. This is your workspace. You said woodworking is your passion and if I can save money, it's a win-win."

"How do you figure that?" she asked.

"I'm getting the impression you're not happy with my surprise. However, let me explain myself. It's a win-win because you can work and follow through with your dreams. You're here at the Blake Corporation so I know you're safe, and at my disposal," I clarified.

"So that's your master plan?"

"Am I wrong?" I looked at her sideways, trying to remain calm. I didn't quite know her angle, but I knew that part about listening was bullshit.

"No, you're not wrong. I knew that was your plan when we walked in. I wanted to see your reaction if I didn't accept."

"Baby you don't want to see that. I have to admit that I'm relieved. Liven up yourself because we'll be up all night, trust and believe."

I watched as she examined all the equipment. I spared no expense and gave her the best of everything. She had every tool imaginable and her own office.

"Junior, I'll be able to be creative with all this equipment. I can't wait to get started," she said with excitement and passion.

"You won't have to wait long. I'm starting you out with a smaller project until I see what you're working with. We just won a bid on a property rental with forty units. This is the perfect opportunity to show what you're made of. I need cabinets for forty kitchens and bathrooms. When you look at the cabinets they need to say high-end and custom-made. You can work out the details with Juanita, the head of design. She can give you a more accurate picture of what we need. Of course, you will need to hire your own staff. Do you think you can handle all of this?"

"Yes, with my own staff, I believe I can." She was high as the moon which made me happy, knowing I was responsible.

"I'm counting on you, Chass. Don't disappoint me. I know you can do anything you put that wondrous mind to. Let's bounce, we have so much catching up to do."

Chapter 26

Chasity

Junior surprised me to no ends with my personal wood shop. My love for him magnetized to heights unimaginable, and losing him would devastate me. It would be equally as hurtful as the loss I've already endured. His mind was mysterious and full of slight malfunctions, but his sex was miraculous and magnetizing. I researched his behavior online and he didn't fall into the bipolar criteria. However, after much investigation I found him. They referred to his type as The Possessive-Man-Syndrome and every article advised me to run fast. Junior met the bulk of the symptoms, but not all.

I knew in my heart I would never let Junior control me to the point of losing myself, but I knew how to submit. I watched Aunt Dumpling do it with Uncle Kenny. In turn, she always got what she wanted. I was in knee deep and loving most of it.

My phone rang, and I saw Destiny's number on the screen. "Hey, Dee! What's good?" I asked.

"You know I start college in a week, even though I'm not staying on campus. Uncle Jon is having a party for me and I want you to come. Khalif is going to Penn because he's so smart, and I'm going to Temple."

"Destiny, that's wonderful news! I'm glad you're not going away. Of course I'll be there, just give me the details."

"It's this Saturday at Uncle Jon's. I invited all of my friends, and Uncle Jon is going all out. I'm so happy I don't know what to do with myself!"

"I know that's right. I would be happy too if I were you."

"Are you happy, Sis? If Junior gives you any problems, I will beat his ass for you."

"Girl, please. I am jubilant and you called at the perfect time, because Junior gave me my own woodshop! You know, my dream job. Uncle Kenny would be so proud of us."

"I know. Sometimes he shows up in my dreams. I wake up thinking he's there until I realize it was just a dream."

"What do he say? I wonder why he doesn't visit my dreams." I asked, slightly jealous of a dead man's dream.

"Let me rephrase, I just dream about him often, before you have a heart attack."

"What happens in your dreams?" I was dying to know.

"Alright, one time I dreamt he forced us to watch the Super Bowl. My mom was in the kitchen cooking, and you asked if we could go upstairs to play. He said, "Fuck dem punk ass Barbie dolls, this here is history, girls. Nah, y'all staying your little asses right here with me."

"He was always cussing. You're just like him," I responded.

"I know," she laughed. "He would always threaten to whip our little asses, but never followed through. I remember when you called him out and dared him to beat you. You even went in their room, got the belt, and said," "Whip my ass, Uncle Kenny. I dare you with your punk ass." "He was so mad that day and I honestly thought you were a goner."

"I remember not caring. I wanted to sleep over Jennifer's house and he said no, as usual, so I went off."

"Yes you did! And you talk about my mouth. I called to tell you something else, and I'm crossing my fingers you won't get mad."

"What? Tell me!"

"I went to see Daddy's son, and he looks just like him," she said. She called Uncle Kenny daddy because he was the only father she had known.

"I'm not mad, Dee, but I'm not ready for that."

"I figured you would say that, but when you are, I'll go with you. He's so cute and came right to me when I picked him up. We got us a handsome little brother."

"I bet," I replied, unenthused. "What's his name?"

"He's a junior. His name is Kenny."

"I'll let you know about that, but I will be at your party. What should I bring as a gift? It's not like you need anything."

"I don't, but I saw these diamond earrings I want. I would ask Uncle Jon, but he's already doing so much with the party."

"I tell you what. I'll get them as my going-away-to-college gift, and we can spend some time together before the party. I miss you. I know I've been preoccupied with Junior, but now I can relate to the way you felt about Khalif."

"You must feel wonderful. Khalif will marry me, and I hope Junior has the same plan."

"We'll see. I'll call you Friday."

"That's what's up. I'll see you then." She hung up.

Junior left for work, but my first day wasn't until Monday. I called Jeff to make sure he was on board. He said yes and that he had a few workers in mind. Jeff estimated that five men would get the job done. I had interviews set up, but I trusted Jeff and if he wanted to put his men down, I had no problem with that.

I went into the kitchen and placed some turkey wings in the oven, knowing they would take forever to cook. I bought all the ingredients for my own strawberry margarita and hoped it tasted as good as Uncle Jon's. When I took a sip, I was pleased. I turned on Junior's surround sound stereo system and surfed all the XM stations. I found the old school R&B and sat in the living room. *Chante Moore's I Gotta a Man at Home* blared through the speakers, and I remembered Aunt Dumpling loved this song. When she played it, I'd be upstairs singing along, wishing for the day I had a man at home. Junior was complicated, and we stayed on shaky ground, but he was my man. The music continued to get better. *Jagged Edge, I Want to Get Married* followed, and I was in my private circle of love.

A knock at the door broke my groove. "Who is it?" I asked.

"It's Calvin, Ms. Chasity. Junior explained that I'm not to leave for any reason, and I need to use the bathroom."

"Of course, Calvin," I replied and opened the door. "It's down the hall on your right."

"I know where is. Thank you, Ms. Chasity," he responded.

"Calvin, please call me Chasity. I'm only twenty-two. That makes me feel old."

"As you wish," he replied and headed to the bathroom.

"Would you like a sandwich, Calvin? I know you must be hungry," I asked when he came back into the room.

"No thank you. I'll get something when my shift is over."

"And what time is that?" I asked, knowing Junior might be home late.

"When Junior gets here."

"Who knows what time that'll be? I'll make you a quick sandwich and no one has to know. I won't take no for an answer."

"If you say so, Chasity. I am starved."

"I knew it. I can't have my protector running around hungry. That could interfere with your performance," I joked. I had just purchased fresh rolls from the market and I made him a healthy turkey and cheese sandwich. I handed him a bottled water, but he insisted on eating outside. That was probably for the best because if Junior came home early and saw that, who knows how cray-cray would react.

I returned to my strawberry margarita and the next song that came on was *Anthony Hamilton's Cool*. Uncle Kenny used to sing this song to Aunt Dumpling when she was mad at him. He'd sing, *If you're cool, then I'm cool, then we're cool. Quit your worrying, Dumpling – aaaaaaaaaaaaw, quit your worrying girl.* I stood up and gyrated my hips to the smooth beat, performing as if I were on someone's stage. I was so into the song that when Junior snuck up behind me, he scared the shit out of me.

"So this is what you do when you're alone. Exotic dancing, babe? Dance for me," he requested.

"You sure you can handle it? I wouldn't want you to get upset when you see my moves."

"I saw your moves when you danced with Track," he said, with his face slightly distorted.

"If you keep bringing that up, we will have a problem," I replied, ready to attack.

"Dance with me." He wrapped me into his embrace, and we slow grinded to *Nothing Even Matters*, by *Lauryn Hill* and *D'Angelo*. "You've been on mind since I left you this morning. It's my hope you will consider starting tomorrow and take me out my misery," he whispered as he gazed in my eyes.

"You can't stay away from me now, can you?" I asked, unrestrained by his touch.

"Nope, so what's up? You rolling with me tomorrow?"

"Yes, but I need to take Friday off, because I promised Destiny I would treat her to a pair of diamond earrings. She's having her graduation party this weekend, and I need to be there." As soon as I said it, it was as if the music stopped, because he loosened me. His mind was on overload, and I waited to hear how going shopping with Destiny was not a good idea.

"When were you planning to inform me?" His mood dissipated quickly as he scratched the top of his head.

"When you got home. I just found out today when she called to invite us to her party. I have to get her a gift, and now that I can afford it, I want to make up for her graduation," I explained.

"Earrings, huh? We can go to my jeweler, and she can select what she wants."

"She wants to spend alone time with me. I'm positive she would not take kindly to you tagging along. What's the problem?" I asked with a baffled expression, even though I was fully aware of why he was mad.

"I see you tryna start shit so I'll give you some time," he replied and went into the bedroom. I just shook my head, because I had every intention of going out with my sister.

Instead of chasing after him, I checked on the turkey wings. They needed another forty-five minutes. I put on a pot of rice and sautéed broccoli in butter and garlic. I turned up the radio and made another margarita when I finished preparing the food. I turned the radio up as I sipped my delicious drink and changed the station to old school rap. Uncle Kenny was a music connoisseur, and he taught me to love that time in music. DMX was blazing through the speakers when I heard Iron Man summoning me.

"Chasity, come here now," he yelled.

Of course, I ignored his request because the margarita said fuck him. If he wants me, he can bring his old, controlling ass in here. I danced and sang along, "What these bitches want from a nigga, rrrrra—what these bitch—."

"Chasity, did you hear me calling you? I know you heard me." He answered his own question.

I turned the music down and said, "You wanted me?"

"What's really good with you? I come home early because you been on my mind, but this isolating and now ignoring me? Tell me what game we're playing now."

Suddenly, the liquor halted my brain and in a second, drunkenness consumed me. I stared at Junior, swaying from side-to-side. It was time to give him a taste of his own medicine. "Is that a passion mark on your neck, bastard? You messing around on me already Junior?"

"Fuck you talking about? You put this shit on me."

"I don't suck that hard, liar. I bet it's a one of those model chicks you got walking around your office."

"Let me save you before you start drowning," he replied as he strolled towards me. "It's obvious you can't control your liquor." He grabbed the glass out of my hand. "This," he said, referring to my margarita, "is a no-no. Where's the rest so I can get rid of it?" He stormed into the kitchen before I could answer and found the bottle of vodka and margarita mix. I heard him pouring it down the drain.

"Why are you pouring my liquor out? You are too controlling, Junior. You're suffocating and stifling me. Maybe Uncle Jon was right, I should stay with him and see you whenever."

"Whenever, huh? How quickly we forget. Just the other night you vowed your obedience. Oh, I got it now, you only listen when I'm fucking you. You love my dick more than you love me."

I was drunk, but not intoxicated to where I didn't recognize reverse psychology. "You're a control freak and that's all you need to know. As of today, I'm no longer on house arrest, and I will drive my car and live again," I replied with my hand on my hip as I rolled my neck. It was time to identify if he was a violent control freak or a non-violent one. I could barely deal with control period, but to add physical abuse was intolerable.

"You know what. Do whatever you want. Leave, stay, drink. I don't give a fuck. And since I'm only good for one thing, I'm not giving you no more of this." He grabbed his dick. "It's time for me to pull back. You will no longer invade my space or monopolize my time. What the hell is burning?" he asked, sniffing the air.

"Your dinner. Enjoy, asshole." I stormed off into the bedroom. I hated his place because there was no privacy and nowhere to hide. I jumped into the bed, pulled the comforter over my head, and went to bed early.

The next morning, I woke up in Junior's hold. Somewhere between the night and the sunrise, Junior found his way back home. I never felt him embrace me through the night, but I was overjoyed that he did.

"Where are you going?" he asked as I attempted to get out of the bed.

"To the bathroom. Shouldn't you be getting ready for work?"

"You coming?" he asked in a childlike voice I could not deny.

"Yes, but I need to stop by my house and pick up a few things."

"That's cool, is it okay if I join you in the shower?" he asked, which was unlike him because he rarely asked permission. His specialty was demanding and regulating.

"Sure, I would love that. Hurry up before I change my mind," I teased, knowing what he wanted. Unexpectedly, he refrained from touching me, other than when he washed my back. "Junior, you don't want no loving before we leave?" I asked, hopeful.

"We have plenty of time for that. You're my woman, and I can have you anytime I want—right?"

"Yes, anytime!"

"Good, let's pick up the pace," he replied and stepped out of the shower.

When we arrived at my house, I unarmed the alarm as soon as we stepped in and everything appeared to be intact. I told Junior to make himself at home while I checked out the place.

"I'm going with you, superwoman. You don't know what can lurk inside these walls," he explained.

"Fine, have it your way," I replied as I walked into the kitchen. I opened the fridge and the foul smell almost knocked me out. I knew I had to clean it before I left. Junior followed me upstairs, and I checked Destiny's room first. When I stood in front of Uncle Kenny and Aunt Dumpling's room, I paused.

"What's wrong, babe? You okay?" Junior asked.

"I hate going into this room," I replied.

"I'll check the room, baby." I waited in the hallway until Junior came out and then escorted him into my bedroom. I watched as he surveyed my belongings, and his eyes focused in on my end tables. "Damn, those tables are superb," he said as he further inspected them.

"I made them," I proudly stated. "That was the first project I did without Uncle's Kenny help. He was so proud of me. You would've thought I hit the lottery instead of made tables."

"I'm proud too, and this makes me feel confident with you running the woodshop. I'm impressed, Chass. You shock me each day." I smiled, because just last night, he was over me. I grabbed the duffel bag out of my closet and threw as much clothes and shoes as I could fit into it. I grabbed my journal and the pictures from Uncle Kenny's safe.

"Once I clean the fridge we can leave," I explained as we went back downstairs. Junior helped me clean out the refrigerator, making it go much faster, and I enjoyed watching him do domestic work. "Junior, I want my table upstairs to go in my new office. I was thinking they'll fit inside your truck, and I can follow you to work."

"That wondrous mind of yours is always ticking, but I'm trying to keep up. Give me the keys and I'll make sure you get the tables, Chasity. Issue resolved."

"But I need my uncle's truck too. Face it, Junior, your condo is too small for my two cars and all your stuff. We should stay here. I'm tired of not knowing where I belong. I need to be in one residence."

"You belong with me, wherever that may be. You might want to think about selling or renting this place," he responded.

"Why would I do that, Junior? I mean, you can put me out anytime you want. I need to have something to fall back on. So, I take it you don't want to live here."

"That would be correct. I'm a city boy, babe. But let me work on something. I'm tired of you complaining about space and privacy. For now, we have to make the condo work. Deal?"

"Fine, but only because I love you." He smiled while bear hugging me. We left for the office but I was uneasy about it, knowing we would be the talk of the office.

We arrived at the job, and I couldn't help but recall our escapade in the woodshop. Junior held my hand as he escorted me inside. Everyone happily spoke, but did a double take when they saw him holding my hand. He smiled and greeted them all back, which had me delirious. During the short time I worked for him as an intern, he never spoke to anyone.

"We're going up to my office first, then we can work out the rest of the day," he said as I followed him.

"Junior, I hate to dampen the mood, but we need to figure out shopping with Destiny tomorrow. I want to hang out with my sister alone," I pleaded

"I know you do, but we can't always get what we want when we want it. I'm sure there will come a time when that will be possible. You're right, don't dampen the mood, baby. You'll have your shopping trip, but you won't be alone. It will just feel like you are, okay?"

"Umhum," I pouted. "What am I supposed to do all day, Junior?"

"You can start by giving me an early morning treat," he replied devilishly.

"Sorry, but I can't."

"Fuck is you talking bout? You pretend to be sleep and don't give me none last night, and now you continue to reject me. What's really good, ma?"

"I offered this morning but you turned me down, and now it's too late because my period came on when we were my house."

"Fuck! I wanted some meat before I started my day. Why didn't you tell me?"

"I didn't know my period was the headline news of the day. I figured I'd tell you when the time was right, which is now. Please don't tell me you have a problem with something I can't control. God is responsible, so you need to deal with him." I rolled my eyes.

"Chill, I'm just saying if I knew, I wouldn't have gotten my hopes up. It's cool, babe, now I know. If you want to go check out your new workplace, knock yourself out," he replied. Before I walked out the door he said, "And Chass, don't leave the property. If you need something, call me. Also, try to limit your contact with the men around here. Until everyone knows that you're off limits and mine, be cool. I'm sure you wouldn't want their unemployment on your head." I glared at him as if he had bumped his square head. I must have stood there a minute too long, because he followed up with, "Are you well?"

"Yes, but you're clearly sick," I said and exited his office.

Once I entered the shop, I admired the equipment and thought about all the stuff I could create. Equipped with every machine imaginable, I was ready to craft my way to Heaven. I noticed furniture in my office that was not their last night. I examined the tacky desk and chair, knowing Junior was responsible. Before I became further disgusted, the phone on top of the desk rung.

"Hello?" I answered.

"Are you upset with me? I hope not, because I won't be able to get any work done, and I have some important phone calls to make. You cool?" Junior asked.

"I'm cool, but very bored. And who told you to put this ugly desk in my office?"

"If you don't like it, I'll have it removed immediately. My bad."

"Please do, I want to make my desk."

"A ton of wood is due to arrive this morning. As soon as I get the word, I'll call you back. I hope you can get started on that desk today to occupy your boredom. It's going to be a long day, baby, so strap in and I'll check on you soon." He hung up before I could protest.

I waited all day, but wood never came. I called Jeff, and he assured me he had a few reliable men in need of work. Junior explained that the company would handle the accounting, but I had to provide the workers. A five-man team would be sufficient, along with a receptionist. While I was off in Neverland, my cell phone rang and it was Destiny.

"What's up Dee? I was about to call you. Tomorrow's shopping trip is turning out to be more trouble than I anticipated. Junior wants to come along or have security there. I just wanted one normal day, spending time with my little sis."

"I know, but Uncle Jon thinks it for the best. You know, I don't care who comes along. Maybe I'll get more gifts. I say the more the merrier."

"So you don't mind if he comes?"

"No, he can come. And by the way, you almost messed up the shopping spree when Junior called Uncle Jon last night."

"Why did he call him?"

"To say how you want to risk our lives to be alone. Uncle Jon was livid, saying you're just like your mom and that the shopping trip was off. I had to think of something quick, but you know I saved the day. I'll see you and Junior in the morning. I can't wait," she said and hung up.

Junior gets on my nerves with this control shit. Now he got Uncle Jon thinking I am defiant. I was tired of being a prisoner in someone else's home. Honestly, I didn't think Track would hurt me. He wanted Junior dead, but he wanted me as his woman. I failed to recognize the need for all my protection. I understood what Junior was saying, but how much could one person take? The office phone rung, and I knew it was only one person.

"Hey, Junior. What's up?"

"You and everything about you. Come upstairs, we're about to leave," he requested.

"Okay, see you soon." Instead of going home, Junior took me to Uncle Jon's, and I wondered what was up. "Why are we here, babe? The party is not until Saturday."

"Chasity, you said you wanted to go shopping with your sister and spend more time with her."

"Aww that's so sweet Junior. I do miss chilling with her. Are you staying with me?" I asked.

"Nah!" he spat. "I mean, your period is on, and I can't be around you without touching you."

"I can remember a time you were afraid to touch me. You brought me here because of my period? I can't believe you. Your mind is really twisted. Just so you know, I get a period every month. Is this what I have to look forward to?"

"Yes, for now, until I work that out. Don't get mad, Chass. You'll see me every day."

"I don't care," I barked as I got out of the car and slammed the door.

"Yo! Why you tripping?" he yelled after me, but I was already inside the house.

That next morning, Destiny woke me up early, saying Junior was downstairs waiting for us. I showered and picked one of Destiny's outfits to wear, then met Junior in the kitchen. He was watching the news while helping himself to the breakfast cooked by Uncle Jon's private chef.

"Did you sleep well, babe?" Junior asked.

"Sure did. Actually, it was the best sleep I had in weeks," I replied, grabbing a croissant with the chocolate filling inside. He ignored my sarcasm and continued to watch the news. Destiny came in and we left shortly after.

At the jewelry store, I realized I left my wallet with all my credit cards at Junior's. I hated to ask him for the money since I planned to give him the cold shoulder.

"Junior, can I talk to you for a minute?"

"Talk," he replied, slightly agitated.

"I promised Destiny I would get her a pair of diamond earrings and I left my card back at your place. Can you loan me the money until we get home?" I asked.

"Yeah, I got you. You can come back tonight. I prefer you near than far. I'm glad to hear you slept well, because I got none."

"That's for being an asshole, but I forgive you," I replied, but we both knew I was being untruthful.

"Destiny, pick out whatever you want," he instructed.

"Whatever?!" she responded excitedly, and I knew he wanted to take it back.

"Within in reason, but enjoy yourself," he responded.

Destiny walked away with a pair of two-carat diamond studs, a pair of diamond hoops, a tennis bracelet, and a heart shaped pendant made with pink diamonds. He asked if I wanted something but I declined, still acting stank. I was only hurting myself because I wanted a pair of those diamond hoops.

"Thank you so much, Junior, and Chasity. I can't wait to take some selfies with my new bling," Destiny said, happy as a butterfly.

"Anytime, Destiny. I never welcomed you to the family, so please accept this small token as a belated gift."

"I accept!" she said loudly. "Chass, you should get something, you know you want to."

"Trust me Dee, I'm good. The thrill is gone, but I'm happy you're happy. I'm ready if you don't want anything else, Destiny."

"Come here," Junior demanded, escorting me out of the store. "This toddler behavior and fucked up attitude stops now. I don't like that shit, and I hate cussing at you to get my point across, but it's like that's the only language you understand or respond to. We both know you want something. Take my card and go shopping. I'll be waiting in the food court so you can spend time with Destiny. Calvin will give you enough space that you won't even know he's there. Happy now?" he asked.

"Whatever." I brushed him off.

"Nah, fuck that whatever shit. Give me an answer before you upset me further." This was one of those times where you ate the cake like Anna Mae.

"Yes," I replied as I snatched the card out of his hands. "Come on, Destiny."

Three hours later and exhausted, Destiny and I finished our shopping spree. Junior was on the phone when we arrived at the food court, but as soon as he spotted us he hung up and strolled over.

"From the looks of all the bags, you ladies appear to have enjoyed yourselves."

"I did, I love shopping. One can never have enough clothes," Destiny responded.

"What about you, baby? Are you happy?"

"Yes, Junior," I replied, trying to be convincing, but he knew I was placating him. When we got back to the house, Destiny wanted me to spend the night and surprisingly, Junior stayed too.

The next day, Uncle Jon was overflowing with joy as he gave Destiny a party suited for the stars. It was a beautiful August day, and he spared no expense. Destiny invited the entire graduating class from her school, and Uncle Jon transformed the backyard into paradise. The pool was full of aspiring young adults laughing and playing. As the deejay played the music, the dance floor lit up with each beat and changed colors accordingly. The massive pink tent that covered the buffet had an array of food. There were several food stations, from seafood, to Italian, to soul food. Uncle Jon even had a chef handling the grill for all your hamburger, ribs, and hot dog needs.

"Pops went ballistic," Junior commented.

"I know, right. I'm definitely playing on the wrong team."

"What?" Junior spat.

"Did I say that out loud?" I smirked.

"It would benefit you to remember what side you chose because there ain't no turning back now." He looked at me sideways.

"Trust me, Junior I'm aware of the prison and custodial care I chose."

"Good, so we understand each other," he replied, being a smart ass.

"I know I'm about to get turned up at this graduation party. You can stand over here and let your mind wonder off to Never-Never Land." I left him standing in my dust while I went to stir up more trouble. I knew my next move would cause a whole commotion.

I went to my room and took a quick shower. I inserted a fresh tampon and changed into the bathing suit I purchased with Destiny at the mall. I stared at myself in the mirror and admired the yellow two-piece string bikini. It definitely left nothing to the imagination, and it was the perfect tool to fuck up Junior. He thought I forgot about him reprimanding me at the mall, but it was still fresh on my mind, and it was time to strike back.

When I got outside, I surveyed my surroundings and people were everywhere. The football field backyard filled with graduates, their parents, and Uncle Jon's business associates was the perfect game location. I walked out and the young boys, including the white ones, took notice. I made my way over to the pool and dipped my foot into the water to see how cold it was.

"Pumpkin," Uncle Jon summoned me. "Here's my beautiful niece, though I prefer her with a little more clothes on." *Not you too, Uncle Jon,* I thought. "Did Junior see you dressed like this?"

"Not yet, but it's a pool party, Uncle Jon. Everyone has on their bathing suits, so I don't see the problem."

"Yes, they do, but none quite like this. I'm waiting on Destiny's gift to arrive but if you need protection, you can find me in my study."

"Protection from what? I can't get no more protected than I already am, Uncle Jon."

"When Junior finally spots you, just run to me," he said as he walked away.

From every angle of the backyard, multiple guests stared at me. I ignored them and went over to the buffet. I placed some crab cakes and shrimp on my plate and headed back out the tent. As I was devouring the delicious seafood, I saw Junior on the other side of the backyard talking to a couple of men. He was oblivious to what I had on, that is until his friends gawked at me, and Junior turned around to see what they saw. His expression went from calm to garbled, and if looks could kill, I would be six feet under.

He made his way towards me with speed. I placed the plate on the table and hurried to the pool. I could feel him getting close, but I refused to see that awful look on his face. It was too late to turn back now.

"Chasity." I heard him say, but I jumped into the cold pool and instantly regretted it. However, I continued to ignore him.

"Can I play?" I asked the graduates, who were engaging in a game of volleyball.

"Sure, we could always use another player," a Justin Bieber look-a-like answered.

Before I could take my position, I felt an arm wrap around me and a kiss on my neck. "Be cool, I don't want to embarrass you in front of all these people," Junior whispered. "Sorry guys, but she'll catch you all another time," he stated as he turned me around to face him. "You're rebellious and spiteful, but I got something for that ass in a week. Showtime is over. Pops," he yelled when Uncle Jon came back. "Can you bring us a couple of towels?"

"It would be my pleasure, Son," Uncle Jon replied, looking at me with that I told you so face.

"Chass, you really bugging the fuck out. You had to know I would have a problem with this when you took it off the rack. Therefore, the only logical excuse is, you're trying to test me, and I forewarned you about that. Now, I'm angry." When he said that, Uncle Jon came back with the towels. "Cover yourself up and go straight inside the house," he demanded. I remained silent the whole time, not wanting to ruin Destiny's party with me and Junior's dysfunctional relationship, but I had every intention on setting him straight once we were alone.

I did as he wished and went up to my room. I spotted Carlton talking on the phone at the other end of the hall, but when she saw me, she quickly hung up. She waved as if it was nothing, but that bitch looked suspect. Maybe Destiny was on point with her observation. Before I could contemplate any further, Hurricane pushed me into the room.

"Junior, what is your problem? Don't be pushing on me," I spat, ready to whip his ass. I never got into a fight until I had to beat Kali, but I knew how to hold my hands. Uncle Kenny taught me how to box, specifically to defend myself against boys, and that is why Kali received a man's ass whipping.

"You're the one with the problem," he responded as he backed me against the wall and wrapped his hands around my neck. He had me so hot, and I was mad that my period was on because this would have been the perfect time for him to beat up my pussy. "Do I look like a child to you?" He tightened his grip around my neck, and I was seconds away from gasping. "Answer!"

"I can't because you're choking me," I replied. I started rolling my eyes around in my head, trying to appear as if I was about to pass out, which only angered him further.

"This is the shit I'm talking about with your dramatic ass," he said as he shoved me on the bed by the neck. He was on top of me before I could recover from the slight vertigo episode I had just encountered. He pinned my hands down and stared at me with a crazed love visage. "I want to fuck you up so bad, Chasity. You hear me?" he asked while squeezing my wrists snugger. "I want to fuck you up for wearing this G-string bikini in public. I gave you a specific dress code to abide by, but you! You want me back in jail, don't you?"

"No I don't, Junior. I love you and you know that."

"You let that word roll off of your tongue with ease, but your actions are deceptive. I'm not convinced of this love you proclaim for me. You know me enough to know that this get-up would not go over well. You know me enough to know that I have your best interest at heart, and I'm trying to make you happy. Finally, you don't know me enough to know my anger or my wrath. Please don't ever disrespect me like that again. I know you're fearless, but you don't want none of this," he explained, never taking his disgruntled eyes off me.

"I'm sorry. I just wanted to get into the pool and enjoy myself. Everyone else had on bathing suits."

"It wasn't about getting into the pool, baby. You deliberately tried to get under my skin. I know you, and I'm on to your shenanigans. You'd be wise to follow that one command. You see, some men like to flaunt their woman's body and show that they have the best eye candy. Not me, I don't want no man looking at you in a lustful manner. You're my woman, and no other man will appreciate you the way I do. Trust me on that. Your body is beautiful and sexy, designed for me only. I know what I got and don't take kindly to you informing others. You caused a spectacle out there, and I can't have that." He released my wrists and snuggled next to me.

"Junior, do you love me? If you said it, it would make all the difference. I feel it inside, but I would like confirmation."

"You know how I feel about you. Action speaks louder than words, and that's where I got you. You tell me how much you love me, but you never really show me. You're a struggle to deal with. Me, my actions are clear, so I hope that answers your question," he replied, nibbling on my ear. "I want you so bad, baby. When do your period go off so you can receive your punishment?"

"Not for a couple of days, but I can help you out in another way."

"How?" he asked, curious as a cat. I pointed to my mouth and then to his penis. "You're not ready for that, Chass. I can't have your lack of knowledge in that department around my dick, sweetheart. I would have to teach you."

"There's no better time like the present," I replied as I pulled at his wet shorts. When he didn't resist, I unzipped his shorts and pulled out the best part of him. I massaged his meaty sausage, bringing it to its full potential before I bent down and began the process of sucking a dick.

I started out with just the head, sucking and licking as if it were a lollipop. I peeped up and saw him make faces of enjoyment, which I had never witnessed before. I continued to devour his manhood, providing him with uncontrollable pleasure.

"That's right baby, you're doing good. It feels so good," he moaned. I was going in hard, as if I was a pro. After a while, Junior began assisting me my pushing my head further down his immense penis. It went downhill after that because I didn't have a deep throat. I started choking on it and he hollered, "Fuck, Chasity! You bit my dick, man. Stop, I told you, you weren't ready," he spat while holding his dick as if he were protecting it from me.

"I'm sorry, Junior, but you shouldn't have grabbed my head. You don't have a little penis, and I was trying to take my time," I replied, embarrassed that I had failed.

"I think you fractured my dick," he said, inspecting it like the value it was. "It's cool, babe. I knew it was too soon for that, but you were aggressive so I gave in. You just need a little more practice. In the meantime, I'll just have to wait until your visitor leaves to enjoy that sweet pussy of yours," he responded and kissed me on the forehead. At the time, it was an unwanted gesture, a pat on the back for a good try.

"I'll do better next time, I promise."

"That's cool, baby. Listen, I'm ready to leave this place. You fulfilled your obligation to Destiny, and it's time to bounce. Put on some real clothes, and meet me downstairs so you can say your goodbyes."

"Junior, the party won't be ending no time soon. What are we going to do when we get back to the condo? I want to stay a little while longer."

"I know you do, but you should've thought about that before you decided to bare my essentials to the world. I'm still mad, but I do care a great deal about your feelings, and I prefer for you to be happy rather than sad. However, we're still leaving, so get dressed quickly." He got off the bed, buttoned his pants, and left out the room.

When I reached the backyard, Destiny was opening up her gifts and Uncle Jon was right by her side. I didn't want to disturb her happy moment, so I searched for Junior and silently left to destination Ice Cave.

Chapter 27

Kenny

C hasity was leaving for college soon, and I still felt as if I didn't have enough time with her. She had bought so much joy into my life, and seeing her go away reminded me of when I lost her as a baby. Over the years, I tried to find the similarities between us, but she was her mother's twin. She was the spitting image of Cat, and it was damn right eerie. Dumpling held us all down, and I would be eternally grateful for her loyalty and dedication. I went to have a talk with Chasity before she left for Lincoln University the next morning.

When I got to her room, her music was blasting, and she was dancing around the room. She had a ton of shopping bags and suitcases scattered throughout her room. The moving van would come in handy because all of her stuff wouldn't fit into my truck.

"I see someone is happy to be leaving the nest!" I said.

"I am happy, but I'm not happy about leaving you, Uncle Kenny. You're my rock and I love you so much. Are you crying?" she asked.

"Hell nah. You got those candles burning and they're messing with my eyes."

"Yeah, right. I see those tears in your eyes. Just man up and tell me how much you will miss me, and how your life will be hell without me," she replied, being flip. That's how I always knew she was mine. She looked just like Cathy, but she had my DNA with that slick tongue of hers.

"I see someone is full of themselves, but straight up, I need to holler at you. Turn the music off and let's talk." She obeyed and plopped on her bed, knowing it was time for one of our many hearts to hearts. "Pumpkin, you know my love for you runs deep. You're more than a niece or a daughter, you're my everything, and it's killing me to let you go. It seems like just yesterday you were following me around like my shadow, wanting to do everything I did. Now look at you, a beautiful and intelligent young adult."

"Thank you, Unc. You can thank yourself for the way I turned out. You took me in and loved me as your own. You're the best thing that happened in my life," she cried.

"Listen, let's cut out all this mushy shit because we ain't no punks. And just like everything else we've been through, we will conquer this too. Chasity, you are a strong and unique woman. The way you think and handle situations impresses the hell out of me. It's as if we're cut from the same cloth."

"We are cut from the same cloth, Uncle Kenny. You're more than an uncle or father, you're my everything, and I will miss you," she mocked, lovingly.

"See that's that shit I love about you. When you meet your husband, he'll be one fortunate son-of-a-bitch. But let's get something clear, I don't want to meet no boyfriend of yours, unless he's asking for your hand in marriage."

"Stop already. I'm not even interested in boys, Uncle Kenny."

"You better not be interested in no girls either. I hear and see your generation, and anything goes nowadays. I'm happy to hear boys are not your priority though. I will miss you, but I knew this day was coming."

"If you don't want me to cry like a punk, you should stop now," she replied, trying to hold back her tears. But she didn't know it was me who was fighting.

"You're right. When you finish packing up, meet me downstairs. I'm taking everyone out to dinner."

"I'll be back for Thanksgiving, so don't fret, Unc. You'll see me real soon. I'll be down in a few," she responded as she turned her music back up.

Four Years Later

Chasity was excelling in school and as a result, she was graduating with honors next week. I couldn't be prouder. She was coming home and wanted to work with me, saying it was time to make her own money. She wanted to learn everything there was about carpentry, but I insisted she take business and said if she still wanted to do construction after college, she could. Now she was forcing me to follow through on our little deal. Since she left, there was an unexplainable void. I loved Destiny and Dumpling, but I still felt lonely. I resorted back to my old ways, and I was fucking around with this young girl named Yolanda. She was sexy and did things that Dumpling stopped doing a long time ago.

I had strong feelings for Yolanda, but I loved Dumpling with all my heart. The thought of losing her under any circumstances was unthinkable. She was my rock, but new pussy was so delightful. However, I worried my life was about to change, because I wasn't sure if Dumpling would forgive what I had done. I had fucked up and gotten Yolanda pregnant. I didn't condone abortions, but I was sure this would fuck up my life as I knew it. Dumpling, always exact with her intuition, had suspected I was messing around, but there's no way she knew things got this far

For the past month, I focused on getting my business affairs in order and making sure my family was good in case something happened to me. I made sure my life insurance policy was straight, and I talked to Jon to make sure he would hold my family down. I didn't have any plans to vanish, but a sinking feeling was heavy on my mind. I believed Yolanda was carrying my child, but I wasn't taking no chances. I had my DNA frozen because I planned to tell Chasity that I am her father soon, and it was also a precautionary measure for the baby Yolanda was carrying.

Two days before Chasity's graduation, I wrote two letters to Chasity and one each to Jon-Jon, Dumpling, and Yolanda. I mailed Jon his letter and included the letter for Yolanda, with specific instructions on how to handle my children.

Dumpling was extra with the constant arguing these past couple of days, and she was getting on my nerves. I had a lot shit on my mind and tried to keep my cool.

"Kenny, I know you're cheating on me, and I want a divorce," Dumpling stated, angering me on purpose, knowing I hate the word divorce.

"I'm tired of you accusing me of this shit all the time. It's like you can't sing a different tune. When you get the proof to present, then we can talk, but until then, stop fucking with me, Dumpling."

"I don't need proof, asshole! Your behavior this past year says you're cheating on me. You can deny it all you want, but after Chasity's graduation, I'm filing the paperwork. I already talked to a lawyer and saved my money to pay the fees. You gave me a lot and took care of me for most of my adult life, but I will not eat the crumbs off your mistress' plate. We've both sacrificed a lot to make this marriage work, but since you checked out, so am I."

"Whatever, Dumpling. I tell you this, that will lawyer will die, so you better know what you're doing. Stop threatening me with divorce because that's never happening. The only way you're getting rid of me is if I'm six feet under. Tell me how to make this right, baby," I said, trying to comfort her, but she rejected me.

"It's over, Kenny," she spat as she walked away from me. Although she had threatened me many times, something about the look on her face alarmed me. I pray constantly that she stays with me when I tell her about the baby. However, while I was in the shower, Yolanda called Dumpling and told her everything.

"I knew you were up to no good, you bastard! I gave up my dreams to take care of you and these kids. I allowed you to manipulate me into believing I owed you my life because you gave me a better one. A baby, Kenny? When the doctor said I couldn't have any more kids, you said you were good with that."

"I was, Dumpling. I fucked up bad. I don't blame you for wanting to leave me, but I can't breathe without you. We can fix this, baby. You're my wife, Dumpling. We took a vow for better or worse," I pleaded.

"You know, I always thought that part was overrated and misinterpreted. I've been here for better or worse, bitch, but I will not stick around for disrespect. Let's get through Chasity's graduation, and when things settle down, we'll talk to the girls. I think it's best we leave your adulterous behavior and that bastard baby a secret for now. I can't imagine how Chasity and Destiny will react, knowing their super hero is the scum of the earth."

"Don't drag them into our dirty laundry. We can work this out between the two of us," I warned. Nevertheless, my expression didn't go off well, and she looked at me like *nigga please*. We were running late, so we put it to the side and hit the road. My baby was graduating, and I couldn't miss it for the world.

An hour into the drive, Dumpling broke down inside the car. She bawled and talked shit to herself, but she got my attention when she said, Bill, the young boy who cuts the grass, ate her pussy.

"I shoulda let Bill have his way with me instead of just eating my pussy. Then maybe this shit wouldn't hurt so bad!" she cried.

"What the fuck did you say?" I asked, ready to whip her ass.

"You heard me! I shoulda let him fuck me, you cheating dog," she repeated.

"You shoulda let him fuck you?" I repeated. "You let this bum nigga eat your pussy?" I yelled. Without giving it a second thought, I smacked the shit out of her, which was my biggest mistake.

"You're hitting people now, motherfucker?" Her ungodly response revealed that my relationship was over. She regained consciousness and threw a left hook.

The car swerved, but she continually hit me. I tried to get control of the car while blocking her blows, but was unsuccessful. I hit the back of a moving truck, and the next thing I knew the car flipped over several times. On impact, I knew we wouldn't make it. I looked over at Dumpling's barely visible face and said, "I love you my wife." She stared at me and closed her eyes. *Damn.* A few moments later, everything went dark.

Chapter 28

Jon-Jon

Twelve years earlier

"Jon! I found King over at a motel in Camden, and he's not alone, either. I hate to be the bearer of bad news, but Renee is in there with him," Calvin advised.

"Perfect. I can kill two birds with one with stone. You sure she's there?" I asked.

"Yeah. We followed him from the pool hall, and she pulled up to the motel shortly after. How you want to handle this boss? You know Jersey could pose a problem if we go over there shooting up the place," Calvin responded.

"You make a good point, but I have a quieter plan. One that will leave no traces of us, and one which they truly deserve. Renee, what the fuck! None of these bitches are loyal."

"You had a loyal one in Leila. She was one of kind."

"I agree. I need to make a stop first. Call in more reinforcements in case we encounter opposition."

"I already got that covered. I just needed you to say the word. We out," Calvin replied. "It will be two in the morning when we reach the motel. They should be asleep, but just in case, I'm prepared," he said as he screwed on a silencer. I have a little care package in the trunk and the spare key to their room. Just say the word," Calvin explained.

"Word, nigga, let's do this," I replied.

The room was dark inside as Calvin and I stood outside and listened. He discreetly unlocked the door, pushed it open, and turned on the lights. I quickly closed the door behind us and stared King and my adulterous wife in the face. It had been a month and a half since Tray and Cat's murders, and I had finally found the ingrate. A week after their deaths, I received a tape in the mail of my wife and King, compliments of Tray. I sat on the information, but tonight was the perfect time to put them both on blast.

"Wake up, pussy. You too, bitch!" I barked, and when they saw Calvin and me standing over them, they knew it was their last day on God's great earth.

"Jon, please! It's not what you think. He forced me to come. He said if I didn't he would kill you. I was just protecting you," Renee begged.

"Save your excuses for the devil, whore. I'm done with you. King, you have two options, my man. You can either take one to the head, or go out high as a kite," I explained, showing him the pure heroin I had in my hand.

"Fuck you, Jon. You already know you're gonna have to shoot me, nigga."

"Have it your way," I responded as I pointed the gun to his head.

"No, please Jon. We'll take the drugs," Renee pleaded.

"That's a good girl. Now, come to daddy and sit in this chair," I instructed. Calvin prepared enough heroin for the ride of their lives. They were lucky I was being so kind. "King, shot to the head? Or a more logical route?" I asked again.

"Fuck you. I've been fucking your bitch since the day you said I do, nigga. I killed Tray and Cat for the hell of it. I don't give a fuck about dying," he spat.

"I knew you would feel that way." I placed the gun in Renee's hand and fired two shots to King's head.

"Please, Jon don't do this. I'm so sorry for deceiving you. I'll disappear and you'll never see me again."

"Baby, you should've thought about that before you deceived me. I gave you everything, and you betrayed me for this loser. Listen, this will be painless, and don't worry, since you enjoy fucking King so much, you can pick up where you left off in hell." Calvin administered the heroin, and we watched her die. Out of respect, I held her hand to let her know she was not alone.

"Boss, let me tidy up. You can catch a ride back with Bullet and his crew," Calvin said.

"Thanks, man. Your loyalty means everything. I lost good friends in Tray and Cat, but now they can rest in peace."

Present Day

My decision to end Track's life had me somewhat torn. I took him in and gave him a spot on the team, knowing King didn't give a fuck about the young lad. I had intended to speak to Junior about a truce since there was no real beef, just a misunderstanding. However, word on the street is that the Blake's are all dead according to this belligerent fool. Each day I thanked God I left the drug game alone. When I think about the idiots running things now, it's no wonder there are senseless killing sprees in the city almost every night.

"Hey, Calvin. I've been sitting here thinking about how to handle Track. The streets are talking, and I really don't care for what they got to say. We have a slight problem that needs to be taken care of ASAP."

"I know where he lays his head. Just tell me how you want to handle it. He's having a birthday party next week. From what I hear, he went all out," Calvin replied.

"Taking his life on his birthday is not my cup of tea. I'm not getting any enjoyment out this, and I wish he would've left Junior alone. I'm trying to live a peaceful and happy life, but this punk wants to start a war he can't win. No, I want this done immediately. He won't make it to his party. Give me until tomorrow to work out everything. I'll call you in the morning. And Calvin? I will always be grateful and indebted to you."

"Your fam, Jon. You know how we do," he replied as he left.

"Carlton," I yelled, and magically she appeared. "Damn, that was quick. Were you standing outside my study?" I asked.

"No, I just walked up, wondering why you're taking so long. I want to make love and you're playing games."

"That's all you have to say! We need to talk first. All these trips and vacations you take have to stop. No more. The next time you travel, it will be with me. Where is Anastasia? I haven't seen her in forever."

"She's with my mother. She wanted to stay and play with my nieces. Come on baby, let me show you how much I missed you," she seductively said, and I followed her lead.

Chapter 29

Track

I made a large profit over the weekend, and the extra money would come in handy for the big birthday bash I was hosting next week. I had the drug game on lock in North Philly and was about to expand my empire by taking over Southwest. My soldiers were going hard and bringing in paper by any means. I loved my life, but I was missing something of substance. She was indisposed, and I had to change that. She was feeling me at Junior's birthday party, but I would have left her alone had Junior respected me. And the incident at Fat Larry's proved to me that this nigga had to go. He should've stayed in the construction lane. But since he wants to crossover, I'll remind him what a street nigga is.

"Boss, she's here," Tweet said.

"Send her in," I instructed. A few minutes later, a vision of loveliness walked in, but she wasn't the main course, just a quick appetizer. "Carlton, baby. What's up?" I greeted her with a hug.

"I'm pissed at you. Why didn't show up at the cabin? I went overboard for your ungrateful ass," she spat.

"Hold on, baby. I called and told you I couldn't make it. I thought you understood. I mean, I really do appreciate all the trips and effort you put into making me happy, but sometimes my business takes precedence. I tell you what. Let me take you somewhere new and exciting. What about Italy?" I suggested, knowing that would never happen unless she was paying.

"That might help you out, but that's not the reason I'm here. I came to warn you."

"Warn me about what?" I asked, fully tuned in to what she had to say.

"Jon-Jon is planning to kill you and anyone who looks like you. I heard him talking about it yesterday, and he was on the phone all morning."

"Hold on a minute. Tweet!" I yelled. He was in my office within seconds. "You gotta hear this shit. Carlton just informed me that Jon-Jon got a hit out on me, because I know his punk ass won't do it himself. Please, Carlton, tell us this big plan to end my life," I pleaded.

"I don't know everything, but this morning I heard him talking about the basketball team you sponsor and the upcoming game this weekend. One of his business associates owns the security company you hired. He's planning on replacing them with his men," she snitched.

"This is some good information, Carlton. I must say, it's the best news I heard all day. Thank you for your loyalty. I'll find a creative way to reward you. You're more than just a good fuck, you're an awesome ally as well."

"I care about you more than you care about me, but I'm willing to give you more time. If you told me to pack up my stuff and move with you right now, I would do it in a heartbeat. Anyway, I have to get back, but I wanted to warn you."

"Not so fast, sweetheart. Tweet, can you give us a moment." When he left, I grabbed Carlton, bent her over my desk, and pulled up her skirt. She was wearing a white lace thong, and when she rose her leg up, I dropped my pants quickly and went in for the kill. "You missed this dick, didn't you?" I asked as I inoculated her vagina walls.

"Yes, Track. You're the best lover," she moaned.

"Better than grandpa Jon-Jon?" I asked as I smacked her ass and dug deeper.

"Yes! You're so big, Track, and your dick feels so good. Fuck me hard and stop playing," she commanded. I placed her in a squatting position on top of my desk, reinserted, and rapidly roughed up the pussy. She was crying out in ecstasy, which excited me. I turned her around and spread her legs. "Track, don't stop," she yelled as she played with her clitoris. I dived back in and annihilated her with jabs.

"The next time you fuck grandpa, think about me," I groaned. Her cantaloupe breasts jiggled around with each thrust, taking my enjoyment to another level. Her breasts fell to the side when she was on her back, and I had to control them. I grabbed one and sucked the nipple extra hard, making her cry, showing her how a real man fucks. I lifted her up from the desk and devoured each breast, taking turns. She provided assistance by bouncing up and down on my Johnson, bringing sweet satisfaction. I pulled out before I came inside her, and she continued with her mouth, drinking every bit of me. "Damn, Carlton, you're the truth, baby."

"If we were together, there would be so much more in store," she replied as she grabbed a tissue and wiped her mouth.

"I can imagine," I replied. Although she was a good lay, that's all she was. She would fuck around on me with the next nigga. It didn't matter if he was or wasn't a rival of mine, she could never be trusted. What if the bitch tires of me and brings unnecessary strife into my life? "You better get back. You don't want him to get suspicious," I said after the stimulation had ceased.

"You're right, but what's the plan?" she pried.

"Don't worry your pretty little head. Thanks for the heads up, and be sure to act normal. Call me when you can," I instructed before she started in again on our nonexistent relationship. When she left, I called Tweet.

"Yo, my nigga! You hear that shit! I knew Junior had a problem, but Jon-Jon? This nigga thinks he slick too, but luckily the gods are on my side this time."

"Carlton came through. We need to strike back hard. I'm talking the whole fam, dog. So, what's the plan?"

"It's simple. He made it easy for me." After I explained the plan in detail to Tweet, he informed all my men. It was on and popping now. I would take care of Jon-Jon first, then Junior, and finally, Chasity. I'll be her shoulder to cry on once they're out of the picture.

Chapter 30

Chasity

A month had passed since I started working for the company, and we were ahead of schedule. Junior took the finished cabinets to the building site because we ran out of room in the workshop. I suggested he rent a warehouse off site, but that would put me in another location, and we all know he wasn't having that. Jeff brought three men with him to the team, Cory, Bobby, and Jose, and I hired my receptionist, Natasha.

My workplace was a happy space. We listened to music and laughed often, but we also worked hard and fast. Jeff showed me so many ways to use the machines, and currently I was working on a bedroom set. Junior's bed was comfortable, but outside of that, it screamed nothingness. I needed something to occupy my time, because Jeff had the cabinets under control.

Destiny started working at the company after school a week ago. I begged her to work downstairs with me, but she wasn't having that. She said there was too much dust and debris for her taste. Instead, she opted to be Domencio's personal assistant, but we saw one another every day.

"Chasity, Jeff is going to that seafood restaurant we love. Would you like something?" Natasha asked.

"No, I'll probably have lunch with Junior or Destiny, but thanks for including me."

"Of course," she replied and left. She went to college at night, and I admired that she worked full time while taking on a full course load.

When she completed her work, I allowed her to study, because she did over and above her receptionist duties. She reported our payroll to human resources and acted as my personal assistant. Often, she invited me to hang out, but I always had an excuse. Although I wanted to take her up on the tempting offer, I refused to set myself up for failure. Junior would never allow it, and he was too important to risk. I gave her excuse after excuse until one day she figured it out and chilled.

At lunchtime, I called Junior to see what he wanted, but he didn't answer. Destiny hadn't come in yet, so I went up to Junior's office. While I was on the elevator, three young men got on and turned away immediately when they saw me. *Junior and his paranoia,* I thought. When I got off the elevator, Samantha, Junior's new secretary, stopped me, which never happened before.

"Excuse you," I said, ready to check this bitch.

"I'm sorry, Chasity, but Junior is in an important meeting and asked to not be disturbed."

"Who's in there with him?" I asked, wondering who was so important.

"I'd rather not say, Ms. Chasity."

"If I have to tell you one more time not to call me miss, you will anger me. Is it a male or female he's meeting with?"

"Uh, woman," she replied, and her behavior was suspicious. I waited until she sat back down and charged through the door. "Chasity!" I heard her shout. My mind went into a frenzy when I saw Junior embracing Kali.

"What the fuck are you doing, Junior?" I screamed. My mind was telling me to kill this bitch first, and torture Junior later. I rushed towards Kali, and strangely, Junior stood in front of her.

"Chasity, this is not what it looks like," he reasoned.

"You take me for a fool, Junior. Do I look like I got my head screwed on backwards? You were hugging this bitch. I thought I told you to stay away from us!" I directed my attention to Kali.

"Listen!" Junior scolded as he shook my shoulders hard. "I need to finish talking to Kali. When I get home I'll explain everything, but right now, I need to you go back to work. Better yet, go home, baby. Please don't make me ask again. I'll call Calvin," he replied, dissing me.

"Did you fall down and bump your fucking head? You're choosing this bitch over me!" I yelled, wanting to kill them both.

"This is not about a choice, Chasity. I thought I told you I'll explain everything later. Goodbye, baby. I'll see you at home," he replied as he pushed me out of his office. *What the fuck?* I thought.

"You don't have to explain shit, Junior. Take a good look at this face, because it will be your last look." I stormed off and caught the elevator to the basement. The wheels were turning, and I had to get the hell out of that building before I caught a case.

"Natasha, can I see you in my office right now?" I asked once I reached the woodshop. "Listen, I don't know you like that, but you seem genuine and cool, like a person who knows how to keep a secret."

"Sure, your privacy is guarded over here," she responded, providing the right answer. However, I really didn't care until after I made my escape. Junior would be punished for this incident, and I didn't want to hear shit from him.

"I need your help leaving this building without Junior's knowledge. Once you drop me off, you can take the rest of the day. If Junior asks where I am, just tell him you haven't seen me since lunch."

"I got you, but what's the plan? Junior has security everywhere, and everyone knows you're not supposed to leave," she asked with a confused expression.

"I know, but I have a plan. Actually, I've been planning it for a long time, just in case. This is what I need you to do. Pull your car around back to the equipment lot and park in front of the window. You can't miss it, because it's the only one. I'll climb out the women's bathroom window on the first floor. Normally there's no one back there, so let's hope that's the case."

"Okay. I feel like I'm in a Mission Impossible movie, and I'm excited to help," she replied.

"A lot of drama, I know, but just like in the movie, we will succeed in our mission. I'll leave first, and a minute later you follow. I'll be at the window waiting for you. Put my number in your phone and call if you have any problems," I explained before leaving.

I hurried to the women's bathroom on the first floor, but was stopped by Calvin. *Damn!* "Chasity, Junior called and said I should take you home."

"Yes, Calvin, but you have to give me a minute. My stomach is killing me, and I was on my way to the ladies' room."

"No problem. Take your time. I'll be right out here waiting." *I just know you will. Too bad you're about to be in trouble for losing me,* I thought.

When I got inside the bathroom, I went to the last stall and climbed on top of the toilet. I looked out the window, and when I saw Natasha pulling up, I opened it. I climbed out, jumped into the back seat of her KIA, and ducked down.

"When you get out of the parking lot, make a right on Columbus Boulevard and haul ass!" I instructed. When we got past the shopping mall, I came up for air and gave her directions. Five minutes later, we arrived at Junior's condominium and I had little time to make my move. "Thanks again, Natasha. You looked out, girl and as promised, you can go home. I'll be honest with you; I don't know what will happen to the woodshop, because I'm not coming back."

"For real? You think Junior will fire us?"

"Who knows what will happen once he finds out I left his ass. I'll call Jeff, but you haven't seen me since lunch."

"Okay. Good luck, Chasity."

"Good luck to you too." When she left, I went down to the garage, hopped into my Infiniti, and raced away like a NASCAR driver.

I had my identification and credit cards on me, and that was all I needed. I drove to Jenkintown and switched cars. I switched my car with my uncle's truck inside the garage. I raced inside, grabbed a few things, and got the hell out of Dodge.

Chapter 31

Junior

My reign of thoughts towards Chasity was at an all-time high. I loved this woman, and for the past couple of days, the thought of confessing my love and proposing to her rambled my brain. I was trying to figure out if this was my demise, knowing Chasity was a difficult woman who loved to stir pot, but I had devoted my heart to her a while ago. My emotions remained nameless and unascertained verbally, but my physical love shone through.

When we were at the jewelry store, I glanced at the engagement rings and saw a design I liked. I made a mental note to have my jeweler find the perfect stone. She was a Scorpio, something I should have been privy to immediately, because she was very sexual and willing to try new things. As I sat in my office thinking about popping the big question on her birthday, which was two weeks away, an unexpected and unwanted visitor came to see me.

"Junior, a Ms. Kali Johnson is here to see you," my secretary informed.

My initial response was to have security throw her ass out, though I was curious of what her angle was. "Send her in, Bridgette," I instructed.

When she walked into my office, admittedly, I felt a brief attraction. She was a beautiful woman and an unfaithful bird. "To what do I owe the pleasure of this abrupt and bizarre intrusion?" I asked.

"Junior, please listen before you throw me out, because I know your patience runs thin. I have two very important things to discuss with you. First, I didn't cheat on you. When you got life in prison, I thought I'd die. You left me out in the cold. I had nothing, and you never once asked your father to help me."

"Let me stop you right there. I have no desire to travel down memory lane. I don't give a fuck when, how, or why you betrayed me. The damage is irreconcilable, and I would have thought you've moved on from that. I know I have. It's been what? Twelve years!"

"Trust me, Junior. I don't want you, and I am over you. However, when I look at our son every day, he reminds me so much of you. It's time for you to know the truth."

"What the fuck is you talking about? Our son? What games are you trying to play, because I'm ready to take you out your misery with that bullshit!"

"Bullshit? Let me refresh your memory. When you went to court, I was pregnant and didn't know. After the sentence, I had to look out for me, because you went into a deep depression and shut me out. I came to see you and you refused my visits. I wrote letters telling you I was pregnant, but you never answered. Did you get any of my letters, Junior?"

"Yeah, I got them, but I never read them. Like you said, I was going through my own hell being imprisoned at eighteen. I wasn't fucking with no one."

"My point exactly. I had to make a way for Jordon and me. Dre was a friend first, and over time he became the love of my life. When you abandoned me and Jordan, he took care of us, and we moved to Baltimore."

"You think you can come in here with this lame ass story and I'm supposed to take you seriously?"

"Maybe this will help," she replied and placed a picture on my desk. I studied the picture of the eleven-year-old boy and lost my breath. It was like staring at my twin.

"How the fuck could you keep something like this away from me for twelve years? You no good bitch. You come in here with this news, trying to fuck up my life."

"I'm happy you're not denying it. I mean any fool could see that's your son. I didn't mean to cause you any discomfort, but I'm dying. Jordan needs someone," she explained and sobbed. I know in the past I wished death on her, but I hoped God knew I was just playing. "I'm sorry to hear that Kali," I said, trying to change the tone.

"I've been struggling with breast cancer for the past six years. I was in remission for a long time, but somehow the cancer spread and progressed. I've been through every type of treatment you can imagine, but the time has come for me to get my affairs in order." She continued to cry.

I truly felt for her. I got up from my chair and embraced her. My mind was still comatose from seeing the picture of my son. Just as I was about to let go of Kali, Chasity barged into my office. *Fuck!*

I could tell she was unhappy with my response to her, but I had to sort out this shit with Kali. After I escorted her out of my office, I told Kali to take a seat. Chasity's threat didn't go over my head and I needed to make sure Calvin took her home. I haven't seen her that mad since I fired her. I was uneasy now, and something was telling me I handled the situation wrong.

"I'm not trying to cause no problems with you and your girlfriend. She is crazy about you. I have the bruises to show for it. But it's time you take your son. I told him about you, and he agrees that he should stay with you instead of my mother. She's on a fixed income and can't manage his finances. Jordan goes to a school for extraordinarily gifted kids. He's a genius, and he's very mature for an eleven-year-old. I have life insurance, but it's only enough to bury me. Jordon's school tuition is eighteen-thousand dollars a year. I won't be able to rest in peace if I thought he'd be kicked out of that school. He was attending one in Baltimore but I found out they had a chapter near Philly, and we transferred."

"If he's my son, you can rest well, because he will never want for anything. Is there anything I can do for you? Pops can get you the best doctors. Maybe there's a chance to turn this thing around."

"It would have to be an act from God, Junior. I've come to terms with my disease and made my peace with God. I'm not afraid of dying, I'm just afraid of leaving my son behind. Listen, I'm about to leave. We can work out the details later. Here's my number. Call me when it's a good time to meet Jordon. I'm leaving in two weeks to check into a private hospice care center. They're well-known for making your last moments comfortable."

"Let me talk to my lady and my family. And, for the record, let's let bygones be just that. I'm here for you and Jordon," I replied.

"Thanks. I didn't expect for this to go so well. One more thing, Junior. Beware of Track. When he took me to the hospital, he swore on his dead father he would end your life."

"Tell me something I don't know, but thanks for the heads up," I replied, and she left. I studied the picture of Jordan and there was no doubt in my mind, but I was still getting a test. *Me with a son. I don't know how to be a father. God, what's really good?* I asked. Seconds later, Calvin burst into the room.

"Boss, Chasity's gone! She went into the bathroom but never came out. I had the receptionist check, and she said it was empty. I checked after that and the bathroom window was open."

"Fuck you mean she's gone? She couldn't have gotten far. Did you search outside?" I asked, ready to lose my fucking mind.

"We did a thorough search, and she's gone. I never left the bathroom entrance, so I'm pretty sure she's not in the building."

"Yo, get more security and meet me downstairs." As soon as I grabbed my cell phone, it rang. I saw it was Pops and immediately picked up. "Pops, we got a problem. Chasity is missing."

"Find her, Junior. We got a bigger problem than that. You need to come see me immediately, son. Certain shit cannot be discussed over the phone."

"Pops, I need to find Chasity first."

"Hold on, Junior," he said. "Destiny, have you spoken with Chasity today?" She said no and Pops came back on the line. "This shit could be serious. When did she go missing?"

"Less than an hour, why?"

"Meet me at your condo. We need to talk in person," he instructed and hung up. I wanted to turn back the clock and start the day over. Before I had a panic attack, I grabbed my keys and raced home.

When I got home, I searched the whole condo. She wasn't there, but her belongings were untouched. Calvin informed me her car was gone, and I was about to go ballistic on somebody.

"Calvin, tell me what happened again."

"I want you to know that I feel fucked up about this shit. I care for her too. She was holding her stomach and told me she had to use the bathroom. I figured she had to take a dump because she said her stomach hurt. After about fifteen minutes, I told your receptionist to go check on her. She came back and said no one was in the bathroom. I went inside, checked all the stalls, and saw that the window was ajar. The entire security team searched the inside and outside of the building."

"I fucked up everything. I might have a son, but my now my world, my life, is missing. I have to find my baby, Calvin."

"We'll find her. I feel confident she left on her own and not by force. She'll turn up. Chasity is a strong but loyal woman. She has a great heart."

"Calvin. I don't want to hear that shit. I know what I got or what I had. I'm trying to overlook the fact that she out slicked us, and you let her get away."

"I understand, Junior. I'm willing to take full responsibility. I will do everything I can to make this right. There's something else you need to know. Your father ordered the hit on Track, but that shit boomeranged on all of us. It's like this nigga knew we were coming. I'll let your father fill you in on the details, but Track and his boys killed four of our men last night."

"What the fuck. Why am I just finding this shit out? What if this motherfucker has Chasity!"

"I highly doubt that, but we can't take no chances. We can't find this nigga, and no one seems to know his whereabouts." The anxiety and helplessness I felt was on one hundred. I grabbed a Corona out of the fridge, but I needed something stronger. I remembered flushing the liquor down the drain once I saw the effect it had on Chasity.

"Oh my God, Junior. I can't believe I didn't think about this earlier. When I put the car in the storage garage, I told Mike to install a tracking device as you instructed."

"That's right. How the fuck did I forget that?" I replied. "Get him on the phone now." I watched in anticipation as he called Mike and handed me the phone. "Yo, Mike, I need you tell me where that Infiniti is located, now! It's an emergency, man," I demanded.

"Just give me two minutes while I put it up on the screen," Mike responded. Two minutes later, he told me where the car was. Chasity was at her house.

"Thanks, man." I hung up. "Calvin, we need to get to Chasity's house. That's where the car is," I said, already out the door. "Call Pops and tell him to meet us there," I instructed.

When we arrived at her house, Pops and Destiny were already there. I saw them, along with an extensive security team, searching the garage. I jumped out of the car and dashed to Pops.

"Is she here?" I asked in a panic.

"No, Junior, she's gone. It looks like she took the truck and left. I called in favors from all my important contacts. I'm sure they will come up with something. I'm just waiting to hear from my contacts at the airport. We'll get her back, Son, but you need to relax. I see that distorted look in your eyes and I don't like it. We will handle this situation," he explained.

"Like you handled Track?" I replied.

"Calvin is a good man, but he needs to be reminded where his true loyalty lies. That was an unfortunate mishap and that too will be resolved."

"Whatever," I spat and ran into the house. I needed to check the house for my own sanity. I ended up in her room and saw she had been there. Her closet was almost empty. *Why are you running, babe? What I did, was it so bad?* I thought. I sat on her bed and prayed. Moments later, Destiny interrupted my prayer.

"Junior, what did you do to my sister? I know you did something because Chasity don't act like this. She's always been reliable and happy. Ever since you came into her life, she has been obsessed with you. She barely takes interest in me anymore, and now I fear she's in trouble," she cried.

"I'm sorry, Destiny. I never meant to hurt your sister. I—I love her, you know. I want the best for her, but I don't know how to show her the proper way. I promise you this, when she comes back, I will marry your sister. You can hold me to that," I replied while embracing her.

"Junior, let's go back to my home. We have a lot to discuss, and I want you to stay close," Pops said when he came into the room.

"Pops, I'm not a little boy. We need to talk. I don't even know where to start with all the shit that happened today."

"Destiny, come, we're going home. And don't worry your pretty little head. Chasity will be home soon, I promise," he said, and I prayed he was right.

Domencio and Wayne were at the house when we arrived. Pops told me to follow him into his study because he didn't want to talk in front of them. Domencio was never in the drug game. Pops forbade it, but he couldn't stop me. Conversations like this stayed just between us.

"Junior, what happened today to make her just up and disappear?" he asked.

"Kali came to see me to give me some important news, and she misunderstood something she saw. I needed to finish my conversation with Kali, so I basically told her to go home."

"You told Chasity to go home? Junior, I'm not around her every day like you are, but I know enough to know that she ain't having that."

"Clearly, but she's taking this too far, Pops. I can't live without this girl. She's my future. I just have to get her back so I can show her."

"You should've thought about that before whatever it was she saw. What did she see?"

"I gave Kali a hug after hearing about her tragic circumstances, after she told me I have a son. She showed me his picture.
I'm ninety-nine percent sure he's my son."

"Do you have the picture?" he asked, stunned I pulled it out
of my pocket and handed it to him. "Yes, he looks exactly like
you did at that age. Why would she keep this a secret?" he asked.

"She gave me some bullshit ass excuse. I decided to forgive
her, because she's dying of stage four breast cancer. She wants
me to raise him."

"What's his name?"

"Jordon," I replied.

"That's a good, strong name. When can I meet my grand-
son?"

"I have to work out the details, but soon. I still have to get a
paternity test. I heard you can buy them over the counter."

"Junior, I haven't even met the boy, and I can see that he's
your son."

"I agree. Jordon is safe, and I want to meet him as soon as
possible, but Chasity is my main priority right now. The anxiety
is building up inside, not knowing where the hell she is. If Track
is responsible, who knows what this nigga will do? His reputa-
tion when it comes to kidnapping is well known."

"Junior, we will get her back and I doubt he had her. She
probably left to get away from you, son."

Chapter 32

Chasity

The sweet smell of freedom lingered in the air, and I was in my dream place. The chains, locks, and barriers were unbound and I could finally breathe again. Everyone had to be worried, wondering where I was and why I disappeared. My actions were selfish, but I desired this time alone to get to know me. Junior was crippling me with his dysfunctional love, and I had to find an outlet. To add further humiliation, that bastard had the nerve to have his arms around that bitch. He would pay for that. I'm sure there was a logical excuse for his actions, but there was no way I was giving him leeway or cutting him any slack.

I booked a quick vacation to Alaska, the land of my dreams, and it was all I had imagined it to be. I took residence at the beautiful Lodge. The rooms were small, individual lodge cabins, and I was having the time of my life. It was day five of a nine-day package, and I had already seen much of what Alaska offered. In addition to my newfound freedom, I had a new white family from Canada that welcomed me into their circle. I met the Cougars on day two of my vacation. When they saw me dining alone, they asked me to join them. Initially, I thought they were trying to be nosey, but they were genuinely interested in me. Bob and Mary had two children, Jeremy and Jessica. Bob was a surgeon and Mary was a stay at home mom. Jeremy was all about adventure, while Jessica followed me everywhere I went. She reminded me of Destiny at that age.

I was meeting them at the main lodge. We were on our way to the adventure activities at the ski club. We had already visited museums, national parks, and the infamous pipeline. I saw caribou, moose, and deadly brown bears. I even tagged along for fishing. That wasn't really my thing, but hanging with my new family, anything was possible. They were daredevils and encouraged me to let loose.

I heard a knock at my cabin door. Jessica was on the other side, urging me to hurry. "Chasity, we're all waiting for you. Come on! We're going to have the best time. Aren't you excited?" she asked, jumping up and down. Her baby blue eyes and sparkly smile could light up a stadium.

"I'm coming now. I know this is a dumb question, but have you ever skied before?" I asked, feeling out of my element.

"Of course, we come here every year, and we have plenty of ski resorts back home. Don't be scared, they have beginner's courses."

"I'm not scared, lollipop," I replied, calling her by the nickname I gave her. "Let's go."

"Hey kiddo, I didn't think you were coming," Bob said when we reached the lobby.

"Yes, we were concerned, honey. Is everything okay?" Mary asked.

"I'm fine, I just overslept," I replied. They showed so much sincerity towards me, and I felt at home with them.

We all boarded the bus. It was cold as shit outside! I had never experienced cold like that before. You had to respect the Alaskans that lived in secluded areas and off of the land. Bob explained that temperatures drop below 50 degrees.

"I'm so happy you joined us, Chasity. We've enjoyed your company these past few days," Mary said.

"It's been my pleasure. Thanks for including me as a part of your family this week. I dreamt of coming here for a while now, and I know I wouldn't have done half the stuff we did if I was alone," I replied.

"What do you mean a part of our family for this week? Your family, period, and we will keep in touch young lady," Bob said.

"Yeah, you're the best," Jeremy added.

"You guys are going to make me cry," I responded sincerely. Their family worked as a unit, and Bob communicated well with Mary. He wasn't possessive or controlling like somebody I knew. He was a successful doctor, and it was clear he loved his family much.

"Chasity, tell us about your family. You told us what you do for a living, and I'm surprised and impressed. I admire anyone that follows his or her dreams. Do you have siblings?" Bob asked.

"I have a sister. Actually, we're cousins, but we consider ourselves sisters. She started her first year of college last month."

"Wonderful! And your mother and father?" he asked, but when he saw my expression change, he continued, "Did I say something wrong?"

"No, but it never gets comfortable when someone asks about them. They died when I was ten years old. I moved to Philadelphia where my uncle and aunt raised me."

"I'm so sorry to hear about your parents, Chasity. Your uncle and aunt did a good job, because you turned out just great."

"Yes, may their souls rest in peace."

"They passed on as well?" he gasped.

"Yes, unfortunately," I responded, and put my head down.

"Were you and your sister raised by relatives after they passed?" Mary pressed on.

"No, I raised Destiny. That's her name. My uncle and aunt were in a fatal car crash on their way to my college graduation. That was two years ago, but it feels like yesterday."

"You've endured great losses. I can relate. I too lost my parents at an early age, and my grandmother raised me. I know how you feel, kid," Bob said.

"You're a strong woman Chasity." Mary reached over and touched my hand. My new white family was all that and a bag of chips.

"You know, Chass, oh do you mind if I call you that?" Bob asked, and I shook my head no. "Every summer we spend a part of our vacation in Ocean City, Maryland at our beachfront home. We would love it if you would come down next summer and hang out with us. You can bring your sister along. We would love to meet her," Bob suggested.

"Absolutely! Thanks, Bob. You're cool."

Our day was full of fun and adventure. I was afraid to ski, but I tried snowboarding, and it was on the list of my top ten life experiences. As the day went on, my skills improved, and I moved up to the intermittent level. Bob, Mary and Jeremy went to do some real skiing, while Lollipop and I snowboarded.

We continued to enjoy the great state of Alaska, but the day before we were all leaving I became extremely ill. Bob was worried sick, saying they pushed me to do too much. Although he was absolute in his assessment, I would never tell him that. Their last name should have been, The McCrazies because they were down for anything. Today was rafting, and I was somewhat happy I fell ill. I dreaded it from the time they invited me, but I was trying to be just as adventurous as my new family, to prove I had survivor skills.

Bob checked all my vital signs and my temperature was normal, which relived him. When I described my symptoms, he ruled out a cold or virus. He explained that he was going to the town's pharmacy and would be right back. I had thrown up the entire night, and I couldn't hold anything down that morning. I felt light headed and exhausted. Whatever it was, I had never experienced it before.

I had to get better before tomorrow, because it was unimaginable getting on three different planes feeling the way I did. I sucked on a few ice chips and my stomach settled. When Bob got back, I had already packed so I would be prepared for tomorrow, regardless of how I felt. I heard a knock at the door and when I opened it, Bob and Mary were standing there.

"Listen, Chass. I did every test I could with the limited devices I had, however, I need to rule out one last thing," he explained as he handed me a pregnancy test.

"You never told us you had a boyfriend, but a beautiful girl such as yourself, well we just assumed. If we're wrong, I apologize for both Bob and myself," Mary explained. "When he described your symptoms, they sounded familiar. I had those same feelings with both of my children."

This was awkward as hell, and I was embarrassed. "Okay, I'll take the test," I replied quickly, knowing it was a possibility.

"Just follow the instructions on the box. You'll be fine. We'll be right here waiting," Bob said.

As I waited for the test results, I tried to recall the last time my period was on and believed it was when Destiny had her party. That was damn near a month and half ago. *Oh my God. Could it be true; could I really be pregnant with Junior's dysfunctional baby? God tell me it ain't so,* I prayed as I glanced down at the stick and it slowly turned pink. Tears welled in my eyes, as I silently broke down, not wanting my new family to see my uncertainty. Once before, Junior told me he did not want kids and that having a woman was already too much to ask. I washed my face and regained my composure before heading back out.

"Your observation was correct, Mary. I am pregnant."

"I'm so happy for you! I told you, Bob, you might be a doctor, but momma knows best," Mary said. She reminded of me of a dark haired Cameron Diaz, and you could see she kept her body in shape. Bob was half-handsome, but I saw the appeal. Their kids were beautiful too.

"Thanks," I replied, but they heard the skepticism in my response.

"Hey, we'll give you some privacy. You probably want to call the father and give him the happy news. We'll check in on you later. Since it's nothing serious, we can still go rafting, honey," Bob said to his wife.

"Yes, the kids will be thrilled," she replied and kissed him.

"Thanks again for everything guys. Your support means more than you know."

"We're glad we could help," Bob replied, and they left.

I plopped down on my bed and cried myself to sleep. I woke up and insomnia hit. I was packed and tired of Alaska, and anxious to get back home. But the more I thought about it, I was unsure what I was going back to. I wondered what Junior was doing and how he was getting along without me. They hadn't crossed my mind because I was preoccupied with my freedom. Destiny and Uncle Jon had to be worried sick, but I had to figure out some things on my own, and now I had bigger fish to fry with my pregnancy.

Before we headed to the Anchorage airport, The Cougars and I exchanged contact information and promised to keep in touch. My flight was departing first, so I hugged them and boarded the plane. I thanked God for the first-class seat and was happy that I spent the extra money. I prepared myself for the nine-hour flight, and the two stops in Boston and Chicago.

I was pooped when I landed in Philly without a real plan. I knew if I went home, Junior would find me there, and Uncle Jon's was out of the question. Once I got my bags, I had to remember where I parked my truck in the parking garage. After fifteen minutes of searching, I found it. Once I paid the astronomical parking fee, I drove to a small motel on City Avenue and checked in. I wanted to keep a low profile and stay where no one would look for me. They were reasonable and had an extended stay program. I paid for one month in advance, hoping that gave me enough time for me to figure out my next move.

One month later

I was stressed, lonely, and spending too much money. After I checked into the motel, I found an obstetrician right across the street. The office visits were ridiculous, and I had to sign up for that new health care program, which was not cheap. I was paying seven hundred dollars a month, but that was a small amount as opposed to the cost of having a baby.

I was on my way to get a sugar test. When I asked the doctor why I had to get it, she explained that my hemoglobin was high, whatever that meant, and they needed a more extensive test. Once the test was over and they finished poking every vein in my body, they explained that I had gestational diabetes, which occurs in pregnant woman.

I had to change the way I ate, and I was living around nothing but fast food. I needed a place with a stove and kitchen so I
could cook the healthy meals required to control this thing. I
didn't even like the way that shit sounded, so I knew I had to rid
myself of it. I had two more days before I had to either pay more
money, or get the balls to go home where I belonged.

I had isolated myself from Junior and my family. Destiny and
Uncle Jon did not deserve that, but Knucklehead had it coming.
Hugging that bitch and dismissing me as if I meant nothing was
foul. However, I missed his fine ass. I blocked him from my mind
throughout this whole process, but I was in my feelings and
wanted my man.

After little deliberation, I went home. It was time to face the
music and get back to reality, whatever that may be. I was unsure
of my career goals, and my dreams of becoming the best female
carpenter in the state were disappearing, but I knew the baby
inside me was a brand new dream, which I cherished.

When I got home, I was happy to be somewhere familiar.
Once inside, I realized I was alone. The house was lifeless and
strange. No aunt, uncle or sister in sight. Immediately, I knew I
could not stay for long. After lugging my suitcases and bags full
of souvenirs into the house I had to take a breather, and I noticed
I was tiring quicker. I didn't enjoy that feeling. The doctor said it
was okay for me to exercise within reason, and I had every
intention on joining a gym. I was three plus months pregnant and
recovering from morning sickness. I noticed it had stopped three
days ago, and I was feeling normal again.

Once I caught my breath, I walked into the kitchen and
opened the fridge. It was empty, but I was happy Junior and I
cleaned it the last time I was here. At least I had a fresh start. It
was the end of November, but this cold was miniscule compared
to the cold I felt in Alaska. I had a newfound appreciation for our
zero below degrees. I had to get to the market, and I needed a few
outfits. I left the bulk of my clothes at Junior's, plus I was already
having a hard time buttoning up my jeans.

When I got outside, I noticed that my truck was running low
on gas. Going to the supermarket was one thing, but I definitely

was not about to pump no gas. After exchanging cars, I was tired and realized it would have been easier to just pump the damn gas. Nevertheless, I was happy to ride in my car. From the time Uncle Jon gave me the car, I never could drive it, and y'all know why.

I purchased enough groceries to last a few days, figuring that after I slept in my bed, I would feel energized to do more. I still needed some clothes, and I didn't want to go far, so I went to Cheltenham Mall to pick up a few things. As I headed back to my car, several black SUVs surrounded me. My first instinct was to run, and that's exactly what I did, however I ran straight into one of the security man's arms. Shortly after, I saw Junior and Calvin racing towards me. *Damn, I'm caught*, I thought.

Chapter 33

Junior

Two weeks had passed since Chasity went missing and I was about to fucking lose it. Horrible images clouded my mind as we used every lead we had to find her. I was losing hope until we got a call telling us she had landed on a flight from Alaska. We were two hours late getting that news, and she had already left. *Damn! She went to Alaska without me. At least she's safe,* I thought as I continued to mentally berate myself. My overbearing hold on her was not something she could sustain, and as a result I pushed her away.

The one positive out of this whole tragedy was my son, Jordon. Kali brought him over the day after Chasity disappeared. My condo was too small and unsafe, so Pops took us in temporarily, until I could find a suitable place for Chasity and Jordon. My relationship with Jordon was growing stronger each day, and I thought back to two weeks ago when he arrived.

"Jordon, you remember the man I told you about?" Kali explained. "I would like to introduce you Johnathan Blake, your father. You'll be staying with him from now on."

He glared at me and said, "It's nice to meet you, however I'm only here because my mom is going to Heaven. My education is important to her and I will not let her down. If you pay my tuition, I will bring home straight A's and you won't have no problems out of me. I'm well-behaved," he said, selling himself as if he were up for auction.

"Listen, Jordon, you don't have to self yourself. I can see with these two eyes that you're my son. It will be my pleasure to care for your needs and get to know you." I walked over to him and shook his hand. "Would it be to awkward if I gave you a hug?" I asked.

"Yeah, but I'm sure we'll work our way to that," he replied, and I had to respect his wishes.

"Jordon, I'm Johnathan Senior, but you can call me grandpa. I'm thrilled to welcome you into the family and pray you allow us to make up for lost time," Pops said sincerely. His dreams were coming true, and our family was growing.

"I'm your Uncle Domencio. I never thought I would have a nephew! Welcome to the family, young boy," Domencio said, while giving him pretends jabs. "You like video games? Because I have every game imaginable!"

"I play when I'm not studying, which isn't that often. I prefer reading," Jordon replied.

"Reading is the key to success, son. I like reading too, but I have done little reading for a while. You're making me want to read again. We can go to the bookstore tomorrow if you like." His face lit up, which pleased me. I introduced him to Carlton, Anastasia, and Destiny, but Destiny was too heartbroken over Chasity to engage with him. She greeted him and excused herself, but I wasn't mad. We had a common interest, and I felt her pain.

When Pops found out Kali's hospice was in Jersey, he worked his magic and found a place closer to us. Jordon could visit her every day, which made him happy. He was a genius, much smarter than I imagined, and investing into him was a gift.

A week after he arrived, I was in Pops study drinking a glass of scotch while wallowing in the void I felt. Jordon came inside and asked to talk.

"What's up, Jordon? Come sit down beside me," When he took his seat I said, "What's on your mind, son?"

"I was thinking I could call you dad—on one condition though."

"Shoot," I replied.

"I need to know why you're so sad. It's as if you're faking happiness, and that bothers me." He was a good son to be concerned about his father, and he brought me so much joy in that moment.

"Is it that obvious?" I asked, faking a smile.

"Yes, I hope it's not me." He held his head down in shame.

"Not at all, I'm so happy you're in my life. There's just one thing missing."

"What's that?"

"My lady. She disappeared right before I met you, and I can't find her. I'm worried to death, but I have only myself to blame."

"What's her name?" he asked with interest.

"Chasity, and she was my angel. I let her fly away."

"If she loves you, she'll come back. I tell you what, Dad. We should prepare for her return." When he called me dad, I was putty in his hands. My son made me love him more each day.

"What do you have in mind?"

"Are you going to marry her when she comes back?"

"Yes, that's my plan. Her birthday was two days ago, and my plan was to propose then."

"Don't worry, Dad. I can help you get her back, because I know what girls like," he boasted.

"What makes you the expert at eleven years old?" I asked, fascinated he cared enough to offer.

"Trust me, all you need is one day with me. I'll show you the ropes."

"I trust you, son, but there's just one problem. We don't have the subject."

My concentration and focus were impaired, and I appreciated Domencio and Wayne for stepping up to the plate. A little over a month had passed since my baby left, and my emotional state worsened. She didn't go home when she landed, which frightened and angered me. There were moments when I thought of holding her and asking her to be my wife, but then there were moments when I could see me torturing her little defiant ass. Spending time with Jordon got me through the most hideous days. He and I planned a surprise for her, and although her whereabouts were unknown, Jordon kept hope alive in my heart. He was positive and inspiring. I couldn't wait for them to meet and prayed she accepted him, because Jordon was here to stay.

Even Destiny was coming around, and she helped us with the surprise. She took off the rest of the semester after some objections from Pops, but softened the blow after she promised to return. She was worried to death, along with the rest of us, and I felt especially sorry for her. When she turned down the shopping spree I offered, I knew she was hurting. Kenny Jr was over here often, and his visits brought a rare smile to her face.

As for me, I was drinking more than usual and knew I had to get a handle on it before it turns into problem. However, I still opted to grab a Corona out of the fridge while I watched the news. I stopped going to the office a few weeks ago, not wanting my torment to spill onto the employees. I enjoyed seeing their smiles instead of their fear or carelessness towards me.

I stood in the family room staring out at the backyard. I never noticed how calming the leaves were, and I wished Chasity was by my side. She's everything I need, and I know God designed her just for me. Although she was missing, I was confident that once we reunite, I would take possession of her and make it official.

An hour later, Calvin stormed into the family room. "Junior, we got movement on the Infiniti. We need to go now!"

"When did the signal come through?" I asked while putting on my kicks with the quickness. I grabbed my coat and Calvin was on my heels.

"Fifteen minutes ago, but dude just called and informed me," he replied.

When we got inside the SUVs, we found out that the car had stopped, but shortly after she was back on the move. "Where the fuck is she, Calvin?" I yelled.

"She's driving down Cheltenham Avenue right now. We will get her, Junior, but you have to stay calm." Calvin responded.

"Yo, man! Speed this shit up! We need to get there now!" I yelled.

"Junior, they're saying the car stopped and parked in the mall," Calvin announced.

My anxiety was about to kill me. I had to get to Chasity before she vanished again. "We can't fuck up this time. I need to have Chasity in my custody today! I can't live another second without her!"

"We got her, Junior. We'll be there in less than ten minutes," Calvin assured me.

When we pulled up to the mall, we spotted the Infiniti right away, but it was empty. My men were in place, and within minutes I spotted her walking out of the mall. We surrounded her, and she took off running back towards the mall, but Calvin was on that ass.

I jumped out of the SUV and ran to get my future wife. I lifted her in my arms and hurried to the SUV. When I placed her inside, I noticed she was heavier in the hips than I recalled. When we pulled off, I noticed it wasn't just the hips, her face was slightly plump, and those jeans needed to go to charity.

"My car, Junior!" she yelled, more concerned with it than me.

"Don't worry, baby, you'll get your car, but first I need to know why you left and tried to break me?" I asked tenderly, hoping to have a happy reunion. Now that she was in my presence and I knew she was safe, anger was on the horizon. I was fighting hard to suppress my emotions.

"Junior, you know why. You chose your ex over me! Not to mention I was tired of the boundaries and chains. I needed a break to figure out what I want. You broke me when I saw your arms around another woman. And not just any woman, your ex! How do you think that made me feel?"

"I'm sorry you saw that, but it meant nothing. Dismissing you the way I did was the wrong way to handle that situation. But the news I received, I believed warranted my behavior. Chasity, when you disappeared, you fucked me up, baby, and that shit won't happen again," I said. She appeared to be ignoring me while indulging in the soft pretzel she was eating. She was going in hard as if she hadn't had a meal in months, while it was clear she was eating everything under the sun.

"You need to explain to me why you hugged Kali, after all we've been through. You should be happy I left, because I was out for blood. You and Kali were close to meeting your maker," she replied, while taking another big bite off the pretzel.

"Really? Funny you should say that, because Kali informed me she was dying of breast cancer, after she told me I had an eleven-year old son. I felt sorry for her, and when you walked in, you saw me giving my condolences. I didn't want you beating up a dying girl, and I needed to get to the bottom of her claim," I replied, and her face softened.

"I'm sorry to hear about that, Junior. For real. I feel bad for beating her the way I did. Had I known, I would've let her slick tongue get a pass. Are you sure it's your son?" she asked, still eating the pretzel, and I was happy she was almost done.

"Yeah, he's definitely mine. He's at Pop's, and he knows all about you. I told him you were the love of my life, and he planned something nice for your homecoming."

"How did he know I was coming back, Junior?"

"He didn't, but I think he did it to keep my mind occupied. He's a wise young man, and I hope you'll love him like I do."

"You love him, Junior. This must be the real deal because you don't love no one. I'm sure over time I will love my new little cousin, but as far as you and me, I'm done trying. I deserve better than what you've provided, and it took going away for me to realize that."

"So you went to Alaska alone, ate off the land, and now you discovered your worth?"

"Yes, I did, but I wasn't alone. I faced my fears and challenged myself beyond anything I ever imagined. Life is too short to be imprisoned."

"Fuck was you with?" I spat, throwing nice Junior to the side.

"My new white family, The Cougars. They included me into their circle, and by the end of the trip, I was officially like fam," she smiled at the thought. This was not my ideal reunion.

"So you want us to just be friends? No ties, no connections? Come on now, you know better than that, baby."

"Take me to my house, Junior. I want to continue being alone," she requested.

"I'm taking you to Pops. Everyone has been worried about you. And poor Destiny. She hasn't been the same since you left. She dropped out of school stressing over you. So while you were out in the fucking wilderness living it up, our lives were falling apart!" I barked.

"She dropped out of school? I never thought my leaving for a month would have that effect on her."

"Almost two months, to be correct. You're fucking selfish and spoiled. I was going out of my mind over your ungrateful ass, praying for your safe return. Don't worry though, your wish is about to come true."

"Whatever," she said.

"And another thing, the new fat girl look is not a good fit on you. Whatever you've been eating, you need to stop immediately."

"I'm sure someone else won't have a problem with the additional ten pounds I gained." She rolled her eyes and stared out the window. I wanted to smack the shit out of her.

"Yo, Calvin! Speed this shit up before I do something we'll all regret." She ignored me for the rest of the ride.

Once we reached Pops' house, she jumped out the car, and I was right behind her. She went straight into the study, knowing that's where Pops would be.

"Uncle Jon, I missed you!" she shouted and ran into his arms.

"My prayers have been answered," Pops responded while holding her tight. I had never been so jealous. He pulled out his phone and called Destiny. "Destiny, Chasity is home! Get your tail down here now!" he demanded.

Within seconds, Destiny stormed into the study. "Chasity, thank God you're safe! I thought I lost another family member. Please don't disappear again, sis. I really do need you in my life, but it looks like you need me more. Maybe we should go back to living together, because when we were under the same roof, you never pulled anything like this," she explained, while tears ran down her face.

"That's because she's selfish and only thinks about herself. I would never knowingly hurt you Chasity, and you want to treat me like shit!" I interrupted.

"Fuck off, Junior!" she replied, and directed her attention back to Destiny. "I'm sorry, Dee. I didn't think I would hurt you. I figured you were happy living with Uncle Jon. I was being selfish. I promise not to disappear on you, but if I have to go, I will let you know, okay?"

"Okay, I'm so happy you're home. We can stay up all night, catch up, and watch movies. Uncle Jon gets the new movies the same day they come out in the theaters." Destiny's voice was full of enthusiasm.

"Sure, but I'm getting old, so I'll stay up as long as I can," Chasity replied, and they both laughed.

"Girl, you gained weight. You might want to do some sit-ups, or treadmill, or something! But it don't look bad." Destiny said what I was thinking. You could tell they were raised in the same house because Destiny didn't hold back her tongue either.

"Whatever," Chasity replied, giving her the same answer she gave me. I noticed Pops was looking at her peculiarly, and I wondered what was on his mind.

Jordon walked in and Chasity stared at him in awe, or maybe it was shock. Everyone was silent until Jordon spoke. "Dad, is that Chasity?" he asked.

Before I could answer, she said "Yes, I'm Chasity, and you must be Jordon. It's a pleasure to meet you."

"The pleasure is mine," he responded shyly. "You are pretty, and I'm glad my dad let me plan your surprise."

"Jordon, I don't think she's interested anymore. Let's just hold off on that for now," I replied, thinking marriage was the last thing on mind.

"Man," Jordon pouted, and I could see the disappointment on his face.

"Junior, don't be in a haste. Let's just wait for a more appropriate time," Pops added.

"No, let's not put it off. Jordon, I'm very interested, and I can't wait for my surprise. Can I have it now?" she asked.

"We're not quite ready, but if you give me until tomorrow, you can get it then," Jordon replied.

"I can't wait! You were the mastermind behind a surprise for someone you don't know. I'm impressed. Can I have hug?" I watched as she embraced my son, which softened my heart.

"I know everyone want to spend more time with Chasity, but I need to talk to her. Can you all give us a few moments alone?" Pops requested.

Everyone dispersed, and I went to get a Corona from the fridge. Jordon followed and said, "Dad, Chasity is beautiful. You should've kissed her."

"What do you know about that? You kissed a girl before?"

"Of course, who hasn't," he replied as if I was a moron.

"I hope I get the chance, but we need to give her some time to adjust to being home. You understand, right?"

"I guess," he responded and left.

Chasity was on some other shit, and I didn't know what game she was playing, but I was definitely getting to the bottom of her behavior.

Chapter 34

Chasity

After my capture from the mall, finding out Junior had a son and seeing Destiny so upset, filled me with guilt. Admittedly, I was punishing Junior even after his explanation, knowing there was a legitimate excuse, but I was not playing by his rules anymore. The lockdown had suffocated me, and the taste of freedom was still fresh. He purposely hurt my feeling with the fat jokes, and insecurity invaded my confident mind. Even Destiny had to put her two cents in. They were in the dark about my weight gain, trying to figure out what happened, but Uncle Jon was on to my ass. He asked to speak with me alone and once everyone left, he addressed the issue directly.

"Chasity, come over here and let me look at you," he requested.

"Okay, Uncle Jon. I want to apologize for any pain or unnecessary worry I caused. I just needed a little me time."

"I get that, but it wasn't a good time for you to leave, and it had nothing to do with Junior. I asked him to protect you, and I asked you to be patient. Nevertheless, I will sleep well tonight knowing you're under my roof again. Now that we have that squared away, how far along are you in your pregnancy?"

"Uncle Jon!" I retorted.

"Don't Uncle Jon me, young lady. I assume that's my grandchild inside," he said, sure of himself.

"That's crazy how you just knew, but the father thought I was away overeating! I'm a little over three months."

"Chasity, you're glowing. Your skin is clearer than I remember, and that slight baby bump is one I'm familiar with. You added to my happiness, and I can't wait for my grandchild to arrive! When are you planning to tell Junior? Don't drag your feet with this, Chass. Junior deserves to know, and he's been doing a great job with Jordon. I know he will make an excellent father."

"Yeah, I hope so. I will tell him soon, Uncle Jon. I promise."

"You have until tomorrow morning. If you don't tell him, I will, and I hate to be a snitch. And, your sister dropped out of school. But she enrolled in beauty school. Everyone is not college bound and she admitted she in that category. Don't be upset with her, pumpkin. I'll get her a nice salon when she finishes school," he said, defending her spoiled ass.

"I got it," I replied. "I'm tired and need a nap. Oh, and Uncle Jon? Can you have your chef come and cook some healthy food? When I was at the doctor they told me I have diabetes, the pregnancy kind."

"Oh my! You need to stay away from sugar and salt. I will call him tonight, and we'll hire him full-time."

"I have a dietary sheet that shows the kinds of foods I should be eating."

"Of course, we'll give it to him in the morning. Go get some rest, Pumpkin. Be sure to spend time with Destiny when you wake. She's really missed you."

"I will."

I went into the kitchen to tell Destiny I would take a quick nap. Jordon and Junior were watching TV, and Destiny was eating a bowl of cereal. "Chasity, you want some cereal?" Destiny asked.

"Nah, I'm cool, but can you hand me one of those bananas. I can't have all that sugar," I replied, instantly wishing I could take it back.

"Why, what's wrong with you? I know you gained a few pounds, but you still look good," she said, trying to make up for the comment earlier.

"Just hand me the damn banana, Destiny!"

"Don't snap at me. I'm not the one who had everyone on edge. You should take your own advice."

"And what would that be? If I can recall, you never listened to me, so obviously that shit didn't work."

"Yo, watch your mouth, Chasity. The cussing and foul mouth stops now," said Junior. I ignored his sorry ass, but I made a mental note to watch my language around Jordan. Still, I didn't see the problem. Uncle Kenny cussed us out all the time, and Destiny and I turned out just fine.

"Back to you, girlie. We can watch movies after my nap," I said, changing the subject.

"Can I watch too?" Jordon asked.

"Sure, the more the merrier. I hope you like scary movies," I replied.

"Not really, but if you sit next to me, I'm sure I can get through at least one."

"Don't let me find out you're a scaredy-cat like your father! I think I can manage that. I'll meet y'all in the family room in two hours."

"Two hours!" Jordon warned. He was a miniature Junior.

"I got it, Jordon. Destiny, I meant to ask you, where are Carlton and Anastasia?"

"Uncle Jon put her out. I have to tell you about that. They're history, but I miss Anastasia."

"I guess a lot has happened! Okay, I'll see you later."

When I reached my room, I noticed my clothes neatly put away inside the closet. There were boxes everywhere, and I wondered why, but was too exhausted to inquire. Moments later, Junior came into the room. I pretended to be asleep, but he always seemed to know when I was faking. He eased into the bed and whispered, "I know you're not sleep, baby, and I want you to know that you got my heart and I love you. Please turn around and face me." I turned around, because I could not believe he finally said it.

"Say that again, Junior?" I asked when we were facing each other.

"I love you, you knew that. I'll say it again and in front of the entire world if that will please you. I love you, Chasity Smith, and our life together is just beginning. You still love me, baby?"

"Yes, I do, Junior. I never stopped loving you. I just needed you to say it. The confident me felt it, but hearing you say it makes all the difference. Thank you."

"Can you stop with all the hatred towards me now? I haven't slept well since you left. Let me lay in your arms and rest, baby." I opened my arms, and within seconds, Junior had nestled his head into my bosom. "Your breasts feel so good, and they got bigger just like the rest of you." I ran my fingers through his hair as he dozed off.

"Junior, I will gain more weight, and I hope you won't mind too much," I said, before he drifted into a coma.

"Why, what's wrong with you?" he asked, barely audible.

"I'm pregnant, or I should say, we're pregnant."

He raised his head up and said, "You're pregnant? Damn! I should've known. When you first left, I felt lightheaded and nauseous, but blamed it on the stress on my chest. Why didn't you tell me right away, babe?"

"I thought you would be unhappy. I remember that night we discussed kids, and you were unenthusiastic, saying that was the last thing you want."

"At the time, I didn't know that's what I wanted. But I love you, and I will love our baby," he responded with a passionate kiss. I realized just how much I missed his lips. "I'm about to make everything right. I want to make love to you so badly, but when I tell you I haven't slept, please believe me, baby. Just lay with me," he requested as he rubbed my belly.

What began as a nap turned into a deep sleep, and we didn't wake until six the next morning. Junior gazed into my eyes, and it was both romantic and spooky because he never blinked.

"Is everything okay?" I asked.

"Now that you're by my side, life is grand. Thanks for coming home. I got the best sleep of my life. I feel revived and ready to get back to work. Are you hungry, baby? You're eating for two now. I want to apologize for calling you fat. It all makes sense now."

"Whatever, Junior." We snuggled together for the next two hours, until there was a knock on the door. "Come in!" I yelled.

"Dad, I wanted to remind you about the surprise for Chasity. It's ready, and so are we," Jordon explained.

"I'm so excited, Jordon. I'm sorry about last night, but tonight it's on and popping."

"That's okay. Get dressed. Grandpa said the chef is here and breakfast will be ready soon."

"Thanks, Jay. We'll be down soon," Junior replied. I was impressed by how their relationship developed in such a short period, and was happy to see that Junior had parenting skills. Their communication was effortless. "Come on, let's get dressed. We have a long day ahead of us and you need some new clothes. We can't have you suffocating my baby in those tight jeans you love so much."

"Our baby, Junior. I agree. I need comfort, not style. They have maternity jeans I can get."

"Our lives are about to change. I need to know you're sticking around this time."

"I am, promise."

"That was very convincing," he replied, being smug.

"I give you my word, I'm not going anywhere. I want to be a reflection of you and I feel blessed to be given a chance. I trusted you when you professed your love, and I need you to return the favor."

"Fair enough, now let's take a shower together like old times," he suggested, getting me hot.

"I'm too fat, Junior, and you didn't help my morale any. Let's just bathe separately until I'm comfortable, okay?"

"My bad, babes. I was mad at you and that's all I had. You're nowhere near fat. I want to explore your pregnant body. Follow me," he said as he pulled me off the bed. I followed, hoping he would penetrate me and make my day.

I took off my clothes and Junior stared at me as he leaned against the wall, looking sexy. He was fine on the regular, but he had certain facial expressions and body language that made me weak. It was awkward because on the norm, I would not hesitate to strip. He strolled over and placed his hand on my stomach. He ran his fingers through my hair and kissed my lips.

"I remember now how wonderful your touch is!" I moaned.

"Let me make sure you never forget it," he replied as he undressed.

His hands performed wonders on my body as he caressed every inch. He held my face up to his, and his kiss was full of passion and desperation. I was floating and fully submersed into his will, submitting with ease. Making love to Junior was my comfort zone, because this is where his emotions towards me were undeniable. A river was flowing between my legs, but I anticipated the foreplay, knowing Junior is the master in that department. I wrapped my arms around his neck while lifting one leg and grinding on his penis. He had a beautiful dick, and the way it made me feel was like magic.

"I missed you so much, baby, and I'm sorry for leaving you. Make love to me, Junior," I demanded.

"You're not running the show, sweetheart. It's my turn to show you whose boss," he said, while sticking one finger inside my vagina. "You're not ready for what I'm about to do to you." He bent down on his knee, lifted my leg as far as it could go, and ate my pussy at a thirty-degree angle, providing a new sensation.

"Sheeesh, ooooh, Junior! I can't take it. You're trying to drive me crazy!" I cried. He ignored me and continued to ravish my genitals. As his snake tongue licked my clitoris, tears fell from my eyes from the pleasure. He slid his finger inside me again when he came up for air.

He stood up and said, "Turn around and spread your legs." I assumed the position, ready for my misery to end, when suddenly Junior slammed into my pussy as if he were a Mack truck. I lost my breath and balance, but Junior was right there to put me back in position. "Where do you think you're going?" he asked as he repeated the wanted assault on my walls. His speed became rapid and his hold was tight, making escape impossible. "You leave me and think you can get away with that. Open up and let me in!" he demanded, while grabbing a fist full of my hair and fucking me like a bitch.

"Junior, I'm sorry!" I moaned.

"You should be, taking this good pussy away from me and worrying me to death. If you leave me again, I will kill you. Do you hear me?" I couldn't answer because I was hypnotized by Junior's fucking skills. "Answer me," he yelled and smacked me across my ass.

"Yes," I bawled and backed my ass up, pushing into him and giving him full access. That move sent him over the edge. He pulled out of me and carried me back to the bed. He quickly locked the door, ran back, and was inside of me again.

"Baby, I love you so much, don't fuck with my heart like that," he lustfully reprimanded as he placed my legs behind my head, gunning my pussy down. "You feel better than I remember, baby. This pregnant pussy is so sweet. I need to taste you again." He extracted his dick and went under the umbrella once more. "I want this pussy wet, Chasity, because you're getting fucked now, but I'll make love to you tomorrow. Do we have an understanding?"

"Yesss!" I moaned.

"Good," he replied as his tongue spiraled across my clitoris, sending my body into an uncontrolled dwelling where I lost your mind from delight. He continued to devour and possess me, as if he got joy out of torturing me. He was everything.

"Junior, I can't take it no more, please baby," I pleaded.

"You can't take it, huh? Alright, get on top," he directed. I climbed on top and gently slid down his shaft. Before I could please him, he cupped my hips and jabbed every crevice of my womanhood. It was a constant gallop, reminiscent of riding a horse. He sat up, grabbed my neck and placed one of my legs over his shoulder. "Aaah, baby, stay just like that. This feels so good. You're fabulous," he moaned, never slowing or stopping the pace. Junior was in the fuck-you-hard zone, and who knew when it would end. I strapped on and enjoyed the ride. "You got me lost in your love, Chasity. Do you love me?" he asked, slowing down the rhythm.

"Of course," I replied, shivering. "There's no one else but you. It's always been you." As we kissed, I suffocated his penis with my vaginal muscles, sending him into an ejaculation frenzy.

He sighed like a snake and said, "That was the best sex I ever had. Don't ever leave me again, Chass. You knew I loved you from the beginning. I know I didn't pronounce it, but I expressed it, and there was no reason for you to leave."

"Junior, I needed you tell me how you felt. I hoped you loved me, but I wasn't sure. I'm not leaving you now or ever, and I pray I don't have to keep proving it."

"Dad, we're leaving. Grandpa said we'll meet you there, so hurry up!" Jordon yelled through the door.

"Okay, we'll be down soon," I yelled back. "I'm about to miss my surprise fooling with you."

"Trust me, the surprise ain't going nowhere," he replied.

As we drove, it hit me that this was my new life, and I wasn't sure if things were moving too fast. Although I was pregnant and Junior said the magic words, I felt overwhelmed. I glanced at Junior. His strikingly handsome face weakened me, and I released any doubts I had. I was where I belonged.

"What are you over there thinking about?" Junior asked.

"You, our baby, and the future. What's the surprise, Junior? You can tell me. I promise to pretend when we get there."

"You're not a good liar and I love that about you, but Jordon planned this whole thing and I'm not saying shit."

"Punk," I said jokingly as I punched him in the arm lightly.

"Keep the compliments coming, baby, so tonight when I'm fucking you, I can add them to the long list."

"You don't have to be crude, Junior."

"I disagree. I was too soft on you before, making love to you the way I thought you wanted, but we see where that got me. It's time for us to be one and put all the one-sided shit on hold. Tonight, I'll teach you how to please me. Don't get me wrong, I love making love to you, but when you misbehave, I just want to fuck." He leaned over and planted soft wet kisses on my neck. "I love you."

"I love you too." He pulled me into his arms and I melted. Me and cray-cray, he's my boo thang.

Twenty minutes later, I noticed we were driving around a winding road and wondered where we were. Soon thereafter, we drove off the road and into a driveway, leading to a massive Victorian-style mansion. It was a beautiful home, but the closer we got, the more I noticed an update would not hurt.

"We're here, Chass," Junior said.

"Whose house is this?" I asked.

"A friend of mine. He let me borrow it for the day."

"Is my surprise inside, or do we have to go somewhere else?" My patience was running thin.

"Calm down. I can feel your body becoming anxious. Let's go inside so you can relax. I don't want you stressing our baby."

"I'm just confused, but I'm ready. I hope Uncle Jon got me another car."

"Why do you get so excited about his gifts and not mine? How do you know I didn't get you a car?"

"Yeah right, Junior. Let's go." I laughed.

"You got jokes, but that's just another strike added to the list. You're making this easy."

"Junior, I'm not afraid. Bring it on, baby."

"Your wish is my command," he replied, grabbing my hand as we walked inside.

The home was more beautiful on the inside, but it looked abandoned, as if the prior residents just left. I was truly dumbfounded at this point, so I just followed Junior. He led me into a room and when the lights came on, people screamed, "Surprise!"

I looked around and saw Uncle Jon, Domencio and his woman, Jordon, Jeff, and Calvin. The room was decorated like a five-year Olds birthday party, with balloons that said Happy Birthday and Welcome Home. I finally spotted Destiny, and she was holding a little boy, who I assumed was Uncle Kenny's son.

"Oh my God! I don't know what to say. Thank you for welcoming me, Jordon. You made me so happy. Can I have a hug?" I asked.

"Sure," he replied, happy with himself. I could see the pride on his face as he walked towards me. He wrapped his arms around my waist and hugged me tight. "I'm glad you're home, because my dad is happy now."

"I think you had more to do with that than me, but we're family now and we can make each other happy," I responded.

"The real surprise is coming soon. Let's get some ice cream and cake first," he suggested.

"Deal." I greeted everyone and thanked them for coming, and I saved Destiny for last. She stood in the corner with Kenny Jr, waiting. When I stood in front of her, Kenny stared at me and rubbed his sleepy eyes. He reached his hands towards me, wanting me to pick him up, and I hesitated.

"Chasity, he wants you. Take him before he cries," Destiny demanded as she placed him in my arms.

He lay his head on my chest and his little fingers gently pinched my skin. He was holding on tight, and I couldn't deny him. I propped him up on my shoulder, placing him in a more comfortable position, and he was out like a light. I held him the entire time while mingling and wondering why they had the party here. They could've easily had it back at Uncle Jon's beautiful abode. The house was huge, but there was no furniture and I was itching from dust. I was about to tell Junior I was ready to go when he asked for everyone's attention and for me to join him. Destiny took Kenny, and I walked over to Junior.

"You must be curious why I brought you here. I can see it on your face." He smiled and pecked me on the lips. "Let me take you out of your misery. You damaged me and stole my heart when you disappeared, and I will not make the same mistake again. I need you and I'm only half of a man without you," he said and kissed me again, "This house belongs to us if you like it. I wanted to build a home from the ground up, but I knew you wouldn't go for that. I found a place you can renovate, remodel, and do whatever your heart desires. This is where we'll start our family. Does that make you happy?"

"Yes, I am! You did all this for me. You must love me, Junior."

"I'm trying to tell you. Jordon started the process of planning your surprise party, and it escalated from there."

"I helped with everything, even the..." Jordon stopped speaking when Junior looked at him.

"Shhhhh, lil man. We're about to get to that part."

"What part?" I asked.

"The part where I ask you to become my wife. Chasity, will you marry me?" he asked, as Jordon handed him a black box. He opened the box and a perfect, round cut diamond blinded me momentarily.

"Yes, baby, I will marry you!" He placed the ring on my finger, and it fit perfectly.

He pulled out another box and said, "Jordon picked out the first ring, but this ring is for special occasions." The new ring was ridiculous.

"What size is that ring?" I blurted, because it was humongous, and I would never feel comfortable wearing it.

"I got you, babe. I told you this is for special occasions," he whispered. "The other ring is an everyday ring, but there will be times when I need everyone to know you're taken. We'll put it in a safe for right now and pull it out when needed, It's ten carats," he bragged.

"You're a mess, you know that? But I love you, flaws and all."

"Likewise, baby, Likewise."

"Since everyone is in a good mood, I too have something to share," Domencio interjected. "This is my lady, Savannah, and we're also pregnant. I'm not quite ready for marriage, but I'm ready to see what the future holds," he explained and kissed Savannah. She was gorgeous, reminding me of the singer Mya.

"This is truly one of the best days of my life. My family has tripled in size and I'm a happy old man. I never thought I would have grandchildren, nor a daughter, but now I have two. Destiny, will you join me?"

"Yes, Dad," she replied, as she walked towards him. Everyone did a double take.

"Yes, Destiny is officially my daughter. I legally adopted her a day before her eighteenth birthday, and I feel complete."

"Now all you need is a woman, Uncle Jon." I added.

"Once you two tie the knot, please call me Dad or Pops, Pumpkin."

"We can start now, Pops." He embraced me, and his cologne smelled so good. When he finds the right woman, she will be one lucky bitch. He walked over to Savannah, hugged her, and said "Welcome to the family."

"Well, there you have it. To the Blake's!" Junior said. "Jeff, I have to steal you away from the office for a while. I need your help with this house. Since you did such a good job with Chasity's flip, I know you could work wonders here. Especially since there's no budget. Whatever my baby wants."

"Anything for Chasity. Plus, you're the boss. I go where I get paid," Jeff replied.

"I know I'm not family, but I look at you all as family and I will do everything in my power to keep the Blake's safe," Calvin spoke.

"Calvin, you are my most loyal friend, and you are considered family," Uncle Jon said.

"Junior, I don't mean no harm, but this place is making me sneeze with all the dust. Can we go home until the house is fumigated?"

"I'm ready when you are. Everyone, let's take this party back to Pops' house. Jordon, are you ready?"

"Yes, Dad."

Everyone except Jeff went back to Pops house. He said he had a date, and if everything worked out, he would introduce us. He was a trip, but I was happy Junior brought him along for the crazy ride. When we got home, the chef prepared salmon, teriyaki shrimp, crab cakes, lobster, and scallops, along with seasoned red potatoes, Caesar salad, and string beans. I tore that food up and felt blessed to have a chef. After dinner, Savannah, Destiny, Jordon, and I watched movies, while the men drank in the study. Finally, a secure family that loves us, I thought as we laughed at *Ride Along* featuring *Kevin Hart*.

As promised, Junior fucked me silly that night, and I fell deeper in love with my fiancé.

Four months later

Life on the ranch was grand, and I felt a great sense of love. Junior treated me like a queen and catered to my needs and complaints. He made Christmas a dream by taking Jordan and I to Paris. We visited Rome and England on our two-week vacation. Jordon missed a few days from school, but his teachers all agreed it would be an opportunity of a lifetime. Jordon was a wonderful child, and he helped me keep Junior in check. Pops was even dating. He courted Paige a month ago, and she took the bait. Everyone approved of her, including Junior, and I admired her strength. She was a surgeon who had little time for Pops, but when they connected, everyone saw the special bond developing between them. She was a striking Caucasian woman with her own money. Pops asked her to move in, but she declined, wanting to take things slow. He was understanding and patient, two qualities I hoped Junior would master.

We had just gotten back from the NASA Space Center. Jordon went ballistic when we arrived there. He was definitely in his element, and when we had lunch with Astronaut Bill, the light in Jordon's eyes was bright. He had so many questions, and Bill was patient with explaining and educating him. He was impressed with Jordon's intelligence. We spent the weekend exploring the adventures of the space center and I had to admit, it was one of the best trips I had encountered.

Jordon was happy, and he told us often. However, when Kali moved into the mansion, I had to find a huge amount of inner strength to hold my tongue. When Jordon asked Junior if she could stay, I was fucked up. Junior put the weight on me by telling me it was my decision. I contemplated it, and on the third day, Jordon asked me to go with him to the hospice.

When we arrived, he asked me to join him to meet his mother, unaware I had beat her ass not too long ago. I was reluctant, but just like his father, I could not deny him. I walked into the room slowly and waited until Jordon embraced his mother.

"Mom, this is Chasity, my dad's fiancé. You remember? I told you all about her! I wanted you to meet the person who's been taking care of me." She sat up slightly and glanced at me with a smile.

"It's nice to meet you, Kali. Jordon has told me so much about you, and it's a pleasure to meet the woman that raised such a great kid," I greeted.

"Thank you, and the pleasure is mine. Come closer, Chasity. I can barely see you from way over here." I walked closer and sat down on the chair beside her bed. "Oh my! You look like you're ready to pop any day now. When is your due date?" she asked.

"May sixteenth, but I'm ready to have this baby. It's becoming more and more difficult to just take care of my hygiene. That can take a minute," I laughed.

"Trust me, I know what you're going through, but this is the price we have to pay for the sin, you know. Jordon, can you give us a few minutes, sweetie? I need to speak to Chasity alone. Can you go get me a soda from the vending machine? Here's a dollar," she instructed.

"Should you be drinking soda?" I asked.

"At this point it don't really matter. Go now, Jordon, and I'll see you in a few minutes."

"Okay mommy, I'll be right back," he replied and exited.

"Chasity, the last time we met was a disaster, to say the least. I want you to know that I forgive you, and I had that ass-whipping coming. Trust me, I would have done the same thing if it were my man, may he rest in peace. Jordon speaks highly of you, telling me about the time you spend together. Of course, I'm hurt I won't be around to love my son, but I'm overjoyed that he will have you. I just ask that you love him as a mother would. You'll find out about that kind of love real soon, and I pray you embrace Jordon."

"You don't have to worry about that. In the last few months, I've come to love your son. He made it very easy. He's bright, handsome, and loveable, and I vow to be there for him always, even if Junior is ever out of the picture. You see, I know about loss more than I would like. My parents' death came as I hid in the attic. I was raised by my aunt and uncle, and they died in a car crash on their way to my graduation."

"Oh my goodness, I didn't know! That must have been hard on you."

"Yes, it was the worst, and I was left alone to take care of my sixteen-year-old sister. But a year later, the Blake's came into my life, and now I have a family again. So I know how Jordon will feel, but I will be there to help him get through, and I promise to keep your memory alive."

"I believe you, Chasity. I can sleep better knowing you will be there for him."

"I'll be here for you too, Kali. Whatever you need me to do," I responded. I felt the need to hug her, so I stood up and embraced her. "Your son is in good and capable hands," I whispered. Jordon came back, and we chilled until visiting hours were up. I promised to come every chance I could, and the satisfaction on Jordon's face encouraged me.

That was two months ago, and she moved in last week. After I agreed, Pops hired around the clock medical staff to provide her with the best care, but I was underwhelmed. It was fine while she was at the hospital, but now she was invading on my attention. I understood her disease was more important than my common pregnancy, but I was annoyed. However, that was just the beginning of my discomfort that week. Junior walked into the bedroom and handed me a prenuptial agreement.

"What's this?" I asked, dumbfounded.

"Read the top of the page, baby, and don't tap your feet on this. I'm ready to get married, and this is the only thing standing in the way." When I remained silent he said, "What's the problem, Chass? Just look it over and sign on the dotted line. I'll be back for the questions I know you'll have."

I looked at the paperwork and got a headache after reading the first line. A half hour later I finished reading the ridiculous document, which verified Junior's mental disorder and the fact that it was progressing. The financial settlement amount in the event of divorce was not the problem, but rather the section that listed Additional Clauses was insane.

"Junior!" I yelled, ready to cuss his monkey ass to hell.

Chapter 35

Junior

I thanked God each morning for Chasity, Jordon, and our little girl, Lela, who was on the way. It was Chasity's idea to name her after my mother, and I had no objection. When I saw my daughter on the ultrasound, I was in awe at technology. There was no doubt the baby was a girl. I thought it was impossible for me to experience this much love, and I was desperate to marry Chasity within the next couple of weeks. Jeff told me the house was almost complete, and it was obvious Chasity had been uncomfortable since Kali moved in.

On her second day at the house, Kali was severely sick, and I felt sorry for her. She was hysterical and going on and on about leaving Jordon. I held her hand, and of course Chasity walked in at that exact moment. Surprisingly, she joined us and held Kali's other hand, which both relieved and shocked the shit out of me. My love for her escalated to an unforeseen scale. I thought this shit would fade, but she was unshakeable, and it was time to take full ownership of her.

I planned to fly to Vegas for a quick ceremony, and then she could do whatever her heart desired for the family. The prenuptial agreement was holding up the process. In my heart, that would prove her love and I was praying she just signed. When I handed her the papers, she looked lost. But if she thought I was marrying her weak and unarmed, she was deluded.

When I walked into the study, Pops was on the phone, so I poured myself a glass of Patron. I was counting the minutes before Chasity confronted me, and I wanted my mind to be relaxed. Seconds later, I heard her screaming out my name. Pops wrapped up his call when he heard the drama queen. She stormed into the study, but took a few moments to catch her breath.

"Junior you have lost your fucking mind! You are fucking crazy if you think I'm signing this shit!" she hissed, and flung the documents towards me.

"Yo, fuck I tell you about that mouth while you're carrying my seed? Calm down. Now," I insisted.

"What's wrong, Pumpkin? Why are you getting yourself and the baby so upset? Junior, what was that paper she threw at you?" Pops asked.

"A prenup, and before you defend her, I'm not getting married without one."

"Well, that settles that. This marriage is off, and you can kiss my ass!" she barked.

"You think you're worth half my money? Nah ma, you got me twisted. I'm worth a quarter billion dollars, baby, and you like to run and disappear. Chasity, for your own good, sign the fucking papers." I demanded.

"Let me see those papers, Junior," Pops said as he snatched them out of my hands.

"Focus on the Additional Clauses at the end, Uncle Jon," she said.

"What happened to Pops?" Pops asked.

"I love you no matter what I call you, but Junior just shot down any chance of you becoming my father. There's an Infidelity Clause, Baby Clause, Career Clause, and a whole host of bullshit. He's trying to control and take my identity away from me!" she cried and left the room.

Minutes later, Pops said, "Son, you truly are special. This agreement is ridiculous. Do you want her to leave again? As I recall, you were a step away from losing your mind and having a breakdown. No woman would sign this shit, and you don't deserve Chasity."

"A woman that loves me would, and Chasity will submit. Just stay out of it, Pops."

"Dig your own grave, Junior. She loves me unconditionally, and that came straight from the cat's mouth. I will take care of her and my grandchild. She doesn't have to bow down to your narcissistic ass to feel loved."

"Pops, I see you're in your feelings about this shit, so I'll give you some space," I said and went into the kitchen. "What's up Jordon? What's that you're watching?" I asked.

"A program about black holes in the Universe. Did you know that we could be living in a black hole and not even know?"

"Is that right?"

"Yes. Why is Chasity so upset, Dad?"

"Not you too, Jay. We need to be on the same team and you need to have my back sometimes," I jokingly replied.

"I do, but I remember you were so sad when she was away. If she were my lady, I would try to make her happy every day. She's sweet, and we have so much in common. If you don't want to treat her right, when I turn eighteen, I'll gladly take on the responsibility," he smirked.

"Don't make me find out you're plotting on my wife," I replied, while play fighting and throwing soft jabs.

"Jordon, your mom wants to see you," Chasity interrupted. Jordon ran over and gave her a tight hug. He glanced at me and smiled.

"Yo, take your hands off my woman, Jay. She's mine," I said.

"I belong to God, and you can hug me as much as you want, Jordon," Chasity smugly stated.

"I know, but from now on, I'll hug you when grumpy isn't around," Jordon replied.

"Chasity, stop playing and come here," I demanded.

"Junior, not now. Trust me. You don't want none of this," she spat and left out the kitchen. Jordon followed, leaving me feeling abandoned.

Chapter 36

Chasity

I was drifting off as I snuggled with my pregnancy pillow. When Junior walked into the room, I pretended to be sleep, but he always knew when I was faking. He got into bed, eased over, and rubbed my belly. I pushed his hand away and tried to turn as far away from him as possible.

"I see you're still mad, baby, but don't push my hand away again. I'm sorry the papers upset you and I never thought you'd react that way. Turn around and face me, Chass."

"No, there's nothing more to say. Just leave me alone and find yourself a puppet, because I'm not that girl," I replied.

"Correction, you are that girl, and I will only ask one last time. Turn around and face me, now," he demanded.

"Kiss my ass, Junior, and leave me alone!" Within seconds, he slid the back of my pajama pants off and kissed my ass. "Stop playing, Junior," I yelled, trying to get away from his hold.

"You said kiss your ass. Come here, where you think you're going?" he asked. His sexy grin and hypnotizing eyes weakened me. "It's time for you to understand the severity of this situation. Me, you. We are one. I told you before that God loves me, and I'm not letting go what he designed for me. You're my Mary, and I know how Joseph must have felt protecting and caring for her. I can't live without you, and if you will grant me this one wish, I promise to cherish and give you your heart's desires."

"That's sweet, Junior, and I love you too, but I'm sure Joseph didn't ask for an agreement or have all these stipulations. He obeyed God with sacrifice, knowing she was not carrying his child. If I'm Mary-like, then you need to step out on faith."

"Did you take a bath yet?" he asked, changing the subject.

"No, I was too distraught to bathe."

"Let's take a quick shower so I can rub you down with cocoa butter."

"I'm tired of the smell, and I'll take a shower in the morning," I replied while trying to turn over.

"Get up, let me show you something real quick," he responded as he helped me out the bed. He escorted me to the full-length mirror and said, "Take off your clothes." I stood in the mirror naked, wondering what he was doing. "Look at your stomach and tell me if you see one stretchmark."

I stared hard, but I could not see one. "No, and what's your point?"

"Turn to both sides and tell me what you see." I looked at my hips and my skin was smooth and silky. I shook my head. "That's my point! Your ass is intact as well, because I'm taking care of the body that belongs to me. Don't fuck up the progress. Let's take shower so I can maintain my goods."

"You get on my nerves," I nagged, but submitted. As promised, Junior rubbed me down, and we went to bed.

The next morning, I woke to an empty bed. I sat up and spotted the agreement on the side table. Junior was not giving in, but neither was I. After dressing, I went downstairs to the kitchen where I found Paige and Uncle Jon kissing.

"I'm sorry, I didn't mean to disturb you guys, but I'm starving."

"Don't be silly, Chasity. I was just saying goodbye. I'm on call the entire weekend and I won't see you until Sunday, my darling."

"I'll be counting the hours," he replied.

It was all I could do not to barf, though I was truly happy for him. When she left, I said, "Where's Junior, Uncle Jon? He knows I have a doctor's appointment today, and I'm already running late."

"He went to work, but I can take you to your appointment."

"Okay, but he doesn't like to miss my appointments. I guess he's giving me some space."

"Maybe. I think you two need counseling. I see issues with the both of you."

"Whatever, Uncle Jon. I'll be ready after I eat."

"Okay, pumpkin. I have to change clothes and check on your sister."

"Uncle Jon, wait! I decided I do want to take that DNA test. I want to know if Uncle Kenny was my father."

"I'll take care of it." He left, and I enjoyed a healthy breakfast, thanks to our chef.

Before we left, Uncle Jon told me to have a talk with Destiny, because he believed she was hiding something. I hadn't noticed anything, but I was too busy being pregnant, dealing with Junior and Jordon, and tolerating Kali. I called her as we walked out the door.

"Destiny, what's going on with you? Is there something you need to discuss? I know I've been neglecting you, but I want you to know that I'm here if you need to talk."

"I don't know what you're talking about, Chass. Everything is fine," she replied. Just then, four vans surrounded the car, and several men with ski masks came straight toward us.

"Oh shit! Destiny! Some men are about to kidnap or murder me and Uncle Jon!" I yelled into my cell. "Call Junior and tell the security in the house to get their lazy asses out here. We're about to be goners."

"Oh shit," I heard her say, right before one of the masked men shot Rodney, our driver, in the head. Another pointed a gun to Uncle Jon's head and forced him into the Evade. A third grabbed me and shoved me into a van.

"Help us!" I screamed constantly, but it felt as if it was falling on deaf ears. When we pulled off, Uncle Jon's security let off shots with no regards to us, and the kidnappers returned fire. I had to duck down in the nasty ass van to avoid the gunshots. *If I make it out of this shit, I'll be sure to tell Junior to fire those incompetent fools.* I was not in the mood for this bullshit and figured Track was behind this brutality. I'm tired of living in fear, and if that means Track has to die…so be it.

Chapter 37

Track

I returned to Philly from a much-needed vacation, but I still had some dirty laundry to wash. Word on the street was I was hiding, but that was not the case. I took Carlton and Anastasia to Mexico for a few months. I handled business while she enjoyed the beauty of the country. I felt comfortable with Carlton, but I would never fully trust her. If I'm keeping shit real, she's a thot, and the way she did Jon-Jon, that bitch would do me the same. However, she was very useful in my mission to take out the Blake's. She gave me their address and I had my boys watching the place.

After a week of surveillance, I decided today was the day. I just got the call telling me they had Jon-Jon, but I still needed pretty boy himself in my custody. I was waiting patiently for my guest to arrive at a warehouse I owned in the Kensington area. It was time to settle our differences, and for him to pay for killing my father. Although that piece of shit sperm donor never gave me anything, it was the fucking principle of it all. Who knows what would have happened between he and I when I got older, because Jon-Jon took that possibility away from me. He thought I didn't know, but I'd known that shit for years, even when I hustled for the snake.

Revenge is always sweetest when you're the one supplying the ingredients. Those idiots believed this shit was over Chasity, but that was just the icing on the cake. Yeah, I was feeling her, but not enough to start a war. Junior cemented the war with his disrespect, but Jon-Jon started it when my father died. You reap what you sow, and my day is coming, but it's not today.

Minutes later, I heard a female voice pleading and wondered what the fuck was going on. Then my men brought in Jon-Jon and Chasity.

"Yo, why the fuck did you bring her along? I didn't request her, Bean. Yo, you slipping dog."

"I didn't have a choice, Track. They were together, man!"

"Look at you. You're ruined. I guess that's Junior baby you're carrying. You let that nigga impregnate you. Damn!" I said, staring at Chasity, feeling fucked up that she would have to die. I getting slightly uncomfortable, and that protruding belly did not help.

"Track, please just let us go. You and Junior need to talk your differences out instead of all these dramatics."

"Dramatics, you say? Chasity, I'm truly sorry they brought you here, and this kill will hurt more than any of the others. I want to you to know that I'm hurting inside, baby. I would rather love you than hurt any part of you."

"Where's my uncle, Track?" she asked, forwardly and fearlessly.

"He'll be joining us soon, but you should be more worried about yourself, and that baby inside. Oh, I forgot, you're a tough girl. On the real though, you beat the shit out of Kali. I just wish you chose my team to fight on"

"You're correct. I am tough, but I'm in a vulnerable situation, which I'm sure will work at your advantage. I'm asking you nicely to let us go. I've lost so much already, and I can't bear to lose my uncle."

"But your uncle didn't consider me at all when he put a hit out on me. Again, I apologize for my idiot boys involving you. I'll take care of them the same way I plan to take care of you. Chasity, don't worry, I will not lay hands on you, and your death will be painless." My speech was interrupted when my men came in, dragging Junior in front of me. "Ah, finally, the great Johnathan Blake has arrived. Now we can get the party started."

Chapter 38

Junior

Chasity, Jordan, and the baby weighed heavily on my mind as I sat behind my desk. These past few months, I tossed around the idea of starting a new business with Chasity. However, she was challenging me and putting up a good fight. The prenuptial agreement was a flop, but that was just my security blanket. If Chasity had obeyed and signed, I would've shredded it in front of her. I was looking for affirmation of her love so we could move the fuck on with our lives.

Moments later, Calvin barged into my office. "Boss, we got a problem. Talk to Destiny. She's on the phone." My heart dropped, because I knew it was bad news.

"What's wrong Dee?" I asked, preparing myself for the worse.

"They took Chasity and Dad! They—they--took my sister!" she yelled into the phone.

"Calm down, Dee," I replied, before turning my attention to Calvin. "Calvin, get that special gear and let's roll. Tell me what happened, Destiny."

"I was on the phone with her and suddenly she screamed they were kidnapping them. She told me to call security, and you." She was sobbing and shrieking at a high pitch.

"Where were they going?"

"She had a doctor's appointment. Dad said he would take her."

Fuck, I forgot about her appointment. "Do you know if she has her phone?" I asked while jumping into Calvin's SUV, because I was moving as we talked.

"I don't think so, because shortly after she told me about the men, the phone went dead. Junior, please find my sister. I will die without her," she cried.

"What the fuck did security do?"

"By the time they got out there, they were at the front gate. So they shot at the vans, and the kidnappers returned fire. I'm scared."

"Listen, take two security men and Jordon to your house. I'll call you back soon, and don't worry." I disconnected the call. When I glanced at Calvin, he was already on the iPad looking up Chasity's phone's location. When she got back from her little trip, I placed tracking device in her phone and on several other items. Because of the ongoing threat from Track, I insisted she carry mace spray and an illegal Taser. She refused to carry the gun I purchased for her, but compromised on the other items. I prayed she had them with her.

"Junior, the phone is a half a mile from your father's house. They probably threw it out when they saw her talking. I'm pulling up the other service to check for the spray and Taser. It's a good thing you thought about that, Boss."

"Yeah, but she might've taken another pocketbook. If she left with Pops, she felt safe. I'm praying she's carrying that new Chanel bag I bought."

"Prayers answered, we have their location. I'm calling in backup, but I have two vests in the back and a small arsenal. We can do this. I'm not letting anything happen to you. We're less than ten minutes away. They are in Kensington."

"Good looking. If anything happens to them, Calvin, I will demolish Track and kill his entire family. I should've handled this instead of letting Pops take control. My fucking unborn baby, man. This nigga trying to take my world away from me?" I asked, about to break down.

"Calm down, Junior. We're almost there. You ready?"

"Fuck you mean? My family is in severe danger. I'm killing everything in sight."

"When we get there, I want you to follow my lead. You haven't held gun in a long time."

"Calvin, save that shit."

"We're two blocks away," he said as he glanced at the iPad. When we pulled up on the block, the signal directed us to an old warehouse. "This is how this thing will go down, Junior. We gone park on the next block and check this shit out."

Calvin parked the car around the corner, and we geared up for war. He never lied when he said he had a small arsenal. After putting the vest on, I had my choice of handguns. I chose the Glock with the silencer, all the while praying we made it in time. As we approached the back of the building and searched for a way in, Calvin pushed me back against the wall and shushed me.

"We got one at the door. On my count, take him out," Calvin explained. With the quickness, I revealed myself and shot the doorman in the head.

We crept up the steps and cautiously opened the door. I overheard the other thugs inside and proceeded with haste. When I burst into the room, I immediately took out two of Track's men. I heard a gunshot coming from the other room, and Calvin let off several shots, letting the whole world know we were there. He killed the other two men in the entryway, and I ran to door, hoping I was not too late.

Chapter 39

Chasity

After I was shoved in the van and shot at by my own people, one of the kidnappers threw my phone out of the window. When I realized they put Uncle Jon in another van, I knew I had to man up and fight. Today was not a good one to be fucking with me, let alone kidnapping me and my uncle. My feet were swollen and my back was in severe discomfort. If they thought I was losing another family member, or myself for that matter, they were in for a rude awakening.

The longer we drove, the angrier I became. I was trying to keep my cool for the baby's sake, but I was fired up. *How dare these bastards take me from my front door?* Uncle Jon's security was horrible, and I felt bad for coming down so hard on Junior. He was paranoid for good reason, and when I get out of this mess, I'll be sure to inform my baby that I finally understand. I figured by now Destiny reached Junior and he sent an army out looking for us, or at least I hoped so. The thugs parked in back of a warehouse, and my dread increased, knowing this would not end well. It was like a scene out of a gangster movie starring me, and my temper started to rise again.

"Don't be pulling on me so hard! Can't you see I'm pregnant, fuck face?" I snarled when one of the kidnappers yanked me out the van. He forced me up the stairs and into the warehouse. Once inside, fear consumed me, but I would never let them know I was scared. My intentions were not to beg for my life, but to fight. Another loss was unacceptable, because I had a daughter to birth.

We went through another door, and I was forced down the steps. That's when I saw the bastard himself, reclined in his chair as if he were a king. I wasted no time asking where my uncle was, and he wasted no time showing me his true colors. The situation was far more severe than I had anticipated. Moments later, they bought Uncle Jon in, and I raced to his aid. He was badly beaten and blood was oozing from his temple.

"Now we can get the party started," Track said.

"What party, Track? Why are you doing this? Please don't say it's about me, because I'm not worth this."

"Don't flatter yourself, baby. You're cute, but we know the truth. Ain't that right, Jon?"

"I don't know what truth to which you're referring, Track. You started this war, talking recklessly and threatening my family. You would do the same thing."

"Yo, sit his ass down in this chair and tie him up. Make sure that shit is secure, Burnie."

"No, get the fuck off my uncle!" I yelled, while punching Burnie with several blows. He mugged me so hard that I fell to the ground. I took a minute to inspect my stomach, which was fine, but something felt off on the inside of my body.

"Nigga, did I tell you to put your hands on her? She shouldn't even be here," Track barked before shooting him in the head. His blood splashed on me and Uncle Jon. "See, baby, I told you he would pay. Cutty, tie him up. And as for you, Chasity, I need you to calm down before you get hurt. I told you I got other plans for you," he said as he helped me up from the floor. "I tell you what, stay close to me for right now." He pulled me into his arms and began to taunt Uncle Jon.

"Track, do what you want with me, but I of beg you, please let my niece go," Uncle Jon implored.

"Her presence is unfortunate, but I'm sure my father, and your wife for that matter, didn't have a choice either. Tell me, how is it that my father, who never did drugs, was found with a needle in his arm?"

"You seem to have all the answers, but this newfound love for your father is shocking. I recall a man that never claimed you.

When you were hungry, I fed you and gave you a home," Uncle Jon responded.

"Everything you gave me I worked for, pussy. I was the one in the streets grinding for you and your newfound uppity family," Track thundered.

"Fuck dis nigga, Track!" Bull said, as he hit Uncle Jon in the head with a pipe.

"Stop!" I yelled. "You're a bitch ass nigga. It takes all of y'all to torture and punish one man. If I wasn't pregnant, I would beat your ass like a dude," I cried. I attempted to run to Uncle Jon, but Track pulled me back.

"Not so fast, little momma. That tough girl role won't get you far with Bull. I told you I got you, Chasity. You won't suffer, I promise," Track said and kissed my neck. "Bull, I'll handle it from here. Take Cutty and check on the shipment."

"You sure? Why you playing, Track?" Bull asked.

"Nigga, just do what the fuck I asked you to do!" Track yelled, and Bull reluctantly left. *Yes, this is what I've been waiting for,* I thought as I discreetly rummaged through my pocketbook. Junior insisted I carry a can a mace and a Taser. This was my only chance, and I was taking it. Track was the true Psycho, and our time together was nearing its end. "You feel better now, Chasity? You're right, torturing your uncle would be a bitch move, so how about I just put a bullet in his head," he said as he pointed his gun at Uncle Jon.

I flipped the top off the can of mace and sprayed him in the face. *That shit really works,* I thought as he grabbed his eyes from the burn and I went in for the kill. I pulled the Taser out and shocked his ass into Kingdom Come. He fell yelling to the floor, and I grabbed the gun out his hand.

"Quick, Chasity! Untie me!" Uncle Jon implored.

"But he's still moving! Oh my God, he's getting up!" I panicked and shot him in the head with a gun I snatched off the ground.

"Chasity, untie me now," he demanded, but right then, we heard gunfire coming from upstairs. I didn't have time to be untying Uncle Jon. Instead, I backed up against the wall and aimed at the door. As soon as it opened, I closed my eyes and emptied the gun. When I opened them, I spotted one man at the bottom of the steps and another laid out on the rail. I noticed the watch on the man's hand at the bottom of the steps, and knew Junior had the same watch. Uncle Jon was screaming to get untied, but something drew me to the man I had just killed. What I saw next took me into premature labor.

"Junior, oh nooo!" I bawled. "Uncle Jon, it's Junior! I killed him! Please, oh God, tell me I'm dreaming. This can't be real!" I bent down and saw the blood draining from his neck. "Junior, I'm so sorry, I was trying to protect our baby, please forgive me," I cried.

"Pumpkin, look at me," Uncle Jon said coolly. "Help me, so I can help you, baby. Untie your uncle," he demanded.

I got up and felt an indescribable pain in my abdomen. I knew something was wrong. "Uncle Jon, I think I'm going into labor."

"That's why I need you to get over here, now!" I hobbled over, untied Uncle Jon, and felt another contraction. "Oooooch," I screeched.

"Come on, Pumpkin. We need to get you to a hospital." Uncle Jon inspected Junior when we reached the steps. He angered me when he kicked Junior in the leg and said, "Wake your ass up, Junior. We need to bounce." He bent down and smacked the life back into Junior, and he moaned. *Thank you Jesus,* I silently prayed, no longer mad about the kick.

"What the fuck! I'm hit, Pops!" Junior sighed.

"The bullet just nipped your neck, so you should be grateful. Wrap this tie around it and let's move! Calvin, are you hit?" Uncle Jon asked.

"No, Boss. Just a little fucked up from the impact. I called for backup and they should've been here already."

"Good. I need you to call housekeeping and take Junior back to my house. I'll take Chasity to the hospital, but Junior can't go. Get Paige on the phone, now." Uncle Jon demanded.

"Oh my God, I shot Calvin too. I'm going to hell. Junior, I didn't mean it. I thought you were one of Track's men. Calvin, please forgive me," I begged.

"I forgive you, Chasity," Calvin assured. "Boss, I have Paige on the phone."

"Baby, I can't go into details, but I need you back at the house ASAP. Bring your tools, because Junior needs a bullet removed. No, baby, I'm okay, but he needs your help. I'm on my way to the hospital. Chasity appears to be in labor. I know. I'll see you when I get home." Uncle Jon said.

I glanced at Junior and he was staring at me with a dead, unfamiliar expression. I knew at that moment our relationship was irreparable. Junior had many strange expressions, but this one was especially eerie. Another contraction came, and then my water broke. "Uncle Jon!" I screamed.

"Let's get you to the nearest hospital," Uncle Jon said.

Once upstairs, I saw several bodies scattered around the room and instantly became sicker. Back up security was coming in as we were leaving, and even in the state I was in I felt sorry for them, knowing their fate of unemployment or possible death. Two of them broke off from the group and escorted us to the hospital.

This cannot be happening without Junior, I thought, while Uncle Jon took over as my support system. We were in the final stretch, and I was about to score. Lela refused to wait, and she was emerging into the world a month and a half early.

"Push, Pumpkin, we're almost there! Man, I can see the head! You can do it, sweetheart!" Uncle Jon cheered.

"Yes, one more good push, Chasity!" Dr. Simmons concurred. I pushed one more time and when she came out, it was as if I let out a huge shit, relieving me from an unbearable constipation. I melted into the pillow, trying to catch my breath. I glanced at my daughter as they were cleaning her up, and I could see she had a head full of hair. When they handed her to me I thought of Junior, because she looked just like him. She weighed six pounds one ounce, and she was seventeen inches long.

"She's beautiful. Right, Uncle Jon?" I asked as I doted on my beautiful little girl.

"Yes, she is. Just like her mother. She looks a lot like Junior's mother, Lela. You made me the happiest man in the world, and I owe you my life."

"You don't owe me anything Uncle Jon. I know you love me, and you will make a great grandfather. I would do almost anything for you because as an adult I can actually protect the ones I love.

"There's no doubt in my mind that you mean what you say. I can never repay you for today," he said sincerely.

"We could go on all night, so I'll change the subject. I'm naming her Lela Cathy Blake. Although she may not have her grandmothers around, she'll carry their names."

"That's sweet and a wonderful gesture. As soon as we get home I'm spoiling all my girls, and I will treasure every moment with my family," he promised. Once everyone left the room, he said, "Pumpkin, you are a phenomenal and brave woman. You showed no fear back there and impressed me unlike anyone. I don't know where you got that controlled gangster mentality from, but I'm thankful for it."

"Uncle Kenny. Although we lived in the suburbs, he was ghetto as hell and could cuss up a storm," I laughed. "Most of my classmates were white, so I started speaking like them. When Uncle Kenny heard me say their slang, he snapped. He explained that it was one thing to attend an all-white school, but a completely different story if I continued to talk cracker. He even threatened to whip my ass, which he would never do, because he couldn't even bare me being mad at him."

"I couldn't bare it either, and I can see why it was easy for him to love you. I need to check on Junior and hire new security. I'll be back soon with the whole gang.

"Okay. Please tell Junior that I love him and we have a beautiful little girl who can't wait to meet him. And, Uncle Jon, there was something in Junior's eyes that killed me. I don't think he wants to be with me anymore."

"He would be a fool if that's the case. I doubt he feels that way. I'm sure once the shock wears off, he'll be back to the Junior you love. Though, I'm still trying to see it. either way, you don't have to worry about your future. I told you, I got you."

"I know you do, but you don't have me the way he does, and I can't imagine my future without him. We have to fix this Uncle Jon. I'll need all hands on deck for this one."

"Anything for you. I'm leaving, but I'll be back as soon as I can."

"Please get Destiny, Jordon and Kenny Jr. up here. I can't wait for them to see her."

"Right away." He kissed me on my forehead and left.

That evening, Uncle Jon and Paige brought the whole crew, along with gifts, balloons, and teddy bears. Everyone was overjoyed, but the one that truly mattered was home getting bullets pulled out.

"Uncle Jon, how is Junior? He's going to be okay, right?"

"Yes, he will be just fine. One bullet caught his thigh and another nipped the right side of his neck. He'll survive, and when he wakes, he wants to Facetime. Here's an iPad so he can have a bigger picture."

"Thanks everyone for coming. I didn't have a baby shower, but this is the next best thing. Destiny, get over here and give me hug," I demanded.

"Chasity, you scared the shit out of me. We have to be more careful, sis, because I thought I lost you for real. Lela is so precious. My mom and dad would be so proud. I wish they were here, but I'm happy for our new family and I can't wait to babysit."

"Me either. Jordon, are you happy?" I asked, hoping he didn't feel second best.

"I'm happy, and I'm going to protect her and you. That's what big brothers do!"

"Thank you, Jordon. I love you." He didn't say it back, but I knew in time he would. He still had his mother, and I wondered how she was doing. I decided not to mention it and risk dampening the happy occasion.

Once they left, Junior and I Facetimed, but I was more of an afterthought. He was unable to hide his disdain for me and focused his attention on Lela. I tried to ask how he was doing, but he cut me off and ended the Facetime. My feelings were hurt, and I became paranoid at the thought of him not loving me anymore. He had to know that I didn't intentionally try to hurt him. I relied on our love and believed once we were together again, our love would conquer all.

The next morning, they told me I was being discharged, and I was more than ready to get the hell out of there. As I was packing my belongings, Uncle Jon called with the sad news that Kali had passed away that morning. I know this sounds heartless, but I was relieved, yet still sorry for Jordon. I just couldn't imagine going home to my ex-fiancé and his dying ex-girlfriend. I was ready to be a mother to Jordon without the haunting of her sickness.

That evening, I was overwhelmed with just having a baby, Kali's death, Junior's dismissive behavior, and killing a man. I wanted to rectify things with Junior, but Jordon needed me more. I focused on his needs and assured him I was there for him. He took it very badly, and I was not surprised because he loved his mother. He cried himself to sleep in my arms, and I related to his pain. I waited until he was in a deep sleep before I went to check on Lela. She was with her father in one of the guestrooms, which he obviously took residence in recently.

"Hey, Junior. She's beautiful, right? I think she looks just like you, but Uncle Jon said she reminds him of your mother." I said, trying to feel him out.

"She's a gift from God, and I will cherish her all the days of my life. I think she may be hungry," he replied, placing her in my arms and leaving the room. I called after him but he ignored me. Tears fell from eyes, because he was done with me. His disposition showed a void when it came to me and for the first time, I was afraid to approach him.

Chapter 40

Junior

I magine trying to save something you thought was precious, only to have it backfire on your ass. My heart felt as if it were struck by lightning when she riddled me with bullets. After the first shot to the leg, we made eye contact, and she continued to shoot. There is no doubt in my mind she saw me, no matter how much Pops tries to convince me otherwise. She could thank Lela and Pops for her life, because I could barely stand to be in her presence without wanting to choke her to death, so I maintained my distance. Eventually, she stopped trying to convince me of her innocence.

One month later

I was spending time with my daughter when I received the good news that Brock, my childhood friend, was in town. I didn't have many friends, but I considered him a good one. We hung out almost every day from our sophomore year in Junior High until we became seniors. He went to college while I went to jail. He was never into the drug game, but he didn't knock me for my hustle. He was someone I could trust, and I respected him for not allowing the streets to tempt him out of his dreams.

"Junior, did you hear that Brock is back? I invited him to dinner tonight and can't wait to find out what he's been doing all these years." Pops said.

"Domencio just text me with that information. Dinner sounds cool, but I think we should go to a nice restaurant."

"That sounds absurd, Junior, when we have one of the best chefs in town right here. I want him to meet the entire family, and Chasity has been under the weather. I don't want to leave her alone. You may not have noticed, but she's depressed, Son, and she came down with the flu recently. I had to order formula for Lela until she gets off her meds. She can't breastfeed right now."

"Why am I just finding this out?" I asked as I rocked my daughter in my arms.

"Since when do you care about Chasity? I've said a thousand times and I'll say it a thousand more. You are a fool for turning your back on her. She is my hero, and she was only trying to protect us. She had no idea you and Calvin would come through those doors. She showed bravery, and her fearlessness saved our lives. I loved her before, but after the kidnapping, I have a lifetime pedestal to place her on, so you can stand around stuck on stupid and watch her slip through your fingers." He warned.

I repositioned Lela in my arms and tried to ignore that last part of his comment. "Pops, let's do seafood tonight. The chef makes some mean mussels, and Brock loves seafood."

"Chasity loves seafood and everyone knows it. You're not slick, Junior, and you can never fool me. Did you know that she cries every night over you, to the point where I can't even console her? Yes, she is hurting, but the amazing thing is, she hardly shows it. She takes excellent care of both your children, and they would never know she's pain. I watch her with Jordon and he adores her. She prays with him before he goes to bed and then cries herself to sleep. If you weren't my son, I don't think you would matter."

"I see where your loyalty lies, Pops, but my interests lie only with my kids. Had I known she was sick, I would've spent more time with Lela. Now that I know, I'll have her bassinet brought to my room."

"Yeah, you do that," he replied and walked away.

I spent time with my daughter every night, fully willing to be a full-time dad. I changed Pampers and had the feelings down to a science. I even knew when to burp her, so this would be easy "Ain't that right, sweetheart. That's daddy's little girl," I said as I kissed her cheek. She smelled so good, and I loved that she was an image of me. When the bassinet arrived, I placed her inside and went to Chasity's room.

When I walked inside, she was smothered under the covers. She coughed and sounded horrible. She was sick, and I had never witnessed her so vulnerable. She sat up and placed her face into her hands as if she had given up on life. It took her a moment before she realized I was in the room.

"Oh sorry," she said, once she spotted me. "You need to take Lela to Uncle Jon and Paige. They're watching her until I get better," she explained and coughed again.

"That won't be necessary. I can take care of my daughter. I came to get a few Pampers and her blanket."

"Her Pampers are on the changing table. Let me get the things you'll need." I observed her as she obtained Lela's necessities, and she looked worn down. For a second I felt sorry for her, but I quickly blocked that emotion. "If you need anything else, just let me know," she said as she handed me the bag. She jumped into the bed, pulled the covers over her head, and that was my cue to leave.

"I hope you get better soon," I replied and left. That was the most words spoken between us since the shooting.

Brock arrived, and his presence distracted me from my circumstances. Since Lela's birth, Pops had a calm demeanor and with Brock's arrival, he was on cloud nine. He always compared me to Brock, saying I should have been more like him, but I never took it personally. Dinner was delicious and Pops was right, there was no need to go to a five-star restaurant when we had one of the best chefs in the Philadelphia area. Domencio and Savannah came over, and she looked like she was ready to burst. Wayne had stopped by earlier, but said he had to get back to the office. Everyone was there except for Chasity. Brock's interest in Chasity was on an all-time high when Pops explained she was sick and bedridden.

"I can't wait to meet the mother of your child, Junior. I must say, my man, I never thought I'd see the day," Brock said.

"What day?" I replied with a confused look on my face.

"I think we should retire to my study for a drink. Domencio, are you joining us?" Pops asked.

"Nah, I'm taking Savannah home. You ready, babe?" Domencio asked.

"Yes, but I'm sorry I missed Chasity. Junior, will you give her my best?" I nodded, but had no intentions on relaying that message.

Once they left, we retired to the study, and Pops poured us each a glass of his favorite Scotch. I downed mine with one gulp and sat on the couch.

"Brock, don't follow Junior. Take your time with the Scotch. It's meant to be savored, not abused."

"Pops, why is it I can never make you happy? I can move mountains and you'll still find fault with it. Back up off of me and try supporting me for once, instead of showing your obvious disappointment," I said, ready to go to war with him.

"Junior, let it go," he warned.

"Jon, the Scotch is delicious. My preferred drink is Henny, but I'm adding this to my shelf," Brock said, trying to break the tension.

"Sorry my friend, you won't be adding this to your stock. You can't get this bottle any longer."

"Well, I'll be sure to savor it then, as you suggested. Junior, tell me more about Lela's mother. She must be special if she got you to commit to a baby. You have two kids, nigga! The last time I was here we had a different woman every night. I was kind of looking forward to it myself, but you're a family man now, so I'll chill."

"Brock, this girl is trouble. She stole my heart and tried to kill me. Short version, and that's all I have to say about her."

"What the fuck, man? I'm still stuck on tried to kill you and she still breathing!" Brock rubbed his head.

"She will breathe as long as God sees fit. Junior is delirious about the facts, so let me set the record straight. Chasity is a Godsend, and she is the light of my life. She is strong, fearless, sweet, and caring, traits Junior knew nothing of until she came into the picture. You'll meet her soon, because you're staying with us. I insist." Pops said.

"She sounds extraordinary," Brock replied.

"If it sounds unbelievable, then it probably is," I added.

"Junior! Shut up, please," Pops begged.

"Uncle Jon, where are Lela and Jordon?" Chasity asked as she came into the study.

"Speak of the angel. Brock, this is my beautiful niece, Chasity. Come, sweetheart. Are you feeling better?" Pops asked, bowing down to her ass.

"Not really, but I'm tired of being in the bed and want to see my kids. Paige gave me some masks and gloves. I want to hold my daughter. Where is she?" Chasity asked with authority.

"She's with Destiny, Pumpkin, and I believe Jordon is in the pool," Pops responded.

"Thanks, and I'm sorry," she added as she turned toward my friend. "It's nice to meet you, Brock. I would give you hug or shake your hand, but I don't think that would be wise," she said and coughed.

"It's not a good idea for you to be around the kids, either. When I saw you earlier you sounded bad, and you still do," I interjected, ready for her to catch a tantrum.

"You think so? Maybe you're right. I would feel so guilty if either of them got sick," she humbly said, surprising me.

"Well, it was nice to meet you, Brock. But I should get back to bed."

"The pleasure was mine," Brock replied.

"Wait, Pumpkin. I'll tuck you in," Pops said, running after her.

"Junior, tell me something, my man? This shit don't make no sense!" Brock asked when they left.

"Brock, you know you're my man from way back. I trust your opinion, so I'll share this story one time, and you can tell me what you think. You remember Track?"

An hour later, I finished giving him the complete story, and it felt good to have everything off of my chest.

"Damn, man. That was a story that belong in theaters. But you really believe she intentionally tried to kill you? I just find that hard to believe. You said she doesn't like to listen, but she obeyed you a minute ago."

"I was just as shocked as you, because she never makes shit easy for me. She's spoiled and Pops don't help. You see that display that just went down. He's putty in her hands, and she can do no wrong in his eyes. After she shot me in my leg, she opened her eyes and continued to shoot. Both her and Pops tried to convince me otherwise, but that's not how I remember it."

"Do you think it's possible that you saw what you wanted to see?" he asked, doubting me.

"Fuck you! I'm sure of it, and that's what I can't get past. When I try to remember loving her, it gets foggy. Whatever feelings I had been fading."

"I don't believe that shit for one minute. I saw the spark in your eyes when she walked into the room. I know what it is, it's that virgin pussy!" He laughed at his own joke.

"For sure, but she brought more to the table than that."

"Enlighten a brother," Brock said as he poured another glass of Scotch.

"She didn't need me. I'm used to women falling to their knees at the sound of my voice. You know how I do. She wasn't like that, Dog, until she wanted me. Even then, it was like pulling teeth! She got me with her honesty and boldness. When she wants something, she goes after it. She was hell bent on trapping me and almost succeeded. I proposed to her and in return, I get bullets to the leg and neck."

"Were you attracted to her when you first met?" he continued to pry.

"Nah, not at first. She didn't grab my attention until her little tantrum at the meeting. You know me, Brock. Women bow down to a nigga, but this chick was ignorant and inappropriate. The way she disrespected me was punishable by my law, but surprisingly, it intrigued me."

"She hit that ghetto hood rat shit on you?"

"Yeah, but I knew she wasn't ghetto and when I placed her ass in the chokehold, it was as if she welcomed it and she showed no fear. I had to turn her loose from the job because she affected my common sense and placed a spell on me. I thought I was in the clear, but when she showed up here, I knew I was in trouble. Once she announced she was untouched, I was a goner. The game began, and now here we are."

"You mean to tell me you weren't attracted to her when she walked into your office the first time?" he asked, smirking.

"Fuck no! I make it a point to never get involved with work bitches. I have plenty of attractive women working in the building, but I never play where I stay. There are too many women in the world for me to bring that shit to my business. Hoes would be fired after a week."

"Now, that's the Junior I know, but what's different about Chasity? I mean, I've seen some of the women you've baited, and you even put me down with some elite pieces over the years, so forgive me if I'm still trying to take this shit in."

"No need to apologize, my brother. I'll be back to old Junior in no time. Chasity had a nigga going all out, but never again," I explained, trying to convince myself as much as him, because I had just purchased her a Ranger Rover. Her Infiniti was too small to be driving Jordon and Lela around town, I rationed.

"Listen, let's change the subject. I'll be here for the majority of the summer, so we can revisit this another time."

"Agreed. Now let's head down to the basement so I can whip your ass in a game of pool."

The Range Rover came the next day with all the specifications I required. I had a high end-tracking device installed and cameras inside. It was slightly armored, yet sleek. I called Pops and asked him to give the car to Chasity, because I had to keep my distance. I glanced out the window and when he handed her the keys, she did her happy dance I loved so much. However, Pops must have told her I was the giver, because the dance stopped. Brock walked into the family room and surfed the channels. A few minutes later, Scarface made her entrance.

"Junior, thanks so much for the SUV. I was tired of being chauffeured around just to take Jordon to school or Lela to her doctor appointments. You always seem to know what I need before I do. Good morning, Brock. It's good to see you again. I'm sorry again about last night. I must have looked horrible."

"You're very beautiful, Chasity, and I doubt you would ever look horrible," Brock laughed. "You have a lovely daughter, congrats."

"And a son," she corrected. "Thanks Brock, that's sweet of you to say." She was a step away from being pulled by the hair, and Brock was about to go missing.

"I heard you complaining to Calvin, so I figured you could give him a break with all the nagging and get what you want in the process. I'll feel at ease with you driving my children around in that car," I said, interrupting the flirt fest.

She looked at me sideways. "You would feel safe, huh? Oh, I get it now! When I go too far the car will just stop, right? You probably got a kill switch on it, Junior!" She cracked up as if I was comedian and continued to laugh hysterically.

"What the fuck is so funny? The only one that kills shit around here is you. If you want to drive my kids alone, you drive that car you ungrateful...!" I caught myself before I went too far.

"Bitch, right? Say what you mean and mean what you say. Anything after ungrateful is bad, and you don't want to start name-calling, Junior. I came in here to thank you and show my appreciation, but from now on, I'll keep my mouth shut. Brock, sorry about all of this, and I would like to welcome you to this fucked up, dysfunctional family starring Junior Blake." She stormed out and Brock just looked at me.

"You see! That's the shit I'm talking about, and you still didn't get a full dose of her venom."

"Junior, get your woman before it's too late, brah. Yo, you two are hilarious." He left out, leaving me alone with my frustration over Chasity.

That evening, everyone gathered around the table for dinner and Pops had an announcement to make. "Family, with all we've been through, I'm proud to say there will be another addition to the family. Paige and I are pregnant." Everyone seemed taken aback, and Chasity even spit out her drink. "I know this is a shock, but obviously I'm still strong in that department. Also, I asked Paige to be my wife, and I expect you all to welcome her to the family."

After a few moments of awkward silence, Chasity spoke. "Welcome to the family, Paige. I think you guys make a wonderful couple am so happy Uncle Jon found someone to love."

"Thank you, Chasity. I do love your uncle and I plan to cherish him. I'm retiring early, because I don't want to risk losing the child I've dreamt about. At forty-five there are more risks involved with my pregnancy. So Chasity, I can babysit more often! I just adore Lela, and she's a bright child. If you could give me the information on those videos you play for Lela, I'd greatly appreciate it."

"Yes, I can do that. But before we get off track, there's something I need to say. The news of your engagement made me realize that I need to bring this out into the open. Junior, I want to apologize for earlier. I never meant to antagonize you, because I love you. This past month has been hell for me. I don't know if I'm coming or going. I spend all my time focused on the kids and praying you take me back!" she cried.

"Don't cry, Pumpkin. You don't owe him an apology," Pops spat.

"Honey, I think Chasity can handle it," Paige said as she calmed Pops down. I liked her.

"Anyway, I just wanted you to know that I respect you, and I will sign the prenup if that will bring you back. I can learn to be a slave, I mean…a submissive wife, and if you would only give us a chance, I know I can do it."

"Stop it, Chasity! I will not allow you to humiliate yourself and beg for his forgiveness. He's the one that should be on bended knee. Junior, if I didn't love you, I'd disown your ass. This girl has sacrificed and given up her life for you, but you're too shallow to see it," Pops barked.

"Uncle Jon, I'ma need you to calm down. Junior is a king in his own right, and I can't live without him. Junior, let's go away somewhere and talk. Remember how we used to talk for hours? Let's get to know each other again," she begged.

My heart wanted to take her into my arms and hold her for an eternity, but my pride got in the way. I stood up from the table, grabbed her hand softly, and said, "I'm sorry, Chasity." As I was leaving, I heard Destiny call me a pussy which brought back memories and ignited my anger. I stormed to my room, tormented by my negligence and arrogance.

Two months later

Brock is heading back to Los Angeles tomorrow. He had spent the majority of the summer trying to convince me to move to LA and get back with Chasity. I was somewhat sad to see him go, but was distracted by Domencio and Savannah's baby shower. The house was full of unknowns, mainly Savannah's family. Pops planned a lavish party, and I was looking forward to it. The backyard was beautiful, and everyone congregated out there. When I walked outside, Pops asked where Lela and Chasity were.

"I don't know, but she should've been down here by now. The party started over an hour ago. There goes Jordon, let me ask him. Yo, Jay! Where's your sister?"

"She's with Chasity, Dad. Dad can I go over Tyler's house? He has a new stethoscope I want to check out. Please?" he begged.

"Is this party too girlie for you?" I asked.

"Yeah, sort of, but I really want to see his stethoscope, and his sister likes to rub her butt up against me."

"What! How old is this sister?" I asked.

"Fourteen. She's harmless, Dad. So can I go?" he pleaded.

"Yeah, tell Rob to take you and call me as soon as you reach his house."

"Thanks Dad. Love you!"

"Love you too, Son." I couldn't be more proud of Jordon. We bonded as if we were never apart. Speaking of bonding, I was missing my daughter, so I headed to Chasity's room. She and I were now cordial and on speaking terms.

When I walked inside her room, I spotted Lela laying in her crib and noticed that they needed more room. Lela's things monopolized the room, making it look like a daycare center. I bent down and kissed her hands softly so I would not wake her. I heard the shower running, so I went into the bathroom. When I got inside, it was steamy as shit, but I saw Chasity sitting on the shower stall, just allowing the water to run. When I got closer to let her know that I was taking Lela, I noticed she was moaning and using a silver egg-like gadget to jerk off. I stood there until my dick was about to explode watching this freak.

"What the fuck are you doing?" I yelled. She jumped up and the silver egg fell to floor as it vibrated out of control. I watched as she struggled to get control of the vibrating device. "You're going to electrocute yourself, dumb ass. Look at you, you can't even pick it up! And what the fuck is that, anyway!" I barked.

"Get out!" she screamed, but I didn't move.

"Nah, not until you tell what that was about," I replied, still blocking her way.

"What did it look like, Junior? It's none of your business anyway. Please move," she asked as she wrapped the towel around her body. I moved to the side and followed her. I knew she was embarrassed because she couldn't look at me.

"I came to get Lela since you were taking so long. But back to the shower. What if Jordon walked in and caught you sodomizing yourself? I don't think that's a good look ma, and I don't appreciate you doing that nasty shit while my daughter is in the next room."

"What would you have me do then, Junior? Umm, let me think about it a moment. I guess the right thing for me to do is to go find me someone to satisfy my needs, instead of getting carpal tunnel pleasing myself. Next time, knock, because you never know what you might see!" she spat, angering me with her comments.

"Do whatever you want, Chasity, but don't do that shit around my kids."

"Or what? What could you possibly do that you haven't already done? You took my heart and shredded it to pieces, so there's nothing left, baby. Just take your daughter so I can finish what I was doing, and I'll be down when I can." She rolled her eyes and let the towel drop. I watched as she sat on the bed and began covering herself with lotion. I had to get the hell out of there.

I placed Lela in the travel carrier and left hot and nasty alone. Later that afternoon, I went into Pops study to get away from all the commotion and enjoy a real drink. When I looked out the window, I spotted Chasity and Jordon playing with Lela. I was drawn into their interaction with each other and realized I was missing out. I enjoyed my kids, but Chasity had mastered motherhood, and Jordon adored her. She was impressive with the way she cared for my kids. Lela was smart for three months, and she could thank her momma for that. Chasity spent numerous hours stimulating and reading to her. When she walked into the room, Lela would light up and get excited, and I couldn't blame her.

"She is truly a gem, Junior. I was hoping you guys would patch things up, but I see you both are stubborn," Brock said.

"Yeah, I know, but I don't know how to find my way back to her. It's been a while, and I'm still not ready to say I was wrong. I let my misguided emotions destroy my relationship, my world, because that's what I see when I look at her."

"Man, she's right there, and since I've been here, she's been giving you the green light, brah. You need to man up and get out your feelings before you lose the love of your life. Initially, I thought it may be just an infatuation, but I was wrong. A blind man could see you love her. She's the one, man, and you heard that shit from me. God bless you, but I'm not ready to give up my player card yet."

"I hear you."

"I hope so. Anyway, I'm going back to the party, because Savannah got some sexy ass sisters and friends, like beauty runs in packs. I've been here for two months and haven't gotten laid once thanks to you. This has never happened, but I have a chance to redeem myself. I'll see you outside," he said and left.

Once the main party died down, Savannah's family and friends came inside, because Pops knew how to keep a party going. I was holding my daughter when Wendy, Savannah's sister, approached us.

"Your daughter is so beautiful, Junior, and she looks just like you. What's her name?" she asked while touching her hand.

"Lela," I replied, keeping it short because I knew this game oh so well. She was pushing up on me, giving me permission to proceed. I know Savannah told her about Chasity, so she knew there was beef between us from the many dysfunctional dinners. Despite my tumultuous relationship, she was barking up the wrong tree. However, I'm always a gentleman to a beautiful lady, and I didn't want her to feel uncomfortable. I engaged in small talk about Lela, but when Chasity walked in and saw the exchange, I regretted it when I saw the same deadly eyes that took Kali out. She lacked control, and I was worried for Wendy. Chasity surprised me and left the room. I saw Pops standing in the corner watching the scene, and he followed her when she left.

"Junior, if you're ever in Delaware, please call me. I would love to cook for you sometime," Wendy said, throwing her pussy at me.

I just smiled and was happy when Destiny interrupted. "Junior, I'll take Lela for a while. I haven't played with her all day," she insisted.

"Sure, I need to talk you about something anyway. Would you excuse us Wendy?"

"Sure, but I'll be right here if you need me."

"Why would you need her, Junior?" Destiny asked, ready to defend her sister.

"I don't, come on," I said as I ushered her away. "Thanks for saving me little sis. I'm glad to see you got your brother's back. I still have to get used to having a little sister."

"Yeah, and a new sibling coming soon."

"That's right, Pops'. There's so much going on in this family."

"Junior, you need to stop playing with my sister. You know you can't live without her and she loves the ground you walk on. I would suggest taking her away somewhere and marrying her.

Fly her to a remote island and make this thing official. I'm finally happy with my life and want my sister to experience the same thing."

"Yeah, believe it or not, I want her to be happy too."

"Well you need to start acting like it. Oh my goodness," she said and covered her mouth. "Chass, you look beautiful. Where are you going, Sis?"

When I turned around and saw Chasity, I wanted to whip her ass in front of everyone, and it didn't help that everyone told her how beautiful she looked in her hooker attire. I was burning up, knowing this was revenge for Wendy, but she was taking shit too far. She knows I don't play that shit.

I'm going out with Natasha. You remember her, Dee. She worked with me in the woodshop. She invited me to hang out." *I'll be sure to fire her first thing in the morning,* I thought. "Savannah, I hope your enjoyed your baby shower, it was beautiful. I can't wait for little Domencio to arrive."

"You and me both, girl. This baby is kicking my behind," Savannah replied. "Chasity, you're looking sexy tonight. I'm used to seeing you in a Maxi dress or some sweats, but you clean up nice and you look stunning!"

"Thanks, Savannah. I'm looking forward to letting my hair down and dancing the night away. Uncle Jon, can I speak to you for a moment?" Chasity asked.

"Yes, Pumpkin," he replied, and they stepped out of the room.

"You're going crazy, aren't you?" Destiny asked. "That dress is the business, and I would be scared if I were you. You're just going to let her leave in that dress? My, my have times changed, Junior. Oh well, I guess it's really over between you two," Destiny taunted.

"Watch Lela," I said and went to find Chasity.

"That a boy." I heard Destiny say as soon as I walked away.

On my way to find Chasity and Pops, Jordon stopped me in my tracks. "What are you doing here? I thought you left." I asked.

"I did, but Tyler acted like a bitch over his stethoscope so I left his punk ass alone. Plus, his sister wasn't there."

"Yo, Jordon. Who told you that you could use that type of language in front of me? What's really good with you, my man?"

"I apologize, Dad but that's how I felt, and Chasity said I should never be afraid to express myself. She explained that some cuss words are acceptable and good for the soul, though certain words I can't use."

"Really, so what words are off limits?" I asked, knowing he just gave me the leverage I needed.

"Actually, I can say shit, punk ass, and bitch, but only when referring to a man. Don't mention it, Dad, I'll stop if it bothers you. I'm sorry."

"Apology accepted, Jay. I don't expect to hear you form those words again, understood?"

"Yeah," he replied and put his head down.

"Lift your head up and take your shame like a man. Come with me, I want you to see Chasity."

Once inside Pops study, I witnessed him handing her a check and her embracing him. "What's going on?" I asked, breaking up the happy moment.

"None of your business, Junior. Chasity, I hope that satisfies my debt to you, though there's no way I can ever repay you."

"Uncle Jon, would you stop already? You don't owe me anything. Your love and support is thanks enough. Jordon, where were you?" she asked when she noticed us. "I was looking for you earlier because we forgot to finish our designs."

"I went over Tyler's and his punk a—I mean, he acted like a little bi---I mean, girl, so I came home. You look pretty. Where are you going in that short dress?" *Jordon hit nail on the coffin. That's right son, find out where she's going.*

"I'm going out with a friend. It's been a while since I had some adult time. You know."

"I know, but I don't think you should wear that." *Yes, get her ass Jordon.*

"Why?" she asked.

"If you go out in that dress, you will definitely meet someone. Men will likely flock to you, and I want you and Dad to get back together."

"Jordon, I wanted that too, you know we discussed it, but I can't keep my life on hold forever. No matter what happens, I will never leave you. I will always be here for you."

"Pops, Jordon, I need to speak to her in private," I said.

"Alright, but I don't want no shit from you, Junior. Pumpkin, call me if you need me," Pops said as they left. She stood there ready to battle with her agitated eyes and ignorant stance, but this was a battle she was about to lose.

"It appears you're testing me with that hooker get up you're wearing. And before you start with that shit about us not being together, I don't want to hear that. You have kids, and that dress is inappropriate. Before you leave, you need to change before we have a problem," I explained.

"Junior, there's nothing wrong with this dress. Everyone told me I look beautiful. And the fact remains, we aren't together, so I don't see your problem with my get up." That was the response I expected and she should've expected my next move.

I grabbed her by her neck and backed her into Pops desk. She smelled so good and the dress was turning me on. "What? Say it to my face," I dared.

"Say what, dumb ass?" she barked.

"Tell me again what everyone thought of this shirt," I replied as I stuck my hand up her dress. "You don't have on any panties?" I yelled, ready to commit first-degree murder. "You want to die tonight! What the fuck is wrong with you?"

"You're hurting me, Junior." She gasped.

"Yo, I'm bugging, but before I lose all control, let me escort you to your room." I grabbed her arm and ushered her to her room.

"Dad, is everything alright?" Jordon asked when he saw us pass the family room.

"Yeah, we're cool, Jay. Go and enjoy the party. I'll be back soon." When we reached her room, I locked the door and pushed her onto the bed. "Take off the dress or I'll rip it off myself."

"Fine, Junior. If you think the dress is too revealing or sexy, I will take it off," she replied as she undressed. *My God,* I thought when I saw her perfect body again. Her breasts stood at attention, and although she was no longer breast-feeding, they looked full of milk.

"Hurry up and change, and make sure you put on a pair of panties before I knock you out," I barked, needing her to cover herself quickly.

"There's no need for the threats, Junior. You already spoiled my evening with your unfounded concerns for me, so I'll just turn in for the night. You can see your way out and lock the door when you leave," she replied as she opened the drawer to get her underwear. I glanced down and could not believe my eyes.

"What the fuck is this, Psycho? A rubber dick, Chasity! What are you up here doing alone?" I asked in shock.

"Nothing, Junior, just give it back. It's nothing."

"This is some freak shit. Let me see what else you got in there?"

"Noooo!" she screamed. She tried to push me to the side, but it was too late. I found the silver egg, jelly, and another rubber dick that looked like it was the mother of all jack off devices.

"This whole time, you convinced yourself that I was the one who was cray, when all along it was you who needed meds. The only things missing are whips and chains. You need your ass whipped with a bottle." I grabbed the items and placed them in Lela's diaper bag, and she went ballistic.

"Give them back, you selfish bastard!" she yelled as she pulled at the bag. "What do you expect me to do?" She smacked me and it took the strength of Hercules not to body her. "I've had it with you! I'm tired of trying to do everything just right, hoping you will come back to me. But I'm done with that. Me and the kids are we're moving into the house. I passed through last week, and the house is ready."

"We who? Because my kids ain't going nowhere, and neither are you!" I replied and snatched the bag away from her.

"I hate you, and you can't stop me from leaving. Uncle Jon gave me twenty million dollars tonight, and I will fight you in

court with the best lawyers. I'm tired of trying to figure your
mind out, Junior. You win, and I give up. I'm young, rich, and
beautiful. I want to party and experience what it is to be young.
No more of you holding my heart hostage and playing with my
emotions. You can have the toys, Junior, I'll just order more until
I find the real thing. Now, get the fuck out of my room, and the
last nigga that threatened me—well we know what happened to
him." She gave me the meanest expression and covered her head
when she jumped into the bed.

"Chasity, thanks for reminding why we're not together. You
can leave, but you'll be going alone. And if I'm not mistaken, the
last part of your comment was a death threat." I pulled the sheets
back and dragged her out of the bed. I forced her to the floor by
her hair and climbed on top of her. "If you ever threaten me or
mention that day again, I'll forget you're the mother of my child.
Do we understand each other?" I barked while squeezing her
face. "You got one more chance to answer before I snap your
neck."

"Yes," she sighed, and her expression showed that she was
floored, literally.

I gazed into her eyes, watching as they filled with tears and
hurt, and it killed me. "Yo, I didn't mean to hurt you and man
handle you that way. You know I hate disrespect, and I'm still
coping with what happened, but I would rather cut off my hands
than to use them on you." I stood up and lifted her to her feet. "I
didn't mean to spoil your night and I think you should go and
enjoy yourself," I said, feeling bad for the way I reacted.

"I don't have nothing else to wear. That was one of the
dresses Uncle Jon bought last year, and they all fit the same.
Please leave, Junior. I just want to be alone, something I've
become accustomed too and something that brings me peace."

"Fair enough, but it's your own fault you don't have anything
to wear. You're rich by your own account, so act like it," I replied
before grabbing her toy bag and leaving.

When I got downstairs, most of the guests had left. Savannah
and a few of her friends were still laughing and giggling. I
noticed Wendy staring at me and I gave her my famous *you're the*

last person I'd fuck with look and she caught on quickly. I spotted Destiny feeding Lela her bottle and went to get my daughter.

"Where's Chasity, Junior? Did you make things right? If you tell me anything different, I'm disowning you as my brother."

"Listen little sis, that thing you mentioned earlier about getting away...can you set something up for the family while I work on something else?"

"Sure, how soon are we talking?"

"ASAP!"

Chapter 41

Chasity

For the past three months, I've been holding Lela and Jordon down, and Junior was starting to act normal again. I deserved to wear a big fat S on my chest because I was a super mom. I took Jordon to his doctor appointments, school and after school activities. I wanted him to know that I was there for him, and our love was growing. He told me last week that he loved me like a big sister but respected me like his mother. That brought tears to my eyes, knowing I was following in the same footsteps as Uncle Kenny, and I planned to do the same exceptional job.

Junior on the other hand was a hard nut to crack, and I had exhausted all possibilities and hope. No matter what I tried, he shot me down. I put aside my pride and bowed down to him, though he never noticed. I compromised myself many times because I just couldn't imagine life without him. It seemed as if he'd become even more handsome and sexier since we've been apart. I looked forward to dinner, knowing I would see him. I put on a happy smile, but felt desperate and uncontrolled inside.

The first month, I cried every night, and Uncle Jon would come in and console me. He, along with everyone else, tried to convince Iron Man that he had it all wrong, but we all know his mental disorder got the best him. However, when Brock came there seemed to be hope in the air. He was definitely team Chasity and we spoke often. I knew to keep our conversations short and he picked up on that as well, knowing that Junior was crazy as hell. However, his attempts failed, and I was at my wit's end. When I tell y'all I did some desperate shit to get my man back without success I am not exaggerating. The last straw was at Savannah's baby shower. We were on speaking terms, which sent me the wrong message. I thought that meant we would be together soon and move into the house as one big family. My childish dreams went up in smoke when I saw Junior flirting with Savannah's sister. When I witnessed it with my own eyes, my first instinct was to go over and punch Wendy in the neck, but I was a mother now and that would've been inappropriate. Instead, I went upstairs, called Natasha back, and told her I would come to her family's party.

I hurried and put on one of the dresses Uncle Jon had bought me last year. I didn't have many clothes because before Lela was born, Junior bought me everything. He had my body size down to a tee, and when I would ask how he knew what size to get, he'd say he knew my body better than I did. When I glanced in the mirror, I knew the dress was too much for Junior, but not for the average man. Most men would love to flaunt me around, but not Mr. Hibernation. He would rather hide me from the world and keep me to himself, and I was cool with that—until now. I gave my face a quick makeover, sprayed on perfume, and went to face the enemy.

When I got downstairs, all eyes were on me. When I looked around, every man in the room had a bulls-eye view of my badness. My shit must have been tight and I was feeling myself. Once Destiny placed her stamp of approval and I saw the venom in Junior's eyes, satisfaction was a bitch. I stole Uncle Jon away to ask if he and Paige would watch Lela for a couple hours to get away from Junior. I knew I was playing with fire and didn't want to give him any more leg room to whip my ass.

"Uncle Jon, can you and Paige watch Lela while I go out for a few hours? I really need to get out of this house. Please?" I begged.

"You don't have to ask, Pumpkin. I would love to watch my granddaughter, and you deserve to get out. You do know you're taking security with you, right? I know things appear safe, but until I'm sure, I'm not risking my family's lives again."

"Okay, Uncle Jon, but I don't know why you and Junior gave me cars if I can't drive them."

"You'll be able to drive wherever you want soon, I promise. But I'm glad you pulled me away. There's been something I've been meaning to give you for some time now."

"I hope it's not another useless car?"

"No smarty pants. I think this gift is much more substantial. Take a look," he said as he handed me the open envelope. I noticed all the zeros and saw a two in front, but before I could thank him, Iron Man stormed in with Jordon in tow.

His plan to ruin my night worked when Jordon asked me to take off the dress. That bastard used our child against me. I had to change because I was not about to make Jordon feel uncomfortable. I just wanted to feel sexy because I'd been running around in my nun dresses Junior got in Dubai. Another one of the things I did to make him happy, even if he didn't notice. When he asked to be alone with me, I knew it was on. I wasn't really in the mood to fight because I was still getting over him embarrassing me earlier. I was having a wonderful time with my bullet, about to have a wonderful orgasm, when big-head busted in on me. Initially I felt shame, but when I thought about it some more, I could've been doing worse things.

Once they left, the look in Junior's eyes was not just of anger but of hurt and confusion, a combination I had never witnessed. When he escorted me to my room and took my sex toys, shit got crazy. I thought he was going to beat my ass, and he really came close. In the midst of the fight, I gave in and allowed him to get his shit off. I should've known better then threatening him, knowing he already thought I tried to kill him, but he had me heated.

Two days later, Uncle Jon informed me that we were all going on a family vacation. I wasn't in the mood for a vacation because I was too busy trying to find a way to keep Jordon and Lela without facing resistance from Junior. He had made it clear he wasn't going for that.

"Uncle Jon, when are we leaving?" I asked, hoping I had time to go shopping.

"Tomorrow," he replied.

"Dang, why so soon? I need time to get Jordon and Lela together."

"That's all been taken care of, Pumpkin. Did you forget what family you belong to, Chass? Let me refresh your memory — The Blake's."

"Uncle Jon, I need to get some clothes. I haven't purchased much since Lela was born. Can we leave this weekend instead? I mean, what's the rush?"

"I want to leave tomorrow, that's the rush. You have a problem with that?"

"I see where Junior gets some of his ways, but it's cool Uncle Jon. Whatever you want.""Thanks, Pumpkin. If you want to go shopping to get a few things, I suggest you get a move on. Paige and I will watch Lela. That will give us practice for our baby. Chasity, I love Paige, but this old fool has been hurt many times. Women, they're my weakness, but something about her is different. I can see myself having a long future with her. This pregnancy is going to be rough, and I have to watch her closely. Having babies is not so easy at forty-three, and that's why she quit her job. We were told she's a high risk pregnancy, which is another reason why we need this vacation. Comprende?"

"Yes Sir, I think I'll get a move on. And Uncle Jon, Paige will be fine. She's eating all the right things and following the doctor's orders. I'm certain you will have a healthy baby. Before I leave, I wanted to give you that check back. It's feels as if you're buying my love, and I feel uncomfortable. The money is unnecessary because I plan to make my own."

"No one's buying your love, Pumpkin. I always wanted to spoil you, from the time you came to live with your father. I was going to tell you on vacation, but we need to have this conversation now. Kenny was your father and I never believed him, but he was always sure of it. We argued many days before your parents died because I thought he was delusional. When you came, I told you I wanted you but Kenny wasn't having it. He severed ties with me and I never knew why, because he could've been a millionaire with his skills. But it makes since now. He didn't want anyone coming between you two and would never accept my help financially. So the opportunity came when you graduated college."

"The scholarship?" I asked.

"Yes, I wanted to give you a million dollars, but the maximum allowed for that type of money was twenty-five thousand. After Kenny passed away, I called the Dean and asked him to reach out to you."

"For the internship?" I replied, and it suddenly made since.

"Yes. I never knew you followed through until you came to dinner that night. When you called, Pumpkin, that was music to my ears, though I was disappointed you believed I was responsible for your parents' death."

"Sorry about that, but I had to know before I let you into my life."

"I understand. I'm not accepting the money back. Since you've come into our lives, you have changed our whole family dynamic. Not only did you single-handedly steal Junior's heart, which made him a better man, you saved our lives and made me a better man. I'm willing to love again and take chances, because life is short. You play a big part in my joy, and I love you, kid. You will be provided for the rest of your days. So don't go spending it all in one day, even though there's more where that came from."

"Uncle Jon, I don't know what to say. You never cease to amaze me with your loving heart towards Destiny and me. I would save you a thousand times again if I had too, because I love you. You know Junior wanted to kill me and you when I told him. Is he coming on the trip?" I asked, hoping the answer was yes. Although I was tired of waiting and hoping, whenever I was in his presence that spark remained.

"I'm not sure, Pumpkin. He was invited, but who knows. Don't fret over something that you can't control, and Junior just happens to be one of those things."

"Alright, Unc. Let me go and spend some change from my millions."

"That a girl. Go have fun. I'll see you when you get back."

I took Destiny to the mall with me, and it ended up being an all-day trip. I racked up on clothes for myself, Jordon and Lela, not to mention whatever Destiny desired. When we got home, I went to find my baby and check on Jordon. I wanted him to try on the clothes I bought to make sure they fit. I knew his size, but I also noticed he was growing. The house was quiet and Lela was sleeping, so I took the opportunity to pack for all of us. The excitement of going on a family vacation was growing on me. I loved Uncle Jon's house, but I needed a break. After I packed, I was exhausted. Uncle Jon came in and said Lela could stay with him and Paige. That was music to my ears, even though my daughter was sleeping through most of the night.

The next morning the house was chaotic. Trying to get the whole family off to the private jet was a task. Everyone was forgetting something or another, and it was a good thing we weren't taking a commercial flight. Finally, we reached the airport, and a small part of me was hoping Junior would be there with flowers, ready to recommit to me. However, he was not there and I hadn't seen him all morning. I figured he went to work to avoid seeing everyone happy. *He's such an ass,* I thought.

"Paige, you're starting to show! That glow you're sporting is beautiful," I said once we settled on the plane.

"Thank you, Chasity. You're so sweet. I see where Lela gets it from."

"Grandpop, do they have water slides where we're going?" Jordon asked.

"I'm sure they'll have a slide, but if they don't I'll build you one," Uncle Jon joked, and we all laughed. On the plane was Destiny, Uncle Jon, Paige, Jordon, Calvin, Lela, and me.

"Uncle Jon, why didn't Domencio and Savannah come?" Destiny asked.

"Domencio is taking a later flight, but Savannah is too far in her pregnancy to travel. When both she and Paige have their babies, we'll go on another trip."

I thought it was strange that Domencio would even leave Savannah at this stage in her pregnancy. I guess everyone needed a break except Knucklehead. We arrived at an airport in the Bahamas and a private yacht awaited us.

Once we boarded our mega yacht, I couldn't help but fall in love with the deck. As the crew greeted us, my eyes wondered around, and I was ready for the complete tour. Lela and I were escorted to one of the five staterooms, and it was exquisite. I placed Lela's sleeping body on the bed so I could take in the view from my balcony. I was not one who craved luxury, but I felt a part of the elite and these extravagant rewards were appreciated. The white accents against the cherry wood in my room popped. Once the yacht left the dock, I plopped down on the white, oversize sofa and the cushions sucked me in. For this to be the junior suite, it was a dream. I watched Lela sleep peacefully and wished Junior was here.

Once Lela woke up, I placed her inside her stroller and went to find Jordon and Destiny. I found Jordon on the deck in his swim pants.

"Jordon, did you even unpack?" I asked.

"Not all the way. Can I do it later? Please?" he begged. "They have a slide on the boat that leads to the ocean. Uncle Jon said as soon as we arrive at the next location, I can slide."

"Next location, did he say where that is?"

"No, but he said we should be there in fifteen minutes."

"Where is Uncle Jon anyway?"

"I think they're below deck. Chasity, I'm already having the best time! I can't wait to use that slide."

"Me neither, but until then, why don't you come have lunch with me? I heard the chef will prepare anything we want."

"Okay, I want lobster."

"Lobster, young man? You are your father's child. You two will only settle for the best."

"That's not the only thing we have in common," he smirked.

"And what else is there, smarty pants?"

"We both love you," he replied. I was shocked and honored that he finally told me that he loved me.

"Jordon, you just made this one of the happiest days of my life. I love you too, and no matter what happens, we will always be family and I will always be responsible for you."

"I know. Now let's go get that lobster! And tell the Chef I want it smothered in garlic butter."

"Okay, boss man. Now push your little sister, but don't wake her up, because you always do that against my wishes."

"I promise, plus I want to eat in peace. She's beginning to grab for regular food."

"I know, right. She'll be crawling before you know it. Come on, let's go see what they got."

After lunch, Lela was all the way live and I took that time to read her a book. She loved books and the nursery school videos I purchased. She was very alert and growing too fast. She was almost four months, which reminded me that Junior's birthday was in a couple of days. It was hard to believe a year had gone since Junior and I started our relationship. *I have to get this Negro out of my head, because he consumes too much of my time,* I thought.

I glanced towards the sea as I cradled Lela in my arms, and saw a small island in the distance. As we neared, I saw what appeared to be an estate of villas.

"Uncle Jon, are we going to that island?" I asked.

"Yes, Pumpkin. I rented out the island for our vacation, so you can enjoy this wonderful boat or dig your feet into the sand.

"Uncle Jon, you are a true baller, and Paige, you are a lucky woman."

"This I know Chasity, trust me," she replied with a confident smile.

"Uncle Jon, where is Destiny? I haven't seen her since we arrived."

"She's upset because Khalif couldn't come, but I have a surprise for her. She'll get over it," he replied.

"Jon, you just can't say no to these girls. They're the lucky ones," Paige added.

Once the anchor went down, small boats arrived, and the crew assisted us inside safely. On our way to the island I decided this was Heaven, and I was unwilling to let Junior's absence spoil this vacation. Uncle Jon had gone all out.

When we walked inside the beautiful resort-like estate, I felt peace and resolve. The lobby area was decorated with coral linens and bohemian wood. The sheer curtains that swung freely from the gazebos attracted my soul, and I could see myself lounging there for hours.

"Pumpkin, I want you meet my sister, Tina. She and my brother-in-law Rameen will be joining us," Uncle Jon said as they walked up to us.

"Wow, I didn't know you had a sibling Uncle Jon. It's a pleasure to meet you, Tina!"

"Siblings, Chasity. I have two more brothers that you'll meet shortly. Remember, family vacation, and it's time for you and Destiny to meet the entire family."

"I can't wait." I replied, excited to be a part of a big family.

"Please, let me take care of my great niece. When we heard Junior was having a baby, we were shocked and excited. I want you to enjoy yourself and know that your child is good hands. And you can call me Aunt Tina," Tina said.

"I agree, Pumpkin. We can handle Lela. You deserve to relax after all we've been through. Why don't go get settled in your room, and hopefully the rest of the family will be here shortly."

"Are you sure, Aunt Tina? She can be handful." I replied

"Yes, Sweetheart. I raised four boys. I can think I can handle this little princess."

"Thank you so much, and you too Uncle Jon. This is turning out to be a spectacular getaway," I replied, looking forward to the break.

"My brother only provides the best. Welcome to the family dear," Aunt Tina responded as she whisked away with my daughter.

"Miss, right this way," a handsome Bohemian man said. "I'll show you to your room.

"She's staying in the Grand Suite," Uncle Jon said. I looked at him like he was crazy, because he was taking the favoritism too far. "What? Your grand, so what do you expect?" Uncle Jon responded.

"This is our vacation so I'll let it slide, but I'll deal with you later Unc." Morgan escorted me to my grand suite, and although it was a little distance from the lobby, I didn't mind. The landscape was immaculate, and I enjoyed the tropical scenery.

"Here we are, Miss. I'll take your bags in and be on my way," Morgan replied once we reached the top step of my suite. The privacy was nice, but I would've preferred staying closer to the family. However, my mind instantly changed when we entered.

The room was open and bright with its contemporary wood furniture and finishing's. However, the strangest part of all was *Trey Songz, Panty Dropper* softly playing in the background. When I looked to my left, a view of the sea captivated me, and I could see the yacht in the distance. But when I looked to my right, Junior was standing there like a piece of art.

"Oh, there must be some kind of mistake, Morgan. This room is occupied already. I'm sorry Junior, I didn't know you were here. Morgan, I need to find me another room," I said, confused and excited that Junior came.

"You're in the right place. You're exactly where you belong. Morgan, that'll be all for now."

"Sir," he nodded and left.

Junior strolled towards me with haste and I didn't know if he was going to kiss or kill me. But when he pulled me into his wonderful arms and kissed me with hunger of a lion, I felt safe and relieved. I submitted with the same hunger and we were tongue locked for what seemed like forever.

"I missed these lips," he said when he came up for air. "I missed this neck," he moaned while tenderly pecking my neck. "But most of all, I missed this," he seductively stated as he put his hand between my thighs. He scooped me up and carried me into the bedroom. "You miss me, Chass?" he asked as he undressed me.

"Yes, so much Junior."

"And you don't need those toys anymore, right?" he asked as he pulled off my shorts.

"No, I'm good." I replied, anticipating his next move.

"And when we get back, you're throwing them away, correct?" he questioned while dropping to his knees. And before I could answer, his tongue answered for me. Junior's tongue, his beautiful, big dick, and passion recharged all my emotions. He did things to me that will go unsaid, and when we were done, he continued to pamper and love on me.

"Chasity, do you know you're my weakness? I realized a long time ago I can't live without you," he said as he caressed my face. "I've been a fool these past few months and I hope you can forgive me, baby."

"There's nothing to forgive. I know you, and I prayed you would come back to me. I just want to forget the past and focus on our future, Junior. You're all I ever wanted. When I think back over my life, there is nothing that I wanted more than to be with you. I wasn't going to mention it, but I think you got scared of getting married and your unique mind strayed, but your heart was never far."

"You might be right about that. However, over the summer that changed, and I want you to know that I appreciate all of your efforts. I know I shot you down on more than one occasion, but I recognized the change in you and knew I was partly responsible. You're a wonderful mother, more than I deserve, and I hope I haven't ruined the chance of becoming your husband. I've been missing out on my family as a whole, and I want rectify my actions. Chasity? Let's stop the games and the bullshit and get married," he said, pulling me onto his body and squeezing me tight.

"I thought you'd never ask, Mr. Blake."

"Well, there you have it. We're getting married tonight in front of my family. It's time you meet the entire clan. Plus, I have a surprise for you. I hope you're onboard."

"Tonight, Junior? I don't have anything to wear for a wedding and I didn't see no wedding dresses in the gift shop in the lobby."

"Come on, baby. You don't know your man by now?" he replied and lifted me off the bed. "We need to freshen up, and I need to see if all the family arrived. I can't wait to see my uncles!" he said, as excited as a child. Destiny and Paige will assist you in getting ready," he explained as he opened the closet in the master suite. There hung three white, beautiful wedding dresses. "They should fit, but you may need the length adjusted. The resort has a seamstress if needed," he smiled.

"Junior, you planned all of this yourself?" I asked.

"I had a little help from the fam, specifically Destiny. She's responsible for most of it. Once Pops heard his precious Chasity would finally get what she wanted, he rented the island. And here we are."

"Here we are," I repeated. "Junior, are you absolutely sure you want to spend the rest of your life with me? I know you've had your share of women, so why I am so different?"

"You just are."

"Junior, be honest. How many women have you slept with if you don't ever follow up after the second date?"

"Stop with the crazy talk, babe. Trust me, you don't want to know."

"Yes, I do, Junior! It doesn't matter, because nothing will stop me from marrying you," I rationed.

"Okay, no secrets. That's one of the things I love about you, baby. You don't have no shame, and you're honest. You want the weekly number or monthly?" he asked, and I was sorry I even asked if he had a weekly number.

"I was hoping for a yearly number, but weekly is fine," I replied, anxiously.

"Three, on a good week. But there would be times I'd go a month or two without." When he replied he avoided eye contact.

"Three? What the fuck, Junior! You will never be satisfied with my little old pussy. What have I gotten myself into? I can't compete with that shit, Junior!" I spat.

"That's why I didn't want to tell you. You want to know what you got that they didn't?" he asked quickly. "You got my heart. Sure, I've been with plenty of women, Chasity, but never without a condom since Kali. Making love to you was like my first time. I love your pussy, and everything else about you. I cherish you and only you. Never doubt my feelings. The only pussy I'm swimming in is yours."

"That's so sweet, Junior," I replied as he wrapped his arms around me and kissed my neck. All was forgiven.

"You belong to me and I to you. Now get freshened up so we can make this official. I'm getting ready in another room. I'll tell Destiny and Paige to come help you. The wedding is in two hours, and I need you to be on time. I'll have some food sent shortly," he stated, back to bossy Junior.

"You don't want to see if the dresses fit?" I asked, hoping he would stay longer.

"My dick is hardening, and if I stay any longer, we won't make the wedding. And that takes precedence over my lust for you. But don't worry babe, you're getting pregnant on this trip. Once we've said our vows, get ready to be fucked silly!" He kissed me and strolled away.

I was left standing in a daze. I never expected a reconciliation, let alone a wedding. Nor did I think Junior would even be on this trip. I took the gowns out of the closet and laid them on the bed. Though they were beautiful, they were a bit revealing, which made me question Junior's choices. He didn't like me showing off my body in public, so this was confusing. But before I could ponder any longer, Destiny and Paige barged through the door. Paige was starting to show and she looked beautiful.

"OMG! Can you believe you're getting married, Chass?" Destiny blurted.

"Hell to the naw! But I heard you had a lot to do with this. Thank you lil sis! Besides Lela and Jordon this is the happiest day of my life!" I replied.

"We are all happy and relieved, Chasity. I can speak for both myself and Jon that prayers have been answered. It was uncomfortable to say the least. To see two people that clearly love each other fall apart was heartbreaking. But this is a new day, my darling, and this wedding is taking place," Paige said and added a dance on the end of her speech. Destiny and I laughed so hard, she farted.

"Okay, stank butt, you can be excused with that funk," I said.

"It's your day so I'm not going to argue with you. Did you try on the dresses? Me and Paige picked them out," Destiny asked.

"I was about to take a shower real quick," I responded.

"Don't let us stop you. I'll set up the makeup table and when you're done, we can choose which dress to wear," Paige suggested.

When I re-entered the room, it was set up like a small boutique. My dresses were hung in the middle of the floor and a different pair of exquisite shoes sat underneath each dress. There were two vails that hung on the rack along with the dresses. The room had multiplied with staff, Aunt Tina, and an unknown young woman holding Lela.

"Chasity, I want to introduce you to my daughter, Brittany. But we all call her Juju," Aunt Tina said when she saw me staring at the young girl holding my daughter.

"I'm so happy for you, Chasity. We never thought Junior would get married. The family is very excited for you two," Brittany said sincerely.

"Thank you Brittany. I'm just as excited to be a part of this family," I replied. Lela started crying for me so I took her from Brittany and rocked her in my arms. My baby missed me and I had to spend some time with her.

"I just came to introduce my daughter to you before everyone else gets here. A boat of people just arrived, but some won't make it until tonight after the wedding," Aunt Tina explained.

"Everyone else? I asked.

"Yes, there's many more. This is what we call an emergency alert. When Jon calls people come running. He demanded the entire family be here with few exceptions. You'll meet most of the Blake's tonight. Welcome to the family niece. If you don't mind, I'll take Lela so you can continue to get ready," she smiled and swooped my baby up, leaving little room for objections. I watched my new Aunt lovingly care for my daughter and I relaxed.

"Chasity, Junior didn't request anything special for the wedding. But he asked that you wear your hair straight down. I know you like the natural curly look, but I can blow out your hair. I'm

almost finished with beauty school, and I do a mean blow out,"
Destiny said.

"If that's all he wanted than have fun, Dee! I'm not objecting
to anything today. It's all so surreal. I can't believe almost a year
ago, Junior and I first met. I can't wait to be Mrs. Blake!"

"Ladies, we don't have much time. I think you should try on
the first dress, Paige suggested.

"You're right, Paige. I don't know if they will even fit," I replied.

The first dress was a Pronovias short, round-neck tulle dress
with gemstone embroidery throughout the entire dress. It was
beautiful, but more suited for the reception dress.

"You look stunning, Chasity, but now that I see it on you, I
don't see that wow factor," Paige said when I modeled the first
look.

"I agree," Aunt Tina concurred.

"Let's try on the one I picked!" Destiny said.

Destiny's choice was a Vera Wang, leave-nothing-to-the-
imagination dress that was only appropriate for the bedroom or
the strip club. "Where's the rest of the dress, Destiny? You trying
to get me killed on my wedding day?" I asked.

"It looked so pretty on the model. I knew you could pull it
off, but I guess I see your point," she replied.

"This is the last dress, so let's pray for a miracle," I said before trying on the deep V dress with cap sleeves and scattered
crystals around the bodice. The silk organza and crinoline
underlay gave a Cinderella feel, and I was in love.

"That's the one!" Aunt Tina yelled.

"Yes, Chasity, you look like a princess," Paige gushed.

"You look beautiful," Destiny said and started crying.

"Don't cry, Dee. You know I hate to see you cry."

"These are happy tears, sis. I love you so much!

I love you too girl! Now let's stop with all these tears. This is
the day I've been dreaming of, and I can't wait! I'm starving, can
you bring me the food Junior had sent?"

"I'll get it," Aunt Tina said as she placed Lela in her stroller.

"I need to start blowing out your hair," Destiny said.

"And I can work on your nails," Paige added.

An hour later, my hair and nails were done and it was time to put the dress on. When I looked at myself in the mirror I felt beautiful, and I couldn't wait for Junior to see me. We all turned when we heard a knock at the door.

"Come in!" I yelled and Uncle Jon walked in with little Kenny. He ran to me, but Destiny swooped him up before he could jump on me. "Hey little man. When did you get here?" I asked.

"I don't know," he replied while rubbing his eyes.

"You look sleepy. You want lay down with Lela on the bed?"

"Noooooo!" he cried.

"Okay, but I can't hold you until later. I love you."

"Luh yu," he replied.

"He just arrived with the rest of the guests. The place is packed waiting on my beautiful daughter. And I must say, I've never seen such beauty in all my life. Junior is a lucky man, and I hope he can keep his composure. Because when he sees you, oh my! Don't cry, Pumpkin. You're too beautiful for that," Uncle Jon stated and wiped my tears with his handkerchief.

"I'm just so happy to have you in my life, and I love you, Pops."

"Pops. I love the sound of that, daughter. I know you've been through a lot, and I wish all your parents were here to celebrate, but I promise to be a good father and grandfather. Besides Junior, I'm the happiest man in the world. My lovely woman is carrying our daughter, and I look forward to a new life with you, Paige. Destiny, I have a surprise for you, too. I think Khalif is waiting for you downstairs."

"For real, Dad? Thank you so much!" she replied as she put Kenny on the bed and jetted out the door. She was comfortable with calling him Dad, but I barely used the word after age ten, so Pops was my comfort zone.

"I think we lost a member," I said.

"The last step is the makeup. Since you don't want much on, it won't take long," Paige said.

"I'll let you ladies finish up. Chasity, Junior asked me to give you this, and I'm honored to walk you down the aisle and give you a way to my son," he said and handed me an envelope.

"Thanks, Pops. Can I have a moment to read this Paige? I'll be right back."

"Take your time. It's your day. I'll escort you out, honey, and we'll see you in a few," she said.

As I was walking to the balcony, I noticed little Kenny had fallen asleep. I opened the letter and instantly became stressed. Although I told him I would sign the prenup, I thought it was a thing of the past. With further inspection, I noticed all the additional clauses gone and the prenup changed to simple language. It basically said if I leave the marriage that I get half, but if Junior leaves, I get his whole fortune. Again, I'll say it, y'all know what I'm dealing with. I had to talk to him and let him know that this was unnecessary. I searched for my phone when I got back in the room and called him right away.

"I see you got the agreement. I was expecting your call," Junior said when he answered.

"Junior, please, baby. This is way too much, and you're making me uncomfortable. Let's not sign anything and let the chips fall where they may. I plan on spending the rest of my life with you, so there's no need for an agreement at all. You're my dream, and so you will be my husband. Let's build off of that," I replied.

"You're right, baby. I just wanted to put your mind at ease. When I told you about the women, I didn't like the look on your face. I wanted to reassure you of my love."

"When you showed up here and asked me to marry you, that was all the reassurance I needed. Now stop playing and meet me downstairs. I can't wait for you to see me in my dress."

"I can't wait either. Are you ready?"

"I just have to get my makeup done and then I'm ready."

"Not just for today, but are you ready for me—for the rest of our lives?"

"Yes. Are you getting cold feet?" I asked, hoping that wasn't the case.

"Nah, my feet are hot, and I'm ready to get my family back. I'll see you in a few, baby. I love you."

"I love you more," I replied and hung up before he could say anything else. "Paige, do this makeup so I can go marry my man," I demanded.

"Right away, sweetheart. Can you call your sister and tell her to come and get dressed? We're your bridesmaids," she said excitedly. "Lela is the flower girl and will be escorted down the aisle by Jon's niece, Christiana. And of course, Jordon is the ring bearer. You see, you have nothing to worry about. Just relax, they have to wait for you. You're the star.

"Thank you for being here, Paige. It means the world to me. And thank you too, Aunt Tina and Brittany. I'm so happy to have a family."

"You're welcome," Brittany replied, but Aunt Tina was getting her nap on. "She stay sleeping," Brittany said when we heard her slight snore.

"She's probably tired from the flight," I responded, knowing they didn't have much time to prepare. Lela and little Kenny woke up simultaneously, and Brittany gently shoved her mother.

"Watch out now!" Aunt Tina yelled when she woke up. We all laughed so hard at her reaction, and I knew I would grow to love this woman.

"What y'all ova dere laughing at? Give me my great niece so I can get her dressed. And who's gonna dress dat dere boy?" she asked with her southern accent.

"My sister will dress him, Aunt Tina. Brittany, can you go and find Destiny and tell her to hurry her butt up?" But as soon as I said it, Destiny walked into the room. "Dee, I know you're happy Khalif made it, but I'm ready to get married. You need to get a move on."

"I just have to put on my dress and some lip gloss. My skin is flawless so I don't need all that makeup, and neither do you," she bragged.

"I'm not putting much on, Chasity, because you are a natural beauty. I'm just enhancing what God gave you," Paige replied.

"Do your thing, Paige. I just need everyone else to move a little quicker before I have a breakdown."

Once everyone was dressed, we headed out. When we neared the lobby, I could see all the flowers and the many guests that were already seated. They had transformed the lobby in 2 ½ hours, and I was astonished at the results. This was really a wedding, my wedding, and I was amazed. I spotted Junior in the distance and even at that range, he was gorgeous. Destiny and Paige were like two organized party planners. When they finally descended down the aisle, Uncle Jon accompanied me and placed his arm under mines.

"You ready for this, kid? Just say the word and I'll get you out by helicopter," Pops teased. "I'm just kidding, Pumpkin. I'm very happy for you and Junior. You guys make the perfect couple. And don't worry, I will always have your back. You will officially be my daughter in a few moments, and I will watch over and protect you. I love you."

"I love you too, Pops. More than you will ever know. Now, take me to my king," I demanded. The piano played *Here Comes the Bride* and that was my cue.

Chapter 42

Junior

After Savannah's baby shower, I knew I couldn't live without Chasity. I swallowed my pride and took action. I spoke to Destiny, who talked to Pops, and everything fell into place. Chasity had no idea what was in store, thinking she was only going on a family vacation. Pops came to talk to me the day before, and once I reassured him of my intentions, he pulled out all the stops. But what surprised me even more is the encouragement he gave.

"Junior, I know I come down hard on you, son. But you have to know that I'm proud of the man you've become. You're my first born and that's so special to me. Initially, I was against this whole infatuation between you and Chasity, knowing the man you were. I prayed you would settle down one day, but my little faith blinded me when the day came. Chasity loves you for you, Junior and it's obvious you cannot breathe without her. So I give you my blessings and will do everything in my power to make this wedding spectacular with the short time I have to prepare," Pops explained.

"Thanks, Pops. I love you too, and I know you was just being you," I replied.

"Great. Now that we have that squared away, we can prepare for this special occasion. I was able to rent out a private island with enough rooms to cover the entire family. I called in all the Blake's, but it's going to be tricky getting everyone there by tomorrow. By the grace of God, everything will work out."

"Pops, thanks again, and you need to know that I will make Chasity happy. I know you have a special, untouchable spot in your heart for her, but she's in good hands."

"Yes, that's my Pumpkin, and it's a good thing she's marrying you. I don't think I could stomach a stranger," he laughed and we embraced.

When I saw the yacht arrive, I was dying in anticipation to be with my woman again. I prayed her heart still belonged to me and that she would take me back. I watched as they boarded the passenger boat and they touched sand within minutes.

I didn't see her love coming because it blindsided me, but I imagined spending a lifetime with her. She was my unexpected dream and she was a warrior. She was loyal and out to protect what she loved at all costs. I know I was an asshole about the whole shooting, and I still can't explain why I reacted with such contempt. I thought back to that day, and I'm still somewhat confused, but there was no doubt in my heart that she would try to hurt me intentionally. And I could see her taking punk ass Track down too. I just wish I was the one who pulled that trigger. When Pops told me about her nightmares and crying spells it killed me inside.

Yeah, she was my little soldier, and soon to be wife. I saw her walking up the ramp to our suite and pressed play on my phone. The room was set up with surround sound and wireless internet, so I played her favorite artist, *Trey Songz*. I was slightly jealous of her crush, but I had something planned that would change that. She would never see this surprise coming. Though my family was aware, she had no idea.

When she walked through the door, I could see the surprised look on her face hearing the music. But when she spotted me standing across the room, she was happy and embarrassed. She could barely get her words out, believing she was in the wrong room. Once I reassured her she was in the right place, my life began. We made love as if it were the first time, though her pussy is hypnotizing even on a bad day. She agreed to marry me and basically told me to shove the prenup up my ass. I took that lip because nothing was going to stand in our way.

Now, here I stood with Brock and Jordon by my side, waiting to see my lovely wife. When they made their way down the aisle, I had never seen someone so beautiful. Chasity was a vision of purity and strength, and with each step she made, my heart skipped a beat. She chose the dress I hoped she would, because I don't know what Paige and Destiny were thinking with the other two. I was trying to be open minded, but I was happy my baby knew me well. That simple decision made me love her more.

"Here she come, Junior. I'm proud of you, man. You made the right decision. I'm honored to stand as your best man. You sure you're ready?"

"Nothing is clearer, dog," I replied, never taking my eyes off my wife. Her hair was straight, which gave her another look. When she wore her hair in a ponytail, she reminded me of *Chili* from *TLC,* and when she wore her natural curls, she reminded me of a young *Lauren Hill.* Today she was just Chasity, beautiful and splendid, and she belonged to me.

"Who gives this woman to this man?" the official asked.

"I do," Pops said loud and proud. He kissed her cheeks and handed her over to me.

As we stood face-to-face with direct eye contact, she had a youthful, giddy, slightly embarrassed vibe that stimulated me on another level. A tear fell from my eye and I quickly wiped it away, but she didn't miss a beat and kissed me.

"We're not at that point guys," the official said, and the crowd all laughed.

"I love you!" she whispered, and I shook my head.

She had me in a daze, and the only thing I remember after that was when the official asked for the rings. Jordon walked with the ring for Chasity. Before I could get it, Chasity leaned over, kissed Jordon, and told him she loved him. When he said it back, that warmed my heart. Destiny handed Chasity the ring I picked out for myself, and I could see the curious look on her face. When we exchanged rings and were pronounced man and wife, I picked my wife up, spun her around, and gave her the most passionate of kisses. She was smiling from ear-to-ear, and I thanked God in that moment.

"You're all mine now, and I can do with you as I please," I said while holding her tight in my embrace. The guests all stood and cheered.

"I think I can say the same thing. I never believed this day would come, Junior. I want you to know that I'm going to be a good wife to you. No more running away and no more games. Aren't you glad we can just enjoy and love each other?" she replied.

"Yes, and I have a surprise for you later on. What I'm about to do has never been done for anyone. I'm going to humble myself, because you deserve to know everything about me and how you've changed my life. Damn, you look amazing, and I love your hair like that! Don't cut it, baby. I just want to take you back to the room and have my way with you," I said, hungry for her touch.

"We can't leave all the guests, and I want to enjoy the entire wedding ceremony. I can't wait for the surprise, but I'm dying to meet your family, Junior."

"You're right, baby." She smiled and I loved to see her happy.

We joined my family and immediately they embraced her. I wanted her by my side the entire night, but my family had other plans. I watched as she made her way around the room, greeting all the guests at their tables. Hugs and kisses were pouring out, and Chasity was absorbing it all. It was clear that she craved a family, and now she had one.

"Congrats, brah!" Domencio said when he walked up. "We're all happy the dramatics have ceased and things can get back to normal. I give you credit, Junior. I didn't think you had it in you. I think back to all the women I had to appease on your behalf, and I'm glad I don't have to be bothered with that dumb shit no more."

"You had to go there, little punk, but thanks. Yeah, everyone knows she got me, and I'm not ashamed of it. I'm good, brah!"

"Obviously, but better you than me. I hope Savannah is not holding her breath, because she will eventually die from lack of oxygen," he replied and rolled his eyes.

"She's about to have your baby and y'all live together. Sounds like you're already married to me."

"Sounds and reality are two different things. Savannah tried to trap me with this pregnancy, but the only thing she locked down was child support. I'm playing the part, and after I get this paternity test, I'll put her up in a nice place of her own and take care of my child." This nigga was fooling himself, and it was just a matter of time until he realized it.

"Look, you're bringing me down with all the negativity. Why don't you go find anyone else to talk to," I replied as Brock walked up, saving me from this gloomy punk. "Brock, my man. Thanks again for being my best man. Things turned out nice, right?"

"Yo, this wedding is nice, and your wife looked beautiful, Now, don't punch me, I'm just giving you a compliment. You can take a compliment, right?"

"Get the fuck outta here. I see you and Domencio got jokes, but you can save them because here comes all that matters," I replied as Chasity sauntered towards me. "Hey, baby. Did you meet everyone?" I asked.

"Yes, and your family is so sweet. I'm looking forward to spending more time with them," she replied.

"You wish will come true. Just stay tuned. You, me, and the kids are just the beginning."

"Everyone, can I have your attention please?" Destiny asked. "They will be serving the bridal party first, and then everyone else will be served. After dinner, we can all get our party on," she announced. "Chasity and Junior, you can follow me."

After dinner and the toast, I was ready to take my wife and go, but my surprise was still on the way. I prayed she was on board, because this was the only way I could see us living a peaceful life. We danced, drank, and enjoyed the occasion. I had finally loosened up and was ready to present my wedding gift. I informed Destiny that it was time, and she got people back to their seats.

"Chasity, there are no words to express how I truly feel about you. You know I love you, but I don't think you know how much. I know you think I'm controlling, and I agree with that assessment. However, I want you to feel free to be you and do the things that were forbidden before. You and the kid's safety are my responsibility, and I believe this is the perfect option that will suit our circumstance. If you could turn your attention to the flat screens, this will make more sense," I explained.

When the 35,000 square foot home appeared on the screen, everyone ooed and awed, but I was watching Chasity's reaction. Hers was all that mattered. Initially, she looked confused, but smiled a few seconds later, knowing her man.

"That's our new house, Dad!" Jordon yelled from across the lobby.

"Yes, son, and they're adding a special water park for you and your sister. Wifey, does the house meet your standards?" I asked.

"Yes, but we just finished renovating our house back home. But it doesn't matter, Junior. You know I'll go anywhere you are." She responded, submitting to my ego, but I knew she would get me later.

"We'll keep that house when we come to visit Pops and when I have business in Philly."

"Wait, where is this house, Junior? she asked.

"In Atlanta. Actually, in the Buckhead area."

"That's right nephew, come on home," Uncle Jeremiah shouted, and all my family applauded.

"I know we have to work out all the details, but are you riding with me?" I whispered.

"For the rest of my life. The house is ridiculous, but I'm looking forward to moving in," she replied.

"Everyone, I have one more surprise for my beautiful wife. Chasity, would you sit here?" I asked and helped bring in the chair that sat in the middle of the lobby. "Aunt Tina, could you bring my daughter over?" I asked, because I wanted to share this with the females that had my heart.

"I'm so excited!" Chasity said when Aunt Tina gave her Lela.

When the music came on, I sang *Kem's* song *Promise to Love* and had Chasity's full attention. As I showed off my skills, my baby was flabbergasted with excitement. And once I finished serenading her, she gave Lela to Jordon and jumped into my arms. She had tears falling down her face.

"Junior, I didn't know you could sing like that, baby! You just give me more to love and you sounded like an angel," she said as I embraced her.

"Only for my sweet, Chasity. I'm ready to take you back to the room. What's up? You ready to blow this place?"

"No, Junior! I want to enjoy this time with your family. Most of your family are leaving tomorrow."

"Yeah, and most of them live in Atlanta. You'll be able to spend all the time you want," I reasoned.

"Okay, Mr. Party Pooper. Let me say my goodbyes and we can blow this place," she said and made her rounds around the room.

Jordon was enjoying spending time with his cousins, which confirmed my decision to move my family. We had offices in Atlanta and Miami, but there was no way I was taking them to Miami. Atlanta was perfect. I was just concerned memories of her parents would cause a problem. But so far, so good.

"Junior, you did good, son. I'm a little upset that you're taking your family away, but I understand. I was thinking of starting somewhere new as well. I'm happy with Paige and I'm about to become a father at fifty-one. Don't be surprised if you get a neighbor. I can't imagine not seeing my grandchildren," Pops explained when he walked up. "Junior, I love you!" He hugged me and walked away. The last time I received a hug with substance was when they released me from prison.

For the next week, I enjoyed my wife and kids. This was the first time I was able to spend time with them all together. We spent our time between the island and the yacht, and I was in love with my family. I never believed this would happen to me. But I can't live without the funny face girl that stole my heart.

It took us a few months after the wedding to relocate, but it was worth the wait. I was impressed with my new home, and we had everything we needed. And as I predicted, I impregnated Chasity but not with just one, but with twins. Pops and Paige secretly married right before my little sister Penelope made her arrival. And yes, Pops followed me to Atlanta and gave the old house to Domencio. He and Savannah moved in and had a beautiful baby boy. Domencio insisted he be a Jr. The Blake's had multiplied, and this was just the beginning.

Chapter 43

Chasity

The Aftermath

Okay, so much has happened since my wedding, but let's start there. When Junior surprised me with the home, I was slightly agitated, but after viewing the slideshow that evening, the house was a dream. I looked forward to starting fresh. The night continued to get better when he sung to me. I was surprised and pleased. His voice reminded of me Joe's the R&B singer. He was smooth and sexy with his expensive suit that I know he paid a fortune for. I thanked God at that moment that he didn't make a career out of that voice. I wouldn't have stood a chance.

A month after the wedding, I found out I was pregnant, and two months after that, I found out I was having twins. I gave birth to two healthy girls, Marley and Mavin. Junior wants five kids, so this helped narrow that number down. However, I had a rough pregnancy and was uncomfortable carrying two babies. I had plenty of help with Aunt Tina and Uncle Kareem staying in the guesthouse during the week. Aunt Tina insisted on being Lela's nanny, but when the twins came, she called in reinforcements. Aunt Fiona arrived, and she was much different from Aunt Tina. Aunt Fiona was married to Uncle Jacob, Pops other brother, and she was slightly stuck up. Paige had no tolerance for her, and whenever she would speak, Paige would leave the room.

Oh, I forgot to mention, Pops and Paige moved down here and live within walking distance. Paige and Penelope visited daily, and Junior's country family came over every Sunday. I enjoyed it because Aunt Tina and Aunt Fiona would go at it like two enemies, but then turn around and have each other's back. If someone tried to interfere with their beef, they would start defending each other and giving compliments. I went through this shit daily. I remember the day Junior tried to show his authority in front them. That didn't go over well.

"Chasity, why you get out of bed so early? You know I can't sleep without you," he warned as he walked into our massive, beautifully decorated kitchen.

"Nigga, please. This girl has four kids to tend to. You're just one man. And why you always sniffling and leaching onto her? Give this poor girl some breathing room. Since you were a kid, you always been bossy. Take some sleeping pills and leave this young woman alone," Aunt Tina emphasized.

"Aunt Tina, when are you going home? I'm still trying to figure out how you and Uncle Kareem are living in my guesthouse," Junior said as he yawned.

"Oh, no he didn't! Junior you're out of order, and we have something special for folk like you. It's called a hanging, and if you ever talk to my sister-in-law that way again, we will roast your ass. Now, see your way out of this here kitchen, because this ain't no place for you," Aunt Fiona spat.

"Junior, I'll be up in a minute, baby. You want me to bring you breakfast?" I said, ignoring my aunts.

"Yes," he relied and left.

"You need to stop letting that boy run your every move. Take Destiny for instance. That girl moved down here and opened the hottest beauty salon in Atlanta. She's living her life to the fullest," Aunt Fiona said when Junior was gone.

"Yeah, ain't nuttin special bout dat boy. Besides the fact he wealthy and handsome, he just like any old other trifling man," Aunt Tina added.

"You see, he is special, and it takes a unique woman to deal with his thought process. I don't mind the way he loves me."

"Unique, huh? We'll see how long that lasts. Every woman needs that me time. Why don't you go out with those new friends you hang out with?"

"I do go out with them, but I'm good you guys. Leave my man alone."

"Okay, you're the boss. But you ain't giving him none of the breakfast me and Fiona cooked. Make it yourself," Aunt Tina said.

"Aunt Tina, stop playing. I'm taking my man some food," I replied as I fixed his plate. I heated it, grabbed him a bottled water, and headed out.

My aunts were crazy, but I especially enjoyed Aunt Tina. She reminded me of my real father. Destiny didn't want to move because of Khalif, but Pops wasn't playing that so she came to Georgia kicking and screaming. Pops found her the best location in the area and opened a shop that no one could rival. Destiny hired the best in the business, and I frequented her shop often for the facials and massages. Khalif flew down her on breaks, and they seemed to work out the distance.

Junior and I joined a church, but I still had trouble with the cussing. Lord knows I try to put forth effort, but some words just fit more. I met Sheree, Jennifer, and Mariah at church, and after getting to know them, I found out they were extreme hypocrites and used the church as status. However, Junior played basketball and golf with their husbands so I tolerated them. Sheree was light bright damn near white, and she loved to throw shade. She always came at me about my clothes, and one day I overheard her talking about me to the other ladies.

"Girl, you see that big ass house she lives in and handsome husband of hers? I wonder why the bitch always dress like a poor chick," Sheree said.

"He probably just filling her ass with babies and keeping all that money to himself. She looks like she licks that man's ass," Mariah added. "I mean, he is fine as shit and if he were my man, I'd lick that ass too." They laughed, but I noticed Jennifer didn't say anything. The old me would've confronted her and beat her down, but the new me had better things to do.

I told Junior what they said, and he was pissed. He was not only mad at them, but he was mad at me. "I keep telling you to go to shopping and you keep ignoring me. How many time do we have to go through this? And fuck them bitches. They're jealous of you. This is what you're going to do. Invite them over for dinner this week, and wear one of the forbidden dresses. We'll shut them up once and for all.

Later that week, we hosted the dinner and Junior surprised me with a sexy Hermes dress. When the girls arrived with their husbands, neither them or their men could take their eyes off me. Since our wedding, I had a new found love for *Kem*. His music was playing in the background and I had a decorator come and set the mood. Junior openly showed his affection in front our guests. The husbands were uncomfortable and so was the wives, because clearly they didn't get that type of love. Junior kissed and nibbled on my ear while rubbing my body. To add insult to injury, after dinner and small talk, he asked everyone to come outside. When we got outside, there was a Bentley coupe sitting in the front of our mansion. I jumped up and down with excitement while my haters stood on the sideline. That night was full of surprises. But the biggest surprise of the night was when he agreed to let me go on a girls trip with the ladies. I thought he was just fronting in front of the men, not wanting to display his control. I declined out of good faith but Junior insisted.

This brings us to the present day. Last week we hosted a dinner with the girls and their husbands. Junior was drinking and enjoying conversation with the men. We all were having a good time, when Sheree asked if I would go on a girls trip with them. I declined, saying I didn't want to leave the twins so soon. The husbands were all for their wives going, and a couple were a little too excited in my opinion. I guess Junior didn't want to seem controlling, so he insisted I go along. I was shocked, but he explained that I deserved a vacation after enduring that rough pregnancy. I didn't care what his reasoning was, I was happy. He even gave us the jet, and we headed to the Dominican Republic.

We were having a wonderful time until day three. The ladies wanted to go to a strip club and I knew better, so I declined. Sheree tried to start her drama with the control shit, and I kindly explained that there's nothing they would see that's better than what I got at home. After they left that night, I poured me a drink and my cell phone rang.

"What's up, babe you can't sleep?" I asked.

"No, and I need you to get packed. A car will be there shortly. You're going to strip clubs now, Chasity?" Junior asked.

"Junior, I'm not even going to respond because you are tripping."

"Don't respond, just get ready. You should be packing while we're on the phone. Imagine my heartbreak when Ricky called, saying Sheree said you were going to strip club. Did you hit your head?" he yelled.

"First of all, I didn't go to the strip club. They left and I'm in this rental house alone, besides the staff. Secondly, don't yell at me for something I didn't do. I know what I have in you and would never risk it over a strip club. You have to trust me, and trust me in the world without you all the time," I reasoned.

"You're right. I'm sorry for yelling. I should've known you better that. Are you packed yet?" he asked again.

"Junior!" I yelled. "I'll be ready when the ride comes, but you're on punishment. I'll talk to you later," I said and hung up.

I left a note for the ladies, informing them I left and that I would send the plane back for them on Saturday. When I got home, Junior was at the door waiting. The vision of him released my anger, and I was ready to make love to my husband.

"Did you have good flight?" he asked as he embraced me.

"It was okay," I barely replied.

"Don't be mean to me, Chass. I missed you and three days was three too many. You should be rewarding me for even letting you leave me."

"Junior, this was your idea. I'm going to bed, are you joining me?" I asked, ready to just fuck. I needed the release.

"Of course, but come here. You know you ain't running shit, right?" he asked as he kissed my neck, making his way to my lips. "I see you trying to act tough, but this is my pussy, and I don't need an invitation." He lifted me up and carried me to our bedroom. His sex was unbelievable, and that was his control over me. God forbid his dick ever went limp, because his crazy alone was not enough to keep me.

THE END

www.ingramcontent.com/pod-product-compliance
Lightning Source LLC
Chambersburg PA
CBHW062019170626
46813CB00001B/224